MIDNIGHT ATLANTA

THOMAS MULLEN

ABACUS

First published in Great Britain in 2020 by Little, Brown
This paperback edition published in 2021 by Abacus

1 3 5 7 9 10 8 6 4 2

Copyright © Thomas Mullen 2021

The moral right of the author has been asserted.

A CIP catalogue record for this book
is available from the British Library.

ISBN 978-0-349-14420-7

Typeset in Garamond by M Rules
Printed and bound in Great Britain by
Clays Ltd, Elcograf S.p.A.

Papers used by Abacus are from well-managed forests
and other responsible sources.

Abacus
An imprint of
Little, Brown Book Group
Carmelite House
50 Victoria Embankment
London EC4Y 0DZ

An Hachette UK Company
www.hachette.co.uk

www.littlebrown.co.uk

For Jenny

TOMMY SMITH NEVER wanted to start a story with a body. It seemed wrong, contrary to nature. The ultimate inverted pyramid: first there is the cold finality of death, the foundation of life turned upside down; then some colorful quotes sprinkled below, a smattering of details about the richness of a life once lived; followed at the bottom, like forgotten memories, by a few thin paragraphs no one ever reads. Telling a story that way, Smith felt, reduced a person's life. Especially considering the fact that the majority of people he wrote about had never been deemed worthy of being in a story until they were dead.

He did not like perpetuating this cruelty.

Yet as a crime reporter for the *Atlanta Daily Times*, the only Negro daily in America, it was his job to report facts and meld them into stories, to form some coherent narrative out of the flotsam and randomness of life.

And this is a story that starts with a body.

The shot woke him up.

Or was there a second shot? Smith would wonder that, later, when he wished he had been awake already, when he wished he could travel through time and better experience a moment he had missed, a moment that despite his lack of participation would turn out to be one of the most important in his life. And him slumped there in his chair, a flask in his lap.

His head felt fuzzy from sleep and drink, his limbs so very heavy. He thought he heard a shout, maybe. Then a crash, definitely.

It took him a second or three, but the solidness that had prevented his arms and legs from moving finally turned liquid and he sprang up. *The hell was that?*

Footsteps, above. But he lived on the top floor.

Wait, where was he?

In his office, that's right. He'd had a short date with Patrice, only one drink, then he'd walked her to her meeting at the Oddfellows Building. He'd leaned in for a kiss, which she'd granted, a short peck but with a winning smile that held such promise that he only felt slightly insulted she wasn't going to skip some dull business meeting for more time with him. Too excited to go home, he'd come to the office to pour himself another drink and type a few pages of a longer piece he'd been tinkering with. He'd thought he'd been alone in the building, but then Mr. Bishop had dropped by and they'd chatted, hadn't they? Then Bishop had returned to his office upstairs, and Smith had tried again to write. Apparently, the prose hadn't flowed as well as the bourbon, because he'd fallen asleep at his desk.

He called out the name of his boss, whose office was upstairs: "Mr. Bishop?"

Silence for a few seconds. The footsteps had stopped.

He tried to turn on his desk lamp but found that the bulb had burned out.

Think. That had definitely been a shot, a pistol. He knew the sound well. He hadn't dreamed it or imagined it. He wasn't in France, slowly trudging across Europe, and he wasn't walking his old police beat with Boggs at his side. He was here in his office, late at night. A place guns did not typically go off.

He stepped out of his office. The hallway light was on, the other offices dark. He crept down a perpetually messy hallway, ever crowded with stacks of papers. He reached the stairs to the second floor.

"Who's up there?" he demanded in the Officer Voice he hadn't deployed in so long. Deep and commanding, willing to brook no dissent. Loud enough to shake the framed articles on the walls and cause any ne'er-do-well to question the direction his life had taken. The Officer Voice could be surprisingly effective. But when Smith had used it in his old life, he'd had a sidearm and a club on his belt, and a partner beside him.

Footsteps again, quick and heavy. Someone upstairs did not like the Officer Voice.

Smith stepped into his colleague Jeremy Toon's office, remembering that Toon, a baseball fan, kept a Louisville Slugger propped in the corner behind his desk. It wasn't a firearm but it would have to do.

The office had suffered a few break-ins in the old days, Smith had been told, but not in many years. Partly thanks to the city's colored cops, now in their eighth year on the job, and partly because the *Daily Times* contained nothing worth stealing, unless the thieves were bibliophiles or had always craved their very own typewriters.

Smith crept to the base of the steps. Steps he knew to be very creaky indeed. Once he started walking up, he'd be a perfect target, trapped in the long stairwell with nowhere to hide. He tried to recall which steps were the loudest.

The floor above him remained quiet. Either the person up there had fled (the fire escape?) or was keeping still, waiting in ambush.

He took a step, then a second. The bat already slippery in his hands.

His third step was a bad choice, creaking loudly. So, element of surprise gone, he charged up the rest of the way. He found himself in the second-floor hallway, a light glowing above him. The hallway felt wider than the one downstairs only because it wasn't lined with as many stacks of newspapers.

A door behind him led to a bathroom. It was nearly closed but not latched, so he kicked it open and the door swung clear and banged into the wall, no one there.

He heard a low moan. Coming from Bishop's office. Then the sound of traffic, a car driving past, louder than it should have been: a window must be open, despite the night's January chill.

He crept forward until he was nearly in front of Bishop's open door. Pressed his back against the wall. This would make a lot more sense if he was holding a gun. He waited a beat, then quickly leaned over to get a look inside.

No one fired at him, no one leapt out of a corner. No one was there at all.

Except there, on the floor. The sound of something crashing before, he realized now, had been Arthur Bishop falling.

The publisher lay not completely flat but close, the room too cramped with its massive desk and chairs and side tables and stacks of books for Bishop's tall frame to fit. He lay mostly on his stomach, but one of his shoulders was wedged against the side of the desk, and his legs were bent. One of his hands pressed against the floor, fingers taut, knuckles up, the Oriental rug bunching from the pressure. His other hand, the left, was inside his jacket, like he'd been looking for something there, and the wide-eyed look on his face confirmed he'd found it.

Blood soaked the rug beneath him in an expanding circle.

The window behind his desk was open. Smith wanted to go to Bishop first, but he couldn't risk the fact that a gunman might be hiding on the fire escape, so he ran to the window, looked out and down. No one. Behind the building was a narrow alley, then another building. If the gunman wasn't hiding in another room, he'd made his way down the fire escape just as Smith had crept up the stairs, and he was long gone.

Bishop wasn't, not yet.

Smith dropped the bat and helped Bishop roll onto his back. Bishop's eyes were still open wide, the pupils moving the tiniest bit.

"Hang in there, Mr. Bishop, you hang in there."

Smith knew the odds a man could survive a shot to the center of the chest, and he knew how long an ambulance would take to get to this neighborhood. He grabbed the phone off Bishop's desk nonetheless and called the hospital. Then he hung up and dialed a number he knew so well.

Seconds later, just as he noticed that the low moan from his boss had stopped, his previous boss answered the phone.

For seven years and nine months, Sergeant Joe McInnis had been serving as the lone white cop in the Negro precinct. He had walked into plenty of rooms with murder victims, but this was the first time he'd received the call from a man who used to be one of his officers.

The office of Arthur Bishop smelled like cordite, McInnis noted before he'd even stepped inside. The cramped room felt cold from the open back window, yet the scent of gunfire hadn't faded.

Smith had claimed Bishop was still alive when he'd called, but he wasn't anymore.

The body was warm, no pulse, eyes open. He lay on his back, arms bent in that cluttered space, as awkward as every other murdered body McInnis had the misfortune of viewing. Folks who died in their sleep often looked as peaceful as that phrase implied, but people who were killed never looked restful, their bodies tense and crooked as if still containing the energy to do all the things they never would.

Behind McInnis stood two of his officers, Boggs and Jones. The latter was a wide-eyed rookie, now viewing a murder victim for the first time in his life. "Don't touch anything," McInnis reminded him.

Boggs, however, was a seven-year veteran, having witnessed all manner of crime scenes. The real reason McInnis had chosen this pair to come along, though, was that Boggs and Smith had once been partners. They had started together in April of '48, part of the inaugural class of Negro officers McInnis had been tapped to lead. The light-skinned, square-jawed Boggs was strict and deeply serious. He had struck McInnis as too intellectual for the job in '48; he still seemed more at home when combing through police records or encouraging kids on the sidewalk to stay in school than when confronting a violent felon, yet the years had toughened him. In contrast, Smith had always been a handful, chafing against rules and regulations as if they'd been designed specifically to annoy him. He'd resigned only two and a half years after they'd started.

McInnis figured Boggs would be able to read Smith better than McInnis ever could.

McInnis was not unaware of the fact that he was the only white man present, though he'd grown used to this. He had not signed up to be the lone sergeant to the Negro officers, but once he'd been made to understand that he couldn't turn down the assignment, he'd resigned himself to doing the best job he could. At first, communication had been a challenge. Sometimes a comment or situation would seem to register with his officers on different frequencies than it did him, codes with unexpected meanings, complex understandings he couldn't quite fathom. Sometimes the translating and rephrasing and explaining grew onerous, exasperating, for him and for them. He worked hard to overcome this, and the misunderstandings had become less common over the years, something he took a not insignificant amount of pride in.

But stress made things worse, and cops were almost always stressed.

As McInnis knelt beside the body, trying to get as good a look as he could without disturbing the scene, Boggs and Jones stood at the entrance, Smith behind them. McInnis smelled booze, and, among haphazard piles of paper that seemed to cascade into each other, he saw a single glass on Bishop's messy desk. A tiny amount of what looked like whiskey at the bottom.

McInnis carefully stepped around the desk, where a drawer was half open. He did not see a gun or a shell casing, at least not yet. No blood on the windowpane, nothing unusual on the fire escape.

"Jones, go down and check the perimeter of the building and the fire escape, look for a weapon or blood or anything else that shouldn't be there."

"Yes, sir."

Blood spatter along one of the bookshelves to McInnis's left. So Bishop hadn't been at his desk when he'd been shot. If Bishop had been moving from behind his desk and toward the shooter, the blood could have come from his back. McInnis slowly moved in a circle, seeing a smaller amount of blood on another bookshelf, possibly from Bishop's hand as he'd fallen. Or possibly from the assailant's.

McInnis walked out to Smith and Boggs in the hallway. He folded his arms and stared at his former officer. Who smelled like liquor. McInnis thought of the glass on the dead man's desk. He studied Smith's clothes, searching for signs of blood or a struggle, but apart from the lack of a tie and his top two buttons being undone, which in Smith's case was likely a stylistic insouciance, nothing looked off. Smith was handsome, dark-skinned, with a rakish charm the other officers had seemed to envy.

His eyes usually weren't this wide.

"Homicide will be here soon," McInnis explained. Homicide meant white detectives; the Negro officers were only beat cops, as none had been promoted to sergeant or detective. Most white cops in Atlanta despised the Negro officers; they'd tried to sabotage and undercut them from the very beginning, and even now, seven-plus years into this racial experiment, most still seemed to hope that the Negro cops would all be fired or would just mysteriously disappear one day.

Homicide detectives would be overjoyed to find a drunk Negro in the vicinity of a dead body. That meant this was McInnis's case for maybe a few minutes.

"Tell me, what happened?"

"Right before I called you, I heard a shot, or shots."

"Which? Shot or shots?"

"I don't know. I was ... asleep. I'd been working on a story downstairs—my office is the one below that room," and he pointed down the hall. "I heard a shot, or shots, I don't know, and it woke me up. Then I heard a shout, a man's voice. Could have been Bishop, could have been someone else."

"What did he say?"

"I couldn't tell. I heard a slam, it must have been his body hitting the ground. Then footsteps, the shooter probably, and I called out to Bishop, asked if he was okay. I grabbed that bat," and he motioned to a baseball bat on the floor of the hall, which McInnis had already spotted, "and came up the steps. He was lying on his stomach, just barely holding himself up with his right hand, and he was moaning. I rolled him over, I touched the windowpane when I looked outside, I made the call on that phone, but otherwise I didn't touch anything."

Smith had seemed shaken at first, but his recitation of facts seemed to be calming him. Like this was a few years ago and he was recapping just another crime scene to his sergeant, the discipline and old habits forcing this chaotic event into a clarity that allowed him to take the next step, and then the next.

"Did you see anyone?"

"No. I heard movement, like I said, but by the time I got here, the shooter was gone. The window was open, so I'm figuring the fire escape. Then I called you. No more than two minutes after hearing the shot."

McInnis took a hard look at Smith. "You've been drinking."

"Yessir, it's late and I was blocked on a story. It's what we writers do. I got a flask on my desk downstairs. But I'm not *drunk*."

McInnis wondered how differently this might have gone if Boggs alone had responded to the call. How differently would Boggs and Smith have behaved without a superior officer present? Without a white man present? What other secrets might have poured forth?

"Did you shoot him?"

Smith's eyebrows shot up. Perhaps he was so thrown by the body that he hadn't thought that many steps ahead. Perhaps he was drunker than he claimed and couldn't think clearly. Perhaps he'd been friendly enough with the dead man that he was still coming to grips with his loss and hadn't yet realized, with the kind of cagey strategizing Smith had always seemed to excel at, that he was in serious trouble.

"No, sir. Sergeant, it happened exactly like I said."

McInnis kept his own mouth shut, just watching Smith. Giving him some more silence, to do with as he pleased.

"I did not kill him. I liked the man." A pause. "Well, maybe didn't *like* him so much, but I admired him."

Already Smith was contradicting himself.

McInnis stepped closer and put a hand on Smith's shoulder. He seldom touched his officers. "You know you're going to be interrogated tonight. You know they're going to want to clear this case fast, and that means driving it right over you. So if you didn't do this, then you need to give us something, right now."

The whites of Smith's eyes were tinged red, either from drink or from the horrific way he'd been awoken.

"Sergeant, I have no idea what happened. None."

McInnis took back his hand. They felt awkwardly close together.

"Can I take another look inside?" Smith asked.

"From out here, yes."

McInnis stepped back and let Smith walk up to the threshold. Smith took in the scene again, then said, "His desk is never messy like that. All those papers everywhere."

"He might have leaned on them, messed them up when he stood," McInnis noted.

"Or whoever shot him might have been looking for something. Didn't have time to clean up after he realized I was coming."

Smith stared a moment longer, shaking his head.

Boggs couldn't resist saying, "Bad night to be drinking."

Smith scowled at his ex-partner. "It's just *alcohol*, preacher's son. It don't make me no killer."

"Smith," McInnis said, "once Homicide shows up, any way they slice it, you're going to be spending the night in the station, understand? You need to stay calm and not push their buttons." Smith had always been an expert button-pusher, like with the "preacher's son" comment.

"Yes, sir."

"I can call you a lawyer," Boggs said. "My father knows a few."

Smith nodded, sweat running down his cheeks now. The hallway was not warm.

"I need to pat you down," McInnis said. "Sorry, but that's how it works and you know it."

McInnis didn't linger on the look in Smith's eyes, just stood there and waited the two seconds it took for Smith to hold out his arms. Smokes in his shirt pocket, a wallet with eighteen bucks in his right pants pocket, keys in his left. Nothing else. McInnis hoped for Smith's sake that whatever gun had killed Bishop was a different caliber than any Smith owned.

"What else can you tell us?" McInnis asked after he'd finished. "Was he sleeping around or worried about money, did you overhear any heated arguments recently?"

Smith uncharacteristically silent for a spell.

McInnis pressed, "Who would've wanted to hurt him?"

"He's the owner of the paper, so plenty of folks would want to hurt him. I mean, you don't read this paper, do you?"

"From time to time." But not, in truth, that often.

"I read it," Boggs said. "Your stories first, every time."

That didn't surprise McInnis; Boggs no doubt read four or five newspapers every day.

"We cover politics, crime, society, everything. Make a *lot* of folks angry. You should see some of the hate letters we get, especially lately. There's this lawsuit against us, and now the Attorney General's trying to—"

"What lawsuit?"

They heard sirens. Getting louder.

"Jesus Christ," Smith said, the reality seeming to hit him all the harder now that a squad car was here. Car doors slammed shut. More sirens in the distance. "I can't believe this."

The same kinds of white cops Smith hadn't been able to stand working with were almost here, and this time they were coming for him.

PART ONE

Three Days Earlier

1

THE WHITE PRISON guard appeared uncomfortable with the idea of allowing these three men to converse alone.

A motley collection they made. On one side of the table: the young Negro prisoner, thin arms jutting through his too-big striped prison shirt, hair in need of a trim. On the other side: the short white attorney, gray hair slicked back with a lotion the guard could surely smell even from so many feet away. And beside him, the wild card: the "attorney's assistant," tall and nearly as old as the attorney, white hair at his temples, but skin the same color as the prisoner's, though a shade lighter. Who had heard of a Negro working with a white attorney like this?

Arthur Bishop, the salt-and-pepper-haired man in question, began to worry that the guard suspected he was there under false pretenses.

In which case, the guard was right.

Atlanta did in fact have some Negro attorneys, but they were fewer in number than Negro doctors or Negro dentists, Negro business owners or Negro insurance men. In fact, Bishop would have bet Atlanta had more Negroes running million-dollar businesses (Atlanta Life Insurance Company, Atlanta First Credit Union, the Colored Hair Care Emporium, etc.) than Negro lawyers. It wasn't that colored folk couldn't learn the law; the problem was that no one wanted a Negro lawyer representing them. If you were on trial for theft or murder or assault in the South, the only thing a Negro lawyer would do for you is incur the wrath of white judges who couldn't stand the sight of a dark-skinned man speaking in measured tones about statutes and jurisprudence and whatnot. Better to have colored folk check your heart and your teeth and your bank accounts, but let a white man defend you if, God forbid, you ever found yourself at the mercy of a white jury.

Which is why Randy Higgs, twenty-three and soon to be on trial for rape, was being represented by Welborn T. Kirk, whose skin could not have been more pale had he spent the last ten years in a North Georgia cave. Despite his courtly name, he hailed from a small firm that represented more than its share of indigent clients.

"We'll be all right, Joe," Kirk told the suspicious guard. "If he manages to break those chains I'll holler real loud, awright?"

Joe shook his head. "Your funeral. You got fifteen minutes."

"Nah, Joe, I believe I get an hour for visits like these," and Kirk, still standing, shuffled through the papers he'd already laid across the desk. "Filled out the L-5 paperwork right here." He offered a manila folder to the guard. Bishop could just barely spot the tip of a five-dollar bill sticking out.

Joe's beefy face appeared bored, perhaps even mildly insulted, as he took the folder, opened it, and pretended to read through the complex legal jargon of the L-5. Then he handed it back to Kirk, minus Abe Lincoln.

"Sixty minutes, then."

The white guard walked away and positioned himself in the far corner, leaving the three of them sitting at that long table bisecting the narrow room. Along one side were the visitors, the attorneys and relatives, and on the other side sat the doomed in their striped clothes and funk of twice-weekly showers.

"One hour is not long as these kinds of interviews go," Bishop said. He had already checked the space for microphones, spotting none. And the lack of a two-way mirror left him slightly reassured. Still, they needed to keep their voices low so as not to be overheard.

Bishop had, in his many days as a journalist, sat in even less hospitable places than this. He'd conducted interviews in backyard shacks, at roadside work camps, at crime scenes, and in combat zones, across several states and abroad. Still, prisons made him enormously uncomfortable, in ways this white lawyer could not appreciate. "We'd best begin."

Bishop wore a brown tweed jacket over a tan shirt and red tie—not his best attire by a long shot, but he hadn't wanted to overshadow the white attorney whose assistant he was pretending to be. He did not like the fact that he was here under false pretenses, as it felt like an ethical violation to this old-school journalist, but he had accepted long ago that the skewed rules of Southern justice sometimes meant he had to bend his own.

"Mr. Bishop is the man I told you about," Kirk told his young client. "He's the publisher of the *Atlanta Daily Times*."

Higgs was imprisoned here to await trial because a young white woman, eighteen, had accused him of rape.

"Nice to meet you, sir," Higgs said. *Decent enough manners*, Bishop thought. He didn't know the kid's family, which had made him even more reluctant to come. If he tried to aid every poor Negro who may have been unjustly accused, he would manage to do little else. The ability to wisely choose one's battles was one of the keys to Bishop's success.

As publisher and editor-in-chief, Bishop was both an award-winning writer and an astute businessman. He owned not only the *Daily Times* but also seven smaller papers in five Southern states. Thanks to a network of train-riding vendors, who sold the paper to passengers and at stations, and thanks to the train porters themselves, who deliberately and neatly left well-read copies at small Southern stops and cities across the North and Midwest, the *Daily Times* and its affiliates boasted a readership well into the hundreds of thousands.

The white lawyer said, "Why don't you tell Mr. Bishop exactly what you told me."

Higgs looked dead at Bishop and said, "I didn't do it."

Bishop almost wanted to smile at the naïveté. "A bit more detail would help," he said. "Mr. Kirk already told me, for example, that you and she were lovers."

Higgs nodded, looking down. Still embarrassed to talk about sex, and on trial for rape! He'd best get used to that right quick.

"But I never did that. Never . . . *raped* Martha. We were, the two of us were, we were a couple. I mean . . . she was the one who, you know."

"I'm afraid I don't know," Bishop said, folding his hands on the table. "The only way this can work, young man, is if you speak honestly and completely. That means no 'you know how it is' and no 'that sorta thing.'" *Be explicit*, Bishop's favorite writing instructor had drilled into his head many years ago. Nowhere was that harder to do, but more important, than when covering the finer points of love and sex in the Jim Crow South.

"All right," Higgs said, still talking to his lap. "She was the one who . . . who got things going. Who started it."

Kirk surreptitiously passed Bishop a pencil. The guard had refused to let Bishop bring a pen into the room, but apparently the guard had not frisked the white lawyer as thoroughly. Bishop opened his notebook and placed it in his lap, blindly scribbling notes at crotch level so as not to be seen.

"She initiated a romantic relationship?" he asked, spelling it out.

Eyes up, finally. "Yes, sir."

"Forward, was she? Bit of a Jezebel?"

"No, sir," and Higgs appeared insulted, "I mean, she's the one who started it, but she's a good girl. I don't want to be saying bad about her."

Bishop glanced at Kirk, two older men wanting to shake their heads at the folly of youth. The young woman he didn't want to say anything bad about had *put* him here. She was but one person, yet she had set in motion a vast machinery fully capable of crushing Higgs, a veritable army of Confederate wrath that, once set to march, was unlikely to be stopped. And the kid blanched when Bishop dared call her a name!

"She's falsely accused you of raping her and you don't want to be saying bad things about her?"

"I just don't . . . It ain't her that's doing this, sir. It's her family."

"She's certainly playing along with their wishes, isn't she?"

No response. Again Higgs stared at his hands, manacled together and attached via a chain to the desk in front of them.

"You still think she's your Juliet, despite where you're sitting right now? This is your little twist on Shakespearean tragedy? Except, only one of you will die."

Higgs looked up, lost among the references. "I just want to set the record straight, sir, that's all. Mr. Kirk said your paper might could help with that."

"I make no promises, young man. A lot of variables go into whether or not I publish a piece. And I'll be honest, there's a lot about this that makes me disinclined to print a single word. But I'll hear you out if you tell me your story, starting from the beginning."

Kirk added, "And don't forget to mention the love letters."

Bishop asked, "What love letters?"

"The ones she sent him."

Bishop looked at Higgs, who nodded. Then back at the lawyer. "When were they sent?"

"We have two, the second of which was sent three days before she filed the charge. Meaning two days *after* the night she claims the first rape occurred."

"The letters are dated?"

"And we have the postmarked envelopes, in matching stationery." Kirk grinned. He knew what got a journalist's attention; solid documentation was always top of the list.

"Where are they?"

"The letters are in a safe place."

"I'll need to see them."

"We can arrange that."

Bishop thought for a moment. He reached into his pocket, popped open his watch. "All right, young man, we're down to fifty-two minutes. Let's hear your love story."

2

SMITH WAS DONE with Bertha. They'd had their laughs, it had been fun, but that fun had been so long ago. Now he just hated her. She was recalcitrant, she would never do what he asked, and every time he tried to push the buttons that had once caused such joyous music, all he received was frustration.

He pushed her buttons again, but they jammed.

"Goddamn it!" He X'd out the word and started again. Checked his watch—shit, ten minutes until deadline. Bryan Laurence, the fastidious news editor, would be knocking on his door any minute now to complain, remind him of certain realities, time-honored practices, the need for careful editing, the respect for their hard-working typographers, stereotypers, and engravers, who had much to do and couldn't be expected to rush *their* jobs just because Smith needed extra time with *his*.

So he kept typing on Bertha, the black Victrola 600 he'd been using since he'd started at the *Daily Times*. The K stuck, the E only worked half the time (the E! Hardly an uncommon letter), and the Y was so wobbly he expected the strike pad to fly off every time he used it. He found himself trying to use words without Y, omitting adverbs from his lexicon, using "claims" or "states" instead of "says," though he knew Laurence wouldn't truck with that, as Laurence believed even such neutral-sounding words contained within them hidden bias, secret meanings. Such bias was everywhere, all but impossible to purge from your prose.

"*Hate* you, Bertha," Smith muttered, dying cigarette dancing in his lips, as the E failed him again. He silently vowed for the umpteenth time that this would be the last story he wrote with

Bertha, while knowing that the paper once again would deny his request for a new typewriter.

Final sentence, period, the closing *30*, then he hit the cartridge release lever and unspooled the sheet. He carried it through the narrow, box-filled hallway, his trophy flapping in the breeze, and laid it on Laurence's immaculate desk.

Though lined with stacked bookshelves, this was the cleanest room in the building. Despite Laurence's hectic schedule, he somehow found time to dust daily. His life was an unceasing battle against chaos physical, grammatical, and metaphysical. Every one of his pencils, laid out in a perfect line on his desk, was kept sharp enough to draw blood.

"In record time," Laurence said, theatrically glancing at his watch. On the wall behind him, a framed photograph of Ida B. Wells silently judged all visitors.

"Hey, I needed to wait on the official police report. You still know I get those faster than any other reporter." Any other *Negro* reporter, at least; the white reporters had great access to the Department, which typically stonewalled Negro writers. Smith had just enough contacts on the force to get what he needed, though it still took arm-twisting and patience.

"So you've told me, more than once." With wavy hair, green eyes, a Grecian nose and very light skin, Laurence could have passed for white had he wanted to. He'd sometimes used his appearance for journalistic purposes, traveling among whites to report on events Negroes weren't supposed to attend. He'd witnessed three lynchings in rural Georgia and Alabama, blending into the bloodthirsty crowds and recording the horrifying details for his stories.

Rumor had it those experiences had stolen something vital from his mind, unhinged certain doors. A few years ago he'd suffered a breakdown, disappearing for a week. His fellow reporters had feared he was dead. Then a letter to Mr. Bishop had arrived from a doctor, explaining that Laurence would need some time off. Three months later Laurence returned, apologizing for his absence and asking not for his old reporter job back, but a different one: news editor. Mr. Bishop had agreed, but the rumors were rampant: Laurence had been institutionalized, he could no longer stand being in crowds, or in open spaces, or in the presence of white people.

Since returning from his mysterious disappearance, Laurence seemed to be his impeccable, thorough self, demanding perfection from his reporters. But there was also this: no one had seen him walking anywhere outside the building and its sidewalk in forever. Every morning, very early, his wife dropped him off in their Ford and then Laurence, fedora pulled low over his eyes, quickly walked inside. They repeated the routine after work each night. Not one employee could vouch for seeing him anywhere else save this property since 1951.

Laurence started reading, reaching for the red pen he always used to eviscerate Smith's copy. Smith loathed that pen. Eyes down, the editor asked, "Surely you don't intend to hover there while I do this?"

"I just like to overhear it when people say '*mm-mm*, that's good!' when they read my stuff."

"I will return your 'stuff' when I'm ready, Mr. Smith. Run along."

Back in his office, Smith lit a cigarette that didn't feel as triumphant as he'd wanted it to. He opened his window and stared out at Auburn Avenue, watching tendrils of his cigarette smoke unravel out of his cramped office and into the cold air, the circular pattern reminding him of paper on Bertha's rotator, the words escaping ineffably into Atlanta. His work felt so intangible, in his mind one moment and released the next into the great world, where he feared it made no difference, the impact as diffuse as this bit of smoke in the planet's atmosphere.

Deep thoughts, he laughed at himself. He should be drinking.

Smith caught up on reading his peers' work in that day's edition. A Massachusetts senator wanted to add a measure to the upcoming education funding bill that would punish states that continued to resist the Supreme Court's *Brown* school desegregation ruling. Alongside that ran a story on Southern governors' insistence on "interposition," their belief that certain states did not have to follow the year-and-a-half-old Court ruling. In other news, the governments of Liberia and the Soviet Union had signed an agreement establishing diplomatic relations.

Smith glanced at the sports pages and read about an upcoming boxing match, checked the Nightlife Review column to see which acts were coming to town. Even checked the News of the Churches section, because sometimes a good way to keep tabs on the sinners was to keep close watch over the angels, too. Advertisers were still paying the bills, with space bought by Manishewitz Wine, the Gate City Barbershop, Kongolene hair straightener, Southern Wire & Irons' Burglar Bars, and radio station WERD.

Smith put down the paper and watched pedestrians on the street. He didn't like admitting it, but it was moments like these— when he should have been feeling triumphant—that he missed the excitement of his old job the most. The adrenaline of filing a story hardly compared to that of chasing down a subject and getting him in cuffs.

Then Mr. Bishop, moving at a faster pace than was normal for one so reserved, walked in. As was his style, he began the conversation without greeting or preamble: "I think there's something to this Higgs case."

Tall and thin, Arthur Bishop never slouched, not even when his head nearly hit the top of a doorframe, as it was doing right then. His very posture one of moral rectitude, which Smith, a waltzer and gallivanter and sashayer, found vaguely comical, even if it did keep him on his toes. Bishop wasn't the kind of boss you wanted to make mistakes around.

"How so?" Smith asked. "Seems like exactly the sort of story you usually don't want to touch."

The conservative Bishop, proud of the megaphone he'd built, was wary of using it on stories he feared might cause his readers more harm than good. The paper covered crime *very* carefully—too carefully for Smith's tastes. (More than once, Bishop had killed one of Smith's pieces for being "inflammatory.") The *Daily Times* certainly covered instances of police brutality against Negroes, and cases where Negroes were arrested under demonstrably false charges, but those tended to be short pieces, matter-of-fact, dry. Nothing like the throat-clearing screeds in the communist *Daily Worker* or the *Chicago Defender*, America's most widely read Negro paper (a fact that irked Bishop), which proudly used its outspoken coverage of the South's inequities to encourage Negroes to migrate north. But reporting on the South was a very different job indeed for those editors and writers who had to live down here every day.

"This case seems worth covering," Bishop said.

"Great. What's the scoop?"

Bishop thought for a moment. "Let me do some digging first." He was famous for being tight-lipped about stories as he worked on them.

Smith changed the subject. "How was Montgomery?"

Bishop had driven there earlier in the week. "It was a productive trip."

"You check up on the boycott?"

Bishop wore a displeased look, as if Smith had passed gas. "I did not. I was busy on other things."

The bus boycott in Montgomery had been going on for close to two months, astounding those observers who were paying attention. The young reverend who led the newly formed Montgomery Improvement Association, M. L. King, Jr., was a native Atlantan, the son of a prominent local minister whose congregation worshipped half a mile from the *Daily Times*.

The paper had run a few pieces on the boycott, and Bishop himself had written an editorial offering support. He'd offered criticism, too, arguing that a legal assault crafted by steely lawyers would have been far better than some strange economic gambit in which maids and laborers voted with their feet. And he'd disparaged the smallness of the group's demands: they weren't even asking for an end to bus segregation, only that already-seated Negroes not be asked to relinquish their seats to whites who boarded later, and that the company hire some Negro drivers. Privately, Bishop had argued that the boycott was a well-intentioned but poorly conceived idea, unnecessarily confrontational and likely to incite violence against the most vulnerable members of the community.

"It's been going on for a while now," Smith noted. "Story's getting bigger. We could at least knock on his father's door and see if—"

"We've had these conversations," Bishop cut him off. "Stick to crime, Smith."

With that, Bishop marched off to his office, so Smith's phone rang to keep him company.

"Hey there, Smitty," came the familiar voice over the line. "I got a body for ya."

✦

By the time Smith made it to the victims' tiny apartment, an ambulance had taken one man away and the other lay dead and very bloody indeed on the floor, awaiting a hearse.

"They're not just brothers but twins, right?" Smith asked Deaderick, a white cop.

The handle of a cleaver rose out of the dead man's back at about a forty-five-degree angle, a fatal hypotenuse. The wood floor beneath was so soaked with blood Smith was sure the ceiling below must be dripping. He'd have to check downstairs, for his story. Thinking, *good detail.*

"Yep," Deaderick said. "This here is Larry and the one on the way to the hospital is Lenny. Trust me, Lenny ain't gonna make it either. Wounds were *deep.*"

Most of the stabbing victims Smith had observed shared an odd thing in common: usually the attacker put a blanket over the body. The first time he saw that, he'd been struck by the sentiment. Whether the killer was a woman or a man or an adolescent, they had been so overtaken by rage or bloodlust that they'd stabbed again and again, furiously. Then later, when the fury subsided, some shame took hold and they couldn't even look at what they'd done. So, a blanket or sheet or quilt, hiding the act.

The fact that nothing covered Larry bespoke the madness of a moment ago, both brothers stabbing each other, no one winning.

They were on the third, top floor of a decrepit building in Darktown, a ramshackle structure that seemed to shift when the winter winds picked up. At least this place had a bathroom; plenty on this block still used outhouses.

"We been looking for these two for that jewelry heist few weeks back," Deaderick explained. "This is their place, but they were never here when we checked. Must have left town for a spell, then figured the dust had settled. Anyway, appears they had an altercation over how to split the proceeds."

A Bowie knife, still glistening, lay on the floor a few inches away from Larry's left hand. On his right wrist he wore a gold watch. Smith checked the make of the watch, scribbled it into his notebook.

"So he was the lefty?" he asked.

"I suppose so, Smitty. It matter?" No one on earth called him "Smitty" but Deaderick. The cop had invented the nickname, perhaps thinking he needed some affectionate way of referring to Smith, something above "boy" but beneath full-on respect. Smith hated "Smitty", but he put up with it.

Deaderick pointed out the open silverware drawer where the brothers had found their weapons. "Oh, and guess what Lenny used to do for a living, when he wasn't stealing. C'mon, guess."

Smith sighed. Deaderick enjoyed these scenes too much. As did the writers for the white papers, who wrote their stories of Negro crime with unrestrained glee, like dazzled anthropologists crossed with stand-up comedians. (*The husky youth moved with ferocious speed, wielding his primitive, razor-sharp weapon in his meaty fist— but for the last time!*)

Smith guessed, "Butcher."

"Hey, give the man a cigar! Actually, butcher's assistant, but close enough." Then Deaderick held his hands out in the air, stretching invisible headlines between his index fingers. "*TWIN KILLING IN DARKTOWN. CAIN KILLS ABEL, ABEL KILLS CAIN FIRST.*"

"Don't quit your day job."

"Why not? Worked out for you, didn't it?"

Had it worked out, Smith wondered? He was a former cop turned crime writer. And before that, he'd led a tank battalion during the war. Which meant that he'd witnessed far too many scenes like this, or worse.

During his time on the force, Smith had seldom experienced the good fortune of working with any decent white cops. To this day, the white and Negro portions of APD worked separately. Negro cops were only permitted to patrol Negro areas, so, if all went right, they should never encounter white officers outside of the station, except on the rare occasions when a white person committed a crime in the Negro neighborhoods, in which case white officers needed to be called for assistance, since only white cops could arrest white offenders. White cops were almost uniformly rude and dismissive, if not outright hostile, popping racist jokes and epithets aplenty.

So Smith never would have suspected that, after leaving the force, one of his more helpful sources in the Department would be a white cop.

The first few times he'd encountered Officer Pete Deaderick at crime scenes, the thirtyish Deaderick had seemed like just another corn-fed white man with an air of quickly evaporating patience when in the presence of Negroes. Yet over the years the two had developed something approaching a rapport. Deaderick had actually complimented Smith on his writing one day, which shocked Smith, who hadn't thought any white cops read the *Daily Times*. A few days after that, Smith had called Deaderick when he'd needed more information on a crime involving a wealthy white lady and a Negro maid whose allegedly poor service had led to a heated exchange, which then led to assault with a deadly weapon (again, knives; the damn things were everywhere). Smith had scored one of his better scoops that day, and Deaderick had become a reliable source.

Smith found Deaderick tolerable enough, but he remained well aware of this truth: Deaderick only acted agreeable because Smith now occupied a lower rung on the totem pole, a mere reporter taking down notes from this important white cop.

If Smith had still worn a badge, Deaderick probably would have hated him.

Smith glanced at the blood-speckled walls, the blood on the doorknob, the blood in the hallway outside. Lenny had tried to run before collapsing, where the police found him. On the floor of the kitchenette sat two satchels, one of them unzipped and full of cash.

"You sure they won't be able to stitch Lenny up at the hospital?" Smith asked. "He definitely won't survive?"

Deaderick blew air out his lips. "That ambulance that came for him? Let's just say it took its sweet time getting here, you catch my drift."

Smith could have caught it one-handed and blindfold. He would have loved to use a quote like that, to note the white officer's cavalier attitude about the value of Negro life and the city's lack of urgency when it came to helping colored folk. But then Deaderick would never talk to him again, and one of Smith's best wells of scoops would run dry.

Another compromise Smith would try to justify to himself, later. First, he had a story to write.

Less than a mile to the west, Gauthier's Catering sat on the northern side of Auburn Avenue, its windows filled with light even on overcast afternoons like today. A bell rang as Smith opened the door and breathed in an aroma that made him almost weak in the knees.

"My God, what are y'all cooking?" He'd skipped lunch and felt tortured by the scent. It was thick in the air, tangible.

"We're making ..." The young woman at the front counter,

who had been placing freshly baked scones under a glass dome, stopped mid-answer when she recognized Smith. "Oh, *hello* there." Her expression not kind.

He recognized her as well, too late. She certainly hadn't been wearing a baker's cap and white apron over a gray smock, with some flour in her right eyebrow, when he'd met her at a dance club. He couldn't recall her name, as it had been a few months, but he remembered the venue and the bottle of wine they'd shared, and the bedroom.

"You got some nerve showing your face after all this time."

He smiled, still drawing a blank on her name. "I seem to recall you enjoying yourself."

"And I recall you never calling me back once, and ignoring those notes I left." Was it Lenore? Lorene? "Why you play it that way?"

"I've just been real busy with work and all." It was times like these when he wondered how he got himself into such trouble, why the pursuit of pleasure always seemed to cause pain. "But I may finally get some down time this weekend."

Her face softened. Lottie, that was it. "You have my number."

Did he? He had no idea. "I do, Lottie." He flashed his winning grin. "But until the weekend comes, I'm still all work. I need to ask the proprietor a few questions. She around?"

"You'd best call, though," and smiled as she walked off.

Moments later, Patrice Gauthier, the shop's owner, emerged from the back. She shook her head.

"Tommy Smith. So that's why Lottie's so moony-eyed."

Despite the hubbub and clamor of the kitchen, she spoke in a voice just above a whisper. At first he'd taken her tone for flirtation, but it turned out she spoke like that to everyone. As if telling the world, *if you want a piece of this mind, listen close.*

"I have that effect on people," Smith admitted. "It's hard to turn off."

"That must be a terrible burden."

Lord, how many women in this building did he have a history with? He had met Patrice three weeks ago, when he was reporting on a rash of burglaries along Auburn. The same night that a jewelry shop next door had been broken into, someone had busted a small safe in Patrice's back room, making off with two hundred dollars. Their interview had turned into a dinner invitation, and because he could tell she was a fine lady (already a widow, having run the business with her husband for years, until his car accident) he took her to a fancier restaurant than was his norm, steak and red wine from Burgundy, then chocolate ganache for dessert, which wasn't remotely the sweetest part of the evening.

"Actually, I'm here for a story."

"I'm afraid this story won't end for you the way the last one did."

She stood nearly as tall as him, in the same get-up as the other woman, minus the silly hat. Her straightened hair pulled into a bun, her skin light, her perfectly plucked eyebrows arching in a way that had always made him feel studied, probed, judged, and her lips pressed tightly together as if to say, *you will never kiss these again*. He found himself wondering, as she clearly did, why he hadn't called on her again.

"The police have found the two men who stole from you," he told her. "They're brothers, Lenny and Larry Fletcher. They stabbed each other—one's dead, the other's in the hospital and probably won't make it. Police found the jewels from next door and a whole lot of cash."

"Did you take a photo of the money before it disappears into some officer's pocket?"

He should have thought of that. He didn't trust Deaderick enough to assume all that cash would make it to an evidence room. "I'm sorry, no. But I was hoping to get your response to the fact that the thieves are, well, no longer at large."

She raised only her left eyebrow. He'd always been impressed by people who could do that. "Am I a suspect?"

"No. They killed each other. I just—"

"You just had to see me again." No smile. Just reporting a fact. Yet his smile returned. "Phrase it however you'd like."

"Oh, I get to write it myself? Lovely. How about," and, just as

Deaderick had done earlier, she used her hands to project invisible words into the air around her, "*THIEVES FIND THEY CAN'T TAKE JEWELS WITH THEM TO THE AFTERLIFE.* Or maybe, *ONE-NIGHT-STAND ARTIST SHOWS HIS FACE AGAIN AFTER DISAPPEARANCE.*"

He should have expected this. "Look, I'd sort of assumed we had an understanding."

"Oh, I think I understand you just fine."

Something started sizzling on a pan. Smith knew how it felt.

"I'm sorry. I didn't mean . . . " But what did he mean? He found himself at a loss, and he wasn't sure if it was some power she wielded over him with those commanding eyes, or if she had just pointed out an essential meaninglessness to his actions.

"Look, if you want to be chasing after twenty-two-year-olds like Lottie, go have your fun." Lottie was only twenty-two? Maybe he should have guessed that. Patrice was, admittedly, more mature than most of the women he'd wooed. He wondered if that's why he'd never called her back. "I have quite enough trouble right now without having to deal with you, Tommy Smith."

"What kind of trouble?"

"You didn't notice how I have fewer people working here? I thought you reporters were observant."

"I did notice, I just figured they were delivering or serving some customers."

"You figured wrong. I have far fewer customers than I used to."

"I'm shocked. Way this place smells, I could eat the air in here. I'd eat that counter if you had a sharp enough knife."

"Most white folks aren't feeling the same way."

"I thought a lot of your customers were white folks." Indeed, her fine French cooking seemed overtly aimed at upper-crust white patrons, much more so than other caterers in this neighborhood. No ribs or corn bread in here.

"That used to be the case. Until my orders dropped off a cliff."

"Since when?"

"A few weeks. I had to let two part-timers go already, and if it doesn't turn around fast, I'll have to let go of some more."

"Any idea why? Can't be they suddenly decided they don't like the food."

"I shouldn't have brought it up. I'll be fine." She shook her head. "Anyway, if you don't mind, I do have *some* work to do. Is there anything else you need? Any other reason you just *had* to come see me?"

"There are plenty of reasons to see a lady like you. But for right now, I wanted to see if you had a quote for the story, on your thieves killing each other."

Her expression pained him, partly because he wasn't used to seeing it in a woman's eyes: a look of utter disappointment in him.

"They got what was coming to them," she said. "As all men who act like little boys eventually do."

⚡

Arthur Bishop, working alone in his office long after the current issue had been put to bed, reviewed his notes from his research trip to Montgomery. The police record, the porter's story. The other information he'd learned, some not yet substantiated, but certainly enough.

He had called the man's office earlier and been given the runaround, as often occurred. This time he called him at home.

When the man answered, Bishop introduced himself.

Then he said, "I know what you did."

3

LATER THAT NIGHT, Officers Lucius Boggs and Marty Jones walked their beat down West Hunter Street.

Both wore gloves and APD jackets over their uniform shirts, and both wished they could exchange their uniform caps for woolen hats, but the Department didn't allow that. Their lack of squad cars had always grated, but especially in the dead of winter, and when the wind was as vicious as it was tonight. Boggs had taken to wearing long johns and had told his rookie to do the same. Jones had only been on the force four months. Boggs knew it was a sign of respect how McInnis always gave him the new blood, but it still annoyed him to constantly be training someone.

He felt like a de facto sergeant himself, not that he was paid like it.

Hunter Street was the main thoroughfare of the West Side. Negroes had started establishing this neighborhood as a crosstown rival to Sweet Auburn a couple of decades ago, first the professors who valued the proximity to Morehouse and Spelman and Atlanta University, then the other professionals. Boggs had heard his father note that many of his wealthiest congregants had moved out here, leaving behind the more crowded Sweet Auburn, which sat on the east side of town. Boggs could tell the reverend worried about how the exodus would affect his church, and his community.

They walked past the home of Reverend King, whom Boggs and everyone else had only recently started thinking of as "King Sr." because of the sudden popularity of the man's son. Boggs was a few years older than King Jr., having met him once or twice as kids. Their fathers often came together for community gatherings and political affairs, from voter drives to meetings with the mayor and police chief. Still, it was surprising to hear how the young preacher was leading the boycott in Montgomery. Boggs felt a curious mixture of fear for King and his family, envy at the man's sudden notoriety, and pride as a fellow Atlantan and preacher's son. Boggs too knew what it was like to have a sense of duty impressed upon you from childhood.

"Hey," Jones said, stopping. "Somebody's in that car."

Boggs squinted to see what Jones was talking about.

"There," Jones pointed to a long sedan with prominent tail fins. Its lights off, hot air pumping through its pipe.

Still squinting, Boggs stepped closer and saw the silhouettes of two fedoras. Sitting in a parked car at half past midnight on a near-freezing January night. Across the street and two doors down from King Sr.'s house.

"I see them," Boggs said.

"We just passed Reverend King's."

"I know. Let's say hello to the drivers."

He took the lead, walking with his right hand resting on the butt of his billy club. He wondered if there was any chance King had arranged for bodyguards, nervous about being made a target due to his son's actions.

And if so, were these men the bodyguards or the people King needed guarding from?

The man in the driver's seat was smoking and the passenger was lighting a cigarette, the windows cracked. Closer still and Boggs saw that they were both white.

The passenger let out his first puff and his eyes widened, making eye contact with Boggs.

The passenger elbowed the driver and seemed to mutter something. The driver too looked up, then the headlights flicked on and Boggs lost them in the brightness.

The engine revved and the car lurched from its parking spot.

"Stop! Police!" Boggs called out, hand still on his club, but already the car was in the middle of the road, driving at such a speed that jumping in front to stop it was not an option.

Boggs got a good enough look at the driver's profile that he would be able to recognize him again, he hoped. Both men white, early thirties, in fedoras and ties and overcoats. The car a newish, white Chrysler two-door.

After the car passed, Boggs reached for his notebook and pencil. He jotted down the car's tag number.

He had feared something like this, but had expected the culprits to look different. These weren't peckerwoods in a pickup laden with baseball bats and ax handles, but men in suits driving a decent car. Boggs's mind raced to *plainclothes cop*. But why? If white cops were keeping watch to protect the reverend—unlikely on its face— they certainly wouldn't drive off at the sight of two uniforms.

He glanced around the neighborhood but didn't see any lights flickering on. Neither his shouts nor the car's engine had been loud enough to wake anyone.

"Should we knock on King's door and tell him?" Jones asked.

Boggs considered it for a moment. "No, let's let them rest. We'll tell McInnis," and he shook his notebook, "and find out who they were."

4

WORKING THE 6 P.M. to 2 a.m. shift meant McInnis slept late most days. Except for mornings like today, when his wife was out running errands and the phone rang, because the school principal was telling him to come pick up his eldest, Jimmy, who'd just been in a fight.

After an uncomfortable meeting with a skeletal principal who'd reminded McInnis of the boy-hating nuns of his Catholic school youth in Savannah, he drove home with his fifteen-year-old. Jimmy's hair was mussed considerably, and his knuckles had been bloodied, but he'd lacked any injury other than a small cut on his lower lip. Two buttons had been popped from his shirt, which bore a couple spots of red that did not appear to be his blood.

"I work hard all night so you can go to that school and learn," McInnis said. "And learn how to do something with your brain that might involve you not having to work all night like I do. I'd best never have to come in there for you again, understood?"

"Yessir."

Two other boys had been sent to doctors' offices, the principal had explained, and two teachers had been required to pull Jimmy off one of them. Jimmy was henceforth suspended, and McInnis would likely be receiving some medical bills.

He marveled at the fact that his easygoing son could inflict such damage. This was his first fight, as far as McInnis knew. After four blocks of silence, he asked, "So who was it?"

"Chet Taylor and Roy Iles."

He didn't know the first name, but the second was an old friend, McInnis had thought. "What was it about?"

A pause, and when Jimmy's voice came, it came quietly. "Nothing, sir."

"That's not an answer. What happened?"

Another pause. "They called me a nigger lover."

Interesting how the principal had failed to mention that element of the brawl. McInnis wondered if she'd even known about it, or was simply afraid to bring it up.

"Why'd they say that?"

No answer. Jimmy might have done that slouch-shrug thing he'd become so fond of in lieu of actual vocalization, but McInnis was watching the road.

"Well?"

"They said my old man was a nigger lover, too."

He'd reached a stoplight, so he turned to face Jimmy. "That right?"

"Yessir. That's when I popped Roy. He went down fast, then it was me and Chet for a spell."

McInnis kept a heavy bag and a speed bag in his garage, and he'd given his son lessons in the basics. He hadn't thought they'd sunk in, but maybe the kid had been practicing.

The light turned green. "How'd this happen to come up?"

Another silence, long enough for McInnis to think perhaps no answer would be forthcoming, until Jimmy finally said, "I assume it's on account of your job, sir."

"How would he know my job?"

"It's not like it's top secret, sir. Roy's friends with Chris Mayfield, and Chris's dad's a cop."

McInnis couldn't think of an Officer Mayfield off the top of his head, but he'd long realized that his own name was well known by every cop in Atlanta: Sergeant Joe McInnis, the only white cop who worked with the colored officers. Increasingly viewed as a traitor working behind enemy lines.

He had been stunned when informed in early 1948 that he would be banished to Negro Atlanta to be the eight rookies' sergeant.

He didn't have anything against Negroes, but why should he be the one to bear the Jim Crow cross for his people's sins? After he'd been given the order, he'd been so upset that he'd told his wife he would quit. Bonnie had managed to talk him out of it, tactfully reminding him of their mortgage and three children.

Still, why him? Chief Jenkins had even sat down with him, explaining that McInnis should take the assignment as a compliment. This was an important job, and Jenkins needed a calm, strong fellow who could lead these rookies through uncharted territory. A man who wasn't a bigot, a man who hadn't been initiated into the Klan like so many other Atlanta cops. Or so Jenkins had claimed. More likely, McInnis had been chosen not by the chief but by someone lower down, someone who had wanted to punish him for being the kind of cop who was not a *company man*. McInnis had been one of the lead officers in a controversial sting two years prior, an investigation into illegal gambling operated by crooked cops, and the fallout had cost several officers their jobs. In a way, it had cost McInnis his job, too: because he had dared to punish dirty cops, he was seen as a backstabber.

When they'd needed to banish someone to run the new Negro precinct, he was their man.

It had been nearly eight years now, and he was proud of how he'd molded his once-green recruits into capable officers—doubly so because of all the resistance they'd faced from most other white cops. Their once lawless neighborhoods still had plenty of problems, but they were safer than before. None of his men had been killed in the line of duty. None had been shot. The Negro precinct had started with eight officers, and though they now numbered fifteen, plenty had left the job, for various reasons: some had gone back to college; one had decided to become a teacher; and a few had angrily cited the Jim Crow rules under which they had been required to work, deciding they could not continue to serve as policemen who weren't allowed to walk beats in white neighborhoods or drive squad cars or arrest white lawbreakers.

Not only had McInnis worked with Negroes all day, he was

possibly the only white person who worked in that part of town all night, especially in those first five years when their precinct had been at the Butler Street Y. So as not to alarm the children, he and Bonnie had not told the kids about his transfer. Jimmy had been seven at the time, Erin two years younger. McInnis had never been one to talk about work, but after the transfer a new layer of silence dropped down like a glass wall in the middle of the dining room table. The kids knew he was a policeman who risked his safety to protect people and put food on that table; they didn't need to know that he did it in neighborhoods that their friends' parents wouldn't dare set foot in.

It hadn't been until a couple years ago that he realized Jimmy knew more details about his job. It had started with an innocent question or two, hesitant attempts to confirm bits of schoolyard gossip. McInnis had eventually explained that, yes, he worked with Negroes, but they were all fine men and the job he did was no different than what he'd done in his earlier years on the force.

Today's conversation surprised him. It felt so odd, the way kids aged into things before you were ready. You try to control their lives as best you can, yet suddenly you realize there's another pair of eyes observing everything you do, forming opinions about your performance.

In the car, Jimmy asked, "It's not really true, is it, sir? I mean, you don't . . . *love* them, right?"

McInnis smiled at the awkwardness and innocence of the question. "'Nigger lover's' not a literal phrase, Jimmy. It's a word white trash use against anyone who doesn't make it a point to bully Negroes. I do not *love* any particular Negro, no. But I work with them. We solve problems together. That's all."

Silence for a few beats. "All right."

He sensed that Jimmy needed more. "At the end of the day, they can be good or bad, like any white person. They're just folks."

He had never really voiced it this way before. It felt strange on his tongue.

"Okay."

He thought for a moment. Silence with his son seldom left him feeling uncomfortable—they could fish or work on carpentry projects for hours without talking—but this one did.

"Are the kids at school talking much," he asked, "about the schools desegregating?"

"Not much. Teachers bring it up from time to time. But we don't talk about it."

McInnis wondered how that could be true. The *Brown* decision seemed to be all some people wanted to talk about. McInnis's wife, Bonnie, had never given much thought to politics, but she'd become galvanized by the schools issue. A meeting for the parents of high school students was coming up soon, inconveniently scheduled for McInnis's one night off; Bonnie was expecting him to join her there. He was not looking forward to it.

"It sounds like it's not going to happen anyway, right?" Jimmy said. "Mrs. Fletcher said the Supreme Court says we don't really have to move fast, plus the governor's coming up with ways to stop it."

"It's complicated." He didn't care to extend this conversation. And he honestly wasn't sure how he felt about what had become an all-consuming issue for so many of his friends and neighbors. Only a couple of years ago, the concept of integrated schools would have been absurd, laughable. Now it was imminent, unless white Southerners and their elected officials took action.

His attitudes about Negroes had evolved. Was that the right way to put it, he wondered, *evolution*? Perhaps that was the wrong metaphor entirely, fraught with primitive imagery. Maybe we were cursed with imprecise words, doomed by language. But he knew he was a different person than he'd been in '48. His work with men like Boggs and Smith had broadened his understanding. At the same time, if fears over integration were *already* leading to fights at school, he had a hard time visualizing a peaceful process ever occurring. Putting it off a few years, so people could get used to the idea, would probably be best—and that would spare his own children the trouble.

"Regardless of what anyone says about me or about you, I don't expect to have to pick you up from school like this again. Understood?"

"Yessir."

"If someone says something like that to you again, you take it up with them outside of school hours, and off school property." He pulled into the driveway and gave his son a hard look. "And you do it in a way that he'll never say another word to you, got it?"

5

"**MOTHER*FUCKER*,**" **BLACKMON NEARLY** spat at the new *Look* maga-zine in his hands. "Motherfucker, motherfucker."

"Why even read it?" Smith asked.

Blackmon threw the magazine in the garbage, where it belonged. "Did you read it?"

Smith wanted to say no, but he admitted, "Yeah."

Blackmon fished it back out of the trash, unable to ignore it. He kept reading. "Motherfucker."

"Who runs something like that?" asked Jeremy Toon. He'd been a writer for the *Daily Times* for more than a decade now. An industrious Morehouse man, Toon had annoyed Smith back when Smith had been a cop and had to fend off Toon's questions. But now that they worked together, Smith often found himself asking Toon's advice.

"It's newsworthy," Smith admitted.

"Cracker motherfuckers," said Blackmon as he kept reading.

Look's lead story, published yesterday, was the confession of the two white men who had killed fourteen-year-old Emmett Till for allegedly talking to a white lady. They had been exonerated in a sham of a trial last summer. Not only had they gotten away with it, but now, only months later, they were boasting about it in print. Paid for the story and forever immune from prosecution.

Blackmon threw the magazine away again. "If we don't start drinking soon, I'm gonna throw up."

He and Smith shared the small office, which was bearable only because they were seldom there at the same time. This was one of those times, as they awaited their editors' word on rewrites.

Toon sat on Blackmon's desk, the only space for a third person. Writing at the *Daily Times* meant being cramped, overtired, and underpaid.

"In other news," Smith said, wanting to change the subject, "Bishop says he wasn't in Montgomery to cover the boycott."

"Why was he there, then?" Toon asked.

"Wouldn't say."

"Mother*fucker*," Blackmon muttered as he picked the magazine back up and read more.

A few months ago, Blackmon had been sent to cover the trial of Till's killers in Mississippi. He'd later told Smith and Toon about some of the differences he'd noticed between that and other trials he'd covered over the years, such as the fact that white reporters had worked the story. Lots of them. Because of all the press, it was the first time Blackmon had felt reasonably safe enough to dress in jacket and tie while sitting in a small-town Southern courthouse, dispensing with his usual method of dressing like a laborer so as not to make himself a target of offended, envious rednecks. The good news was, there now seemed to be strength in numbers while covering such atrocities. The bad news was, lynchers were getting off as easily as ever, *and* the colored writers were now at risk of being scooped by white papers.

As if television news wasn't a big enough threat to what they were doing. Smith didn't own a TV yet, but he was saving for one.

"Motherfucker."

Toon asked Smith, "You gonna go to that reunion?"

"What reunion?" Blackmon asked, tossing the magazine yet again.

"Veterans of the 761st have been getting together in a different city each year," Smith explained. He'd received an invitation the other day. "It's Chicago this time."

Before being a cop, Smith had served in the 761st Tank Battalion, known as the Black Panthers. A Negro reporter named Trezzvant Anderson had been embedded with them, and his mythologizing articles had made the all-Negro 761st famous. The hours Smith had passed talking to Trezz, during the brief parts of their slog across Europe when he hadn't been completely consumed with trying to stay alive, had planted the first seeds of journalistic interest in his mind.

Reporter hat always in place, Toon said, "You should go. Write a story on it."

Smith rolled his eyes. "Write a story about my own battalion's reunion? Nah, I ain't that narcissistic."

A slight pause, then Toon burst out laughing. Blackmon chuckled too.

"What?" Smith asked. "What did I say?"

"*You?*" Toon shook his head, smiling. "*You*, not that narcissistic?"

Blackmon reached over to Smith's desk and found, under a pile of papers, one of Smith's many mirrors. Imitating Smith, he held it in front of his face. He licked his finger, ran it along his upper lip. "Wait, wait, I can't hear you over the beauty of my perfectly maintained mustache."

"Fuck you both!" Smith grabbed the mirror away, smiling despite himself. Before putting it back, he couldn't help glancing at his reflection.

Toon and Blackmon noticed, pointing and laughing harder still.

Leaving the building later, Smith was trying to decide whether he'd join the usual gang for drinks at Ruffin's Royal or whether he'd be smart and save money with another meal of beans and franks in his tiny kitchenette, when the breeze carried a trail of expensive perfume his way.

Next, the sound of her heels, and a sigh, perhaps because she was running late, or was annoyed at some other way in which life had let her down. He turned and saw her striding toward him, the makeup on her light skin perfect, the dark blue hat worthy of Sunday church, and the hand clutching her shawl bedecked in enough gold and precious stones to set off a mining expedition in California.

"Evening, Mrs. Bishop."

"He's in there, I trust?"

"He is, but he ain't as finely attired as you are."

"He forgot, I'm sure. We're supposed to be going to a benefit at Spelman. Is he presentable enough?"

Smith didn't care to get involved in their domestic squabbling. "Doesn't have no ink stains on his cuffs, that what you mean."

"The man wasn't always this forgetful."

Something about Victoria Bishop always set Smith on edge. Perhaps simply because his powers of charm did not seem to work on her, making her a rare woman indeed. She was a good deal older, of course, so it's not like he *wanted* to flirt with her, but still, even old ladies swooned around Smith, fussed over him, indulged in dirty humor they'd otherwise never condone. Maybe it was because she was the boss's wife. Maybe it was because she was so pale she was practically white, a generation away from producing children who might pass—actually, maybe that had already happened. The Bishops didn't have children, as far as Smith knew, but maybe they did, and their progeny had fled to greener pastures, pursuing success as doggedly as their father had but without all the old roadblocks.

"You aren't married, are you, Mr. Smith?"

"No, ma'am."

"Don't 'ma'am' me, I'm not that old."

"Sorry. But no, I'm not married."

She scrutinized him. "Some men would then say, 'I haven't found the right woman yet,' but I can see that wouldn't work for you. You've found all the women, just haven't found a reason to stop, have you?"

This was hardly the sort of conversation to have with your boss's wife. "Well, marriage seems to come with a lot of downsides, and as for the upsides . . . I don't seem to be missing them."

"I'll bet you aren't."

His words might have felt true a short while ago—they had *always* felt true—but they tasted wrong in his mouth now. The way the fellows had laughed at him a moment ago, and that awkward visit to Patrice's kitchen. And the fact that a few young ladies had recently used the dreaded O-word in describing him. Still in his mid-thirties, he didn't *feel* old, but yes, many of his peers had settled down. They didn't seem particularly *happy* about matrimony, and none had experienced anything like his success as a ladies' man, but still, he fixated on that look in Patrice Gauthier's eyes, her dig at him for chasing younger women, her implication that what he saw as success was actually a kind of failure.

Or maybe he was overanalyzing the simple fact that he wanted to see Patrice again.

"Sometimes, Mr. Smith, I fear you've got the right idea after all."

With that, she cinched her shawl more tightly around her throat and left a bemused Smith behind in a jet stream of perfume that, he figured, cost more per drop than the bourbon he would soon be sipping.

RELATIONSHIP CONSENSUAL, LETTERS SHOW

Woman's Own Words Cast Prosecution Claims in Doubt

by ARTHUR BISHOP

Randy Higgs, 23, has claimed since his arrest for rape last week that the alleged victim, an 18-year-old white woman, was in fact the instigator of their relationship. Documents newly revealed by his attorney bolster this claim.

"I don't care what other people say, you and I are meant to be together," the alleged victim herself wrote in one letter. "Dearest, I know we need to keep secret, but let us not allow that to dim the passion in our hearts," she wrote in another. That second letter is postmarked two days after the alleged attack occurred.

Mr. Higgs claims he is innocent of all charges and that his arrest is the result of a misunderstanding between the alleged victim and her relatives, who do not approve of her affection for a colored man.

"They want all the blame to fall on me," Mr. Higgs said during an interview at the prison where he is currently awaiting trial. "But it's not right. It's only because of the shame of her family that things have come out this way."

The letters themselves seemed to anticipate that response. In one, the woman warned Mr. Higgs that they needed to keep their affair secret from her father because "God only knows what he'd do if he found out."

State attorneys said they doubt the letters are genuine, and that even if so, they do not disprove the allegations against Mr. Higgs.

"We have a solid case, and no amount of ridiculous ah-ha revelations can change that," said Assistant District Attorney Dan Cross.

Mr. Higgs's attorney, Welborn T. Kirk, said that he intends to submit the letters as evidence at trial, if the state continues to pursue the case. Mr. Kirk said he would also call handwriting experts and have the letters fingerprinted if necessary, to prove their provenance.

The trial is scheduled to begin in February.

6

NIGGER I WILL hunt you down and pluck your eyes out with my thumbs. I will tear off your fingers one at a time. I will strike the match and watch you burn.

Two days after the *Daily Times* ran Bishop's story about Randy Higgs and Martha Hunter, some readers were proving to be very offended indeed.

"Seems more graphic than usual," Toon noted when Smith finished reading the four-paragraph missive. True, Smith had read other livid letters-to-the-editor before, but this was one of the worst.

"Tell the mailroom to wear gloves for a little while," Smith said. "They get any more of these, no one touches them with bare hands. I want to get clean prints."

Toon nodded. "Our hate mail isn't usually so specific." He pointed out a couple passages in which the writer referred to the Higgs piece. "White folks don't read us enough to be offended by any particular story. Usually they just hate that we exist."

This was merely the most sadistic of several angry letters they'd received. Smith read through the others, skimming them when he saw they weren't threatening bodily harm. He checked to see which writers had signed their names. One of the names made him do a double take.

"Cassie Rakestraw," he read. "I worked with a Rakestraw once. A white cop. Wonder if she's any relation." He checked the return address, in Kirkwood. The Officer Rakestraw he once knew had lived in Hanford Park until 1950, when several colored families, including Smith's sister, had moved there. Within months, all the whites had fled.

He put down her letter (which attacked Bishop, criticized the paper, and argued that this "only proves why coloreds do not possess the maturity and good judgment to be schooled with white children") and picked up the scarier letter again. Like all the others, it was handwritten, which could be useful later. Block letters had been employed in hopes of disguising the sender, but Smith knew there were experts who could make connections, should that be necessary.

Smith slid the letter into a plastic bag and handed it back to Toon, telling him to place it somewhere safe.

That afternoon, Smith typed on Bertha again, filing a story on a quartet of deaths that authorities were attributing to poisoned bootleg whiskey; it was the worst incident since '51, when forty-one died and scores were left disabled by booze mixed with wood alcohol. Smith figured this had a shot to lead the next edition, as the police were concerned a flood of deaths was imminent. He handed his story to Laurence, who waved him away dismissively.

In the hallway, Smith saw three men in impressive suits speaking in hushed tones with Mr. Bishop. Seeing that they had attracted attention, Bishop invited them upstairs to his office.

"What's going on?" Smith asked Toon after watching Bishop and the others exit.

"The paper's being sued for libel."

Smith couldn't help that his first reaction was, "For something I wrote?"

"No," Toon laughed, but his tone was otherwise serious. "For something the boss wrote: the Higgs story."

Laurence appeared, handing Smith his now marked-up copy. Having overheard their conversation, he explained, "The family of the alleged rape victim is suing the paper, and Bishop personally. They have the state Attorney General on board. He's indicting us for violating decency laws."

Smith asked, "For reporting on a rape case?"

"For alleging that the white girl was having a consensual relationship with a colored man," Laurence said.

Nothing surprised Smith when it came to ways white men abused power.

"They can't win," Toon said. "I reread the piece again this morning. Every allegation was printed as a direct quote from Higgs. They can't sue us for a source's opinions."

"That doesn't matter," Laurence said. "White folks didn't like that we ran the piece, so they're out to punish us for it."

Racial politics in Atlanta were especially complicated by its role as the state capital. The city cultivated a reputation for relatively moderate racial politics, at least compared to the rest of the South; Mayor Hartsfield understood that Negroes constituted a large chunk of his voter base, and he governed accordingly, throwing them a few bones, like hiring Negro cops. Over at the State House, however, Governor Griffin was a race-baiter, pandering to whites in rural areas (where few Negroes dared vote, as it could cost them their lives) and encouraging the worst instincts of segregationists. The Attorney General was Griffin's tool. This lawsuit seemed a transparent attempt to punish a group of opinionated Negroes in Mayor Hartsfield's backyard.

Being a cop had forced Smith to navigate this tightrope: be the kind of good cop the mayor supposedly wanted him to be, but also play along with the second-class status the state's Jim Crow laws forced him into. He'd walked away from that job, yet the tightrope still stretched taut beneath his feet.

"The last time we had to defend ourselves in a big lawsuit," Laurence said, "we cut salaries to keep the paper running. *And* we let go of a couple of writers." He patted Smith's shoulder. "You've been warned."

That night, Patrice was outside locking up her storefront, clad in a long gray coat that swirled above her black leather boots. When she wasn't cooking or managing a kitchen, Smith had noticed, she tended to be a stylish dresser, showing off her status.

"Did the Department return your money?" Smith asked.

"Is this for a story, or your own personal information?"

"Just for me."

"Not yet." She looked like she was in a rush to get somewhere. Or just wanted to keep him on his toes.

"Look, I wanted to apologize."

She looked puzzled. Or theatrically pretended to be puzzled. "For what, exactly?"

"For vanishing after that one time, like you said."

"It's nothing. You have many women. And I have never been without my suitors, thank you very much. So don't feel no pity for me, Tommy Smith."

"I wasn't saying that. I was just . . . I wanted to see you again."

She seemed to reassess him. "Here on a sidewalk? Or someplace more romantic?"

"I'd settle for a sidewalk if that's all I can get. Or, maybe dinner?"

"That place you took me to last time worked out pretty well, didn't it? But I have plans tonight."

"He as charming as me?"

"It's a Board of Commerce meeting, actually. So I give you the slight edge on charm."

He had to admit it, she was roughly ten times smarter than most women he wooed. "Some other night, then?"

"Interesting. Does this mean you're promoting me to two-night stand? Or do you just find me particularly . . . alluring because I'm the rare woman who isn't falling all over herself to win you back?"

"Are you going to overanalyze everything I do or say?"

She brightened at the thought. "I might. It's fun. You're a writer, after all. Aren't I required to pick apart your words and be on guard for how you try to manipulate me?"

"You've never struck me as terribly manipulatable."

"I don't believe that's a word."

"Well, you just turn me into a poet. Inventing my own language."

She smiled. "The meeting tonight isn't until eight, so I suppose a drink with my unreliable narrator might make it bearable. But only one."

He offered her his arm and she took it. He'd never before felt so celebratory at winning a single drink with a woman. He would sip slowly.

A few hours later, after the one drink, and after he'd walked her to her meeting, and after she'd offered her cheek for a chaste kiss, he strolled into his office, buzzing with more excitement than he'd expected. He sipped some bourbon from his flask and sat at his desk to do battle with Bertha, not on a deadline this time, but a slower struggle: he was trying to write a longer piece, a sort of memoir of his time as a cop. A project he'd been tinkering with over the years, never getting far.

He heard footsteps on the stairs. He slid his flask back into his jacket pocket, as he imagined Bishop disapproved of drinking at work, regardless of the hour.

"Burning the midnight oil, Smith?"

"Just trying to get something down before I forget it. How about you?"

"The danger of forgetting worsens at my age. So yes, I'm doing the same thing. And I wanted to ask you something. When you were a cop, I know you weren't a homicide detective, but ... I imagine you had a few encounters with murderers."

Smith had to resist smiling at the formal phrasing, *encounters with murderers*. Yes sir, he wanted to respond, I knew me some cutthroat motherfuckers, some baby-killing psychos, and some all-'round sick bastards. Instead he said, "A few."

"In your experience, how often are people caught later because they talked about it?"

"That's about the best way to catch them. People talk. Maybe they don't confess, but they brag about how tough they are and what they've done, and the people who hear them go and tell the cops. Or maybe they mention they scored some money the other night, and the person who hears them knows there was a robbery where somebody got killed, and puts one and one together."

He wondered why Bishop was asking this, his mind first going to the Emmett Till killers, those peckerwoods openly talking about their crime without fear of punishment.

"So for the most part, the ones who get away," Bishop surmised, "are the ones who know how to stay quiet."

"Among other things. Why?"

"I've never asked you much about your old job."

True. Bishop was normally in too much of a hurry to ask anyone anything, unless it was for a story. Which maybe this was.

"I assume you were involved in a few cases," Bishop said, "where you felt confident you knew that someone was guilty, but you didn't have enough to arrest them? Cases where the guilty party got away with it, and you knew it?"

At that point enough bourbon flowed through Smith's veins that he was a poor judge of another person's sobriety. But he wondered if Bishop'd had a few, to be posing such questions. His second thought was that maybe Bishop wasn't talking about the Till killers, but about Smith himself. As if Bishop knew that Smith had once crossed lines he wished he hadn't.

"I can think of a few cases," Smith stalled. "More often than not, they'd do something else wrong, and that second time we'd be ready for them. But, yes, sometimes the bad guys do get away with it. A lot of times."

"That must have been hard to deal with."

"Just like it's hard for us here to deal with writing about all the things people still get away with."

"True. We do what good we can. Best not to beat ourselves up for the failures."

"Well, sir, I don't know that I consider my time as a cop a failure." Smith's voice sharper than he'd intended. But he'd taken that as an insult, too buzzed to let it slide. "I did what good I could, just like I'm trying to do now."

"Of course," Bishop said, realizing he'd offended Smith. "I respect what you did."

"Yeah, well, not everyone feels that way."

Bishop thanked Smith for his thoughts and told him not to work too much later, to get some sleep, but then Bishop failed to take his own advice by walking back up to his office.

The conversation didn't sit right with Smith. He smarted from the weird questions, the sense that the refined publisher had been judging him, and the fear that he'd overreacted. Maybe he was too defensive about his old job, about his own mistakes and need for redemption.

He took another snort from his flask. And another.

The words on the page danced, not a good sign, shifting up and to the right, as if fleeing from possible meaning. He typed, didn't like what he saw, tore the page out, loaded another. Wondered if he'd lost the magic moment he'd felt earlier, if Bishop's questions had dispelled it.

Later, after he'd drunk more than he'd written, and after he'd fallen asleep, the shot in Bishop's office woke him up.

PART TWO

7

SMITH WAS MORE or less sober by the time the white detectives joined him in the interrogation room.

His bladder was about to burst. They'd known he'd had a few drinks earlier, so he assumed that was why they refused to let him use the bathroom. Torture him from the inside. He'd sat in the back of a squad car for at least an hour, during which officers searched the *Daily Times* building and called in reports and gave orders, including an order to proceed to Smith's apartment and search it for weapons (no warrant required, in their opinion), and to walk there slowly, checking in every trash barrel along the way in case Smith had stashed a pistol somewhere. Then two of the uniforms had been instructed to drive him to the station.

When he'd asked if he was under arrest—no one had yet uttered those words—they told him to shut up.

He wondered if Boggs was really calling him a lawyer like he'd promised, or would wait until his shift ended. Or would he not bother calling at all?

Their partnership had not ended with them on the best of terms.

They crossed paths now and again, hellos and how's it goings. There had been times when Smith had tried so very hard to raise the low impression that his morally upright, ethically spotless, annoyingly pious ex-partner had of him. But he'd long abandoned that effortful project, and the new lightness in his shoulders and his feeling of *the hell with what Boggs thinks* had made him feel like he was standing up straight for the first time.

Then why had it also made him feel so hollow? As if Boggs had won. As if Smith had only confirmed Boggs's view that he was mere trash—a no-'count hustler who belonged a few steps below Boggs and the rest of the Talented Tenth.

And here he was in an interrogation room. More confirmation still.

No. He told himself that was the booze talking, the self-pity he normally did not allow himself. This was exactly why they'd put him in this room, psychological warfare, cause him to doubt himself. They criminalized your body first and expected your mind to follow.

Calm down, be smart. Shit, how much *had* he drunk? They no doubt were measuring the contents of his flask, or just drinking from it themselves so they could later claim he'd emptied it.

This was how they got innocent folk to confess. This, and their fists and their billy clubs. The Supreme Court had recently ruled such confessions inadmissible, but federal warnings tended to make their way very slowly down here to the Confederacy. He needed to brace himself for the billy clubs and fists. He needed to repeat in his mind, over and over, that he was innocent and that the best way for Bishop's killer to be found was if Smith and the cops handled this part of the game quickly and cleanly so they could move on.

I'm innocent, I'm innocent, I'm innocent.

Repeating it like a mantra as the minutes dragged slowly by.

And wishing he remembered better what had happened earlier. Because he *had* fallen asleep there half drunk, right? After that strange talk with Bishop? Whatever happened upstairs had happened there without him, right? There was no chance he himself had gone up to speak to Bishop again, to continue that very unexpected discussion about Smith's police work, about how bad guys sometimes get away with it? And maybe more words had been exchanged, and they'd led to an altercation, and he'd lost the memory in a fog of booze and guilt?

Stop, stop, he told himself. They were getting him to doubt himself already.

I'm innocent, I'm innocent, I'm innocent.

"Wake up, boy!"

In walked two white detectives. One mid-career, one a recent promotion. The young 'un was thin and seemed to think scowling aged him. Hair military-short, cheekbones prominent, gaze wary, as if deeply suspicious of all around him. But maybe he only looked that way when talking to a Negro.

The older one, his hair gray, was doing a reasonably good job of keeping his chest thicker than his stomach, but he wouldn't be winning that battle much longer. He leaned his meaty hands on the table, face very close to Smith's.

"See, you done made a mistake already. It's always the guilty ones who fall asleep. The innocent ones, see, they're so danged *nervous* about being here, and they're *insulted*, carrying on about how we got the wrong man, it wudn't me, blah blah blah. But you, Tommy Smith? You just enjoyed the slumber of the damned, now didn't you?"

"I'm tired. I've been here for hours." And Lord God he needed to piss, but he wasn't about to complain to them about it.

"Well, I do apologize for that." The older cop stood tall again. "See, I happen to take police work seriously. I don't believe it's something that should be rushed. And a murder investigation, I'd say that's about the most serious matter a detective could possibly involve himself with. Although I understand you didn't take much to policing."

He wondered if McInnis had told them about his time on the force—had he by any chance vouched for Smith? Would he do that?—or if they'd learned this from his file.

He resisted their bait and asked, "What would you like to know about Mr. Bishop?"

"You get along with him?" the younger one asked.

"As well as any of his reporters did."

"Don't you go dodging my questions, boy."

"Is my lawyer downstairs? You give him real confusing directions in the hallway or something?"

"Watch it with the lip," the younger one said, stepping closer.

Two chairs sat on the other side of the table, but the cops apparently thought looming over Smith was a more effective strategy. "How's a colored like you afford a lawyer? You embezzling from that newspaper? And Bishop caught you, and that's why you shot him?"

Smith tried not to roll his eyes. "You sent men to my place, right? That tiny apartment should prove I haven't stolen or embezzled from anyone. And I did not kill the man. He was my boss, he was a stern boss, but I had no quarrel with him. I was at my desk working late. In my office on the first floor, and he was upstairs, and somewhere past ten I fell asleep. I woke up when I heard gunshots, one or two. Woke me up, but because I was asleep I can't swear how many there were, though your ballistics boys should be able to spell that out for you."

"Nah," the younger one said, "you and him were having some kinda disagreement, and things just got a little bit out of hand, ain't that what happened?"

Smith gave the kid a brief look, then turned his attention back to the older one.

"Y'all have names, detectives?"

"Forgive me for forgetting my manners, good sir," the older one said. "I am Detective Roy Cummings and this hale fellow is Detective Eli Helms. Pleasure to make your acquaintance and all that bullshit."

"And that's the last question *you* get to ask *us*," Helms said.

Smith stared at the kid for a moment.

Helms snapped, "You'd better stop eyeballing me, boy, if you still want to be able to see outta that eye."

There was no such thing as an idle threat when it came to white cops. Just after the war, Isaac Woodard, a Negro veteran riding a South Carolina bus, had been set upon by cops for some imagined offense; they beat the hell out of him and ground their billy clubs into his eye sockets, blinding him for life. That was but one among countless stories. When a cop threatened to mess with your eyes, you believed him. When a white person threatened to hang you,

you believed him. Words possessed raw power, the first draft of imaginations ready to run wild.

Smith cut it out with the *reckless eyeballing*, which was an actual offense on the books. (Just two or three years ago, in a story the *Daily Times* had covered closely, a Negro farmer in North Carolina had been sentenced to *fourteen years* for allegedly eyeballing a white girl.)

"So I'm just supposed to wait here til your other boys finish going through my apartment and can't find a weapon, right?" Smith asked. "And maybe I even have to wait here for you to call all the other *Daily Times* writers and they can tell you that no, there weren't any grudges or bad blood between me and Mr. Bishop, and no one saw me do anything, and then I can finally walk. Right?"

Cummings folded his arms. "Just because you wore a badge for a couple years doesn't mean you know everything."

"And just a YMCA cop," Helms added, using one of the least insulting of the many nicknames for the Negro officers. When the city first had hired them in '48, the idea of those rookies mingling in the station with white cops (many of whom were Klansmen) had proven altogether too much, so they'd had to use a makeshift precinct in the dark, dank basement of the Butler Street Y. The Department had since relented, and now the Negro officers had left the Y and used lockers and desks in the main headquarters.

In headquarters' basement, to be specific.

This was progress.

"You expect us to believe it wasn't you," Helms asked, "and that someone else snuck up those steps past your office and you didn't hear them?"

"I don't know what I expect you to believe, Detective. But that's the truth."

"You must be an awful hard sleeper."

Knowing he was pushing it, but unable to resist, Smith replied, "Yes, Detective, I learned to be a hard sleeper in France and then Belgium and then Germany. Learned to sleep through all kinds of things if I wanted to get any sleep at all. Did you?"

The look of rage in Helms's eyes told Smith he'd guessed right, that this detective had finagled a police deferment from the war.

"If you *don't* have a guilty conscience," Cummings said, "and if you *are* innocent, then right about now you should at the very least be giving us a nice long list of people you think *should* be our suspects."

"Whyn't you ask the Attorney General?"

"What's that?"

"He's suing the paper for libel, or obscenity or something. Because Bishop himself wrote a story about Randy Higgs. You know, the rape case?"

"I know the case," Cummings said, "but nothing about a libel suit."

Smith was disappointed but not shocked. As galling as it was for the AG to sue the *Daily Times*, white papers wouldn't bother covering such a matter. Meaning white people like these cops wouldn't know a thing about it. Separate worlds.

"Higgs claims it wasn't rape," Smith explained. "Bishop printed that statement, along with some letters the so-called victim wrote, and now the paper's being sued for it. So, I don't know, maybe the AG decided a lawsuit wasn't punishment enough."

Cummings laughed. "So you're saying we should make the Attorney General a murder suspect."

"That's a goddamn outrageous accusation." Helms sounded genuinely wounded, as if he and the AG were kin. Hell, maybe they were. This city could feel surprisingly small sometimes.

Smith added, "Maybe not him, but how about the family of the rape victim, the Hunters? We got some angry letters after that story, and some of them seemed like they might've been written by people who knew the family, or *were* family. Letters that threatened murder."

Cummings looked like he'd never in all his days heard a less credible story. "For Christ sake, no way is a white man going into a colored neighborhood in the dead of night to kill a nigger."

Lord, there were so many layers of wrong in that sentence,

Smith didn't know where to begin. Better to just walk past it, try not to drive himself mad sifting through it all. Especially while handcuffed.

Cummings continued, "He'd have to be a damn fool."

You're implying white folks can't be damn fools? It hurt sometimes, how Smith had to swallow his best lines around these people.

He said instead, "You asked me for suspects, and there's two."

"That ain't being helpful," Helms said. "That's sassing."

Smith told himself to breathe and watch the sassing. He'd been cuffed for hours; his shoulders ached and his hands were numb. Helms was just dying to take a swing at him, yet there seemed to be some understanding between the two detectives that they not get physical with him.

At least, not yet.

The Department would not want a former Negro officer booked for murder. Smith consoled himself with this fact. Hoping it truly was a fact. Cops like these—and they were legion—would have *loved* to book every last Negro officer for murder, rape, theft, reckless eyeballing, impersonating police officers, impersonating human beings, anything. But the mayor and Chief Jenkins had put their names and reputations on the line, arguing to Atlanta's white majority that hiring Negro officers would be good for everyone, that crime in colored neighborhoods could best be contained by officers who understood the people who lived there. A Negro officer committing a capital crime—even a former officer like Smith—would be catnip to the segregationists. An arrest alone would be a political scandal for Mayor Hartsfield, which meant no white cop would dare make that move—no matter how badly they wanted to—unless the Chief or some rival with pull gave permission. These two detectives would be risking their jobs if they booked Smith on trumped-up charges, which meant he was safe.

Safe from *arrest*, at least. Which wasn't the same as safe from being roughed up.

Smith knew that if he elucidated these political realities to the white men, they'd pound hell out of him on principle. *How dare you try to tell a white man how the world works*. He had to sit there and not say it, content that they knew it, hopeful they too were not damn fools.

"I don't know who might've killed him," he said. "But I know that as a newspaper publisher, he makes plenty people mad every day. Could've been anybody."

They asked him more about Bishop: did the man have any lady friends, was he a drinker, did he gamble, smoke reefer, etc. Smith explained again and again that Bishop was as upstanding and downright square as they came, yet the cops stayed on the subject of vice, unwilling or unable to imagine a Negro crime motivated by anything more complex.

Smith tried his damnedest to recall the last conversation he'd had with Bishop. He wasn't going to tell these white men about it, but what the *hell* had Bishop been trying to ask him? Something about murderers being caught because they had big mouths, about murder being a line you couldn't cross without becoming something *other*, forever marked.

Then the man himself gets shot no more than two hours later. Smith felt there must be some huge, all-encompassing Answer standing in front of him, but he couldn't see it.

These idiot detectives weren't even *trying* to see it.

"You keep asking about women and drink and I'm trying to tell you, he wasn't like that. He was a damned Boy Scout. Why is that so hard for you to understand?"

He knew why, of course. But he was tired and angry and sick of being insulted.

Yet Helms was the one who took offense. He swung and hit Smith with a right cross.

"You telling us how to do our jobs, boy?"

It wasn't the best punch. Smith had been hit by far worse. He knew he could take this scrawny white man, no problem. If he hadn't been cuffed, or in a police station, or in Georgia, or in America.

He eyeballed Helms.

Helms pulled back his shoulders as if ready to throw the next, but Cummings held up a hand.

The elder detective pulled out one of the chairs to sit down. Scooted real close. He smelled like cigar smoke and Smith saw tiny shaving nicks along his neck.

"Look, Tommy, there are plenty white men wouldn't give you much credit. Who would never dream of saying you're a smart fellow." Cummings's voice had been dialed down a notch in both volume and aggression. A trap, surely. "But I can see you know how to take care of yourself. You lasted two years at the Butler Y, which ain't no small thing, and McInnis vouches for you."

Smith could feel Helms stiffen at this, disgusted at such compliments.

"And because I know you're smart enough, you should only need to hear things once. If you have any information now, or if you find any information later, and if you do not share that information immediately, I will have you booked for obstruction. You'll be thrown in a group cell, and we'll be sure and put you in with some hard fellows who remember you used to wear a badge, who'd just love to pay back an Uncle Tom." He smiled. "You got that?"

"I don't want to obstruct anything. I want you to do your jobs and find out who killed him." *Unless I do first.*

"You lippy bastard!" Helms hit him again. Harder this time.

Cummings shook his head, then stood up. He beckoned for Helms to follow him to the door. Helms stared at Smith, as if daring him to say something more. Smith held his tongue but didn't break his stare. Blood in his mouth, shoulders aching, head pounding.

The detectives finally walked out of the room, Smith eyeballing Helms the whole way.

8

LATER THAT MORNING, McInnis drove to Hanford Park, near the West Side. This was one of the areas his officers patrolled, so he was more accustomed to seeing it in darkness or the hours before summer sunset. At this atypical hour for him, with the angle of the sun sharp, windows gleamed and houses revealed themselves to be more colorful than he remembered.

He rang the doorbell, and in a moment Boggs answered, dressed in a red sweater and gray slacks.

"They're not charging Smith, at least not yet," McInnis told him. "He's been released, just a couple hours ago."

Boggs nodded. "His lawyer called me. He's a friend of my father. Want to come in? Coffee?"

McInnis said sure. He'd had lunch here a few times over the years, as he and a couple of his most-trusted officers gradually tested certain boundaries. He had floated the possibility to Bonnie of their reciprocating with a Sunday brunch or cookout invitation, but her reaction ("What would our neighbors think?") had chastened him.

Some toys lay scattered about, but otherwise the living room and kitchen appeared as spotless as Boggs kept his uniform and desk. McInnis heard someone coughing.

"Lila's home sick," Boggs said as he handed McInnis a coffee cup. "Julie's reading to her in bed."

Boggs had four kids now, the youngest in diapers. McInnis couldn't remember which one Lila was. Taped on the kitchen wall was an impressively thorough drawing of the inside of a fighter plane, as detailed as a military blueprint.

"Your oldest did this?" McInnis asked.

"Sage, yes. He's ten now. Says he wants to be an architect."

"My fifteen-year-old couldn't do that."

They sat down at the kitchen table.

"There's still no murder weapon," McInnis explained. "Homicide combed through Bishop's office and spoke to the widow, but they don't have any solid leads yet. I'm going to the station early to learn more."

Boggs nodded, keeping his thoughts to himself.

"What can you tell me about how Smith's been lately?"

"We really haven't been in touch," Boggs said. "Me living over here and him over there, we don't cross paths very often, except when he drops by a crime scene."

Last night, after the detectives had shown up and taken over, McInnis had walked Boggs to the side and asked him quietly, "You knew him better than anyone. Answer just one thing. Could he have killed someone?" Boggs had hesitated. Looked away. The damn college boy had been trying to formulate a perfect yet evasive response, McInnis saw. Boggs had finally said, "After seven years of this, Sergeant, I believe anyone can do anything."

McInnis didn't buy it then and he didn't buy it now. Surely the preacher's son did not have so dark a worldview? Surely he still divided people into the saved and the damned, still held a belief in man's essential goodness? His answer last night had meant that he thought, *yes, Smith in particular could kill someone*, but he'd needed a way to soften the blow, forgive himself for sounding like Peter before the cock crowed.

This morning, McInnis wanted to know more. He said, "You two seemed pretty close back when you worked together."

"That was more than five years ago."

"And you had a falling-out. Mind if I ask you what that was about?"

Boggs paused for a moment, looking away. "I'd rather not get into it, Sergeant. Just ... personal. I can tell you it doesn't have anything to do with whatever happened last night."

Interesting. Boggs and Smith had both turned in resignation letters on the same day five years ago, shortly following a night in which they had gunned down armed drug traffickers. McInnis had managed to convince Boggs to stay on the force—the bookish Boggs was a good cop, smart, honorable, and tougher than he himself realized. Yet McInnis had happily let the more reckless Smith go.

He'd always had the sense there was more to the story than they'd divulged.

"But you don't have the highest opinion of Smith, is what I'm getting at."

Boggs exhaled, just short of a sigh. "I wouldn't say that, Sergeant. Tommy and I . . . were always very different people. We made things work best we could. But we didn't go about the job the same way. Which you know." He took a sip of coffee. "Whatever happened last night, we have a man gunned down in his own office. I know Tommy had been drinking, and I don't know what might have been going on between them, if Bishop was a hard boss or if he'd threatened to fire Tommy or who knows what, but . . . " He shook his head. "I have a hard time seeing him standing in his boss's office, shooting him dead, and then calling us to report it. That's just cold-blooded. And stupid. I think someone else shot Bishop, and they didn't know Smith was passed out downstairs."

Boggs had seemed harsher in his assessment of Smith the night before, when he'd had less time to think about it. It was as though he regretted what he'd said to McInnis then—*anyone can do anything*—and now he was trying to walk it back.

Which McInnis didn't like.

9

THE BRICK STEPS leading to the Bishops' home in the West End were numerous enough for Smith to expect a butler or maid to intercept him before he reached the top. He was impressed Negroes owned this: the long driveway, the deep porch with white columns, the impressive yard. He felt pride in Mr. Bishop's accomplishments as he walked up the grand steps, but also a hint of envy.

Christ, he envied a dead man.

The door had a brass knocker, but Smith preferred knuckles.

He did not often make it to this side of town. He gazed down the block at the well-kept homes and shiny new vehicles, one of the most desirable streets among the Talented Tenth.

The door opened, a fortyish maid, hair in a bun.

"Morning, ma'am. Is Mrs. Bishop in?"

She looked Smith up and down. Saw his fraying gray blazer that he'd been meaning to replace for a couple years now, his green tie whose perfect knot did not distract from the fact that it was wool and not silk, and his blue slacks that he probably should have ironed and brown brogues that were less fashionable than his stiff wingtips, but which he'd chosen because he expected to be on his feet a lot today.

The bruising on his left cheekbone and his cut bottom lip didn't help. Nor did the fact that he'd been up all night and hadn't showered yet.

"Mrs. Bishop isn't seeing guests today."

"I understand, ma'am, but she needs to see me. My name's Tommy Smith and I work for the paper. I'm the one who found him."

That penetrated her stolid facade. She told him to wait and closed the door. Smith could faintly hear music, the Morehouse marching band practice, perhaps. Because he'd only managed to swing tuition for two years, he didn't consider himself a "Morehouse man"—indeed he felt wildly conflicting emotions whenever he heard that term, or saw a class ring on another man's finger, or heard mention of this alumni club or that fraternal order, signifiers of Negro Atlanta's chosen sons. He'd been given a glimpse of that world, only to be shut out. And then the war came.

A couple minutes passed, long enough for him to wonder if the maid had forgotten about him. Maybe she'd just gotten lost in the massive house. Then she opened the door and invited him in.

A foyer filled with framed photographs and a large historic map of Atlanta. A winding staircase with an engraved oak banister. Crown molding and wainscoting, antique candleholders on the walls, decorative flourishes everywhere the eye fell.

She ushered him to the sitting room on the right, two huge bookshelves and three very comfortable-looking chairs, the kind of chairs that invited you to take a nap, settle in, forget the world's problems; chairs that came with money-back guarantees you would never worry if you settled your backside in them, and with her hand she motioned for him to do just that, and he did. The chair worked, for a minute or so.

Lord God, he was tired. After his release, he had gone home, finding his apartment ransacked by police. They'd taken his guns, as Cummings had told him they would, and trashed everything else. He felt all the more vulnerable without his firearms, and he feared he'd never get them back.

Too exhausted to clean up the mess but too rattled to lie down and sleep, he'd washed his face, downed cold cereal and hot coffee, and called Toon.

News of the murder had spread fast. Toon, Laurence, and some of the others had tried to get into the *Daily Times* building in the middle of the night, but had been rebuffed by police. Laurence and other editors had busily set up contingency plans, if necessary, to print tomorrow's edition at the *Macon Weekly Journal*, the nearest of the smaller papers owned by the *Daily Times*. Laurence had worked the phones, lining up cars and trucks that were ready to drive staff down to Macon and then bring the printed papers back north. It would be a logistical nightmare, but, according to Toon, Laurence seemed to be dealing with the shock of his mentor's murder by obsessively handling every conceivable detail.

Under no circumstances would a day pass without a new edition of the *Daily Times*.

The murder would surely be their front-page story. Toon had told Smith that Laurence desperately wanted to talk to him, hear his report and decide what aspect of it should see print. This was one of many reasons Smith did not want to be anywhere near his colleagues yet. He didn't know what he wanted to share with Laurence, didn't even understand the cocktail of emotions burning in his gut. Sadness and shock at the murder. Anger at the way the white cops had treated him. Sheer confusion over what had happened (Boggs was right—he'd picked the wrong night to drink himself to sleep). And shame at having been on the receiving end of an arrest. His wrists were raw from where the metal had sunk into his skin, and he rubbed himself there, but he would never be able to rub away that particular hurt.

The Bishops' house was old but amazingly creak-free. He didn't hear Victoria coming when she entered through the side door. She wore a long, dark blue dress complete with a gold necklace, even at home in the morning. Her hair was pulled back and she looked like she had very recently applied makeup to a tear-ravaged face. No beauty product could fight grief like this.

He stood, hat in hand. The maid had not offered to take it for him. "Mrs. Bishop, I'm so sorry for your loss."

"Why are you here?" She noticed the notebook and pencil he'd placed on the coffee table. "Not to express your condolences, I'm sure."

She hadn't sat down yet, so he didn't either.

"Well, that's only part of it. I felt I should see you right away. I know this is hard, but if there's anything you can tell me that can help us figure out what happened, it would help to know that sooner rather than later."

"What happened to your face?"

"That's how some policemen like to ask questions."

"Didn't you used to be a policeman?"

"Yes, ma'am. The other kind of policeman, though."

She watched him for a moment. "So you aren't a policeman anymore, but you're here acting like you are?"

"I don't mean to be acting like anything, ma'am. But because of what I used to do, I know how these things go. There are some decent Negro cops, but they aren't the ones who conduct murder investigations. Those are all white folks, and I don't trust many of them. I just hoped that maybe I could help in ways they can't, or won't."

"I find it odd, that you would come here. They asked about you."

"I'm sure they did. I'm the one who called them to the scene. Can we sit, ma'am?"

She considered this for a moment, then she sat and he did the same. The chairs seemed unusually far from each other, but then again, he wasn't often in rooms of this size. The scale of everything felt off.

Even her cats were too big. Two of them entered the room now, slow like sentries. One orange and the other black, they peered at him from the doorway, silent, judgmental, the size of ocelots.

"Do you have any idea who might have wanted to hurt your husband?" Behind him was a mirror, he'd noticed, which meant she could watch herself answer his questions if she was so inclined.

"I already had this discussion with the police."

"And do you trust the police, ma'am?"

"Of course not. But why should I trust you? Am I to repeat everything just because you and I are both colored? Are you privy to some insight they're not?"

"I just think I want to help you more than they do."

"Or help *yourself*. Like I said, they asked a lot of questions about you."

"I'll answer any questions you have about me, ma'am. Your husband wasn't the easiest man for a lowly reporter like me to get to know, but I respected him. I did not hurt him." He let that sink in for a spell. "Now, you do not have to talk to me if you don't want to. But I think—"

"What do you want to know?"

He repeated his question about who might have wanted to hurt her husband.

"I have no idea." The orange cat stalked her way, rubbing itself against her leg. She petted it briefly, then ignored it. It stared at Smith, distrustful, then slunk away.

"What happens to the paper now, ma'am?"

She crinkled her nose. "Are you afraid for your job, Mr. Smith?"

"I was wondering who might stand to benefit."

"There are three voting members of the board, and the board designates the editor-in-chief. Arthur was one of the members, and that seat passes on to me unless his will states otherwise, which would shock me. Another chair is Eric Branford, the paper's attorney, who also happens to be our friend."

Smith remembered something. "Branford was at the office the other day, wasn't he? To talk to your husband about the libel lawsuit?"

"I wouldn't know. But yes, that's the sort of thing Eric would help with. He and Arthur are old friends. And about the board, the third vote goes to our eldest nephew, Crispin."

"The son of the founder, right?"

"The eldest, yes." Smith knew the basics: The *Daily Times* had been founded by Mr. Bishop's elder brother, Sebastian Bishop, in the late twenties. Started as a weekly, as most Negro papers still were. It survived the Depression and weathered frequent attempts from the Jim Crow authorities and even the federal government to shut it down. Early in the war years, Sebastian had been diagnosed with cancer. He appointed as his heir his brother Arthur, a young writer who had been covering crime and local politics for the paper. Under Arthur's leadership, the *Daily Times* steadily grew in numbers and influence. "Sebastian had three children, two sons and a daughter, but they were all minors when he passed away. Their collective vote was held by their mother until one of them reached age twenty-one, which Crispin did a few years ago."

"Do you think Crispin has any desire to run the paper?"

A withering look. "Are you suggesting my nephew traveled down from Boston so he could kill his uncle and get the board to vote him in as the new editor-in-chief?"

"Ma'am, I'm just trying to get the lay of the land. I'm betting the white detectives didn't ask about any of this."

"They did, in a way." She paused, then added, "They asked a bit about our finances, as if they were so shocked we have money they were convinced we must have stolen it somehow. They seemed to think Arthur must have some felon of a brother, or a second cousin who's a flimflam man or Lord knows what. They seemed rather disappointed that we're so . . . legitimate."

Smith asked, "Your nephew Crispin, he's in Boston, you said?"

"He went to Harvard Law and he now handles contract law for large businesses there. When my husband inherited the paper, he also inherited the responsibility to provide for his nephews and niece, which we have done. The youngest, Richard, is at the University of Michigan, and Henrietta graduated from Oberlin two years ago. We have continued to support them, and they get part of the paper's profits. I don't see how any of them would have had a financial motive for killing the uncle who sent them to college and still sends them dividends. They're all many miles away right now, and I'll thank you in advance not to bother them when they come for the funeral."

This was a lot of names to keep straight. Hoping she wouldn't object, he'd picked up his notebook and was jotting things down. "Ma'am, I'm sorry to ask, but how was your relationship with Mr. Bishop?"

"Excuse me?"

"I'm sorry, ma'am, but I'm sure the detectives asked. Did they ask you where you were last night?"

"Yes, and I answered them." He waited for her to elaborate. She didn't.

"I apologize if this seems impolite, Mrs. Bishop, but the other day when we spoke about the downsides of marriage . . . it made me wonder how the two of you were getting on."

"Are you asking me if I was an adulteress?"

"No." He certainly had not asked that, yet it's what her mind turned to first. Interesting. Wouldn't most women wonder if he was asking if the *husband* was an adulterer? Or maybe that's just how Smith's mind worked. "No, Mrs. Bishop, not at all. I just wanted to know—"

"We have been married for fifteen years. We married late and did not have children. Maybe we didn't want any. It's no one else's business, and if people like to assume that means there was something wrong with us, then they can go ahead and gossip."

Being a reporter and being a cop meant asking awkward questions and feeling like a jerk for it. Smith moved on.

"Did he tell you anything about Randy Higgs and the Hunter family?"

"All I know is what I read in the story he wrote."

"He didn't mention all the hate letters he'd gotten? The death threats?"

"No. But receiving hateful letters is hardly noteworthy for him."

"True, but I read some of these. They seemed noteworthy to me, especially in retrospect."

"I agree they're worth looking into. But if you're asking if he seemed especially *bothered* by them, I would say no. One doesn't rise to the station Arthur reached without developing a thick skin."

"Had Mr. Bishop had any problems with other employees that I wouldn't have known about?" One thing that troubled Smith was the same thing that no doubt made the white detectives so interested in him: even though any outsider could have entered the *Daily Times* building at night and shot Bishop, it made particular sense that an employee, familiar with the building and able to navigate its unlit rooms, would have done so.

She looked away. "You know very well he could be an exacting boss. And yes, he did let go a writer a month ago."

"Tim Pinckney, right? For working a hustle?"

She nodded. When Smith had started at the paper, Laurence had warned Smith that sundry business people and "entrepreneurs" would inevitably approach him, asking him to write puff pieces about their business for a small bribe. Any reporters who "worked a hustle" like that would be dismissed. Laurence and Bishop read the paper cover to cover every day, eyes peeled for anything that seemed like a paid piece.

"I didn't know Pinckney very well," Smith said. "Was he angry when he was let go?"

"I imagine he was, but I don't really have any idea."

Smith would have to talk to Pinckney, find out what story he'd been bribed to write, and where he'd been last night. He tapped his pencil for a moment, thinking. "Do you know what Mr. Bishop was doing in Montgomery last week?"

"I don't."

Smith was silent for a spell, wondering if Bishop often left town without his wife knowing why, and if so, if that said anything about their marriage.

She tilted her head, seeming to read his thoughts. "As you know, he was always chasing one lead or another. Sometimes they led to stories, sometimes they didn't. He did not always give me the details on his progress."

"He could be pretty tight-lipped about what he was working on," Smith agreed.

"He'd been working on his memoirs recently. I don't know if the Montgomery trip was related or not, but for the last few months he'd been spending more and more time digging up old diaries to jog his memory. I think seeing people like Langston Hughes and

Richard Wright getting so much acclaim for their memoirs fired his competitive nature."

"Does he have a draft lying around anywhere?"

"He never showed me."

The phone had been ringing in the background, and now the maid appeared in the doorway. "Excuse me, Mrs. Bishop. Reverend Boggs is on the line."

The father of Smith's former partner. Maybe the Bishops attended his church, on the other side of town. Maybe they were friends, two successful community leaders. He scribbled *Rev. Boggs?* in his notes.

Mrs. Bishop stood, as did Smith. "I hope I've been of some help. And I'll trust that you, and Mr. Laurence, your editor, will be very careful about what you do and do not put in print."

"Of course, ma'am. Please let me know if I can be of any help."

Her flat expression seemed to say that he could help the most by leaving now and never returning.

Not owning a car posed significant drawbacks for a reporter. In his first year on the beat, Smith had missed his share of stories by arriving on foot or by bus, late. He'd sometimes borrowed cars from colleagues or whichever lady was in his life at the time, or taken taxis when the drivers actually stopped for him. After a year of that nonsense, he'd finally bought a used, beat-up Ford, but he'd taken it to the shop the previous morning as the engine had overheated.

So, a block away from the Bishops', he waited for the bus.

As he wrestled with his thoughts, he did not at first notice the man watching him. But he noticed him right before the bus pulled up. The man sat in a blue DeSoto at the corner of the intersecting street, his hat brim low. No amount of shadowy hat or newspaper in his lap, which he was pretending to read, was enough to conceal the fact that this man was white. Sitting in a parked car in a Negro neighborhood.

Staking out Victoria Bishop, or following Smith?

Smith climbed aboard the bus, paid his fare to the white driver, and sat in the very back row so he could keep his eye on the car. It stayed exactly where it was.

10

"**TWO GUNSHOTS, BOTH** to the chest," Cummings explained to McInnis that afternoon.

Neither Cummings nor Helms looked like they'd slept much, which McInnis was glad to see; it meant they'd been working the case seriously.

"There's a chance he could have survived one of them," Cummings continued, "but the other would have been fatal even if he'd been shot in an emergency room—hit him two inches above the heart, severing the aorta. We've lifted a lot of prints—odds are they all belong to employees of the paper. We've spoken to his secretary and we're going through his appointment book to see who he might have been meeting with. He worked late a lot, so him being there at that hour isn't strange. The two things I'm particularly interested in are the gun and the bourbon. He was shot with a .38, and Bishop himself owned a .38. There were no bullets in it when the wife showed it to us—it was in a desk drawer in his study at their house. It might have been fired that night, might not. We found no prints on it at all, which is odd, but it's possible he'd worn gloves the last time he cleaned it. We took the gun, and ballistics is checking to see if the bullets are a match."

McInnis had known Cummings back when they'd both been beat cops. It had been years since they'd worked closely together; McInnis's impression had been that Cummings was tough but fair, and smart.

"And the bourbon?"

"He had a bottle in a desk drawer and a glass on his desk, with prints on it, likely his. So at first we think, maybe he's drinking alone."

"But then we notice there's a second coaster sitting there, and the guest chair is pulled up awful close, like maybe someone had been having a drink with him." Helms picked up the story. "But there's no second glass. So maybe it's nothing."

"Or maybe," Cummings said, "this was someone Bishop knew well enough to offer a drink to. Meeting in his office, late at night."

"In which case," McInnis said, "the killer took their glass along with them, knowing it had their prints. Which was a pretty clear-headed thing to do."

Cummings said, "Or, the shooting was a heat-of-the-moment thing, then his or her eyes happened to fall on the glass after shooting him, or they even picked up the glass for a last, nerve-steadying drink, then realized they were holding evidence and had to do something about it."

"And then Smith made noise downstairs," McInnis said, "so the killer runs out the fire escape."

"If we believe Smith," Helms said.

"But why wouldn't the shooter charge down the stairs?" McInnis wondered. "He had a gun. Why jump out the fire escape?"

Cummings shrugged. "He heard Smith and didn't know if Smith was armed. Didn't know who Smith was or how many of them were down there. Maybe Smith even yelled 'police' out of old habit, though he didn't tell us he did."

"And this is all if we believe Smith," Helms repeated.

"Or," Cummings said, "perhaps it was a woman, and she didn't want to encounter someone on the steps, gun or no gun."

The best thing Smith had going for him, McInnis thought, was that no one had found the murder weapon. It was hard to see how Smith could have shot Bishop and called McInnis while the body was still warm unless he'd stashed the gun nearby. More likely, the killer had taken the gun as he fled.

McInnis thought for a moment. "You suspect it was a woman?"

"Right now, we suspect anyone and everyone," Cummings said. "Including his wife. They're a wealthy, childless couple who seemed to lead very different lives. Was it her? Was it a secret girlfriend of his? Was it the husband of a secret girlfriend of his, or a lover of the wife's?"

"You really see a woman rappelling down that fire escape?"

"Not in heels, no. But in flats, sure."

Helms added, "Negresses can be damned acrobatic. I've seen some."

McInnis was tempted to comment on that, but he let it slide for now. He asked, "What did you make of the widow?"

"Uppity bitch," Helms said.

"She was not terribly accommodating," Cummings translated. "*I* am willing to write that off to shock. But we plan on talking to her again real soon. She insisted neither she nor her husband were having affairs, and she wasn't none too pleased with the question. Call me crazy, but I thought she sounded rather defensive about it."

"Extremely defensive," Helms echoed. "Where there's smoke, there's fire."

McInnis had held difficult conversations like that before. Gauging the reactions of the shocked and grief-stricken, trying to parse the difference between guilt and pain, was near impossible. A person's guilt at having not been a better wife or husband or friend could look like an altogether different kind of guilt, especially to a harried investigator rushing to close a case. Double especially to one predisposed to mistrust Negroes.

"If your boys have any dirt on that couple," Cummings said to McInnis, "now would be the time for them to speak up."

"I'll ask around," McInnis said. "Smith told me Bishop's desk wasn't usually so messy. Could you tell if someone had been rifling through it?"

"One drawer was open," Cummings shrugged. "We told people at the paper to call us if they figure out anything's missing."

"Ah, the nigger cops probably just messed up the crime scene looking for the weapon," Helms scoffed.

"My officers don't mess up crime scenes," McInnis eyed Helms. As the Negro officers' sergeant, any insult against them was a perceived knock on him, too. He'd never asked to be put on the front lines of racial division, but here he was. "And you'll treat them with respect."

Helms did a double take. Looked genuinely confused. Either he couldn't figure out what he'd done that was disrespectful, or he couldn't see why McInnis would expect any different.

Cummings changed the subject by motioning to a stack of papers; he explained that they were some angry letters that had been sent to the *Daily Times* over the last few days. "One of their editors wanted us to see them, since a few of 'em threatened violence."

McInnis flipped through the letters. Some were anonymous, some weren't. One of the names, Cassie Rakestraw, struck him as familiar somehow, but he couldn't place it.

He asked, "Do we know if Bishop was in the habit of offering late-night drinks to his employees?"

Helms made a face. "Who the hell knows?"

"It's your job to know, Detective."

"I've delved about as deeply into the habits of Negroes as I care to, thank you very much."

"That's an excellent mindset for an investigator."

"Why don't you focus on your own goddamn—"

"Cool it, both of you," Cummings cut them off. He kept his eyes for an extra beat on Helms, who shook his head.

McInnis looked at Cummings and asked, "What can I do to help?"

"As little as possible. No offense, but the fact that one of your former officers was there at the scene, and is, at the very least, a person of interest ... That makes me want your officers to back very far away. If we need to dig anything up, we'll do it ourselves."

"This is a murder in the Negro community," McInnis clarified. "I know my men aren't detectives, but they can find information you two can't."

"What, with some African sixth sense?" Helms taunted.

McInnis crossed his arms. "They know people in these neighborhoods far better than either of you do. Some of them have met Bishop, are friendly with people at the paper—hell, one of my officers is the son of a minister who's probably had the man over for dinner."

"Look, Mac, this is a damned mess," Cummings said. "We need it cleared fast."

"You need it cleared correctly. Bishop was an important man, with a big megaphone. If we rush through this, we can do a hell of a lot of damage."

"Who's 'we'?" Helms mocked.

"I have been busting my ass," McInnis said, glaring at Helms, "for seven and a half years trying to improve relations between the Department and that community. If you think I'm going to sit on my hands while you do a piss-poor job of investigating the murder of the most influential Negro to be killed on my watch, and sabotaging all my hard work, you are goddamn mistaken."

"No one is sabotaging anything, Mac," Cummings said, trying to be the calm one here. "And I don't do a piss-poor job of anything."

"I know *you* don't." An angry look at Helms. "But this is going to require some tact. The Attorney General was suing Bishop, and now Bishop's dead. This isn't gonna play well in Sweet Auburn. Have you spoken to the Hunter family yet?"

"Who would that be?" Cummings asked.

McInnis explained about the rape case, the story in the *Daily Times* and its relation to the Attorney General's suit, which Smith had mentioned last night, right before Homicide arrived. "I would think talking to Hunter's family and checking their alibis would be a good idea."

"Please don't tell me," Cummings said, "that your time over there has you seeing things the way they do."

"What the hell does that mean?"

"It means of course we're not gonna go bother some white

family over that. Sounds like they're dealing with enough right now. We'll cover the obvious ground first instead of going off on some wild goose chase. As if a white man would head down into a Negro area at night to confront someone."

"Stranger things have happened," McInnis said.

"I'd say I'm seeing something pretty damn strange right now," Helms quipped.

McInnis soon left, realizing that the longer he stayed the more likely he was to take a swing at Helms.

He felt a disquieting sense that the case was being investigated by men of limited imagination. The boundaries governing what Cummings and Helms considered to be believable were too narrow, and skewed. If McInnis did tell his officers to "back off" and leave the detectives to walk down that narrow path, he doubted they would ever find the truth.

Which meant he would need to plan his next moves very carefully.

11

AFTER HIS INTERVIEW with Victoria Bishop, Smith gave in and napped for two hours before crawling out of bed and showing his face at the office, which had opened a few hours late, after the cops finally left.

Laurence had addressed the entire staff, Smith was told, breaking the news to the few who hadn't heard and insisting that they find a way to go on, despite their shock and grief. Four times Smith walked past people who were crying, consoling each other. He dispensed many hugs. Prayers were issued, Jesus' name frequently invoked. The idea of putting out a paper that day felt herculean but all the more necessary, the urgency giving them something to focus on, forcing them beyond their grief, at least until deadline.

The paper would dedicate several stories to Bishop. Smith and Toon shared duties on the murder story itself. Laurence would write the obit, paying tribute to all Bishop had meant to the paper, to Atlanta, to Negro America. He seemed dazed by the magnitude of the task. Smith was concerned about him, as Laurence had not only lost a friend but also had inherited the publisher role, at least temporarily. This would be tough for anyone to absorb, but particularly for a man so fragile.

Laurence's new role might not be temporary: he had long been rumored to be next in line whenever Bishop decided to retire, so Smith figured the board might vote to make Laurence's new position official. Smith wondered unpleasantly about his own comment to Mrs. Bishop: *I'd like to know who stands to bene-fit.* He couldn't see Laurence as a murderer, but the possibility troubled him.

✦

Smith visited police headquarters to request the murder report, where he was rebuffed. Too early, they claimed. He managed to get some scant information by calling Deaderick. He also called Boggs and McInnis, couldn't reach them, and tried Dewey Edmunds, another Negro officer he'd once worked with, and got a few details, not much.

Laurence advised Smith not to insert himself into his story, to leave out the fact that he'd been unofficially arrested and questioned by the police. He didn't have to ask twice; Smith had no desire to put any of that out in public. At the same time, in his sleep-addled state he mused over that phrase, *don't insert yourself into the story*, the impossibility of such advice. Any story has the writer in it, no matter how hard the scribe might try to erase himself.

Smith was nearly finished with a version of his piece when someone knocked on his open door. He looked up and saw Doris McClatchey. In her fifties, she had overseen the front desk for more than a decade. Her thick-framed glasses were always either perched on her nose or lying atop her chest, dangling on a thick black string, as they were now.

"There's something I wanted to tell you," she said, closing the door and then sitting in his guest chair. "I ain't told the cops this."

He'd noticed that Mrs. McClatchey spoke with perfect diction and poise around Mr. Bishop—she could out-stuffy the best of them when she put her mind to it—but in Smith's presence she was more relaxed. In addition to her role as receptionist, she compiled the Among the Clubs column, the biweekly listing of meetings for the African Methodist Episcopal Ministers and Widows League, the Orchid Social and Savings Club, the Jolly Matrons Social Club and the other two dozen or so groups that posted notices. She also was one of the sources for the weekly Social Swirl column, listing bite-sized news about marriages, births, and trips taken by Atlanta's Negro elite.

In other words, she was a professional gossip.

"Those white detectives were asking all kinds of questions about who Mr. Bishop been talking to lately," she said. "They even took my *appointment* book, asked me to *translate* the parts they couldn't read," and she huffed that last bit, insulted by a white person's implication that her penmanship was anything but impeccable (Smith himself had marveled at her neatly inscribed notes many a time).

"Sorry to hear that. They should return the book, but it could be a while." It also meant the white cops had information about Bishop's comings and goings that Smith couldn't access, unless Mrs. McClatchey's memory was as flawless as her handwriting.

Smith had spoken to her earlier, asking if she could make sense of Mr. Bishop's messy desk that night and whether anything seemed missing. She agreed that it looked like someone had rifled through it, but in search of what, she couldn't tell.

"What I wanted you to know," she said now, "and what I didn't tell the police, is that there's a few things that I *don't* put in his appointment book. Things I figure I should be more discreet about."

She wanted to tell him, he knew, but she would take her time. He asked, "Things involving . . . other ladies?"

She raised her eyebrows and leaned back. "*Goodness*, no! That man loved his wife. Mmm-mm. Not every man's as obsessed with that as you are, Mr. Smith. I worry about you, sometimes, carrying on the way you do. Don't you worry about getting someone into a bad situation? Or catching one of those diseases?"

"Mrs. McClatchey, please," and he laughed a bit, "let's get back to that appointment book."

"Well, you know Mr. Bishop was a very strict Republican. He didn't have any respect at all for those communists and socialists and that kind of godless folk."

"I got that message, yeah."

"Well," and she looked around theatrically, double-checking that the door was still shut and she could not be eavesdropped upon, "he wasn't always like that."

"No?" He saw she wasn't going to tell him whatever she wanted to tell him without a long story, so he lit a cigarette and offered her one. She accepted, and he lit it for her. "What was he like before?"

"Back in the day," and she lowered her voice, "*he* was a communist."

"Really?" This indeed shocked him. "When?"

"At least as far back as the Scottsboro Boys."

Smith had been a child then, but he knew the story. When Alabama cops arrested a number of Negroes for the rape of white women on a hobo train, the Communist Party of America had dedicated itself to defending them. In the process, the reds had trumpeted their vision of a world without racial divisions, a world where "we are all workers." Plenty of Negroes had been drawn into the communist fold, intrigued by that vision of a united society.

"He worked for the WPA back then, didn't he?" The Works Progress Administration, part of Roosevelt's New Deal, had provided jobs not only to workers on infrastructure projects but also to writers.

"That's how he survived the Depression. I know he helped Zora Neale Hurston take down old folk tales in Florida and the Georgia Coast, and he did some project collecting old-timers' stories, even heard slave tales from folks who'd been born before Emancipation."

"Was he a member of the Party then, when he was a government employee?" Smith would have figured the government screened for reds then, but maybe that hadn't started yet.

"I don't know all the ins and outs of it," she said after aiming a plume of smoke at the ceiling. "I know he had been a true believer once upon a time. It was something he'd talk about only when he was with his most trusted friends, but, you know, men forget themselves and say things in front of their secretaries that they shouldn't. I got the sense he wasn't proud of his beliefs back then, and didn't want too many people knowing about those days."

Smith could see why. Joe McCarthy's time in the limelight seemed to be over, thank goodness, but he had still managed to take down everyone from Hollywood screenwriters to school board members for so much as expressing sympathy for "fifth column-ists." Bishop himself had written plenty of red-baiting stories the last few years.

"He took over the paper from his brother in '41, right?" Smith recalled.

"Oh, he was through with communism by then, I'm sure. I started here in '43, and I can assure you there wasn't a red bone in his body at that time. I think he was through with them after his trip to Moscow."

"Excuse me?"

The old gossip grinned, so savoring her possession of a good scoop that she couldn't resist dishing it out in portions. "From what I've heard, some time in the thirties he went to Moscow. The Soviets were bringing people in to show off their perfect society and teach their communist theories and so forth. I don't know the details, but whatever it is he saw over there, it must have had the opposite effect of what ol' Stalin wanted. Mr. Bishop always said that after that trip, his eyes were opened, and he was done with them."

"This is interesting, ma'am, but why are you telling me this now?"

She lowered her voice again. "One of the people he went over to Moscow with was Morris Peeples, a lawyer here in town. Peeples used to teach at Morehouse. They were good friends back then. Still are, I think, but the kind of friends who argue a whole lot."

"Did they argue recently?"

She nodded. "Peeples came by here three times the last few weeks. When he'd make an appointment, I'd mark it down in the book as 'Mr. Price,' because with all this anti-communist hysteria, I was mindful of not leaving any kind of a paper trail that might connect Mr. Bishop to him."

"Peeples is still a communist?"

"Oh yes. He's never struck me as the kind of man who hides who he is. I think that's why Morehouse decided to stop putting up with him."

"So Bishop and Peeples were talking a little more than usual lately? What about?"

"I didn't always catch that. But I did hear them arguing about some strike. Seems Peeples wanted the paper to take a more sympathetic tone."

What strike? Smith wondered. The last big strike in Atlanta had come eight years ago, when taxi and streetcar drivers had protested new safety regulations imposed after a number of pedestrians, including the beloved author of *Gone with the Wind*, had been run down and killed.

Was some potential strike or labor unrest looming on the horizon, and Peeples wanted the paper to publicize it, or at least refrain from criticizing it? Bishop would have considered strikes to be nothing but communist propaganda, Smith knew. Worse, strikes by white workers opened the doors for Negro strikebreakers, who were banned from unions. Serving as strikebreakers provided Negroes with badly needed jobs but also set them up for revenge attacks from whites who didn't agree with the idea of an interracial brotherhood of workers. The fear that a strike or protest might lead to racial violence—this was exactly why Bishop was wary of the bus boycott in Montgomery. Smith could imagine how Bishop and a red would have had heatedly different opinions on this.

"Bishop always met with Peeples at off times," she added, "late at night or real early. He did *not* want anyone knowing they were still friends."

"Does *no one* know Bishop used to be a communist?"

"Some do, but it was so long ago now. There was a time when he'd use it to his advantage, you know, saying that he had once been blind but now he could see, that he *knew* what hogwash communism is. But ever since McCarthy started ruining people, he knew to keep quiet."

Which opened another possibility: blackmail.

Maybe Peeples had threatened to go public with embarrassing details from Bishop's past. Maybe he, or someone else, was trying to humiliate the publisher for financial gain, or simply to discredit the paper.

"Let me get this straight," Smith recapped. "Way back, Bishop is so red he travels to Moscow. Then in the mid-thirties he's a writer traveling the U.S. interviewing old folks for the WPA, while his brother runs this paper and makes just enough to keep the lights on. A few years later, Bishop has gone conservative, his brother dies, he inherits the paper, and within another decade he's built it up so that we own half a dozen other papers. Hell of a life."

He thought for a moment. "Did he have any upcoming appointments with Peeples?"

"That's the other thing. They were supposed to meet that last night, here, at nine."

Smith nearly choked on his cigarette. "You saved that for last? That's called 'burying the lede,' ma'am."

"Well, Peeples was supposed to come by around eight, but he never showed—at least, he hadn't as of 8:20, when I finally called it a night."

"Was Peeples, or your pseudonym for him, in the appointment book for that night?"

"No. He'd called only that morning, so I'd just told Mr. Bishop. Didn't bother putting it in the book."

"Ma'am, you not telling the white detectives about this . . . that could be a real problem."

She crushed her cigarette into his ashtray. "Oh, don't you worry about Doris McClatchey. She knows how to take care of herself."

The white detectives had threatened Smith not to hold back if he learned anything. But the thought of picking up the phone and telling them this news was nauseating. And risky: no matter what information he might give them, they'd assume he was holding back more. Maybe the white man who'd been outside the Bishop house the other day had been a cop, following him.

They were not his allies. Mrs. McClatchey's story was one lead this reporter would keep to himself.

12

NATALIE WASHINGTON HAD come to loathe her commute home from the *Daily Times*, but not for the typical reasons of crowded buses or long walks down dark streets. It was all because of the new shadow that had fallen over her life, a shadow with cold eyes, pale skin, and an empty smile.

Natalie had been working at the *Daily Times* for just over two years. Started in the classifieds department, taking down notices, barely a step above secretarial work. A Spelman graduate and former English major, she'd harbored hopes that she could angle her way into the newsroom. Her break came a few months back, when one of the copyeditors took sick and Natalie sat in for her. She quickly impressed Mr. Laurence by catching grammatical inaccuracies he'd somehow missed, earning herself a permanent seat at the copy desk (no raise yet, but progress all the same).

All this forward momentum stopped, three weeks ago, when she met the white lady.

The white lady she still thought of as Call Me Becky.

Natalie had first met her after what had been a normal day. Work, punch out, leave the *Daily Times* building, catch a bus from Auburn Avenue to Five Points for her transfer. At that hour, Five Points was the beating heart of downtown, alive with traffic of all kinds. Cars and buses and streetcars filled the streets, and the sidewalks and crosswalks flowed with pedestrians. The very complexion of the city changed at these hours. White businessmen caught buses north and east to their comfortable homes, crossing paths with the Negro maids and laborers who returned from those same houses, heading back to Sweet Auburn or Summerhill or

Pittsburgh. Like some weird racial relay race, everyone returning to their positions until the next sprint tomorrow morning at eight.

Natalie had been waiting for her transfer bus when the white lady approached.

"Natalie Washington." The lady's smile seemed false. It disagreed with something behind her eyes. "We need to talk about how things are going with Larry Fenton."

Natalie's stomach muscles tensed. All she could think to say was, "Ma'am?"

"Can we talk somewhere more private?"

Larry Fenton headed the paper's sales department. Married, no kids, and his wife was a drinker. A cruel one. He'd been depressed and out of sorts before he'd met Natalie. She hadn't intended to sleep with her boss, but she always had been the sort to take risks, and the first time Larry had kissed her she'd felt too good to question it, so eventually they'd moved on to the next thing.

They'd been doing that next thing for a while.

Since her transfer to editorial, Larry was no longer her boss, but they'd been keeping the relationship secret nonetheless. Mr. Bishop had a strict policy about dress and behavior, and Natalie had heard of past female employees who'd been let go for "fraternization."

"Ma'am, I don't really know what you're—"

"Please, Miss Washington," the white lady said. "I'd hate for someone to overhear what you and Larry have been doing."

Though Natalie walked of her own power, she felt as though she were pulled by another force as she followed the white lady away from the crowded bus stop and toward a metal bench beside a lone, recently planted maple tree, its branches bare.

"I think you have the wrong idea, ma'am," Natalie said after she sat down. "I *work* with Mr. Fenton. I don't figure how you'd even know that, but—"

"I know more than that," the white lady said. Long gray flannel skirt and pumps, smart blue coat and matching hat, like a career woman from downtown or an unusually well-dressed librarian. Early forties or late thirties, her graying hair curling beneath her chin. "It really would be a problem if Mr. Fenton's boss found out what you two have been up to, don't you think? Or his wife? You'd lose your job, and Mr. Fenton might, too."

Natalie felt dizzy. Like some demon had dropped out of the sky and pointed its finger at her, voicing all her secrets.

"I don't ... I don't know what you're talking about." She remembered looking around for help, as if anyone in this sea of commuters might care.

"I think you do."

Natalie would later look back and wish she had been sterner, had told the lady off or just walked away, but she'd been too stunned.

"I wouldn't want that to happen to you. I think I can help you out, if you help me. You see, there are some other alarming things going on at your office, things that could get people hurt. If you can give me some information on that, I can keep your secrets to myself."

"What ... what do you mean?"

"I'd like to know what Mr. Bishop is working on."

Natalie's heart was pounding, but she tried to think clearly. "You're blackmailing me."

"I don't care for that word. It's such a dirty word, Natalie. I'm proposing an equal exchange of information. You give me the information I need, and I will suppress the salacious details about you and Mr. Fenton."

Natalie tried to understand. "What information?"

"What Mr. Bishop is working on."

"Mr. Bishop is the publisher. I don't work with him that closely. Even if I wanted to help you, I couldn't."

"I think you should want to, Natalie."

Natalie stared at her for a spell. "Why are you doing this? Who are you?"

"Call me Becky."

Who talks like that? No one phrases it that way, no one says *call me this* if that's their actual name. It meant, *I have a real name, but you can't know it.* Natalie felt a chill run down her neck.

"And don't you worry yourself with the why. Here's what you need to worry about: we're going to meet right here at this bench, every Monday and Thursday. On Mondays, if you've done a good job, I'll give you one of these." She removed an envelope from her jacket. "Ten dollars, to start. And if you *haven't* done a good job, then your boss will get a phone call. And some photographs."

Photographs? Who was this woman? The night was cold yet Natalie felt beads of sweat roll down her back.

"Either we have an agreement," Call Me Becky said, "or I call your boss before you even get home."

Hundreds of oblivious commuters were dashing to make it to this bus or that streetcar, and so many horns were honking, and buses hissing as they pulled up to stops, that Natalie hadn't realized at first that Call Me Becky was extending the envelope to her, telling her to take it.

Hating herself for it, Natalie took the envelope.

Less than two weeks later, Natalie felt even more nervous than usual as she waited at the bench near the Five Points bus stop.

Today was to be their first meeting since Mr. Bishop's murder.

Everyone at the office was in shock at the news, and though Natalie had cried along with them, she realized she was not entirely surprised. She had felt in her stomach the day she'd met Call Me Becky that this woman with her false smile and sinister eyes was evil, and it would only be a matter of time before something terrible happened.

Natalie had barely managed to eat her lunch, and now as she sat there alone she felt sick to her stomach, her limbs shaky and weak. She tried to steel herself.

Time passed. Call Me Becky had never been late before.

Five minutes ticked by. Ten.

Could Call Me Becky really have been involved in the murder? Natalie hoped she was jumping to conclusions. But then it was 6:45, and then 7:00, and if Natalie didn't catch the next transfer, she'd be stuck here even longer. Already the crowd had thinned, the sidewalks and streets growing quiet.

At their last meeting, just a few days before the murder, Call Me Becky had grown impatient. Natalie had explained that Mr. Bishop had traveled to Montgomery just the other day, though Natalie didn't know why. Call Me Becky had seemed quite interested in this, and frustrated that Natalie hadn't alerted her sooner. "Did he mention anything about train porters?" she'd asked. "Or something about an old murder?" Natalie had said no, not understanding. But the word *murder* scared her. Call Me Becky also asked if Bishop was writing anything about someone named Henry Paulding, but Natalie didn't know.

"You should have let me know sooner," Call Me Becky had snapped.

"How? I don't have your number."

Annoyed, Call Me Becky gave her a phone number and demanded Natalie call if she learned anything about the Montgomery story.

That had been their last meeting. Now Mr. Bishop was dead. Murdered.

And Call Me Becky didn't seem to be coming tonight.

Natalie knew then, as the bus she needed to catch approached, she just *knew* that she would never see Call Me Becky again. This should have come as a relief, but it felt the opposite. The only reason the demon was gone was because it had finished its work.

And Natalie had helped.

The feeling in her stomach grew worse. She stood and hurried over to the nearest trash barrel. Closed her eyes, waited for the moment to pass. Concentrated on breathing as she heard the bus open its doors. She felt her eyes tear up, but she willed herself not to be sick.

By the time the nausea subsided and she had collected herself, her bus was long gone and she was alone in the unforgiving city.

13

MCINNIS WAS WELL accustomed to being gazed at with suspicion, annoyance, fear. A combination of the three crossed the face of Ginny Beth Hunter, mother of the alleged rape victim, Martha.

"Hello, ma'am, my name's Sergeant Joe McInnis. Is your husband at home?"

She shook her head. "He's at work. This about the trial?"

"No, ma'am. I was just hoping to ask some questions about another incident that's occurred."

A hand to her breast. "Oh, dear Lord. Did he get another one? Someone else come forward?"

"No, ma'am, but ... May I come in?"

She nodded and backed up, holding the door for him.

Early afternoon, two days after Bishop's murder. Winter sun flooding through the windows kept the room surprisingly warm. The house spotless. That and the stuffy air made him wonder if the scandal had rendered her a shut-in, staying home and tending her daughter, trying to make her house as orderly as her life was not.

She sat on the orange couch and he took the green chair, a coffee table between them. The house was a bungalow in Grant Park, not more than four miles from McInnis's place. The homes here nothing fancy, but well-kept, much like his own neighborhood. People who worked hard and tended well to what they had. Clean, safe. The nearest Negro neighborhood was not as far as it once had been, unofficial color lines having been redrawn many times just since the war.

"We've been through an awful time, a real awful time. We didn't ask for any of this."

"You have my sympathies, ma'am."

"Y'all did some good work and I'm glad you got that nigger behind bars, but now we have to go through all this trial nonsense. The things people have said about her! I can't believe it's even legal to say those sorts of things about my baby. They should be ashamed of themselves."

She just wanted to talk, he realized, and God bless her for it. The worst were the tight-lipped ones. She was either too naïve or outraged to keep quiet.

He was here on the remote chance the Hunter–Higgs case had anything to do with Bishop's murder. The only major news on the Bishop case since yesterday was a ballistics report that the .38 found in the Bishop house was "unlikely" to be the murder weapon, based on the shell casings present at the scene.

He sat with his elbows on his knees, fingers steepled. "You feel that lots of people are talking about it?"

"Goodness, yes!" Like he was a fool to have asked. "We're all anyone's talking about, seems like. As soon as I show my head, they all hush up and look guilty for it. I couldn't tell you the number of times I've had conversations go quiet just because I stepped into a room."

"Even your friends and neighbors, huh?"

"You really find out who your friends are when something like this happens."

He had to tread lightly. "Why do you suppose so many people are able to believe such terrible things about her?"

"What do you mean?"

"I just wonder why these so-called friends and neighbors aren't circling the wagons to defend her from those allegations. That happens sometimes."

He honestly didn't know what to think about the rape allegation. He'd done some research and it seemed like a strong case, unless the victim was lying: Martha, unmarried and living in her parents' home, claimed she was attacked at 10 p.m., when her parents were out of town. No witness could ID the attacker, but

Randy Higgs owned a blue pickup, and two neighbors claimed to have seen such a truck on that block that night. No one heard any cries, but the victim claimed Higgs had held a Bowie knife to her throat and threatened to slice her if she cried out. Detectives' only piece of evidence was a package of cigarettes left behind at the scene, bearing Higgs's fingerprints. Higgs did indeed own a Bowie knife. The victim's parents had returned from their trip early the next morning, finding Martha huddled in a corner and crying, or so they claimed.

McInnis had looked up the *Daily Times* article Bishop had written about the love letters. Unless the letters were fake, they blew a hole through Martha's story. Perhaps Martha and Higgs had a consensual relationship, and then the parents had come home unexpectedly, so she'd cried rape to avoid the stigma of sleeping with a Negro. If that were true, then not only she but also her parents were lying.

As a cop who uncovered all kinds of behavior, McInnis knew that interracial affairs did indeed occur. Someone was lying here, he just didn't know who yet.

"People who know us and what kind of people we are, they're standing up for us," she said. "It's just, you know, there are some who like to do otherwise."

Before he could ask his next question, she snapped, "It's this trial coming up that's the problem. I'm sorry to say so, but the old way, that made more sense. Grab 'em, string 'em from a tree and be done with it. I know how it was, I heard the stories. This girl lived a couple towns over from me, down in Bibb County, something happened to her once, and they lynched the nigger the very next day, and then the story dies too. You understand how I mean? Decent folk wouldn't talk about it. It's like a cleansing. Almost a religious act. A sacrament. You purge the town with blood like that, and people can walk away knowing it's done. No need for *trials* and *depositions* and all this talk, talk, talk. This may be the *modern* way," she mocked, "but it's just a whole lot of accomplishing not a darn thing. He'll get the chair eventually, sure, but at what cost to *us*? Having to put us through the wringer like this just isn't right."

"The legal process isn't always pretty when you have to see it up close, ma'am. But we try to get things right."

"I cannot believe some people think we should just go along with the Supreme Court and let 'em in our schools. My God, can you imagine?"

"These are strange times," he conceded, not wanting to get into it.

"If there's any way that a little good can come out of this, it's that this will wake people up. I don't want the parents of some other girl to have to go through this. I think people, when they hear about what happened, they'll see how terrible it'd be if we let coloreds in the schools."

Some groups of concerned parents were already distributing leaflets about the case, using it as evidence for why parents needed to "stand up to the Supreme Court." Bonnie had brought one such leaflet home from church the other day.

"Have the newspapers said anything about the case that's bothered you?" he asked.

"Well, of course! We ain't reading 'em anymore! Got to the point where I couldn't bear to even hear the sound of Clarence turning a page, so I finally told the paperboy no more, cut us off, I don't want to see another newspaper til the trial's come and gone. My Lord."

"Any stories out there bother you in particular?"

She watched him in silence for a moment. He'd been wondering where Martha was and then he heard a floorboard creak somewhere in a back room.

"This ain't what you wanted to talk to me about, is it?"

"Well, ma'am, I patrol the area over by Auburn Avenue, in the Negro district. The man who owns the Negro newspaper was shot a couple nights back."

"Good. I'm glad. I read about that, and it made me smile."

"I thought you weren't reading the papers anymore."

She laughed. "Well, I caught that one. It was a happy story, so I didn't mind reading it."

"Happy, huh?"

"The head nigger at the paper that claimed my daughter's a liar and a hussy? Man who'd write lies like that, just to stir up his people and win points at my daughter's expense? He deserved worse than being shot, that I can tell you."

"How did you know he was the one who wrote that story?" None of the white papers had written about the love letters, McInnis knew. They wouldn't have touched that story. Mrs. Hunter only could have known Bishop was the author of that piece if she'd seen the story and his byline or heard someone mention that Bishop was behind it.

"Do you have children, Officer?"

"I do." He didn't bother correcting her to "Sergeant."

"And has anyone ever accused one of your children of having loose morals? Of sleeping with a nigger?"

He thought of the brats who'd called his son a *nigger lover*, but schoolyard taunts hardly rose to the severity of this family's travails. "No, ma'am."

"Well, if one ever did, I guarantee you, you would remember their name. I know the story he wrote and I know his name: Arthur Bishop. When I read that Bishop had been killed, yes, I can put one and one together. And I can put it together right now, too: you're here because you want to know if my husband or one of his brothers did it, don't you? You're wondering if he and I were so mad about that story that we went over and shot that black bastard ourselves?"

"I don't mean any disrespect, ma'am. But it is my job to ask certain questions, and I—"

"Answer's no. And you can leave now."

He stood. "Did you write any letters to the *Daily Times*, ma'am?"

"Why would I write them a letter?"

"They received several threatening letters after that story." He nodded his head out her window as he walked. "Turns out, a few were sent from the post office right down the street there."

She looked thrown, only for a moment. "Plenty of people use that post office. It was probably just my neighbors, standing up for me."

"I thought you said the neighbors were talking bad about you."

"I said *some* were. You think you're so damned smart. And I asked you to leave."

He started toward the door, realizing he'd gotten all he could from her.

"Never thought I'd see the day when a white policeman would take a nigger's side like this."

He stopped. "I'm not taking anyone's side, ma'am. I'm enforcing the law."

"You're just part of the problem. Can't catch the wrongdoers, so you settle for making life difficult for the rest of us."

He put his hand on the doorknob. "We did catch the man who attacked your daughter, ma'am. I also make it a point to catch murderers. If you *do* happen to hear anyone talking about what happened to Mr. Bishop, I'd appreciate hearing about it."

He wondered how he might have handled this conversation differently; if there was any way she could have not hated him.

"I can guarantee," she said, "you will not be hearing a damn thing from me, about anything, ever."

He stepped outside and walked to his car. At least two of her neighbors were watching, one across the street and another two houses down from that one, both women, standing in their doorways. He nodded in their direction; one returned the gesture and the other stepped inside, startled to have been noticed.

A neighborhood just like his. He figured they were still watching when he drove past.

14

"**WEARING YOUR UNIFORM** when you ain't on duty," Smith said, shaking his head as he sat beside his former partner on the cold pew for Bishop's funeral. This was the third day after the murder. "Used to be we couldn't do that."

On the other side of Boggs sat another Negro officer, his young partner. Smith extended a hand and introduced himself.

"Marty Jones," the rookie said as they shook in front of Boggs's chest. Soft voice, watchful eyes. Smith wondered if he'd last on the force.

"Good seeing you, Tommy," Boggs said. Lying, probably.

They spoke softly, seated in the middle of Wheat Street Baptist. The funeral started in fifteen minutes yet the church was as full as a Sunday service, the air growing warm. Satin-ribboned black hats everywhere. The organ music low and sedate, just getting warmed up.

"Used to be," Smith said, for young Jones's benefit, "we could only wear our uniforms on the clock. Not even when we were testifying at trials."

"That true?" Jones asked Boggs.

"It is," Boggs answered. "We're making progress, though. They say we're getting a squad car soon."

Smith scanned the crowd. "You talk to any of the family yet?"

Boggs sounded tired by the mere suggestion. "Are you asking me as a reporter seeking comment, or—"

"As an ex-cop who saw his boss take his last breath."

"You know how it works, Tommy. Homicide runs things. Detectives. We stand down."

"That's always worked out so well."

"We'll find him."

"But you haven't at least talked to the family to offer your condolences, then casually asked a few questions while you were at it?"

"Why else do you think I'm here?"

Smith noticed a few white faces in the crowd. Men as successful as Arthur Bishop tended to have powerful friends in the white community. Such friends, Smith figured, would have disappeared if any scandal had visited itself upon Bishop (like, say, communism). But today they could feel good about themselves for paying their respects to an esteemed Negro, especially one who had always been careful not to rock too many boats.

"Talk to the widow yet?" Smith asked.

"No," Boggs said.

"Well, let me know if you need to know anything."

Boggs turned to face him. "*You* spoke to her?"

"Some of us have to do our jobs."

"Tommy, you need to be careful. And you need to stand down. Detectives may even be *following* you for all we know."

True. He still didn't know the identity of the white man who'd been parked outside the Bishops'. Yet he put on his usual, confident face, saying, "I highly doubt a white detective is in this building." They'd certainly stand out. The white faces in the crowd had the look of business leaders or low-level politicians, not police.

"Nonetheless. You talking to the widow isn't smart."

"I can either wait around for the detectives to do something stupid, or I can act first."

"You always did like acting first."

Smith glanced at the front rows, wondering who was which relative. Then he turned to check the crowd behind him, just in time to see Bryan Laurence walking down the middle aisle, stone-faced. Smith was shocked—he'd never seen his editor out of the building before. Laurence gripped the edge of each pew as he walked, and Smith saw sweat running down the man's cheeks. Being in a crowd like this was nearly killing him, yet he'd known he couldn't miss it. Smith nodded at Laurence but the editor didn't see him, lost in his private terror. He made it all the way to the second row, sitting behind Mrs. Bishop. *Where's his wife?* Smith wondered.

Smith knew last night had been a particularly stressful one for Laurence, as he'd been forced to rearrange the front page at the last possible minute. The lead story in today's edition, no doubt already read by everyone here, reported that Reverend King Jr. had been arrested in Montgomery for allegedly speeding, by driving 30 miles per hour in a 25 zone. Police had initially denied him bond, claiming that the necessary office was closed for the night. Their plan to hold him overnight had been foiled only when a crowd of sympathizers gathered at the station; the cops had finally released him.

The day's edition had been ready to go to press when the *Daily Times'* Montgomery reporter had called Laurence with an update: King's home had been bombed.

The Montgomery reporter was still gathering facts; all he knew was that no one was hurt, as the family had been out. With no time for a proper piece, Laurence shoehorned a one-paragraph bulletin about the bombing atop the arrest story.

The grief in the church felt amplified by tension, everyone no doubt whispering the latest news from Montgomery, asking who knew anything else. Smith hadn't spotted Reverend King Sr. here yet.

"I might not feel the need to snoop so hard," Smith told Boggs, "if I thought *you* were doing more."

"Oh, it's easy for you to criticize, isn't it? Now that you're outside looking in."

"I criticized plenty on the inside, you know it."

"But now you're talking about team business, and you aren't on the team anymore."

All their old arguments came flooding back. Boggs was right: Smith did feel a certain freedom to point out all the maddening contradictions that had so galled him about their job. Boggs sounded hurt, as if Smith was now cheating in a game they'd played fair for years.

"You see a Morris Peeples here?" he asked Boggs. "One of your old professors?"

Boggs almost sighed again. "There, in the third row, on the right. With the goatee. Why?"

"I've been trying to get him to talk to me about some rumored strike," he lied. "You know him well?"

"I took a class with him. Not a terribly friendly man. He's one of those loves-humanity, doesn't-love-actual-people types."

"Sounds like someone I used to work with."

Before Boggs could reply, the officiant was stepping to the pulpit and announcing the first hymn, "Precious Lord, Take My Hand."

Smith had recovered physically from his all-nighter at the police station, but he still felt emotionally crushed. Even a man with a low opinion of the world still retains some hope that it isn't irredeemably bad. He considered himself a hardened realist, yet this new tragedy seemed to be stamping out a hidden optimism he hadn't realized he'd possessed.

Despite not being close personally with Mr. Bishop, and despite being nothing like the stuffy, conservative, not-terribly-friendly publisher, Smith had looked up to him. It was good for his soul to see an upright, hard-working colored man be so successful here in the South. Bishop's good fortune showed that it was possible to succeed honorably, by exposing corruption, shedding light on evil, and uplifting his people.

Smith feared that the investigation into his murder might reveal something untoward about him. The communist past, or God knows what else. If Bishop had done anything corrupt or sinful, if he had been compromised in some way, Smith almost didn't want to know. It would break that last part of Smith's heart, the part he tried to keep hidden, the part his tough veneer liked to pretend wasn't there, the part he most needed to protect. But if he didn't try to find the truth, he'd always wonder what the truth was, and what it predicted of his own path.

It was his job to dig out these secrets, while hoping they weren't as terrible as he feared.

Arthur Bishop was buried in Oakland Cemetery, the grandest in the city. Here too segregation reigned, as the mourners gathered in the Negro section. On the other side of the bluff lay Confederate war dead and city founders, railroad entrepreneurs and early American financiers. A cold wind blew through the leafless oaks and poplars, the ground hard beneath the mourners' feet. In the distance Smith saw the city towers and ever-present scaffolding, always in a hurry to make more and larger, their dizzying progress mocking the past. Then everyone bowed their heads for another prayer as the pallbearers shoveled red Georgia clay onto the casket with a cold finality that mocked all that activity downtown.

Victoria Bishop hid her face behind a veil and her shoulders shook as she was led away by relatives. Smith's throat hurt from trying not to cry.

Among the crowd he spotted other prominent business owners and reverends. According to Toon, the publishers of the *Chicago Defender* and *Pittsburgh Courier* were in attendance, burying their hatchets to honor a fellow literary lion. Newsroom bets had been placed as to whether Langston Hughes or Richard Wright (who was also a communist, according to rumor) would appear.

As the crowd dissolved across the grounds, Smith found himself walking behind Bryan Laurence. Smith was only a couple feet away when he saw Laurence sway oddly. The editor took another step and began to fall to his left.

Smith hustled alongside Laurence just in time to stop him from falling. He wrapped an arm around his shoulder and steadied the smaller man.

"Are you all right?"

Laurence adjusted his fedora, which had tipped from contact with Smith's shoulder.

"I'm fine. Thank you. Just ... haven't eaten all day."

Smith took a long look at Laurence's face—his eyes red from crying, or lack of sleep, or both, and his expression even paler than usual—and waited another beat until Laurence straightened his shoulders and all but shook Smith off.

"Yeah," Smith said, sensitive to the man's embarrassment. He removed his hands but stayed close in case Laurence wavered again.

A young man walked up to them, concern in his eyes. "Are you okay, Mr. Laurence?" he asked in a Northern accent. "I can look for a bench."

"No, heavens no," Laurence said. "I'll be fine once I have some food in me, that's all. I'm sorry to make a scene. I'm all right."

The three of them stood there awkwardly for a moment, Smith and the stranger lingering until they were sure Laurence could walk unaided. The stranger looked somewhat familiar.

"We haven't met," Smith said, extending a hand. "Tommy Smith."

"Crispin Bishop."

That explained the Harvard accent. He had his uncle's high forehead and air of formality, Smith noticed, even though he was still in his twenties.

"I'm sorry for your loss. I worked for your uncle. He was a great man."

"Thank you," Crispin said, nodding. He turned back to the editor. "Are you sure you're all right, Mr. Laurence?"

Laurence insisted he was fine, and they discussed how he was going to get to the Bishop home for the reception—apparently Laurence's wife was ill today, so he'd come alone. As they were talking, two other men joined them. One appeared to be in his sixties, with white hair visible beneath his dark fedora; the other seemed only a few years younger, with horn-rimmed glasses and a particularly impeccable suit. Smith recognized them both but couldn't immediately place them.

"I'm fine, I'm fine," Laurence said. He turned to the white-haired man. "But Eric, if you're headed to the reception, I'll take a ride."

That's right, Smith remembered: the older man was Eric Branford, Mr. Bishop's longtime friend and attorney. He too was on the board. So many people with a stake in the paper's future, all together. And Branford had been at the *Daily Times* office the other day, consulting with Bishop about the libel suit. Hours before the murder.

Smith had so many questions, none of them appropriate to ask here.

The next meeting of the paper's board of directors was scheduled for later in the week, Smith knew. Once a new publisher was named, a new editor-in-chief would be appointed. Opinions varied as to whether Crispin, the eldest child of the paper's founder, would decide to leave his legal career in Boston to continue the family's leadership of this peculiar Southern institution. Some expected Victoria Bishop to seek the position, but no one knew if she had what it took to be a publisher; she hadn't written for the paper in years. Smith had also heard speculation that Laurence too planned to lobby for the editor-in-chief position.

Smith hated that this made them all suspects. Hated the way he thought. The way he'd thought as a cop, the way he thought as a crime reporter. Always looking for the worst in people. Too often finding it.

Laurence's stumble probably meant he was distraught, as they all were. Or maybe he was overwhelmed at being out in public after years of being a shut-in. Surely that was all. Surely there was no deeper meaning behind it.

"How is she holding up?" the old man in glasses asked Branford.

"As well as can be expected, I suppose," Branford said.

"It was hell when I lost Willa Mae," the man said. "But of course ... these circumstances are so much worse."

"It's a nightmare, Clancy," Laurence said. "A nightmare."

Clancy Darden, Smith thought, another of Bishop's wealthy friends, an executive at Atlanta Life Insurance Company. Smith had interviewed him years ago for a rare, non-crime-related story.

The five of them started walking toward the nearest gate, Laurence seeming steady on his feet now.

Smith wanted to keep eavesdropping on the conversation, but he felt like an obvious hanger-on who didn't belong here. His own car was in the shop, so he'd ridden here with Toon; he turned to look through the crowd as he walked, hoping to spot him. His eyes fell once again on professor Morris Peeples, who was walking toward a different gate.

Though Smith had plenty of questions he wanted to ask Crispin and Branford, this seemed the wrong time. Peeples, however, appeared to be alone. Smith decided his questions for the communist couldn't wait, so he walked toward him.

Peeples might have looked slightly more intellectual if he'd actually carried a lectern around with him. But the gray goatee, thin-framed glasses, and brown tweed blazer did the job just fine. Late fifties, short and squat, he walked with a bit of a hunch. Smith could imagine Peeples getting into an argument with the much taller Bishop, and, needing to fight back, reaching for a gun.

Smith tailed Peeples, who was walking toward the western gate. They had reached the edge of the grounds, nearing the stone arch that led to Oakland Avenue, when Smith made his move. "Excuse me, Mr. Peeples?"

Though half a foot shorter, the ex-professor still had a way of looking down his nose at Smith. "Yes?"

The voice didn't go with the look: Smith had been expecting something nasal but Peeples had a deep voice, a toughness to the way he addressed a stranger.

"I'm Tommy Smith, with the *Daily Times*. I know this isn't the best time or place, but I was hoping I could talk with you."

"What about?"

"About Mr. Bishop, sir."

Peeples stood stock-still. The brown scarf cinched around his neck made him appear under siege. "Are you looking for a quote about Arthur?"

"No, sir." Smith tried to sound matter-of-fact and non-threatening as he explained, "I understand you and Mr. Bishop had a meeting the night he died. Which would make you one of the last people to see him alive. So, Mr. Peeples. I was wondering if you could tell me if you saw or heard anything unusual that night."

Peeples had been still before, but now he seemed somehow more still. "I don't know what you're talking about. We didn't meet that night."

Smith had spoken to a few professors and prominent attorneys in his time, and he always showed respect for the men's accomplishments. He knew that to contradict someone like Peeples would be a breach of etiquette, and he hated how often his job cast him in the role of bad guy.

"You were on his calendar, sir. The police don't know this, but I found out."

Peeples shook his head and backed up a step. "What on earth do you think you're doing?" His voice quieter but more panicked than before. Looking over Smith's shoulder. Others were passing them on their way out, some heads turning. Peeples backed up more and Smith followed him to the base of a magnolia where they might not be overheard.

"What do you *want*?" Peeples asked.

Smith held out his palms. "I was just wondering if you saw or heard anything that—"

"We didn't *talk* that night. We were supposed to, but I had to cancel."

Smith nodded. "I didn't know. If you don't mind my asking, why did you need to cancel?"

Peeples clearly understood that Smith was asking if he had an alibi. "I do mind you asking. But if you must know, I'm an attorney and I was working on a case." Then he sighed and seemed to deflate as he added, "Working at home, alone."

They stood silent for a moment as they both contemplated the implications.

"Mr. Peeples, I used to be a cop, so I know how this works. I'm not going to the police, but if *they* find out you were supposed to meet with him, they're going to be suspicious. They're going to want to talk to you. If there's anything you know that can help me figure out what happened that night, then I can solve this and not have to worry about police going after the wrong man."

Peeples thought for a moment. "'Solve this.' You still talk like a cop."

"Bad habits die hard, I guess."

He didn't like how this banter was giving Peeples an extra beat to formulate a new answer, a new story.

Yet Peeples simply adjusted his scarf and said, "I'm sorry, but I can't help you."

Peeples began to step away. Smith was shocked the man would choose to be unhelpful, especially when the potential of police involvement lingered. Smith needed to get more out of him.

"Mr. Peeples, sir, I understand you two were close, that you went way back. Could you tell me if he'd been worried about anything in particular, or if he'd been threatened?"

Peeples stopped. No doubt sensing where Smith was going with his reference to their long history. "I have no desire to drag Arthur's name through the muck, either to your old police colleagues or for the *Daily Times*."

With that, he walked past Smith, the scent of old pipe smoke trailing him.

What "muck," Smith wondered? Communism, or something even worse?

Peeples stopped a few feet away, turning to face Smith. "When you joined the force, did they happen to educate you about the history of the police in this country?"

"They were light on the history lessons, sir."

"Police in America started as slave catchers. Americans didn't even want police at first. Felt too colonial, reminded them of the heavy-handed British. White Americans are all about their freedoms, after all. But then they decided they needed police to keep the runaway slaves in line." He adjusted his scarf again. "I'd say you made the right decision when you switched jobs. But you should still tread carefully. I always assume they're watching, and you should, too."

15

"**IT'S A TERRIBLE** loss for the community," Reverend Boggs said as he gave his two eldest sons, Reginald and Lucius, a ride home from the funeral reception. "I trust they'll find the man responsible?"

Lucius wasn't sure how to answer that. He liked projecting confidence, but he didn't like having to vouch for white detectives. "We're going to do everything we can," he said from the backseat.

"What do you know so far?" Reverend Boggs asked.

"Not much. It's early." Half a dozen people at the funeral reception had asked Lucius variations on this. *You'll find the killer, right?* He'd long grown used to having his community's expectations pressing down on his shoulders. That didn't make it any less challenging, though. "If you know of anything that might help, please let me know."

"I can't think of anything that would lead to murder," his father mused. He had known Bishop for as long as Bishop had run the paper. "For someone who worked in a public sphere, Arthur was a very private man."

They drove in silence for a moment.

"There's something else I wanted to tell you two about." The reverend tapped a file folder that lay on the front center seat. "Reginald, take a look at this. One of my congregants cuts hair at the Crystal Palace. State senators and lawyers and bankers always talk shop there, thinking we Negroes don't have ears. He happened to overhear something about a week ago, and I've managed to confirm the details."

As Reginald flipped open the folder and started reading the top page, Reverend Boggs continued, "The city is planning to bulldoze Darktown and a good deal of Sweet Auburn."

"*What?*" Lucius leaned forward so he could look over his brother's shoulder. Inside the folder was a memo between two city councilmen, followed by a few more memos between them and a developer. Then maps, one of them showing a radically re-envisioned city. The neighborhood known as Darktown, a slum consisting of substandard housing—and a regular stop on Lucius's nightly shifts—had vanished. In its place sat a large civic center and a hotel. Those and other structures, along with two massive parking lots, spilled out further south and east, even erasing a few blocks of Sweet Auburn. "Good Lord."

"They can't do this," Reginald said. "Most of this property is Negro-owned. I've written policies for some of them." He worked at Atlanta Life Insurance Company, one of the wealthiest Negro-owned businesses not just in Atlanta but in the country.

"Legally, they *can* do it," their father corrected. "Eminent domain. Civic improvement, on the backs of colored folks. They have the law on their side, which means we need to fight them with everything we have."

Lucius asked Reginald for the file so he could take a closer look. As he flipped through the pages, he shook his head. "Mayor's stabbing us in the back."

The city had floated a similar but smaller plan a few years ago, "slum clearance" aimed mostly at Darktown. Community leaders like the reverend had managed to stymie the move, yet here the city was again, this time with an even more destructive plan. White folks seemed to think Darktown was cursed, not worth saving, only destroying. In their opinion, funding badly needed housing for the overcrowded neighborhood was a waste of money; better to bulldoze the area and turn it into a civic center and hotels for tourists.

"How did you get these memos?" Lucius asked.

"Your old man still has a few tricks up his sleeve."

The reverend had likely enlisted some white allies to dig up the material, unless a brave Negro custodian had poked around for him. City Hall had no Negro file clerks.

Studying one of the maps, Lucius pointed at an intersection. "This is just two blocks from the *Daily Times*. Did Bishop know?"

"I doubt it," Reverend Boggs said. "If he had, he would have written about it. He would have rallied people to fight it, which is exactly what I intend to do. I just showed this to his second-in-command, Bryan Laurence. I felt bad telling him today, as I know it's not the best time. The man didn't look very good, honestly. But he certainly agrees this is something they need to cover, so I'm heading back to his office tonight."

Lucius leaned back, thinking. Maybe Bishop had indeed known about the plan, and someone had killed him to keep him from writing about it. But Bishop covered weighty topics every day; why would this story be worthy of murder?

"I only got my hands on these documents yesterday," Reverend Boggs said. "So far, the only people I've shared this with are King, Holmes Borders, and Dobbs." That trio—two older Baptist ministers like himself, and the head of one of the biggest Negro fraternal orders—comprised the unofficial, unelected leadership of Negro Atlanta (which had no elected officials because of Jim Crow). "But we need to let the community know. The *Times* will help get the word out."

"This memo," Lucius said, fishing one of them out from the pile. "He mentions something about 'transportation improvements.' Think he's talking about a highway?"

Municipalities across the country were gorging themselves on Eisenhower's new highway funds. The only question, in crowded places like Atlanta, was where to put the highways.

"I noticed that too," Reginald said. "First they'll drop a civic center on a chunk of Negro Atlanta, then later they'll drop a highway on the rest of it." He slapped his knee. "Where the hell do they expect us to *go*?"

"Language," his father chided.

The city still faced a desperate lack of housing for Negroes, and now white councilmen wanted to wipe out several square blocks of Negro apartment buildings. Lucius tried to imagine what it would do to his job. More families on the street, more young men without reliable shelter and food, and with only one way left to take what they needed to survive.

Lucius felt a familiar rage as he read the memos again. Every time he thought the city was getting better—the *country* was getting better—something like this happened. A slap in the face. *How foolish of you to hope.* Like the schools situation. He was tired of hearing from his kids and Julie about how crowded their classrooms were, how overworked the teachers. Some of his kids only went to school for half the time, as their schools had to teach them in two different shifts. And the mere sight of some of their textbooks, tattered and third-hand—looking like the exact same books he himself had once used—made bile rise in his throat. He'd swallowed enough pride to work out of the YMCA basement, and now the headquarters' basement, but to see his children subjected to similar treatment was something else entirely. When the Supreme Court had issued its ruling, he had hoped that his kids might finally have something better, but now more than a year and a half had passed and, if anything, white people were more determined than ever to make sure their schools stayed off limits to Negroes.

"The mayor used us," Lucius said. "He used you, sir, and used me."

Hartsfield loved deploying the Negro officers as props. In the final week before the last election, in '54, Lucius twice had stood in uniform along with his fellow officers before a stage as Hartsfield basked in applause from the grateful crowd. The same dynamic had played out in the previous election, the first since the city hired colored cops. The mayor had hired them because the city's Negro vote had grown so quickly, so every four years at election time he showcased them as a visual reminder to colored voters about who their best political champion was. Lucius had stood at attention as old ladies took his photograph; had posed alongside youngsters who shook his hand and said they too wanted to be cops when they grew up. And yes, he'd felt a surge of pride as people gazed at his perfectly polished brass buttons and shiny shoes and gold badge. Proud to stand before them, even though he'd known the mayor was shamelessly using him as a bodyguard against his Negro flank.

It stung all the more now.

"Yes, he used us," Reverend Boggs said, "just as we have used him, to get your job, to get streetlights, to get a new park, to get plenty else. That isn't the point. The point is, our neighborhood is under assault, and we need to stop it."

Lucius knew he wasn't as good at working out the political angles as his father was, which worried him. He knew from experience that his father would use him, too, for inside dope on the Police Department—his personal spy. Lucius wanted to stop this awful development plan, but he was wary of being made a pawn in some larger power struggle.

"White folk," Reginald said, "they don't even see the difference between Sweet Auburn and Darktown. Whether it's a bum or a businessman, all they see is *nigger*."

"*Language*."

Maybe this development plan had nothing to do with Bishop's death, Lucius thought. Or maybe it did.

He read through the memos again, checking the names of city councilmen, real estate developers, attorneys. Wondering which of these men Bishop might have known personally, and which might have paid him a visit in his office that night.

16

ANOTHER DAY, ANOTHER crime story.

Despite taking the time to attend the funeral, Smith was still expected to produce. That afternoon he penned a follow-up on a previous piece: a judge had fined a deaf man for using obscene sign language and directing it toward another deaf man out on Edgewood Street. Smith would throw out a line or two about the broadening definition of speech, what the ruling meant about obscenity, and whether this was perhaps the first time someone had been fined for offensive speech without employing vocal cords. He feared Laurence would destroy this one.

Smith visited the copy desk to look over people's shoulders and check in on the latest from Montgomery: the mayor who had recently vowed to "stop pussyfooting" and to "get tough" with the boycott was now denying that his words had incited violence, and he claimed he would protect the King family from future bombings. No arrests had been made.

Sitting in his office, Smith lit a cigarette and realized how exhausted he was. And how deeply sad. He and the other reporters were expected to continue as if life were normal, as if their boss was still alive.

It was absurd, but they had no choice.

He flipped through his notebook, dug up a few angles. He made some calls and tracked down the phone number of Tim Pinckney, the business reporter Bishop had fired a month ago for hustling stories. He'd worked at the paper off and on for years; Smith hadn't known him that well, as Pinckney was quiet and away from his desk most of the time and they worked different hours.

Smith reached Pinckney at his new apartment in Memphis, where he'd gotten a job at the *Tri-State Defender*. That year-old paper had been started by John Sengstacke, owner of the *Chicago Defender*, to expand his empire and exert pressure on Bishop's.

Smith asked Pinckney why he'd been fired, and Pinckney was surprisingly candid.

"Hey, there are gray areas, and I stepped into one."

Pinckney confirmed what Smith had heard: he'd been bribed by a builder to write a fawning piece about a new development on the West Side. He'd done a reasonably good job of covering his tracks, interviewing enough other sources to make it seem like a legitimate news piece. But when Bishop read it, he'd smelled a rat, and when he'd confronted Pinckney, the writer confessed to pocketing $100 from the developer.

"I made a mistake. I thought he'd give me a second chance, but I guess Mr. Bishop didn't believe in those."

"Who was the developer?" Smith asked.

"Henry Paulding, white man owns those new places on the West Side. What kills me is my story was fair, too. Not like I was putting lies in print."

Smith was surprised that Pinckney, a veteran reporter in his late forties, would excuse such a stupid stunt, renting out his byline like that.

"Mind if I asked you where you were the night Bishop was killed?"

"I do mind," Pinckney replied. "But you're a reporter doing your job, so I'll tell you. I was here in Memphis at a city council meeting, and if you don't believe me, you can read my impressively detailed story about it when it goes to press tomorrow."

Then Pinckney asked a question of his own. "You look into the Ledbetter angle?"

"What's that?"

"I wrote for that paper off and on for a long time," Pinckney explained. "I heard a lot of stories. That paper survived the Depression, which was a hard time to stay in business. Especially when you're selling to colored folks. Anyway, at some point in the thirties, back when his brother Sebastian was running things, they had to take out a loan from one Dex Ledbetter. You know the name?"

"I do." Ledbetter once had been one of Atlanta's biggest numbers runners and loan sharks. He'd been killed in the late forties, when Smith was a cop. "You're saying the paper was connected to gangsters like Ledbetter?"

"I wouldn't put it like that. Gotta remember the time. White banks would never lend to a Negro businessman, and even the colored banks were hard up. Look, I've heard through the grapevine that the *Defender* took plenty of loans from the Chicago mob back then, too. All I'm saying is, Sebastian took a loan from Ledbetter, at a very high interest rate, and that guillotine hung over his head for a while. But he eventually paid it off."

Smith thought for a moment. "That's a long time ago."

"Which is why I almost didn't even mention it. And I never had any reason to think *Arthur* Bishop was connected to folks like that. But the fact is, his brother had at least *some* underworld contacts, so maybe Arthur did too. Worth looking into."

That night, Smith took Patrice out again. He'd managed to promote their relationship from just-a-drink to a dinner he could barely afford, at a restaurant a block from her kitchen. A mix of Southern cuisine and some Italian, walls decorated with framed photos of Georgia forests and the Italian Alps. Later in the evening, tables would be rearranged and a jazz band would play in the corner, but for now the place was quiet, dimly lit, linen tablecloths absorbing all sound.

"There's something I've been wondering," Patrice said when they were halfway through their bottle of wine, awaiting the entrees. "Did you like being a cop?"

She'd only been able to ask after some wine. He had long

noticed people felt a certain reticence to discuss his old job. It struck him as oddly similar to how no one ever wanted to ask ex-cons what it was like to do time. Maybe it was because most people wanted to avert their eyes from the criminal justice system entirely. A deep-seated fear of one day finding yourself in the crosshairs of the law. Best to ignore it entirely, if you could. Whistle past the graveyard.

"A lot of times, I loved it. Our first day, mayor gave us this rah-rah speech in the precinct, and when we walked up those steps, there must've been two hundred people out there cheering us on. I felt like a god. An old lady even ran out and handed me a bouquet of flowers."

Patrice laughed. "Of course she'd hand them to *you*."

He shrugged, like he couldn't help the blessings the good Lord had bestowed on his cheekbones and eyes. "It was a rush, I can't lie. But it didn't feel that way for very long." He thought for a moment. "We worked hard. Those boys out there now, they're working hard. That ain't no easy job."

"So why aren't you a cop anymore?"

Smith sensed that *this* was the question she'd been afraid to ask. "I guess … I wanted a way to feel those highs but without the lows. The job I have now—chasing stories, being the eyes on the street, trying to get people to understand what really happens in the city—that comes the closest."

The look in her eyes suggested she didn't believe him. "Are you saying you feel like a god when you're typing on *Bertha*," he'd confided to her his nickname for his typewriter, "or trying to get a quote from someone who's had his head bashed in?"

"No. But I feel like I'm doing something worth doing."

"Instead of selling insurance or hair tonic?"

"Hair tonic is a worthy profession. That's some important stuff. How about you, do you like running the kitchen?"

She exhaled. "Do I like it? Honestly, most times I'm running so fast I don't have time to think about like and don't like. Just trying to keep that roof over my and Annalise's heads."

Smith couldn't remember if her daughter was four or twelve or somewhere in between. To be honest, Patrice's motherhood may have been one of the reasons he hadn't pursued her after their one fun night. He hadn't wanted to get involved with mothers, the messiness of families. He regretted that now.

"How's Annalise doing?" he asked.

"She's good." And Patrice smiled. "Raising a child alone isn't easy. But I have a couple aunts who help a lot. Some people thought, after Bernard passed, I should move in with family, give up the business, focus on Annalise. Call me crazy, but I figured I'd have better luck pressing on with the business. And now I have family moving in with *me*."

She gazed into space for a moment, her smile gone.

"In the beginning, I did all the cooking and Bernard handled the business side, but I learned all that pretty quick after he passed. I had no choice. And I like it. I like having something I'm good at, something that isn't just cooking for someone." She paused. "I hope I can keep doing it."

"You said the other day white folks aren't ordering from you anymore?"

"I made the mistake of signing a letter about getting my daughter into a white school." She shook her head. "No, it wasn't a mistake. But it's why white people are suddenly finding they no longer need my services."

He'd heard stories like this. "White Citizens Council put your name on a list?"

"Apparently."

The White Citizens Councils had formed some time after the Supreme Court's schools decision. That ruling had initially stunned white folks, from governors on down, but after the shock wore off, sheer anger kicked in. Now the white South was feverishly mobilizing. The newly formed WCCs held rallies, wrote letters, and made a point of financially punishing Negroes who said or did anything about improving Negro rights.

If a laborer or maid spoke their mind, they would find themselves fired.

If a farmer made the list, he'd learn that his seed supplier wouldn't sell to him anymore, or his bank had called in a loan.

And if a business owner like Patrice offended their sensibilities, her customers stopped calling.

The WCCs were part of the reason Bishop had always struck a cautious editorial tone. Most of Bishop's advertising came from Negro businesses, but some did come from whites, so he strove to find some middle ground where he could avoid offending either his progress-craving readers or his ad-buying white businesses.

Such middle ground seemed to have vanished since the *Brown* decision.

"I'm sorry to hear that," he said, wishing there was something he could do. "I could pitch my editor a piece about whites boycotting Negro businesses. Maybe we—"

"No, no thank you." She shook her head. "Last thing I want is even more attention. All I want is for my baby to finally go to a school that has new books and doesn't close early because they're so crowded they need staggered shifts. That's all my letter asked, and they're acting like I was proposing a revolution."

That disappointed him, but he understood. It was so much easier to be the writer than the subject.

A pall descended. They both took a silent sip of wine.

"You've never told me much about your family," she said. "Parents, siblings?"

"I have a sister, she's married with two kids now. But they moved to Chicago a couple of years ago so I haven't seen 'em. Looked real cute last time she sent me pictures. My mother passed away the year before they moved north. My father died when I was a teenager."

He chose not to go into further details. That when he was sixteen, his parents had told him how they weren't his biological parents but his aunt and uncle, and his sister was truly his cousin. That back in 1919, when Smith had been an infant, his father, a veteran of the Great War, had been lynched for daring to wear his army uniform at a parade. His mother had drunk herself to death soon after, and his aunt and uncle had adopted him.

This was not date conversation material.

Perhaps because of that tragedy, they'd been an unusual family, small, with few extended relatives. Now most of them were gone. Smith had a couple of cousins in the Atlanta area but that was all.

"I'm sorry," Patrice said, without knowing the half of it. "That sounds lonely."

"I suppose it can be." Maybe that's why he had loved the instant family of the army, then of the police force, and now of the newspaper. Maybe that's why he was so quick to jump into the arms of the next woman.

And maybe that's why, years into such behavior, he was still alone.

Needing to change the subject, he asked if she knew Victoria Bishop.

"I've bumped into her a few times, and I catered some dinners they held. But I wouldn't say I know her very well. I'd see her sometimes at the Board of Commerce meetings."

He was about to ask another question when she added, "And now that I think of it, she didn't show up to our last meeting, even though she was supposed to give a presentation."

Smith thought back, remembering his last date with Patrice, before she had to run to that meeting. Just a few hours before Bishop was killed.

"She ever explain why she didn't go?" he asked.

"No, but I haven't seen her since." She seemed chastened by the gravity of what they were discussing. "You don't think . . . ?"

"I don't know. It could be anything." Yet he thought, *Victoria Bishop has no alibi for the night her husband was killed. She was supposed to be at a meeting at that time, but didn't show up.* He wondered if white investigators even knew this yet.

He walked Patrice home the three blocks north, to a bungalow whose impeccably arranged azaleas, hydrangeas, and rose garden looked like they were merely biding their time til March.

When they reached her front steps, he took her hand and kissed it, looking her in the eye.

She laughed. "Why do I get the sense I've become some sort of test for you?"

"What do you mean?"

"Have you taken a vow of chastity, Tommy Smith? Does a girl have to come flat out and ask you for it?"

He laughed too. "I would love to come upstairs, if that was an invitation. But let's just say that we maybe did things the wrong way last time, and I want to try it the right way now. How about another dinner, on Saturday?"

"Well," and she took her chin in one hand, mimicking deliberation, "I'll have to check with my other six suitors. I forget who has Saturdays. But I might be able to bump him for you."

He leaned forward and they kissed, for real this time, and only when they heard footsteps nearby did they break away.

Too charged up to head home, he dropped by the office again.

He had assigned himself a number of research projects, including finding old *Daily Times* stories on Dex Ledbetter, the gangster who once bailed out the newspaper, not to mention any editorials Bishop had written about the communist menace, of which there were many to choose from. He wondered if Bishop had ever named anyone publicly in those jeremiads.

Smith also had asked Officer Deaderick for any legal papers on the upcoming Higgs trial but had been rebuffed—the white man had all but said "not your place" in turning him down.

Smith sat at his desk and read backwards, following Bishop's byline back in time to see whom he'd particularly offended over the last few weeks, then months.

What an impossible task. And deeply sad. He was a reader

chasing meaning from a writer who'd chased meaning, until it had killed him. Writers try to transmute the randomness of life into something coherent, a story, and even if they themselves can't find any true meaning, they hope the readers will find it. Regardless of what Bishop may have thought when he wrote all this, regardless of which tales and plots he'd found most compelling at the time, one of these stories may have had a meaning he couldn't have comprehended. It was the story that would get him killed.

But Lord, which one?

Smith made it back as far as 1952 when he fell asleep.

Once again, Smith woke up at night in his office.

He'd heard a door forced open. The back door, which led to an alley. No glass shattering, no wood splintering.

Whoever it was knew what they were doing.

Surely this was a dream. Was this really happening? So similar to last time, but downstairs, not upstairs. And no gunshot. Yet.

Smith turned off his desk lamp, plunging his room into darkness. No other lights in the building. He stood and crept to the edge of his office, peering down the hallway.

There: a sliver of light, moving. The intruder was using a flashlight to find his way through the bullpen.

Smith backed up and hid inside the crook of his open door, peering through the tiny space between the door's edge and the jamb. The intruder was aiming the flashlight at the ground a few steps before him, so unless he suddenly lifted the beam, he wouldn't see Smith.

The intruder was confident, not bothering to check the open doors he passed. He walked right past Smith. Enough light was trickling in from Smith's open window that he could see the man's fedora and jacket. And skin: the intruder was white.

He didn't know what the white man might be holding in his other hand. Safest to assume the cat was armed.

Smith heard the creak in the stairs as the intruder climbed to the second floor. Smith waited, counted to twenty. Did it again. He heard the floor creaking and could tell the intruder was in Bishop's office.

For the second time in less than a week, Smith fetched the Louisville Slugger from Toon's office. Gripping it with both hands, he climbed the stairs as quietly as he could muster. Again willing himself weightless. Again trying to remember where the creakiest spots lay.

The intruder was loudly opening drawers, moving things around. Confident he was alone, acting like he belonged there.

Smith reached the second-floor hallway. A faint amount of light tiptoed into the hall from Bishop's office, the door wide open. Smith crept, and crept, and crept, gripping the bat with both hands.

Then he stepped into the room and yelled something he hadn't in years: "Freeze! Put your hands up!"

Smith momentarily went blind as the flashlight stared into his face. He worried about what else might be aimed at him.

Still gripping the bat, Smith lifted his forearms to shield his eyes from the beam. The window behind the intruder glowed a bit from ambient outdoor light, and Smith thought he could see, from the movement of the stenciled darkness before him, the man reaching into his jacket for something. Smith stepped forward, nearly tripping over the open drawers of a file cabinet, as the man stepped back toward the window.

The flashlight illuminated nothing but spines on a lower book-shelf now, because the man had dropped the flashlight, and Smith was all the more certain the man was reaching into his pocket for a gun, and yes, there it was now, a gun.

Smith chopped downward with the bat, connecting with the man's wrist. He heard him cry out and the gun hit the floor and he pulled back with the bat and swung crosswise this time, pretty much the way the good people in Louisville intended it to be swung, except at an altogether different target: the man's midsec-tion. All the air the white man had inhaled that day seemed to rush out, papers flying across the room. His fedora came off as he doubled over and fell onto his knees.

Smith kicked him down further. He held the bat one-handed over his head as he stepped over the fallen man and reached with his other hand for the pistol, which he could see only because a faint amount of light from outside was glinting off its steel barrel. He picked it up.

A 9-millimeter automatic. The white man hadn't managed to thumb the safety off, so Smith did that for him.

"Don't move."

"Son of a bitch! You broke my goddamn wrist!" The accent distinctly Northern.

"And you had a gun on me, so we're even." Smith turned on the lamp that rested on a table between the two guest chairs. "Now, who the hell are you and what are you doing here?"

"I'm an FBI agent."

That knocked Smith back almost as much as if the man had punched him. Yet he kept the gun trained on the man's surprisingly young, unblemished face. Looked no more than late twenties, his short hair slicked back and only slightly mussed from the hat falling off. Hazel eyes, cheeks pocked with the kind of freckling that probably looked even worse in the summer. He wore black leather gloves and soft-soled black loafers. Smith saw a bit of the man's white calves over black socks; no knife nor pistol holster down there, but that didn't mean he didn't have another piece hidden somewhere.

This wasn't the same white man who'd been stationed outside Victoria's house. This one was younger, thinner.

"Where's your partner?" Smith asked.

"Right outside."

"Yeah, we'll see about that. Roll onto your stomach and I'm gonna frisk you."

"*You* aren't going to frisk *me*, boy." He started to sit up, leaning on his elbows.

Smith cocked the weapon. "If you move again I'm gonna shoot

an unlawful intruder dead is what I'm gonna do. Now roll over and I'll take a look at your badge, if you really have one."

They stared into each other's eyes for a long, cold moment. The maybe-FBI agent did not seem to like what he saw. He finally lowered himself to the floor, wincing as he did so, then rolled onto his stomach. "You don't know who you're dealing with, boy. I'll have you strung from a goddamn lamppost for this."

Smith backed up, closing the door and locking it, so that, if this man really did have a partner somewhere, Smith would at least delay him. Then he stepped over the white man, leveling the gun at the center of his back as he patted him down with his left hand. He could feel the empty sidearm holster. He removed a wallet from his pants pocket, then stepped back and held it beneath the lamp.

Talbot Marlon, an agent of the Federal Bureau of Investigation. He informed Smith, "I'm going to roll over now."

"Go ahead, Agent Marlon."

"And I'm getting up."

"You can sit up, but you ain't standing yet."

Marlon, sitting now, glared. He seemed to be trying to kill Smith telepathically. "You've seen my badge, and you will return it and my sidearm to me now."

Smith kept the gun pointed at him. "You just broke into my murdered boss's office and you're disturbing a crime scene. We'll see what *your* boss has to say about this." He picked up what he still thought of as Mr. Bishop's phone.

"It's not a crime scene anymore, and you're training that weapon on an FBI agent, holding me hostage against my will." Marlon spelled that out in an outraged but lawyerly tone, as if hoping some unseen assistant would keep good notes for the coming indictment. "You are making one hell of a mistake, boy."

Smith maintained eye contact for an extra moment, then looked away to dial the number. When he was patched through to McInnis, Smith said, "Sergeant, I need to see you at Arthur Bishop's office right away. There's been another break-in. The back door's opened, I think."

"Smith?" McInnis sounded flummoxed. "What's going on?"

"I'd rather tell you in person. Come quick, please. I've got Bishop's office door locked, so knock and identify yourself when you get up here."

He hung up and stared at Marlon, who was shaking his head in disbelief.

Then Smith stepped closer and leaned down. "You can drop that 'boy' shit, Yankee. I don't care what you think you've learned from the crackers down here, but you say that one more time and I will break your nose and say it happened when you barged in like a common thief. I used to be a cop, but they decided I was too rough with people. So try me."

He kept the gun trained on the FBI man as he sat in one of Bishop's leather guest chairs.

⤙

"It's McInnis," the sergeant said as he knocked on the door.

As soon as McInnis stepped into the office, Agent Marlon exhaled. "Finally."

His implication clear: now that a white cop was here, order would be restored.

He couldn't have been pleased that McInnis's reaction was to calmly ask Smith, "What's going on?"

After Smith told the tale, handing McInnis the FBI agent's gun as he did so, Marlon stood up, saying, "I'll take my sidearm and wallet now, thank you."

"I think I'll hold onto them a moment longer," McInnis said. "What are you doing here?"

Marlon scowled. "I don't have to explain myself to city cops." Like they were a step above garbage collectors.

"I say that you do," McInnis countered. "It appears you were looking for something. Find it yet?"

"I'm leaving." Marlon took a step.

McInnis held out a hand. In his other he still held Marlon's gun, pointed at the floor. "No, you're not."

"It's my word against a Negro's. And I'm a federal agent." Marlon seemed apoplectic that the constant repetition of his job status didn't magically end all discussion.

"So I see, but Mr. Smith and I go back, and I don't know you from Adam. You may draw more water in Washington, but that doesn't mean I have to let you break into properties in my territory. Who's your superior officer?"

"Special Agent Gary Doolittle is in charge of the Atlanta office."

McInnis fished one of Marlon's business cards out of the agent's wallet. "I love how these are embossed with the Justice Department's symbol, don't you?" He held it up and Smith nodded. "Wish we could get our cards all fancy like that." He shifted his gaze back to Marlon. "Our seal I like better, though: the phoenix rising from the ashes. It means, *don't fuck with us*, because we've been through hell and we're still standing, and right when you think you got one over on us, that's just us getting angry."

Smith had seldom heard the strait-laced McInnis talk like this, taunting the agent. He loved it. Calling McInnis had been a risk; Smith had figured there was at least a fifty-fifty chance the sergeant would have taken the white agent's side. So far, the risk was paying off.

Marlon asked, "He's really an ex-cop?"

"Yes," McInnis said. "I taught all of my officers to treat federal agents with the respect they deserve. But I also told them to expect respect in return, and your snooping around here at night and unannounced does not qualify."

"Yeah," Smith added, emboldened now, "I was a cop and now I'm a reporter, and I think I just stumbled into an amazing story."

"If you even *think* about writing about this, you'll—"

"He's not going to write anything," McInnis interrupted, "and you're not going to make any threats. Now, your Special Agent in Charge work night hours like you seem to, or is he home in his cozy bed?"

Marlon recited Doolittle's home number from memory. McInnis dialed. Smith could only hear his side of the conversation.

"Is this Special Agent Doolittle of the FBI? . . . This is Sergeant McInnis of the Atlanta Police Department. Sorry to wake you, but I was wondering if you could tell me why your Agent Marlon saw fit to break into the offices of the *Daily Times* newspaper just a few blocks from my station without telling me? . . . Oh, take your time." He cupped the receiver and told his audience with a wry smile, "He's taking the call to a different room."

Marlon shook his head and muttered something under his breath, no doubt about damn fool Southern cops and their strange ways.

"Yes, sir," McInnis continued, now that Doolittle had escaped the presence of his wife, or whomever he slept with. "One of my officers happened upon your man snooping around the office of Arthur Bishop, a recent murder victim. Seems your man fell funny on his wrist and might need to see a doctor about it." Smith waited while McInnis listened, impressed at how McInnis had identified him as "one of my officers," artfully neglecting to mention that Smith was a *former* officer. "I'd like that very much . . . Oh, I do know how to be discreet. I wish I could say the same for your man here. This his first rodeo? . . . Well, we'll see about that . . . Sounds good. You have a great night's sleep."

He hung up, then stepped forward and offered the FBI man his sidearm back. Marlon took it, then McInnis handed him his wallet.

"We'll escort you out, Agent Marlon."

The FBI man retrieved his fedora and managed to hold his tongue as he walked down the stairs, McInnis and then Smith behind him.

"Nice job on the back door," McInnis said as they walked outside via the front. "Didn't make any scratches at all, not that I saw. They teach that in a class in Washington, right?"

Marlon said nothing. Gripping his injured wrist in his left hand, he made off without a word, walking a block east, then cutting north. Either he'd been lying about having a partner outside, or the partner had fled at the sight of McInnis's squad car.

"We just let him go?" Smith asked.

"First of all, there is no 'we.' What on earth were you doing, going after him alone like that?"

"I was asleep in my office and heard him break in."

"Asleep in your office, again? Jesus, Smith, are you homeless?"

"*No*. I'm up late working. I don't get a lot of sleep. But I heard him break in, so I followed him up, and—"

"And once you saw he was an FBI agent, you called *me* instead of letting him go?"

"I had the distinct feeling that if I returned his gun, he'd use it on me."

He found McInnis inscrutable. The sergeant had backed his behavior in front of Marlon, but now he was tearing into Smith. No matter what someone said, McInnis always seemed to say the opposite, which had made working for him maddening.

"I now have a meeting with this Special Agent Doolittle tomorrow morning," McInnis said. "I expect he'll tell me what he thinks I need to know, which might be very little, and then send me on my way."

"Why would the FBI be messing with Bishop's office? If they were investigating the murder, they'd come in with a warrant. They wouldn't break in at night like this."

McInnis looked up and down the street, as if to see if they were being watched. Hell, they probably were. The sudden presence of the FBI made every parked car suspicious.

"These are all excellent questions, and you need to leave someone else to answer them. You're not a cop anymore."

"I had a gun pointed at me just now. All due respect, I think I deserve some answers."

"*I'm* going to get some answers. If there are any I see fit to share with a civilian, I'll do so." He straightened his uniform tie, which he had a habit of doing. "If you're having second thoughts about being a civilian, you may complete a reapplication form and I'll pass it along. If not, then be very, very careful, because I can't protect you like I used to."

Smith didn't care for the idea that he'd been *protected* by McInnis back in the day, like some child, or that he needed protection now. Yet as he stood silently and watched his former sergeant walk off, he feared McInnis was right.

17

NO GUARD WAS stationed at the door to the Atlanta field office of the Federal Bureau of Investigation when McInnis, in civilian jacket and tie, showed up the next morning. In the small waiting room, McInnis told the lone secretary who he was and she invited him to sit. On the coffee table was a small stack of newspapers, including, surprisingly, the *Atlanta Daily Times*. The lead story detailed the aftermath of the bombing of Reverend King Jr.'s home in Montgomery. Reading it, he recalled Boggs's report that two white men had been sitting in a parked car outside Reverend King Sr.'s house late one night. He'd run the tags, which belonged to a white man in town with no record, and had left it at that. He wondered now whether he'd erred in not doing more.

McInnis thought the bus boycott was a ridiculous idea. It seemed dangerously confrontational and destined to inspire violence, as the bombing proved. His officers spoke in support of it, though, telling him it had widespread approval in the Negro community, both in Montgomery and here in Atlanta.

He flipped through the *Daily Times*. He seldom read it, but apparently the Bureau made a habit of keeping tabs on what Negro reporters were covering. Every story on the front page, it seemed, dealt with racial matters. Alabama's governor would soon sign a law declaring the *Brown* decision "null and void" in the Yellowhammer state; Negroes down in Columbus were asking to use the city's all-white golf course; the University of Alabama had agreed to allow a Negro woman, Autherine Lucy, to enroll in classes; U.N. undersecretary Ralph Bunche was predicting the coming end of colonialism. It was like reading dispatches from a different reality, a realm that somehow coexisted with the greater world of white people. McInnis had been operating in this other realm for the past seven-plus years, yet to read their perspective on stories he'd heard differently elsewhere—or, in most cases, hadn't heard at all—was a reminder of how separate from them he remained.

The door opened and Doolittle appeared. Short dark hair beginning to go gray, round face, looked quite comfortable in his gray flannel suit. He introduced himself, shook McInnis's hand with a curt smile, and invited him back. They walked through a long, open office space filled with several desks, a few of them occupied by men in suits and ties, late twenties to mid-forties. No one looked up. At the end they reached Doolittle's private office, and around the corner McInnis could see another, empty room, its walls being repainted.

"Nice space," McInnis said. "Seems large."

"Yes, we've taken over the next-door office to expand."

"So I can expect more federal agents in my fair city?"

"These are tense times, as I'm sure you're aware." Doolittle spoke in a flat Midwestern accent of some kind. "Mr. Hoover is quite serious about rooting out subversives."

Doolittle closed the door behind them as McInnis settled into one of the two guest chairs beside a small table. Doolittle sat in the other chair, rather than at his desk, making this seem more like a polite meeting of peers rather than the dressing down of an inferior. A diplomatic gesture, probably bullshit.

"How are things on the Negro side of the Police Department?" Doolittle asked, managing to make it not seem like an insult. "That's a unique challenge you have."

"I'm happy to talk about our jobs, Special Agent Doolittle, but I have to confess I'll be a bit distracted throughout the chitchat as I wonder what exactly your man was doing last night. And why the Bureau is investigating the death of a Negro publisher."

Doolittle smiled. "Sorry, I thought you Southerners preferred to talk around a subject for a few minutes before getting to the point.

My goodness, I've wasted years of my life down here just waiting for people to finally say what they mean. So yes, let's move right along. Arthur Bishop's murder, while tragic, is not being investigated by the Bureau. I would like to assume the Atlanta police can handle it and bring the perpetrator to justice."

"Then what was Marlon doing?"

Doolittle folded his hands in his lap. "It should go without saying, Sergeant, that what we discuss here does not leave this room. Not even to one of your officers. Or a white officer. I don't have to tell you anything, but I'm choosing to do so out of courtesy."

"I'm so flattered you're taking the time out of your busy schedule to enlighten me."

Doolittle smiled grimly and recrossed his legs. "I guess we've gotten off on the wrong foot. You feel you have a right to know what we were doing last night. Fair enough. What I can tell you is that there was some paperwork in that office that was considered sensitive by the Bureau, and it needed to be removed."

"But we caught your man before he could take anything."

"Before *he* could, yes. But as you just saw, he's not my only man."

Son of a bitch. So once McInnis and Smith had left the office, Doolittle had simply dispatched another agent to steal whatever it was they'd wanted. Even when McInnis thought he'd done well, he was easy to outmaneuver by someone who had him outmanned.

Still, if Doolittle had wanted McInnis silenced, he could have gone straight to his captain, or someone higher, demanding they make McInnis fall in line. The fact that he was even in this room meant that Doolittle, for some reason, wanted to share information with him.

"What was it exactly that you just had to remove from a crime scene?"

"It's not a crime scene anymore, not according to your homicide detectives. They took their photos and did their forensics. We respect protocol, so we waited. But we needed to extricate from that office any evidence that Bishop had ever corresponded with us."

"Why?"

"Well, just like a good newspaper reporter, we protect the identity of our sources."

McInnis thought for a moment. "Bishop spied for the Bureau?"

"That's a harsh way of phrasing it. Mr. Bishop was a patriotic American who was as alarmed as we are by the spread of communism. As I'm sure you know, the reds have been focused for years on rallying Negroes to their cause. They prey on the downtrodden and disillusioned, and Negroes are frequently both. In Bishop, we had a helpful ally. He was a good man, happy to pass along information about subversive activity in the Negro community."

"I didn't realize the Bureau was so friendly with Negro newspapers. I'd always heard the opposite."

"I take it you're referring to the war years. It's true that several Negro newspapers were overly critical of U.S. policies, all that nonsense about it being a white man's war and how colored people shouldn't be involved when they don't get a fair shake here. So yes, the Bureau did meet with several Negro publishers back then, to get them in line. Bishop agreed with our position all along."

There was more to this story, McInnis figured. Vast politics he could only dimly comprehend. The Bureau was run by J. Edgar Hoover, who championed himself as a defender of liberty against the reds and other radical subversives. But during the war, Hoover's boss had been Attorney General Francis Biddle, a strong civil libertarian. All McInnis knew was what he'd read in the papers over the years: the Bureau had shut down the most radical journals, like those that openly supported the Nazis, but Biddle had overruled Hoover several times when it came to shutting down Negro and left-wing papers. That had enraged conservatives, who felt Roosevelt and his administration were socialistic and soft on reds.

Now, years later, Biddle and Roosevelt were long gone. But Hoover still ran the FBI.

McInnis asked, "And Bishop agreed with you so much he became an FBI source?"

"We're only as good as our information, Sergeant. Bishop's murder is a loss not just for Atlanta's Negro community, it's a loss for our country. I would extend my sympathies to his widow if there was a way to do so without ... unmasking him, which I don't wish to do, out of respect for his service. Not everyone in his community would see his actions as heroic."

Quite an understatement. McInnis tried to let his mind run down the various new avenues he saw stretching before him. And he wondered what the real story could be: whether Bishop had in fact been the noble patriotic source Doolittle was describing, or whether the feds had blackmailed him into spying on his own people. Perhaps they had come upon compromising information about him and threatened to ruin him unless he gave them names.

McInnis said, "If Bishop was an informant, that means any of the names he'd given you over the years had motive to kill him for revenge."

"Possibly. But as I said, we pride ourselves on protecting the identity of our sources. No one would have been able to figure out that Bishop had given us information on them."

McInnis didn't share that confidence. Men were far too fallible for that.

"So, these people Bishop told you about," he pressed. "If Negro subversives are plotting something in Atlanta, shouldn't I be informed?"

"There are channels, Sergeant, for how the FBI shares information with APD. If that information isn't trickling down to you, I'm not to blame."

"You just said the reds are focusing on Negroes. And I'm sure you've noticed that most Atlanta officers have little concern for what happens in Negro neighborhoods. So if you think my beat is a breeding ground for reds, there's a strong chance your 'channels' don't give a damn. In which case, I'd like to know specifics."

"Would you really? Or do you just not like the idea of a federal agency snooping around your territory?"

"That too."

Doolittle smiled, like a chess grandmaster entertained by some prodigy teenager's moves. "I appreciate your honesty."

"I bet you're not used to it."

"No, but I remember what honesty is. And I see your point." He took a breath and leaned back, thinking. "A man in your position has certain advantages for the Bureau. Given you're surrounded by Negroes all day, I imagine you come across evidence of subversive activity more than the average cop does."

"So now you're asking *me* to spy for you?"

"No. But if you're saying that my current channels for conveying information to APD aren't reaching you, then I'm suggesting you and I maintain our own, friendly, *two-way* channel about subversive activity in the Negro community. And I don't see a need to notify your superior officers about this conversation. Unless you do?"

McInnis tried not to roll his eyes. "If I ever bust up a gambling ring or a brothel and I have reason to think it's actually a hotbed for folks plotting world revolution, then yes, I will loop you in. At the same time, I only have fifteen men, and it looks like you're about to have far more."

"Our paths will keep crossing, true. Negroes down here are pushing for more and more change. I don't think they've ever made so much noise. And the Soviets are carefully monitoring what happens."

McInnis tended toward skepticism, so the idea of an international plot being worked out in his backyard seemed a bit much. "The Soviets, monitoring what's happening down here?"

"Don't act like that's far-fetched. Communists spread their propaganda through a number of avenues. That Parks woman who started everything in Montgomery, she'd taken classes at a place called the Highlander School, up in Tennessee, that is rife with Soviet propaganda. Negroes and Russians have been cross-pollinating their ideas for years. We have reason to believe they have their sights on Atlanta next."

He picked a file folder up off the table and handed it to McInnis.

When McInnis opened it, he saw a handful of 8 x 11 photographs of a middle-aged white woman. Long dark hair sprinkled with some gray, thick eyebrows, something about her eyes suggesting a ferocity even when all she was doing was walking down the street. In one of the photos she was crossing Auburn Avenue.

"That is Celia Winters," Doolittle explained, "one of the chief rabble-rousers with the so-called Civil Rights Congress. You've heard of them?"

"Remind me."

"They're a communist organization, created when a few smaller red groups combined. The CRC has been making a concerted effort toward recruiting more Southern Negroes the last few years. Winters showed up in Atlanta two weeks ago."

McInnis did the math. "About a week before Bishop was killed."

"Correct."

"She have an alibi for that night? Or any reason to go after Bishop?"

"She'd have plenty of reasons, since they're ideological enemies. As for an alibi, we're working on that."

"Have you questioned her?"

A pursed grin. "Sometimes we learn more by watching. Anyway, we've let your Homicide boys know she's in town, but I figured you should know too. She may look like a sweet little grandmother, but she's a dangerous individual. The longer she's in Atlanta, the more problems she'll cause for you, and us. Keep the folder. It has information on where she's been staying."

Quite thorough information, McInnis saw. They'd clearly been following her for a while and had listed an address where she and her fellow travelers had quietly set up an unmarked office, south of downtown.

"Back to Bishop," he said. "Your removing whatever files you did, that could make it harder for detectives to find whoever killed him."

"If we had any reason to suspect the murderer was someone Bishop had named to us, then I assure you, we would share that information with APD." McInnis didn't trust this assurance one bit. "But I really don't think your Department would care, since they already seem to have found their man. Or, I should say, their woman."

Doolittle paused for effect, then added, "They're arresting Bishop's widow for his murder as we speak."

McInnis hated the fellow all the more for the way he'd parceled out his information like this. It was an added twist of the knife that Doolittle seemed to know more about the goings-on of APD than McInnis did.

"Interesting," McInnis managed to say.

"Interesting and incorrect. That's what I wanted to tell you. It appears they believe she killed him because she was having an affair. He'd confronted her about it, she demanded a divorce, he refused."

McInnis could tell by his tone: "You don't like it."

"I don't. Again, the Bureau is not investigating the murder, as it isn't something we can dedicate resources to when we have so many other fires catching down here. This is left to the Atlanta police, and your colleagues are jumping on her because it's an easy way to close a case while also shutting down a prominent Negro family and institution. Not only do they have no evidence, I happen to know that she's innocent."

McInnis felt he'd been played with this entire conversation. "How do you know?"

"Because, Sergeant, my men happened to be tailing her that night, and she never left her house. She couldn't have killed him. APD is arresting the wrong person."

18

ADDIE WORRIED ABOUT who would feed Mrs. Bishop's cats as she rode the bus home after the shortest shift of her life.

Fifteen years she'd been keeping house for the Bishops. Started in 1941, before the war, with the Depression still going full tilt. She had never worked for a Negro family before. Addie's oldest was in grade school at that time, her husband unemployed but for some odd jobs, and the white family she had most recently worked for had regretfully let her go months earlier. So when her minister, Reverend Boggs, had told her he knew a Negro couple in need of a maid, she had ironed her dress and straightened her hair and said her prayers and, praise God, won the job.

Fifteen years. And now? Mr. Bishop was murdered, and Mrs. Bishop had just been carted off by police.

This was madness. No sense to it.

To be clear: Addie was not blinded with affection for her employers. She knew plenty of other maids who held their employers in higher regard than they deserved, who felt for them something close to a familial bond. The Bishops, however, were not the type to invite such affection. A cold couple. Even in summertime, the house seemed to retain a chill, the china cool to the touch, the silverware like icicles. Their three unusually large cats roamed feral through the house like descendants of sabertooths, crouching at the top of the stairs and gazing down at her as she swept the front hall, as if deciding whether she was worth pouncing upon.

So no, Addie did not love her employers. But she knew Mrs. Bishop wasn't a killer.

That very morning, not an hour into her day, the front door had shaken on its hinges. The mighty cats scattered as if aware of what was coming. Addie hadn't made it more than three steps when the men at the door had barked, "Police! Open up!"

Addie had never had cause to speak to a police officer before. When she'd opened the door, the one in front had demanded, "Victoria Bishop? You're under arrest for the murder of your husband."

Addie had stepped back, mute, shaking her head at all that was wrong with that statement. One of the other policemen had made an annoyed sound and said, "That's not Bishop, you moron. She's just the maid."

The first officer had blushed. Perhaps he had assumed all Negro women wore maid uniforms. He himself had worn not a uniform but a jacket and tie, as did one of the others, but behind them were two cops in dress blues.

One of the uniforms told her to remain where she was while the other men moved confidently into the house. They asked where Mrs. Bishop was and Addie explained she was in her bedroom. She wanted to warn them that she might not yet be decent, as Mrs. Bishop was a habitually late riser, even more so since her husband's death, but she suspected they didn't care.

Addie had just stood there, withering under the remaining officer's gaze. She heard voices from upstairs. She did not hear a struggle. No furniture overturned. The officer was young and kept his fingers by the handle of his holstered gun, wary of a threat Addie somehow represented. Her husband sometimes went hunting, years ago now, but she'd never been this close to a pistol before. She knew Mr. Bishop owned weapons, but he kept them hidden in a closet.

Then footsteps, and down they came: one of the plainclothes officers first, then Mrs. Bishop, face ashen, eyes on each step before her, as if the cuffs on her hands had also bound her feet and she needed to be particularly careful on the steps, and behind her the other two cops, one of them smirking.

"Get her out of here," the first one said, meaning Addie.

The next few moments were a blur, Addie making for the door and then explaining she needed her purse to get home, and the officer, annoyed, following her, and then taking the purse from her to inspect its contents, as if she might be ferreting away a murder weapon. He escorted her out the front door.

Her head spinning. *Murder?* Were they serious?

She had wanted to say something to Mrs. Bishop, express her concern, ask if she needed anything (that's what she did all day, after all). But the white men seemed to bring with them an air of silence, a wall of it. She feared that if she tried to breach that wall, they would strike her.

She thought of the night, years ago, when police beat her neighbor's son, nearly to death. One of her own son's friends. Never the same again. The things she'd had to tell her boys, coach them.

Better it's me dealing with these cops than my boys, she would think later. But right then all she could think about was fear for her body and what they could do to her.

She'd made but the briefest of eye contact with Mrs. Bishop before heading out the door, nearly tripping down the front steps.

Chill morning air clamped itself around her neck and she'd forgotten her scarf inside, but she dared not go back. She walked two blocks to the bus stop, glancing behind herself once to see the officers guiding Mrs. Bishop into one of their squad cars.

Twenty minutes later, the bus had come to take her across town. She'd ridden halfway home when she thought about the cats. She hadn't fed them yet. Yes, Addie hated them, but Mrs. Bishop was in *jail*. When would she get out? What about her precious cats?

Addie got off the bus, crossed the street, and waited for the return route. Her scarf-less neck unprotected from the wind.

How would she explain this to her husband? They'd already been worried that Mr. Bishop's death might lead his widow to move to a smaller house, or leave Atlanta, meaning no job for Addie. But jail? It seemed impossible, so clearly wrong, a mistake that not only imprisoned one person but imperiled another family. Addie and her husband could barely make rent. Two of the boys were out of school and working, but the third was almost finished at Booker T. Washington. How could she feed him the rest of this year with no job?

Maybe she focused on the cats because it was an easier problem to solve.

By the time the second bus had picked her up and delivered her back to the Bishops' home, more than an hour had passed since she'd left. The police cars long gone, the block appeared normal, no sign that the world had gone mad.

Fifteen years had not been enough to make Addie love the Bishops, no, but it had been enough for them to entrust her with her own key. She unlocked the door and let herself in.

All three cats stood in the front hall, tails high on alert. Caesar, Justin, and Nero, all Roman emperors, Mrs. Bishop had explained. Addie didn't know a thing about Romans, but she had smiled politely at the pretension when they'd been introduced, back before she had learned to despise the creatures.

"Come on, now," she told them as she walked quickly toward the kitchen. Out of respect for Mrs. Bishop, she would see that the damn things didn't starve. On the way, she retrieved her scarf from the closet. She reached into the pantry, found the cat food and the scoop. Filled their dishes, their water.

She opened the refrigerator. How long would Mrs. Bishop be out? Would they release her soon, or would all this food spoil? When would Addie be paid next? Should she take something?

She had never stolen from them in fifteen years. Nor stolen from the white family she'd tended before that. But this couldn't be considered stealing, since the food would spoil otherwise. She stood there, holding the door open and thinking.

The brisket: she'd cooked it two days ago. Wouldn't keep another day. She'd prepared enough for guests, but Mrs. Bishop had wound up eating alone that night. Addie hesitated, then picked up the dish.

She was walking out of the kitchen when she heard a car door close.

She glanced out the kitchen's back window and saw that some-one had driven a green sedan all the way up the driveway and behind the house, beside the garage. Like they lived here. Over the half-curtain, she could see a white man in a tan fedora stepping out. Talking to a man whose back she could only partly see, in a gray blazer and matching hat.

Fear drove her into the hallway, still holding the cold dish. She heard something, a metal sound, hard and rough, at the back door. Then a snap and the door opened. It had been locked, she was certain.

They'd broken in.

"Careful," said a voice.

"It's clean, see?" another said. Then a chuckle.

"Lord, those are big cats."

"I hate cats."

"That's because they see into your soul."

"What soul?"

"Exactly."

Addie's heart pounded. It sounded like two voices, maybe three. Were these policemen, too? But she hadn't seen uniforms, and that wasn't a squad car. And they'd broken in.

"I didn't know blacks had cats."

"I didn't know they lived in places like *this*."

"Come on, we gotta hurry before the cops come back."

She felt a chill run up her neck. These weren't cops. She was standing just beside the coat closet. Leaning the heavy dish against her chest, she put her free hand on the knob, turned it, and stepped inside the closet as silently as she could. To fit, she had to lean hard against the many jackets the Bishops owned. She feared that if she moved too much, the hangers would squeak. She had just pulled the door shut when she heard footsteps in the hallway.

Footsteps upstairs. Who were these men? What were they doing here?

She heard doors opening, drawers being pulled. They were in Mr. Bishop's study, or at least some of them were.

Footsteps closer now, in the hallway again. Someone walked right past her.

She heard laughter. Then silence. They were focused in their search, no more banter. She tried to breathe quietly.

She heard mewing. Lord, the cats.

A scratch. *No.* One of the cats was pawing at the door, pleading for something. *Shoo*, she wanted to say.

Footsteps again. The cat kept mewing, louder this time. Which one was it, she wondered? Probably Caesar, her least favorite, the one who seemed to stalk her as she did her rounds. Like it didn't trust her. Like it wanted to see her punished for something.

The footsteps drew nearer.

Caesar, shoo!

She heard the floor creak close by.

Lord, please.

The door opened. Addie found herself facing a stout white man in a gray fedora. Tweed jacket. Wisps of gray hair poking out around his ears. One of his hands drifted to his belt, where she saw a holster and a gun.

His face blank as he asked, "What are you doing there, Auntie?"

"I'm just ... " Her voice shaking. Caesar had already skulked off, no doubt pleased with himself. "I'm their maid."

"Cleaning the closet, were you?"

"I'm just ... " She felt tiny, and absurd with the cold brisket.

"Warren!" the man shouted. "Get down here, now!"

"I can go," she volunteered, her voice as small as she felt.

"Don't you move, Auntie."

Another man joined them. He had thick reddish hair, his cheeks in need of a shave, and a prominent, large birthmark beside his right eye. She heard movement upstairs still, one of them continuing their search. Or their looting.

"What do we have here? Come out of there, Emma Mae."

She stepped out as the first man backed up. The new man had his jacket unbuttoned but she didn't see a gun.

"I tend house for the Bishops. I was just finishing up when I heard you ... come in."

The new man smiled. "Put a scare into you, did we?"

"I just—"

"Strange men walking into your employers' house. I understand. What's your name?"

"Adelaide. Adelaide Dawson." Wishing she'd been quick enough to think up a lie.

"Well, Adelaide, I don't think your services here will be required any longer." He smelled of pipe smoke. "Your lady's gotten herself into a bit of trouble, and I'm afraid you won't be seeing her again. If you were smart, you'd put some distance between yourself and the Bishops. They're bad folks to be associating with."

"Yes, sir."

"You got family of your own?"

"Y-yes."

"Children?"

Her mouth went dry. "Three boys."

He stepped closer. He put a large hand on her shoulder. "Well, the trouble that the Bishop family got themselves in? I'd hate to see it consume you, too. Or your boys, Adelaide Dawson."

She swallowed. "They're good boys."

"I'm sure. You'd best go tend to them. And don't come here again." He squeezed her shoulder. "You keep this little talk just between us, understand? Or maybe I'll need to have a talk with your boys, see what trouble *they've* been getting in."

Her neighbor's boy had been named Anthony. Cops beat him so bad his right leg stopped growing, like it was frozen in time that terrible night. His mother didn't talk much anymore. Had nothing to say to the world.

Addie asked, "You're police?"

"Yes, we are." Offering her no badge or other proof. Lying. "Now, run along."

She stepped forward, still holding the brisket. She hesitated, wanting to return it to the kitchen, chastened by her sin and her witnesses, but she couldn't disobey them and walk the wrong way.

The first man understood her hesitation. "You were taking that, weren't you? Go right ahead. It'll be our little secret." He winked at her. That would be the last image she had of them, because she looked down as if blinded and kept her eyes low, walking to the door.

A third man, younger than the other two, opened it for her, as her thieving hands were full. She said "thank you," but did not look at him as she walked out, hating herself. Hating them.

Young Anthony had been a sharp one, she remembered. And too quick-witted: he'd talked back to the cops, she'd heard, and that's why they'd beaten him. *Too smart*, white folks would say. *Needed to be punished*.

She walked outside.

Maybe they really were cops. Maybe it didn't matter.

Maybe Anthony had talked back, maybe he hadn't. That didn't matter either.

She knew her Bible, so she tried not to think of Lot's wife as she reached the sidewalk, turned toward the bus stop, and glanced sidelong at the strange men's car, committing its tag number to memory.

19

ON THE OTHER side of town, Boggs parked a block away from the house where he'd been raised. Fedora shielding his eyes from the low winter sun, he jogged up the front steps of Clancy Darden's house and rang the bell.

Darden was a former vice president at Atlanta Life Insurance, one of the first million-dollar Negro-owned businesses in the city, where Boggs's brother Reginald worked. Though Darden was a bit young for retirement, he'd left the company a few years ago, as his many property investments on the West Side had accumulated to the point where he now made his living in real estate.

Boggs was here to talk about real estate and Arthur Bishop.

Darden answered the door, dressed as ever in an impeccable three-piece suit and shoes so well shined they could have reflected stars at midnight. He kept his gray hair short and his ties expensive, and on his middle finger he wore a gold ring indicating his membership in the Prince Hall Masons.

"Lucius Boggs! What a surprise. Come in, come in. Coffee to warm you up?"

Boggs declined the offer and followed Darden into his tastefully decorated den. Leather chairs, packed bookshelves lining most of the walls, a framed Jacob Lawrence painting. Darden's youngest were now in college, and along the mantel a row of framed photographs boasted accomplishments: foreign travel, graduations, a wedding. His wife had died a few years ago, Boggs remembered.

They chatted briefly about family. Reverend Boggs and Darden had served on various boards together, and Darden was a not infrequent guest at the reverend's dinner parties. Finally, Boggs asked, "If you don't mind, Mr. Darden, I was hoping to ask you a few questions about Mr. Bishop."

"Certainly. It's such a tragedy." Darden looked down for a moment, then back up. "Are you investigating the murder?"

"I can't honestly say I'm investigating it, sir. Homicide detectives get to do that. Still, I've learned over the years that sometimes I'm in a position to find things out that they can't. And there's something that's been bothering me. What do you know about this urban redevelopment plan?"

Darden pointed to a folded copy of the *Daily Times*; that very morning the paper had broken the story, in a piece written by Jeremy Toon. "All I know is what I just read in the paper."

That disappointed Boggs; he'd hoped Darden might have some inside dope. Then again, most of Darden's investments had been on the other side of town.

"You were friends with Mr. Bishop. Maybe I'm just grasping at straws, but I was wondering: Is there any chance he'd heard about the plan, and was going to write a story on it? And the people involved in the plan, which wasn't supposed to go public yet ... is there any chance they might have tried to silence him, so he couldn't publicly criticize it?"

Darden's face froze for a moment, like he found this theory chilling. "You mean, did someone kill Arthur so he wouldn't cover this story?"

The disbelieving way Darden had phrased it made Boggs doubt himself. "Well, it's just a theory. But there's a possibility the killer stole something from Mr. Bishop's desk the night he was shot, and I can't help but wonder. Since you knew him so well, and you're so tapped into real estate goings-on, I was hoping to hear your take."

"It's ... strange, I admit. But also, Lucius, I'm afraid you might be misinterpreting Arthur's position."

"What do you mean?"

"Well, I don't know this for a fact, since I only learned about the plan today myself, but it strikes me as the sort of thing Arthur would have supported."

Boggs was surprised. "You think so?"

"Why, yes. In fact, I support it too. If you look carefully at what they're proposing, they're going to be tearing down *Darktown*." He pronounced that word with distaste. "Most of those buildings, their time has come. Knocking down the most crime-ridden neighborhood in the city, I can't say I'm against that. That place gives us a bad name, quite frankly. With it being so close to Sweet Auburn, I believe it's best to have it demolished."

Boggs hadn't expected this, but in retrospect it made sense. Boggs sometimes felt his own father was too conservative and concerned with respectability, and a man like Darden was even more so.

"I patrol those neighborhoods, Mr. Darden, and I've seen some bad things, but there are plenty of good people living there. With all due respect, where are they all supposed to go?"

"Well, I imagine they'll go to more adequate housing. Apartments that have toilets and running water, one hopes. I've been in some of those buildings, too, Lucius. I really don't think they'll be missed."

That didn't sit well with Boggs. The block his wife had grown up on was no different than the ones slated for destruction. He'd worked this job long enough to know that there are no bad places, only bad people.

"They're talking about part of Sweet Auburn, too, Mr. Darden," Boggs said. "Knocking down successful businesses, families' homes. They'll take some now, then more later. Your old company's office, maybe. My father's church."

Like the race riot of '06, when white folks attacked Negroes who lived downtown, slaughtering them, destroying their homes and businesses to push them out of the city center. Whites were planning yet another power grab, bloodlessly orchestrated by men in suits rather than hoods, but destructive all the same.

"Let's not get ahead of ourselves," Darden said. He pointed at the paper. "A couple blocks of Sweet Auburn may be affected, but that's it."

"And the whole idea of a civic center so close to Sweet Auburn—it will be like a concrete wall, blocking us off from the rest of the city. That's probably their whole point."

"That may be, but we need the city to keep adding these services if we want to credibly proclaim ourselves the capital of the South. Civic centers are an investment. They bring dollars to the city." Darden shrugged. "I don't mean to be blasé. Change is difficult. And some people will be inconvenienced, yes. But I think once this all happens, it will be for the best. It's progress, advancement. Making sure not a single part of our community is an eyesore that white people can look down on."

"I'm afraid they'll look down on us no matter what, sir."

"That defeatist attitude," Darden said, pointing at Boggs, but smiling a bit to take out the sting, "is one I'll never endorse. Nor would Arthur."

Boggs nodded, to be polite. He didn't dare mention to Darden that his own father was printing fliers calling for community meetings to rally against it, enlisting friends and relatives to post them in shop windows, on telephone poles, and in barbershops. Darden would figure that out eventually.

"In any event," Darden continued, "I doubt this is the sort of thing Arthur would have been writing some exposé about. I really do think he would have agreed with me. So I don't see how this could have anything to do with . . . what happened to him."

Boggs was disappointed in Darden's take on the city, and equally disappointed to hear his theory about the murder shot down. He stood to go, thanking Darden for his time.

"One more thing," Darden said, pausing to choose his words. "Arthur . . . led a very private life, and he had a complicated past. I know it's a policeman's job to be thorough, but I would hate to see all the details of his life dragged out in public."

Boggs wasn't sure where he was going with this. "So would I, Mr. Darden."

"Men like you and I, we know that sacrifices have to be made to achieve success. And that the less successful always harbor grievances. So, please, I ask this as one of Arthur's friends: Do what you can to see that his reputation isn't sullied by the police. I don't want white detectives turning a great man's life story into some sordid soap opera. He deserves better."

Boggs wondered whether Darden was overly concerned about propriety, or if he knew there was indeed something "sordid" in Bishop's past. And if so, whether it would be possible to find the killer without bringing shame on Bishop's reputation. Once more Boggs felt the heavy weight of responsibility on his shoulders. For his people, for his class, for a case that wasn't even his.

"I'll do my best, sir."

20

SMITH FELT CONSCIOUS of the fact that he was surrounded by words, silenced. He stood in Arthur Bishop's office, bookshelves on all four sides, even over the doorway. Some shelves were neatly arranged, some held haphazard horizontal stacks, and one bottom shelf proved unable to contain all that had been stuffed there, books spilling over its edge onto the floor. And then there was the awkward gap on the one shelf where blood had spilled onto a few books, since discarded. Words, sentences, plotlines, countless hours of labor by other writers, entombed all around him.

He tried to piece things together. He'd learned that Bishop was a former communist who may or may not have had a meeting with fellow traveler Morris Peeples the night he was shot; and then the FBI had broken into this very room.

That could not be a coincidence.

Right about then, he knew, McInnis should be getting some answers from the FBI. This room no doubt contained answers, too, but Lord only knew where he should look.

He wondered if Morris Peeples had ever written a book.

Only some of Bishop's shelves were arranged alphabetically. Otherwise the tomes were shelved according to some logic that only made sense to a man now dead. After a good twenty minutes, Smith found, beside a copy of ex-communist Arthur Koestler's *Darkness at Noon*, a slim volume by Morris Peeples: *This Book Is Not Illegal: The Angelo Herndon Case and the Fight for Free Speech in Georgia*.

With no book jacket, he had to skim the first few pages to

understand what it was about. A trial involving a communist in the 1930s, one Smith was too young to have followed, though he knew he'd heard it discussed a few times. He'd have to spend more time with this later.

As he flipped the book shut, he noticed something had come loose, a corner poking out. A photograph had been hiding between the last page and the back cover.

He pulled it out and found himself looking at a much younger Bishop with two other men and a white woman, their arms around each other's shoulders. Everyone appeared to be in their twenties or so, no wrinkles or gray hair, the men's ties almost comically wide. Bishop stood on one end; on the other stood Peeples, with a goatee even then. The third man Smith didn't know. The caption on the back read, *With Morris Peeples, Leon Farley, Celia Winters.*

He couldn't tell where the photo had been taken (a book party, maybe?), but he could look up those other two names. He slid the photo back into the book, closed the cover, and brought it downstairs to his office.

Then he asked Toon if he could borrow his car.

He parked across the street from the Bishops. The curtains were open, so he hoped Mrs. Bishop was in.

He didn't realize she'd already been arrested that morning.

Smith knocked. No one answered, not even the unfriendly maid. He tried the doorbell this time, to the same lack of response. He stepped back and tried to peer in through the side windows, but all he could see was one of those unusually large cats, gazing at him as it lay atop a light blue sofa.

He might have called, but he'd wanted to confront her with his new information in person. Gauge her reaction when he mentioned the FBI and communism, see if he might lead her to open up this time.

He wondered if she could be home but avoiding him. From

where he'd parked, he hadn't been able to see down her driveway, so he walked to the other side of the house to take a look.

A green Buick was parked at the very end, its nose practically touching the garage door. He tried to remember what car Bishop drove, but he hadn't thought this was it.

He walked closer, taking a look inside the car's windows. Old cop habits coming back. The interior was clean, nothing of note.

He turned around and saw that the back door to the house was cracked open.

"Hello?" he called out. "Mrs. Bishop?"

His first thought was that the maid was in the midst of some task, or maybe Mrs. Bishop was so addled with grief that she'd left her back door ajar. He took a step toward it, then stopped when he noticed that the doorjamb was cracked where the strike plate should be.

Someone had used a crowbar to break in.

He would have reached for a weapon, but he carried none. Sometimes on reporting jobs he'd take a revolver with him, but Homicide hadn't returned his guns yet. And he'd already alerted whoever this was to his presence by calling out.

So he did it again: "Who's in there?" His heart rate increasing, he slowly ascended the wooden back steps. With his gloved hands he pushed the door open more. It swung off kilter from the damage. He looked around, stepped into the kitchen. "Come on out."

Two dishes in the sink, a plate of biscuits on the counter, uncovered. Either the maid hadn't been working, or she'd left in a hurry, or she'd been forced somewhere.

Smith reached for the butcher's block and removed a long knife.

The kitchen floor had a serious creaking problem. He hoped the hallways and other rooms did too, that he'd hear it if an intruder tried to sneak up on him.

He'd taken a few uncomfortably loud steps, and was nearly out of the kitchen when something lunged toward him. He jumped back, holding the knife in front of him, then felt like an idiot when he saw one of Mrs. Bishop's feline friends gazing up at him.

He ignored it as it brushed past him. He stepped into the hallway. To his right was a closet door, then the hallway led to the front foyer, off of which lay rooms on either side.

He opened the closet door, which weirdly smelled of food, but saw nothing except clothing.

"Don't move."

He looked up and saw a red-haired white man in a tan fedora pointing a gun at him.

"Drop the knife, now."

Smith complied, gently tossing it down and keeping his hands high, palms out. He heard motion from behind and he couldn't help turning his head to see another white man coming from the kitchen, drawing a pistol from a shoulder holster.

"Who the hell are you?" the redhead asked. He had an unusually large birthmark along his right temple, and blue eyes that seemed unnervingly calm while holding a stranger at gunpoint. He was a big man, but the man on the other side of Smith looked even bigger.

Christ, Smith thought, *first Bishop's office and now his house.* The man's property was like nectar to armed white men.

"My name's Tommy Smith. Who are you?"

A smile from Birthmark. "You're not in the question-asking position. What are you doing here?"

"I ask a lot of questions because I'm a newspaper reporter." He slowly turned his shoulders so he could see both men without moving his head back and forth. "Which is why I'm here. Why are *you* here?"

"We're police," Birthmark said. "Mrs. Bishop's been arrested, and we're gathering evidence." He stepped closer. The big man on the other side did too, halving the space around Smith.

"You have badges?" Smith asked.

"We don't need to show you, boy," Birthmark said.

"Who's your superior officer? I used to be a cop."

"Oh, Christ," the bigger fellow said. "One of the YMCA cops. Got yourself fired, did you?"

"You still haven't convinced me you're cops."

Birthmark motioned to one of the walls in the narrow hall-way. "Put your hands up there and we'll frisk you like a real cop, how's that?"

No squad car, uniforms, or badges. A busted-open back door. Men who wouldn't identify themselves. The professionalism of white cops had never impressed Smith, so it was possible these men truly were police. But he doubted it.

When two men have guns on you, however, you tend to follow their orders.

Smith leaned his hands against the wall and spread his feet apart, the way he would have wanted a subject to do it in the old days.

"Mrs. Bishop was arrested for what?" he asked, hoping to keep them talking.

The bigger fellow, whom Smith hadn't gotten a good enough look at, stepped behind him and checked him for weapons while Birthmark kept a gun on Smith. The man removed the wallet from Smith's back pocket and the small notebook from his jacket.

"Thomas Eugene Smith," he mockingly read Smith's ID. "Of the *Atlanta Daily Times*. My, my."

"Christ," Birthmark said, sounding more concerned than his colleague about the fact that they had a bona fide member of the press in attendance.

"Now, Thomas, this is one story you are not going to write about."

"You're not cops," Smith said. "FBI? You work with Marlon and Doolittle?"

That silenced the men for a moment. They may have exchanged glances, but that was all.

Then something hard and metal pressed into the back of Smith's head. He heard the hammer of a revolver being thumbed back.

Smith went cold. His fingers felt numb like *that*, which didn't make sense, and the hallway seemed to shimmy.

Birthmark backed up, and Smith could see him holding up

a plaintive hand. He said to his colleague, "Sam, c'mon, we got enough problems."

The big fellow, Sam apparently, said, "I think this might well solve our problems."

"I don't think it will," Birthmark said. Smith didn't know who the hell that fellow was, but he loved him like a brother right then. "I think that attitude's caused us enough grief."

The pressure from the gun barrel eased off, and Smith felt Sam's weight shift behind him.

Birthmark said, "But we know who you are and where you live, Thomas."

"If you even think of writing about this," Sam added from behind Smith, "or even telling anyone, I promise, I'll finish the job."

His throat dry, Smith said, "Can you put that away so we can talk like civilized men?"

"This is how we civilize you," Sam said, and Smith felt a thick arm wrap around his neck, squeezing tight.

He instinctively pulled his hands away from the wall and tried to pry the man's arms off him, but he couldn't break free. He tried to kick backwards but all he got was shin, and the man's pain threshold was high because he didn't loosen his grip. A choke-hold—Smith knew it well and had used it himself many times, the blood draining from his head. He tried to spin and knock the man loose, but all he succeeded in doing was rotating a bit, so that he was facing Birthmark, staring at the gun in his hand, when all went black.

21

MCINNIS COULDN'T UNDERSTAND the FBI's angle with the Bishop case.

He tried to arrange it a few different ways in his mind. Assume Special Agent Doolittle had told him the truth. In which case Bishop had been an FBI informant for years, giving the feds dirt on Negro communists. The FBI mustn't have followed Bishop the night he was killed, otherwise they would know who'd killed him.

But they *had* been following his wife. Why? Perhaps *she* was a communist, and Bishop had fed them names over the years to keep them away from her.

No—if she was a communist, the FBI wouldn't care if she was framed for murder. Hell, they might even want to do the framing themselves. So why would Doolittle tell McInnis she was innocent?

He felt toyed with, batted about by a cat's paw. What was the cat hoping he'd do next?

If Doolittle had been lying, and the feds had not been tailing the widow, then maybe she *had* killed her husband, as Homicide believed. In which case Doolittle must have some other reason to plant suspicion in McInnis's mind, hoping to distract him from something else. Was there any chance Bishop *hadn't* been an FBI source, and Doolittle was planting that false information to discredit the dead man? But that made even less sense.

Back at the station, McInnis couldn't find Cummings or Helms, but someone else confirmed Victoria Bishop's arrest. At his desk in the dingy basement, he read through some reports, felt a headache coming on, then decided that since it was still hours before his shift was to start, he should get out and clear his mind.

He hadn't even made it to the basement stairs when he saw his superior officer, Captain Dodd, descending with two unfamiliar men.

"Just the fellow I was hoping to find," Dodd said with bonhomie that felt false.

McInnis didn't trust him, and the feeling was mutual. Over the years Dodd had all but ignored McInnis's requests for better conditions and more consideration for his officers. McInnis usually found it best to go directly to Chief Jenkins, who was a stalwart supporter of the Negro officers, but that only made Dodd hate McInnis more for going over his head.

The two strangers with Dodd wore jackets and ties, unfamiliar badges hanging out of their pockets. Dodd introduced them as Montgomery police detectives, Pearson and Gilbert.

"Welcome to Atlanta," McInnis said as they shook hands. "What can I help you with?"

Rather than return to his cramped office, which couldn't accommodate so many, he took a seat at a desk his officers shared, in what was basically the basement hallway. The Montgomery cops dragged chairs from other desks and Dodd stood to their side, hands in his pockets.

"Well, as I'm sure you know, we've been having trouble with our Negroes," Pearson began. He had a doughy and otherwise unremarkable middle-aged face, which along with his gut gave him the look of a small-town banker or insurance man. Gilbert was thin and with his once-broken nose and pockmarked cheeks bore the look of someone who'd been in several fights and looked forward to the next one. "Things are getting a bit out of hand."

A pause, during which McInnis was no doubt expected to offer sympathy or curse the gall of Montgomery's Negroes. Instead, he sat and waited. His ability to remain still and silent through awkward pauses didn't make him an ideal dinner guest, but it forced people to come out and say what they meant.

"You heard about King's home being bombed?" Pearson asked.

"I did. Are you here because you suspect an Atlanta citizen of doing it?"

"No, no," Pearson said. "Whoever did that is probably local. For all we know, it was one of the Negroes, dynamiting King to drum up sympathy for their cause."

That did not strike McInnis as genius detective work. He asked, "What *do* you know?"

"We're getting sidetracked," Gilbert cut in. "The problem we're here to talk about is King himself."

"We drove out here to check and see if he has a record in Atlanta," Pearson added. "Your captain just helped us with that, but we didn't find anything. Now, he tells us you're the expert on Negroes here, so we thought we'd pick your brain on the young reverend."

Expert on Negroes. He'd heard that before. Usually intended as an insult.

"I don't really know anything about King Jr.," he said. "I've been sergeant to the Negro officers since '48, and I don't even think he's lived here much of that time. I heard he was a student in Boston or someplace."

"Where he got all his damn fool ideas, no doubt," Gilbert said, shaking his head.

"I do know," McInnis said, "that his father is a respected citizen in the community."

"Well, the apple's fallen very far from the tree," Gilbert said.

Pearson leaned forward. "We're wondering, Sergeant, if there's any chance that perhaps some past indiscretion of King's may have been brushed off by the Atlanta police, partly out of consideration for his old man, like you said. And maybe now it's time to revisit that decision."

Pearson was asking McInnis to invent a past charge so they'd have an excuse to arrest the younger King. McInnis glanced at Dodd, hoping to gauge his superior's position on this, but Dodd's expression was blank.

"What indiscretion in particular?" McInnis asked.

"Look," Gilbert said, "King's been in Montgomery less 'n a year, and already he's trying to grind business in our city to a halt. We got maids who can't get to their employers' houses because of the pressure him and his group are putting on them, and now we've got bombs going off. We've heard he's going to be in Atlanta soon to check in on some family matter, so we figured maybe you could help us defuse things while he's here."

McInnis hated Dodd for bringing this to him, and he hated these outsiders for thinking they could call shots in his territory. If Dodd disagreed with them, he could have told them himself. Either Dodd thought their request was reasonable, or he wanted McInnis to make the call so the sergeant could be blamed for whatever fallout came.

"Gentlemen," McInnis said, "we can't allow you to come in and arrest King based on some old Atlanta parking tickets or God knows what."

"No, no, of course not," Pearson said, waving his hand. "We know this is your town. We were hoping *you* would arrest him."

McInnis had been told many times that he had a great poker face, but surely his surprise was registering somewhere. Certainly in his pulse.

"On what charge?"

"Anything."

McInnis turned back to Dodd and asked, "You care to offer your opinion, Captain?"

"Like I said, Mac, you're the expert on Negroes."

"You understand," Pearson continued with his appeal, "we don't even need the charge to stick. We just need King out of Montgomery until this blows over—probably only a week or two. Then the boycott will be broken and things can turn back to normal."

Both Alabamans were watching McInnis intently, hoping they'd won him over.

After a pregnant pause, McInnis leaned forward and folded his hands on the desk. "Now, I understand you're under some pressure over there. But if you're asking me to arrest an Atlanta citizen on a trumped-up charge, the answer's no. And I'd be saying that even if we were talking about some little nobody, and not someone who's been getting press coverage lately. Someone who, as I mentioned, is the son of a prominent minister here. Far as I know, the senior Reverend King considers Chief Jenkins a friend."

Incredulous, Gilbert asked, "A Negro preacher thinks the police chief is his friend? The hell kind of town is this?"

"The kind of town where bombs aren't going off. I'd like to keep it that way."

Pearson leaned back and reassessed McInnis. "It may be easy for you to sit there and judge us because of what's going on in our city. But trust me, we're not so different. King's a Georgia boy, after all, so it's just our bad luck he took his first job in Montgomery. If he was preaching here, then *you'd* be the one dealing with a boycott and all that goes with it. What we're asking for may be a little . . . unconventional, but extreme times require extreme measures."

Gilbert added, "If the boycott continues and we have more bombings, and more violence, you think that'll be confined to state lines? What are the Negroes here in Atlanta going to think when they see what their kind in Montgomery can get away with? For all we know, the older King is planning the same thing here."

McInnis thought again about Boggs's report that two white men appeared to stake out King Sr.'s place on Hunter Street a few nights ago. That car had Georgia plates, but he wondered now if one of these cops could have been in that car, joined by a local friend. And just a moment ago, Special Agent Doolittle had told him that the FBI would be sending more agents into the South to try to contain "subversive behavior," which a bus boycott may well qualify as.

McInnis may not have liked the boycott, but he unequivocally hated the idea of outsiders—be they feds or Alabama cops—trying to exert control over his territory.

Gilbert added, "What we're trying to do is stop things *before* more violence breaks out. We'd assumed a fellow lawman would agree."

McInnis folded his arms. "Yes, I'm a lawman. If you had any actual evidence, or even well-grounded suspicions, of any actual laws being broken by any actual Atlanta citizen, then *maybe* I'd listen and not be pissed off that you're showing your face in my territory and telling me how to run it. But short of that, if you're asking me to dedicate my scant resources to investigating a *preacher* who isn't breaking any laws here, then my answer's gone from 'No' to 'Hell, no, goddamnit.'"

"You have a lack of vision here," Gilbert said after a wounded pause, "and it's going—"

"I have a lack of *patience*," McInnis cut him off, "and y'all can head back to Alabama."

The Montgomery cops looked at Dodd. Pearson asked, "You feel the same way, Captain?"

"I believe Sergeant McInnis has his finger on the pulse of this community better 'n I do," Dodd said. "If you do come upon anything incriminating, of course, let us know right away, and we can go from there."

The Alabamans stood. "Waste of our time," Gilbert grumbled.

"One more thing," McInnis called out when the visitors were nearly at the stairs. "There isn't any chance you've been staking out the home of Reverend King Sr. without telling us?"

Gilbert looked at Pearson, who said, "No. 'Course not."

"Good. Because for you to pull something like that, out of your jurisdiction and in mine, that would really rub me the wrong way. Would make me awful uncooperative."

Gilbert's smirk returned. "As opposed to the very cooperative fellow you're being now?"

McInnis stood and wished the table weren't in his way. "You'd be amazed at how much less cooperative I can be."

"Sorry we can't help you," Dodd said, stepping in front of McInnis's desk to block him from their view, trying to end this before it escalated. He led the Alabamans to the stairs.

McInnis felt about ready to punch a wall, and it wasn't even noon yet. *First feds, now Montgomery cops. What the hell is happening in my beat?*

Dodd returned. "Your social skills remain impeccable."

"They could have asked all that on the phone. They didn't need to drive four hours. They're in town because they're trying to stir shit up, with or without our help. We should get some uniforms to escort them back to the state line."

"Start a political border dispute? No thank you."

McInnis held out his palms. "Sounds like we already have one. Or do you think it would be all right for *me* to drive to another state and ask cops there to arrest one of *their* citizens based on bullshit?"

"Our ideas of bullshit appear to differ," Dodd said, walking back to the stairs so McInnis could fume alone. "I don't know, Mac, maybe you've just been down here too long."

22

SMITH WAS ACCUSTOMED to waking up in unfamiliar places, the fog of alcohol wearing off as he'd roll over beside a woman whose name he didn't always remember. But the pain in his skull wasn't a hangover. And he was outside. When he opened his eyes, the blue January sky taunted him with its brightness.

He felt very cold. He slowly pulled himself up, his head throbbing with every move. He realized he was in Mrs. Bishop's backyard, just a few feet away from the busted door he'd walked through earlier. The mystery men's car was gone.

Based on his experience giving chokeholds, he figured he'd only been unconscious a short while. They'd carried him out here and driven away, hurrying before he could wake up.

Standing brought his headache to a new level. He saw his wallet on the ground so he bent down to pick it up, which took a while. Its contents seemed in order. They'd taken his notebook, though.

He wasn't sure who those men were or what had really happened, whether one of them had in fact talked the other out of shooting Smith, or whether that exchange had been an act to scare him. If so, it had worked.

He was all but certain they weren't cops. Perhaps they'd left him out here and called the real cops to report a break-in as they left. The knife, he remembered. He'd been holding a knife. It had his prints on it. Was it still in the house, or had they taken it with them, to plant somewhere else?

He leaned over, hands on his knees, and tried to steady himself, tried to remember everything the men had said, commit their appearances to memory.

He slowly walked back into the kitchen, saw that the knife he'd taken had not been returned to its normal spot. It wasn't in the hallway where he'd dropped it either.

If they had in fact called the cops, he was wasting precious time.

He left through the back door, walking faster as his head cleared. Back to his borrowed car. He didn't see anyone outside as he drove away, hoping he hadn't been noticed.

*

Back at the *Daily Times* building, he poured a glass of water, downed two aspirin, and dialed police headquarters. Tried for McInnis, couldn't reach him. Transferred back to reception and asked for Officer Deaderick, one of his usual sources. Sipped his old mug of cold coffee and grabbed a fresh notebook.

"What's this about Victoria Bishop being arrested for her husband's murder?" he asked.

"Wow, you're quick, they haven't even announced it yet," Deaderick said. "You didn't get this from me, but she has no alibi and she did have a motive: she's been having an affair, she asked him for a divorce, and he wasn't too happy about it. She claims she was home alone that night, with nary a soul to vouch for her. She was *supposed to* be at some Negro business leaders' meeting but never showed up."

So the cops had found that out. "Who's her boyfriend?" His pencil could not move fast enough. "He arrested too?"

"Luther Bridges. Negro doctor, lives on the West Side. They didn't arrest him, and as far as I know, they don't plan to. They're saying she told her husband about the affair, asked for her share of the estate. Then Bishop goes on a trip or something for work. Couple nights later she meets him at his office, he tells her he refuses to grant her the divorce or give her any money at all, and she shoots him."

"You buy that?"

"Hell, I don't know. It's plenty sordid, and often that's the reason a man gets shot."

"They're certain about the affair? She told me she'd never had one."

"The detectives don't seem to lack confidence, put it that way."

"They charging murder one, or manslaughter?"

"First-degree, Smitty."

Smith thought aloud. "It'd be one thing if they were saying *he* shot *her* because she was having an affair. The angry cuckold, heat of the moment thing. But *she* shot *him*, because he wouldn't grant her the divorce? Come on."

"Hey, I'm just a dumb beat cop. But that's their case."

"You got Dr. Bridges' address?"

"I ain't a phone book, Smitty. I've given you plenty. White reporters don't even know this yet."

≺

He ran to Laurence's office and gave him the news. Laurence called in Toon, deciding this was too big for one reporter. He told Toon to head to police headquarters and get more on that side of the story and told Smith to find the boyfriend. Smith looked up the number and address for Luther Bridges. Called, got no answer. Flipped through the yellow pages for the doctor's business address. Found it, then decided to try McInnis at his house first.

McInnis answered on the second ring, not sounding in the best of moods.

"Hey, Sergeant. What's this about Mrs. Bishop being arrested for murder?"

A long exhale. "I've not been involved, Smith."

"How long have you known?"

"I just got a tip a short while ago."

"What do you make of the arrest?"

"Smith, if you have any questions for the Department, you can reach out to the public liaison office."

"Sergeant, come on, this is me. On the QT, can you tell me if it's legit?"

"*Legit*?" As if the word's meaning had become a mockery. "We never spoke, first of all."

"Of course."

"I trust Detective Cummings. He's a solid investigator. He didn't have enough for an arrest a couple days ago, but whatever he's found since, it was enough to arrest her."

Enough for a real, deserved conviction, or enough to put a Negro away quickly, which was a far easier burden of proof?

"I heard it was about infidelity and money," Smith said, "but no hard evidence."

"No comment."

"What did you hear from our friends with the Bureau?"

"No way, Smith. That's out of bounds for you."

After having a gun pointed at me last night? Smith felt acid rising up his throat.

"Sergeant, I would be well within my rights to write a story about how an FBI agent was rifling through Bishop's office right around the same time APD was supposedly wrapping up its case against his widow."

"I suppose you do have that *right*, but you should think long and hard about the wisdom of a move like that."

Hearing that same exasperated tone of voice, Smith could visualize himself standing at attention in McInnis's old office in the moldy, rat-infested basement of the Y, basketballs bouncing overhead.

"You are a private citizen," McInnis reminded him yet again, "and they're the *FBI*. I wouldn't want them mad at *me*, let alone you. I would be concerned for your safety if you went and ticked them off. Now, I don't know all that's going on right now, but there are some powerful people involved and they're doing things that don't make much sense."

Smith fished in his pockets for a cigarette. He considered telling McInnis what he'd just been through, his assault at the hands of strange white men at Bishop's house. Either they weren't cops, or they were cops who were doing dirty work and didn't want to be identified. He was afraid that if he told McInnis, the white detectives on the case would find out and would want to know why Smith had been at the Bishop house. Those detectives would see a broken door and a Negro admitting he had been inside the building; they would twist Smith's story until he found himself in a jail cell.

He kept this from McInnis, for now.

"I follow you, Sergeant," he said, swallowing some pride yet again. "But it would help if I knew what the feds told you."

"I'm not sure you ever will, Civilian Smith." Smith would have to hope McInnis had at least told Boggs or Dewey or some other Negro cop, with whom Smith might have better luck.

"One last question. Do *you* think she's guilty?"

Another pause. "*Confidentially*, just between us, I am almost certain she's innocent."

McInnis wasn't the only person Smith was keeping secrets from. He hadn't told Laurence or even Toon about the FBI's break-in last night. McInnis was right: writing about it could be dangerous. Because he still didn't know what was going on, he wasn't sure what to tell his colleagues, afraid of putting them at risk somehow.

At the same time, he wondered if keeping it a secret was yet more dangerous. Unsure what the best move was, he briefly wrote out a note, explaining the break-in, the agent's name, and the fact that McInnis had been there. Then he folded it inside an envelope on which he wrote *To Whom It May Concern*, which he put into his top desk drawer. Just in case whatever had happened to Mr. Bishop happened to him next.

He stood to leave, stuffing notebooks and pencils into his briefcase, when he looked up and saw that the new girl from the copy desk was standing in his doorway.

"Don't tell me I made more mistakes," he joked. "I haven't even handed anything in yet!"

"Oh no, I was just, um, coming by to say hello, actually." She sounded nervous. Normally he would have been happy to while away a few minutes chatting with a young lady, but he'd made an ironclad pact with himself not to woo any employees of the paper. "You used to be a policeman, didn't you?"

Lord, he was so tired of this conversation. "It's Natalie, right?"

"Yes. It's just, I've been, you know, thinking about Mr. Bishop and all. And, um . . . "

"Natalie, I'd be happy to give you the lowdown, but another time." He gave her an apologetic smile as he walked right up to her in the doorway. She backed up as he hurriedly stepped past her. "Right now I'm chasing a story."

23

MINUTES LATER, SMITH entered the Gradys. That's how people referred to Grady Hospital, the large H-shaped building on Butler Street, one wing of which treated whites, the other Negroes. Technically one hospital, but it felt more like two, connected by a hallway that doctors and nurses traveled through when moving from Negro patient to white or vice versa.

Smith was hoping to locate Dr. Luther Bridges before anyone else broke the news that his lover was in jail. Notebook in hand, Smith's heart raced as he went after his story. He was an adrenaline addict, and though this certainly wasn't the same as pursuing a suspect on foot, at least he wasn't being shot at.

Although he'd had guns trained on him twice in twenty-four hours now.

He walked through the Negro emergency room and then the crowded hallways, where beds always seemed to be blocking the way because the rooms themselves were filled beyond capacity. So much disinfectant in the air he wanted to light a smoke, but he was moving too fast.

He spied a young nurse he'd shared a drink with a few months ago.

"Well, hello there, Nurse Lois." He put on his most sparkling smile. She had very dark skin, wide eyes, and lush lips he'd had serious plans for until she'd mentioned a husband.

"You can just call me Lois," she said, smiling back. "And you don't look sick."

"I'm looking for Dr. Bridges. He around?"

She pointed to one of the open doors, room number 9. "He's with a patient." She looked at his notebook. "You're a reporter, right?"

"Yes, indeed. While I'm waiting, what do you know about Dr. Bridges?"

"Ah, he's every patient's favorite."

"Why's that?"

"He listens to 'em, treats 'em with respect. He's not always as nice to *us*, though."

"He married?"

"His wife died, I don't know, year and a half ago?"

Smith's antenna shot way up. "That's a shame. What happened?"

"Leukemia." Antenna down. "I never met her, but folks say she was real sweet. I've only been here about a year, but he seemed awful quiet back then." A sad look crossed her face. She broke from it and asked, "Is he in some kind of trouble?"

"Why would you think that?"

"Police came for him yesterday. Other nurse overheard it, said the cops told him he had to go answer some questions."

"In cuffs? They arrest him?"

She said she didn't know, but that the doctor had been back at work later that day. "What's your story about?"

"Now, now, that's for me to know and you to read about." He saw Dr. Bridges walk out of room 9, so he thanked Lois with a wink and walked toward the doctor.

Bridges was looking down at a chart, revealing a large bald spot on the top of his head. His white jacket hung loose over a cream shirt and red bow tie.

"Excuse me, Dr. Bridges?"

The doctor stopped and looked up. He wore glasses and had a small bandage over his left eyebrow.

"Sorry to bother you, sir. I'm Tommy Smith, with the *Atlanta Daily Times.*" Smith extended his hand, which Bridges shook after a pause. "I was hoping I could ask you a few questions, maybe somewhere private?"

Despite Bridges' glasses and bald spot, which couldn't be seen head-on, he was a handsome man. Sensitive eyes, strong cheekbones, tidy beard. Light-skinned, just a touch darker than Victoria Bishop, and possibly a few years her junior.

"I have a very busy schedule today. What's it about?"

Smith kept his voice low enough so they wouldn't be overheard. "I'm very sorry to tell you this, Doctor, but Victoria Bishop was arrested this morning."

Bridges' entire body stiffened. "What? Why?"

"She's being charged with the murder of her husband."

Bridges was thrown off balance: he moved his arm as if about to catch himself against the wall, straightening just in time. Smith stepped closer in case he started to fall.

"Are you serious?"

"I'm sorry, Doctor, but yes. Are you sure we can't go somewhere more private?"

Flustered, Bridges looked at the other doors in the hallway, all of them leading to patient rooms. He managed to walk forward, Smith following, until they reached the end of the hallway, further from the nurses' station. This seemed to be the best spot Bridges could provide, at least in his present state of shock.

"What happened?" Bridges asked.

"Far as I know, the police don't have much. Maybe just a suspicion, and they're hoping that by arresting her, she'll crack."

This was Smith's least favorite part of the job, just as questioning crime victims or families of the newly dead was one of his least favorite parts of being a cop. In order to get the story and find the truth, he needed to pry where people didn't want him.

"That's ridiculous. She didn't kill him. You mean she's in *jail* now?"

"I imagine she's still being processed, yessir. I'm sorry to ask, Doctor, but could you tell me how you knew Mrs. Bishop?"

"We're ... we're good friends." Bridges' visceral reaction to the news seemed strong confirmation that they were more than friends. Then he shook his head, mind racing. "Wait, who did you say you were?"

Smith repeated his name and occupation, and the doctor's

expression hardened. Smith was used to this, anger and grief quickly taking the place of weakness and vulnerability. He feared that the one golden moment when he might get useful answers had already passed.

"I don't need to say a thing to you."

"You don't, Doctor. And I'm sorry I'm asking you any of this, I am. But I was a police officer once, so I know what to expect from here. They're going to hold her a while, longer than they're supposed to, and after her lawyer has made a lot of noise, they'll finally have a hearing, where she'll be charged and *maybe* let out on bail, but probably not." He paused so this could sink in. "They're saying she shot him because she asked him for a divorce so she could be with you, and he said no."

"That's . . . preposterous. Victoria would never do that. She . . . she still loved him." He put his right hand on the top of his head. "Are they going to come for me next?"

"I don't know." The nurse had already told Smith, yet he asked anyway. "Have they spoken to you?"

"Yes." He instinctively reached for the bandage on his brow, then stopped. "They said I needed to come with them and answer some questions. This . . . this is insane." The doctor shook his head again, the man of science confronted with facts that fit no hypothesis.

"What did they ask?"

"Why should I tell you? Why should I be talking to you at all?"

"Like I said, Dr. Bridges, I used to be a cop. I know a *few* officers who aren't dirty. If the investigators have the wrong idea, maybe I can help get them the right one, but only if I know what really happened."

Dr. Bridges considered this for a moment. "They seemed to know that Victoria and I . . . are close. They insinuated that I had killed Arthur so I could steal her away, and her money. It's ridiculous, and I told them so. I have an alibi for that night. I was at a fundraiser for the hospital, and I named several people who could back that up. They made me wait there while they double-checked, but they eventually admitted I was right and let me go."

Smith could imagine the rest. They'd gotten rough with him, enough for the doctor to admit his affair but not to confess involvement in a murder he hadn't committed.

"Is there anything else you'd like to say for the story, sir? To get your side out there?"

"I don't . . . " He stopped for a moment, still flustered. "I don't want to *be* in your story."

"I'm sorry, Doctor. Atlanta police are the ones who've put you in it." He extended a business card, feeling pity for Bridges. Difficult though this was, Smith was giving him his best chance to speak up before other voices did, more dominant narratives to drown his out.

Bridges stared at the card a moment, perhaps reeling at the sight of the familiar masthead, the famous business run by his lover's husband. It added another layer of meaning to the helpless look in his eyes, one Smith recognized from so many others over the years, that realization that they were now part of someone else's tale, not fully a person but a thing being written against their will.

Bridges took the card, then walked back to Nurse Lois and told her he needed to leave.

Smith left, too. He had a hot date with Bertha.

24

"WHAT'S NEW DOWNSTAIRS?" Captain Dodd asked the next morning.

McInnis tended not to show much emotion, so it wasn't difficult to hide his anger at the mild insult behind a neutral expression as he sat in the no doubt deliberately uncomfortable guest chair in Dodd's office. He replied, "Nothing major since yesterday."

Downstairs meant the basement. Even three years after being relocated here from the Butler St. Y, McInnis still didn't feel entirely welcome in this building. Dodd dropping "downstairs" like that added to his feeling of offense.

"Those Montgomery cops still lurking around anywhere?" McInnis asked.

"Not that I know of."

It still enraged him that Dodd didn't feel the same way about them. To Dodd, the need to keep Negroes down supplanted any sense of jurisdiction or territorialism, or even fair play.

They moved on to other matters, including the Bishop murder, which Dodd seemed to take less seriously than McInnis might have hoped.

Then Dodd said, "I wanted to talk to you about your transfer request."

"What transfer request?"

Dodd picked up a piece of paper and reached across his desk. "This ain't your signature? There another Sergeant McInnis I don't know about?"

McInnis took the sheet, glanced at it. Actually laughed. "I wrote this five years ago."

"I was cleaning my office."

"I'm pleased to see my correspondence rates so highly with you, sir."

"Well, you should be pleased, because it happened to catch my eye at an opportune time. Wetherton's decided to retire and move to Florida, something about his wife's kidneys. Or maybe it's her lungs. Anyway, there's a vacancy in Zone Two. It's quiet, which I know ain't quite your cup of tea, but then again, you *are* getting up in years, no offense, so maybe it's time for quiet." He paused. "It's a ticket out of the Congo."

McInnis had been told back when he started his unwanted position that, if he wanted out, he should wait three years before asking. The date on this memo was April 3, 1951, exactly three years into the posting. Chomping at the bit for his release.

"This . . . is unexpected."

"If that's how you say *thanks*, you might could work on your etiquette. And you're welcome."

"Who would take over the district?"

"Who cares? Somebody who's pissed me off lately, and that ain't a short list."

That comment confirmed it: being assigned to lead the Negro officers had never been an honor, nor was it something given to whichever white officer was presumed to be most skilled at inter-racial communication. It was punishment. McInnis had been punished, for nearly eight years now. He'd always known that to be the case, but hearing it confirmed so blithely set a fire in him.

"I'll think it over," he said.

"What?"

"When do you need an answer?"

"I . . . " Dodd was flummoxed. Then he chuckled. "I didn't think it would require much thought."

"I said I'll think about it, Captain. When do you need to know?"

"You are an ornery one, ain't ya? You've been asking for some-thing for years, and now that you're offered it, you ain't sure you want it. Can't take yes for an answer, huh?"

McInnis had wanted to be reassigned for so long that he hadn't even thought to question it. Because of the official silence his request had received, he had long since resigned himself to the job he had to do. He led his officers, he removed dangerous men from the streets, and he involved himself in delicate investigations whose resolutions called for both smarts and tact, almost like disabling bombs. Bombs linked to both Negro and white Atlanta. Maybe Dodd was right that he was just being ornery. But that was his right as a Southerner, especially one who'd been fucked with for damn near eight years.

"Well, it is a lateral move," McInnis pointed out.

"If you think a transfer from East Senegambia back to the real Department is a lateral move, you're in even worse shape than I thought."

There it was again: *you're not in "the real Department" right now.*

McInnis fumed, as he had when Cummings had said *don't tell me you think like them now.* And Dodd himself had said only yesterday, *maybe you've just been down here too long.* As if McInnis's time working with the Negro officers had made him suspect, his years of advocating for them branding him a traitor. It was his goddamn *job*—a tough one—yet they acted as if his success at it meant he was somehow against the white race. He didn't remember so many comments like this when he'd started the assignment; mostly he'd just been teased, pitied. They'd become more common lately. Maybe he *had* changed, but so had everyone else, in the opposite direction. It was the panic over *Brown* and its specter of government-imposed integration, the retreat to opposing bunkers, the growing fear that anything less than hostility to Negroes would imperil the Southern way of life.

Dodd said, "Look, Wetherton's last day is in a month, and I'd like to have someone lined up before then. If I don't hear from you in two weeks, it goes to someone else. Got it?"

McInnis nodded, confused by the situation, confused by his own response. Perhaps this was the best thing to happen to him in years, but he hadn't received good news in so long that he didn't know how to respond. Should he tell his wife tonight, debate the pros and cons with her, or keep it to himself?

He was unnerved by one thought: right after Arthur Bishop becomes the most prominent Negro to be murdered on McInnis's watch, and the day after he refuses to play along with two Montgomery cops looking to railroad Reverend King Jr., he's finally offered a ticket out.

At the very least, Dodd had poor tact. At worst, the timing was not a coincidence.

"Is that all, Captain?" McInnis asked, standing up. "Or can I grab my machete and hack my way back to East Senegambia?"

25

THAT SAME MORNING, Smith sat at his desk making calls when he finally reached Leon Farley, the man he'd seen in the old photo with Bishop, Peeples, and a white lady named Celia Winters. Smith had found Farley's name in one of the *Daily Times*'s reference guides on important Negroes—since the local libraries were mostly closed to the colored, the paper had created a detailed library over the years—and learned that Farley was a Morehouse sociology professor.

On the phone, Smith got right to the point and asked what he knew about Bishop's long-ago trip to Moscow. Farley seemed hesitant at first, but when Smith explained how much he already knew, the professor opened up.

"People take it the wrong way these days. But you need to remember, plenty of people did what we did back then. From scholars to factory workers ... We were genuinely curious as to whether communism and its race-blind creed really could be a cure for the problems in America. In the twenties and thirties, communists were the loudest voices when it came to Negro rights. They said race is a construct of the ruling class. You old enough to remember the Scottsboro Boys?"

"Yes, sir, vaguely." He gazed out his window and saw a woman pushing a pram down Auburn Avenue.

"The Communist Party made the Scottsboro Boys a major cause, before the NAACP even got wind." The National Association for the Advancement of Colored People was the most prominent organization dedicated to Negro rights, recently winning the *Brown* school desegregation decision. "They used that trial to shine a global spotlight on crooked old Jim Crow. That won the Party a lot of fans among Negroes. There was a sense that the Soviets had illuminated a new way, and if only America could adopt some of that, we'd finally get a fair shake here."

Farley paused for a moment, a pregnant pause Smith was used to, first from suspects and then from sources: the interviewees mentally editing themselves in advance. It always made him want to know what they weren't saying.

"A number of Negro communists were arrested in Atlanta back then, charged under some ridiculous anti-insurrection law, with *life sentences* hanging over their heads. So, yes, as you seem to have heard, Arthur, myself, and several others from Atlanta decided to see for ourselves what was brewing over in Moscow. We went there in late spring of 1932. I was there a few months; some stayed much longer. Arthur and I, we were young, in our twenties, but there were famous writers, actors, educators ... we felt like we were the vanguards of our race and our culture, exploring something new and important."

"What exactly did you do there?"

"Some of us took classes, learning about communist theory, collective social planning. Others were there to teach: factory workers with experience running plants here, or agriculture experts trying to help them run farms after they'd run off all the ruling kulaks who used to do it. But Arthur and I, we were there to help with a film the Soviets wanted to make, called *Black and White*. Part art, part propaganda. A way to show audiences that racism could be overcome with a collective workers' society. They brought big-time actors over, and they even had Langston Hughes work on the script. It was fun—we were carousing with famous people, artists and actors, in a world where we didn't have to sit in the back of a bus—but it didn't last. Egos clashing, everyone sleeping with the wrong people—don't get me started on the romantic morals of the avant-garde. Then the Party overlords tore apart the script, stomped all the humanity out of it. Rewrites upon rewrites, the purgatory of official Party rubber-stamping, and then nothing. Silence. Spring turned to summer turned to fall, and for me, once the *real* cold weather started, and it became clear the script would never be approved, that was enough. I left for home in October. And the film was never made. In all honesty, I think that bit of artistic rejection is the biggest reason Arthur turned away from communism. Nothing like a writer's bruised feelings."

"Was Morris Peeples along for that trip? Or Celia Winters?"

"Why do you ask?"

"I understand they ran with that same crowd once. Maybe they still do."

"Let's leave them out of this."

"Sir, I have to ask. I tried talking to Mr. Peeples the other day, and let's just say that the way he brushed me off, and some of the things he said . . . It only made me more curious."

"Morris is a good man. We aren't really in touch anymore, but I feel . . . he's been unnecessarily tarnished by his politics. Years ago, he helped defend Angelo Herndon, a communist who helped organize the poor during the Depression and was arrested for it. Morris stood up for a colored man's right to speak his mind down here in Georgia, and he lost."

Smith had read a few chapters of Peeples' book, which was part political memoir and part legal history. It made for dry reading, but Smith wondered whether anything in that old trial might relate to what had happened to Bishop.

"After Herndon was convicted," Farley explained, "Morris officially joined the Party, but that made him a marked man."

"When I spoke to him, he implied people were watching us."

"Well, I'm sure he *has* been followed around, many times over the years. Anyone from Klansmen, to fascist blackshirts, to police or the FBI, to rivals from the Party. Look, you need to understand, the idea of communism made a kind of sense once, until I saw how rotten Russia was, too, starving its own people in the name of a 'perfect society.' These days, here in America, there are some who would like nothing more than to crucify every forward-thinking

Negro who dared to believe, years ago, that communism might have some answers for our country's ills."

The reference to the FBI set off alarms in Smith's head. What would Farley say if Smith told him some feds had been in Bishop's office the other night? But he was afraid to disclose this, for now.

Instead, he asked, "What can you tell me about Celia Winters?"

"She was from up north, Chicago I believe, and she stayed there. I haven't spoken to her in years. But I know she's still active in the cause, so to speak. She's involved with the Civil Rights Congress."

"They're a communist group?"

A pause. "As far as I understand it, their main goal is tearing down Jim Crow. Anyway, I haven't heard from Celia in a long time. But ... " He stopped himself.

"But what, Mr. Farley?"

"I did hear recently that she was in town."

"Really? Why's that?"

"I don't know," he said brusquely, as if he hadn't meant to say so much. "Just that the CRC was doing something in Atlanta. That's all. Again, I haven't spoken to her in ages."

"Do you know if she saw Mr. Bishop since she came to town?"

"I have no idea, but I'd be shocked if he'd been involved in her group. Look, I'm very sorry, but I have class in five minutes and need to run. You take care." Farley hung up.

Smith was left with the uncomfortable sense that the professor knew even more than he'd said. He needed to find out more about this communist group and what it was doing in Atlanta.

✦

Before Victoria Bishop's arraignment, Smith killed time in his office reading the day's news. Today Autherine Lucy would become the first Negro at the University of Alabama, though she wouldn't be allowed to use room and board facilities; in Chicago, a Negro disc jockey had received approval from the Civil Aeronautics Administration for his stunt to fly over the state of Mississippi and airdrop reprints of the Constitution.

He read through more of Mr. Bishop's old editorials. Rereading one from '47 praising the city's decision to finally hire Negro policemen, he found himself thinking about Patrice's question, *why aren't you a cop anymore?*

He hadn't dared admit to her that he asked himself the same question damn near every day.

Unlike his high-class former partner, Smith had grown up knowing the underside of Atlanta. His father had worked hard for his family, yes, but theirs had been a tenuous foothold in the world, and Smith had never lived far from the numbers runners and prostitutes, the card sharks and con men whom both white Atlantans and upper-class Negroes were now hoping to bulldoze out of existence. People like Boggs rarely walked down those streets, and if they did, they knew to walk right past them without making eye contact. But Smith had been the sort of cat to stop and make conversation. As a reporter, he tried to draw on his knowledge of the hard decisions they faced, the circumstances they lived with, hoping to show them as fully human, nuanced and deserving of respect. But he worried that such work was less meaningful, less useful than what he used to do.

He had felt deep shame on the day, six years ago, when he dropped his resignation letter on McInnis's desk. He had cited the expected reasons: his inability to tolerate the double standards under which the Negro officers operated, the sense that being asked to do his job with one hand tied behind his back was a sure-fire way to get him killed, and his grudging admittance that perhaps he was not suited to a job that was so reliant on chains of command, a strong hierarchy, and an unhealthy amount of "yes sirs." His army time had had its share of mistreatment based on race, sure, but the indignities he had to face back in Atlanta, night after night, felt even worse. At least in the war, the Black Panthers had fought and won their battles, and the Nazis fell. But what were the Negro cops actually accomplishing?

He feared that the people who criticized the Negro cops—*you're only there to make white politicians look good, trick us into thinking they care*—were right. He had wanted to believe that the best way to reform a corrupt system was to force his way inside it, then bend it to heel.

But after more than two years, he feared he had only become a part of the problem.

Until he felt himself lashing out. At his partner, at whichever girl he was seeing at the time, at the people whom he was supposed to be helping. Violence was a necessary part of the job, yet he felt himself becoming brutal, callous, rage made flesh. Rage carrying a gun. Rage with at least some modicum of institutional backing.

And one night he crossed a line, shooting a man he shouldn't have shot.

The next morning he'd woken up literally sick to his stomach, unable to believe what he'd done. His life a trigger he couldn't un-pull.

The only way to try un-pulling it was revoking his own badge, revoking the new rights that he feared were corrupting him. Maybe the best way to reform the system was from the outside after all. Maybe it was better this way. Maybe he had not simply given up.

Damn, but he missed it sometimes.

Smith was lost in Bishop's old editorials when Mrs. McClatchey from the front desk knocked on his open door. "There's an Adelaide Dawson here to see you."

Standing behind Mrs. McClatchey was a woman he didn't think he'd ever seen before: red bandana tied beneath her chin and covering most of her hair, wrinkles stretching from her eyes to her temples, brown coat patched in places.

"I'd like to speak to you about Mrs. Bishop." Her refined voice rearranged some memories in his mind, and he recognized her: the Bishops' maid. Uniformed then, in civilian attire now. Controlled then, nervous now.

"Yes, ma'am." He stood up and removed a stack of newspapers

from Blackmon's chair so she could sit, apologizing for the mess. "How are you, Mrs. Dawson? I imagine this is a rough time."

She huffed at the understatement. "I just don't know what to think. Or do. I can't decide if I should be looking for work or if that's disrespectful. But Mrs. Bishop was always fair with me, and I want to stand by her."

"Hopefully she'll be out real soon." He had a good idea what a strong criminal defense attorney cost, though, and he wondered just how many liquid assets Mrs. Bishop truly had. Fighting the charges might not lead her to sell the house, but maybe she'd lay off her maid.

"I heard you say to her," she spoke cautiously, "that you used to be police."

Maids did know how to eavesdrop. "Yes, ma'am."

"A lady I know, her nephew's a cop. Dewey Edmunds."

Smith smiled. "Yeah, Dewey's a friend of mine. And I'd be saying that even if he hadn't saved my life once."

"I'm assuming I can trust you. You can't tell anyone that I'm telling you this."

"I understand, Mrs. Dawson."

As he waited, she took a breath. "I was there when they arrested her yesterday. Four policemen, all of them white, but only two of them in uniform. And all of them ... there wasn't any doubt they were police, understand? Well, after they kicked me out and took her away, I got on the bus, but then I remembered I hadn't fed her cats." Then she told him what had happened next, the broken-in door, the second round of white men, this time none of them in uniform, none of them in squad cars, none displaying badges. "They told me they were police, too, but ... they didn't seem truthful."

He sat up straighter. He asked her what they looked like, and her descriptions matched the men who'd accosted him only moments later.

"They warned me not to tell anyone I saw them. They threatened my sons." Her face grave, she told him they'd been rifling through the study. Then she reached into a pocket and handed him a small piece of paper. "I took down their tag number."

He could have hugged her. "Thank you, ma'am. This is very helpful."

He picked her brain as to what they might have been looking for, but she had no idea. He probed for more details on the Bishops' marriage, their extended family, whether she'd overheard any quarrels or heated arguments. Did she know the names Morris Peeples or Leon Farley, or a white lady named Celia Winters, or a group called the Civil Rights Congress? He didn't get much out of her. The Bishops' marriage had never been terribly affectionate, and she knew Dr. Bridges as a friend of the family but she'd never suspected either Bishop of having an affair.

After thanking her and escorting her back out, he picked up the phone and dialed Officer Dewey Edmunds to see if he'd run the tag as a favor for an old colleague.

Though a member of the press, Smith was required by Jim Crow to sit in the furthest rows on the left-hand side of the courtroom in which Victoria Bishop was being arraigned. Beside him sat a Negro stringer who sometimes supplied stories of national interest to the *Chicago Defender* and *Pittsburgh Courier*. He saw reporters for the *Constitution* up front.

Victoria was led out in her prison stripes, a woman very much diminished. No gold or pearls, no cashmere or silk. Her straightened hair pulled back in a ponytail, her face not made up. The carefully maintained markers of her class erased.

She was led to a desk at which stood her attorney, Johnny Dormand, a white man from a prominent downtown firm on Peachtree Street. She surely had a Negro doctor and a Negro banker and a Negro insurance agent, but she realized that given how Atlanta's white judges felt about Negro lawyers, hiring one would have been suicide.

The judge banged his gavel. Charges were read. Mrs. Bishop's

"Not guilty, your honor" was loud and clear back in the colored seats. The prosecutor requested she be held without bail. Dormand responded with outrage that a woman of sixty-one years, a pillar of her community, could be so treated.

The judge sided with the prosecution. Mrs. Bishop was led out by the white bailiff. Friends and family watched from many rows away, which again was as close as Negro visitors were allowed.

Out in the hallway, a small scrum of reporters surrounded Dormand.

"My client is innocent, and she will demonstrate that at trial if the state truly does seek to pursue its nonsensical course," he announced. "Their case is flimsy and circumstantial to say the least, and it is our hope that the state will recognize that soon and drop its so-called case before wasting any more time or resources."

"Have they mentioned any evidence to you at all?" asked Joe Yardley, a balding white reporter for the *Constitution*.

"No, and I don't believe they have any."

"It looks like the city has rushed to prosecute a Negro woman instead of finding the real killer," Smith cut in. "Some people are calling it a legal lynching. Do you see it that way?"

"Now, I wouldn't use inflammatory language like that," Dormand said. "People can call it what they like, but I call it incorrect. I can assure you that if the state takes this to trial, they will realize their mistake."

A few more questions, then the lawyer marched off. As the reporters turned to go their separate ways, Yardley couldn't resist shaking his head at Smith.

"*A legal lynching*? That going to be your headline, Smith?"

"What'll yours be? *Mammy On Trial For Killing Unusually Rich Negro*?"

The white man scowled. "I don't write like that."

"Well, I'm glad some of you don't."

It was unusual to see so much interest from white papers. It meant Smith would have competition for chasing down leads. And it meant the narrative being put forth by the cops and the prosecution would be getting some bolded, twenty-point-font support in the white press.

"Look, Bishop was a good fellow," Yardley said. "A restraining influence. I'd hate to see your paper turn into just another reactionary Negro screed without him."

"You react the way you want to react. Don't worry about us."

"We *don't* worry about you," Yardley laughed as he headed for the door. "Never have, never will."

26

"THIS BISHOP CASE is bullshit," Dewey Edmunds said as he racked some weights.

Ninety minutes before roll call, Boggs and Dewey were hitting the weights at the Y after working the heavy bag and jumping rope. Though their precinct office was no longer in the Y's basement, and while they technically had access to the Department's gym, they still didn't feel welcome there. When their offices had been moved three years ago, they'd sat together and voted unanimously to keep working out at the Y so they could have a place where they could speak freely before clocking in.

"It is."

"Yesterday, man, it's all people wanted to talk to me and Champ about. Everybody blaming us for letting white folks frame her like that. We just tell 'em, hey, the detectives have evidence, they say they have a case, but ... " He dropped his weights heavily. Dewey was the shortest of the officers, and possibly the shortest cop in Atlanta, but few dared comment on that because he was all muscle, a former boxer who took no guff. "I don't want to be defending that."

"I know it."

"I don't think the detectives know it. I don't even think McInnis does."

"Talk to him, then," Boggs said, sitting on a bench.

"And tell him what, exactly? That white detectives arresting an old colored lady ain't good for us?"

Boggs sighed. He agreed with everything Dewey was saying, but he didn't care to be burdened by someone's similar anger. "Yes.

Tell him exactly what you just said. Why not? If you feel like you can't, then why are you telling me?"

Dewey stared for a moment. Then he shook his head and wiped the sweat from his forehead with his sleeve.

"I know it sounds crooked and political and bullsh— wrong." Boggs almost never cussed, though that time he came close. "But what can we do about it?"

This wasn't an altogether new experience for them. Trying to uphold the law fairly and effectively while distancing themselves from the worst excesses of white cops, white prosecutors, and white judges was a near-impossible task they'd been struggling with since day one.

Every time Boggs felt like they were making some progress, something like this happened.

He was in a bad mood even before coming in to work. The heat had gone out two days ago at the local Negro elementary school, so the kids had been sent home. Julie was pulling her hair out trying to keep up with three little ones, and word was the furnace would take a week to fix. White kids' schools were fine, their seats warm and their pencils sharpened.

His eldest, Sage, bored senseless, had asked if he could come to the police station with Boggs, which had required another conversation about how important it was for the kids to avoid white cops at all times. Which led to more questions as to why it was all right for Daddy to be around them if they were so dangerous. The hardest questions from your kids were the ones you didn't truly have an answer for, especially when you were trying to rush out the door to get to work.

"There's something else," Dewey said. They were alone in their corner of the gym—they were always the first two cops here—yet he lowered his voice all the same. "Tommy called me. Asked me to run a tag for him."

"Why?"

"Said a car drove up to the Bishops' house a couple hours after she was arrested, and that the men who went in didn't seem like cops. Said they rummaged around the place for a while."

"How would he know this?"

"Wouldn't say. 'A source.' Takes that reporter shit serious. He asked me to run the tags as a favor, and I did."

"Dewey, he's not a cop anymore."

"Crucify me, all right? I just got the info back from Records. Car belongs to a private dick named Warren Floyd. White, forty-seven years old, former cop. Worked APD only five years, quit the force in '43 to join the army, didn't rejoin after. Instead, he became a Pinkerton. Did that nine years, then hung out his own shingle two years ago."

"He was a Pinkerton, huh? Didn't know they had an office down here." The Pinkerton Agency was a private detective firm. Boggs had heard that people with money could hire Pinkertons for pretty much anything they didn't want the police to do: discreetly investigate an extortion attempt, dig up dirt on a rival, provide security. They were perhaps best known for breaking strikes. A lot of the big steel, railroad, and mining companies had hired Pinkertons to protect their strikebreakers from angry unionists over the last fifty-plus years. More than a few times, Pinkertons had been involved in shootings and other violence. But the South had proved inhospitable to unions, so Pinkertons hardly seemed necessary down here.

"A private eye searched the home of a murder victim," Boggs said, thinking out loud.

"*Broke into* the Bishops' house," Dewey clarified. "Right after she'd been arrested."

"What's their angle? Maybe Bishop had written something about an upcoming strike? Or he'd written about, or was planning to write about, the kind of man who can hire private eyes to break in and steal papers."

"Maybe they were there to plant a murder weapon." Dewey folded his chiseled arms. "Some bullshit to close the case against Mrs. Bishop?"

"No one's found a murder weapon yet."

"I think somebody needs to pay this Warren Floyd a visit and ask him."

"Oh, I'm sure he'd be real forthcoming to a couple colored officers."

"Damn it, we can't just *sit* on this," Dewey insisted. "You said yourself you don't like them charging the widow. Maybe this can help us figure out what's going on, and why."

Boggs hated the fact that Dewey was right.

"Okay, but you need to put Smith off for a while," he said. "Lie and say Records is giving you the runaround. In the meantime," and he couldn't believe he was saying this, "yes, you and me can go pay Floyd a visit. Off duty, in our civvies."

Dewey smiled and clapped Boggs on the shoulder. "Oh, boy. This gonna be fun."

27

AFTER FILING HIS story on Victoria Bishop's hearing, Smith lit a cigarette and tried to make sense of all the suspicions and half-ideas that hadn't fit into the story.

He needed to figure out what the FBI had been doing in Bishop's office. And what, if anything, the Randy Higgs case had to do with Bishop's death.

Professor Farley had told him that Celia Winters, the white lady in the photo with Bishop and Peeples, worked with the communist-affiliated Civil Rights Congress. He'd said she lived in Chicago but he'd let slip she'd been in town recently. Smith asked his colleague Blackmon what he knew about the CRC and Winters. Quite a lot: turned out the group had gotten a lot of ink, including some *Daily Times* stories Blackmon had written, for a small-town Mississippi trial of a Negro named Willie McGee for allegedly raping a white woman. McGee had been found guilty back in '48, despite rumors that he and the woman had a consensual relationship. The CRC had turned his legal appeals into a major cause, rallying all manner of celebrities to speak out against Mississippi "justice." The CRC had won quite a lot of press for itself and the communist cause.

Despite the appeals and the publicity, though, the CRC hadn't managed to save McGee's life: the state of Mississippi gave him the chair.

Smith dug through the archives and read up on the McGee case, which, he realized, had a lot in common with the Randy Higgs case here. It made him wonder if the CRC had its eyes on Atlanta, intending to use the coming Higgs trial for more PR. Perhaps

Celia Winters had been in contact with Bishop, asking him to cover the Higgs case. It would explain why she was in Atlanta, and why Bishop had chosen to cover the kind of story he usually avoided. It might also explain why the reds-hating FBI had been searching Bishop's office.

Professor Farley had seemed shaken when Smith mentioned Celia Winters. The woman was toxic, for one reason or another. Why, because she was a communist? Because she was a white lady? Some other reason?

Seemed like a long shot, but it was worth checking.

He placed a call to Darlene Higgs, mother of Randy, whose number he found by digging through Bishop's notes on the case. Whatever might have been stolen from Bishop's desk the night of his murder, the Higgs file seemed to be intact.

She answered on the tenth ring, right when he was about to hang up.

"Hello, Mrs. Higgs, my name is Tommy Smith. I'm a reporter with the *Atlanta Daily Times*."

"A reporter?"

"Yes, ma'am, with the *Daily Times*." Just in case that increased the odds she'd see him as an ally, though he knew it was far from a magic talisman. People still just plain mistrusted the press. "I was hoping to ask you a few quick questions."

"Oh, no. I'm sorry. But we've got enough trouble as it is. Ever since we talked with one of you, we've been getting terrible phone calls. Terrible."

"You spoke with Mr. Bishop?"

"Bishop, yes. He was a polite man, but that story's caused us nothing but trouble. You wouldn't believe the things people have been saying to us on the phone."

"I'm very sorry to hear that, ma'am. I was just wondering if you've been contacted by a group called the Civil Rights Congress, or a woman named Celia Winters?"

"I'm sorry, I can't help you."

She hung up. He hadn't even gotten around to telling her

that Bishop had been killed since running that story. Maybe she already knew.

Digging through Bishop's notes, he found the number for Higgs's attorney, Welborn Kirk. He reached the man's secretary, waited on hold five minutes before Kirk came on the line.

The attorney started by offering his condolences for Mr. Bishop. He sounded guarded but courteous, treating his interlocutor with a respect white people didn't always offer.

"Thank you, Mr. Kirk. I apologize if one of my colleagues has already asked you this, but would you have any reason to think what happened to Mr. Bishop could be related to that story he wrote about the Higgs case?"

"I have agonized over that myself, of course. It's a possibility. But I don't have any concrete reasons to think that, other than the fact that the story made an awful lot of people mad."

Smith read Kirk the names of the few people who had actually signed the hate mail Bishop had received, but Kirk didn't know any of them.

"One other thing I was wondering, Mr. Kirk. Have you or your client been approached by anyone from the Civil Rights Congress?"

A short pause. "Why do you ask?"

Not a denial. But certainly a hint of fear at the mere mention of a communist group.

Smith explained that he knew at least one member of the group had been in town recently, and that the Higgs case seemed exactly the sort of trial the CRC would want to be involved in.

"Randy really doesn't need anything like this in the papers. It would not help his cause."

"Off the record, then."

"I'm still not sure it would be wise for me to answer."

"Sir, with respect, I'm trying to figure out who killed my boss. If some communist group's been sniffing around a case he was covering, it would help to know that."

Another pause. "All right, strictly off the record: I did receive a call recently from a lady officer of theirs, saying they'd like to contribute their legal know-how to the case. I assured her I could handle everything for Randy and that he wouldn't be needing additional counsel."

"Was her name Celia Winters?"

"That sounds right. Apparently she and some others, attorneys, made the trip down here and were . . . hoping I would let them take the reins. I told them no, that Randy already has representation through me, and his best interests would not be served by some . . . suspect political group using him for their own ends."

"Do you know if they've reached out to him personally?"

"You mean, have they written to him in jail or tried to visit? As of a few days ago, which was the last time I spoke to Randy, they hadn't. Certainly Randy has a right to make up his own mind, but I've warned him that working with them would be suicide. We already have the deck stacked against us in this case, but if the judge found out a communist group was backing him, then a guilty verdict would be all but guaranteed."

"Did Mr. Bishop know that the Civil Rights Congress had reached out to you?"

"I'm honestly not sure."

He tapped his pencil on the desk, thinking. "Did Miss Winters leave you any contact information, by any chance?"

She had, and Smith waited while Kirk found her number, a local one, and read it to him. Thanking the attorney, Smith hung up and dialed Winters' number.

It rang with no answer. Which meant it was time to ask Dewey for another favor.

28

MCINNIS FELT UNMOORED by the thought that, after all this time, he could simply walk away from the Negro neighborhoods and his officers. This historically unusual assignment had defined him, for better or worse; had made him a pariah to so many other white cops, had made him internalize things that had once seemed so foreign.

And now Dodd was telling him it could be shed like snakeskin.

He'd grown fonder of his assignment, and his officers, than he'd dared admit. His role here, for all its drawbacks, had come with a clarifying moral purpose. One he'd found wanting at the main Department, which, in his early years as a cop, had been a sewer of kickbacks, incompetence, and corruption. At least his job here made sense: these men should be cops, they should patrol their neighborhoods, they should right past wrongs. He'd been able to look himself in the mirror and know he was doing right by training them and supporting them.

Every time a cop like Dodd cracked a line about "the Congo" or "his boys," he felt his spine stiffen. Those insults weren't meant for him, maybe, yet they hit home all the same.

Leaving this position, and the Negro district, would mean concluding this part of his life.

He recalled what his first days on this beat had been like. Being the only white cop working with a Negro squad had forced him to navigate countless squalls and shoals, small and large, that he hadn't even realized existed. But back on the morning of his first shift in '48, he'd realized he'd overlooked one problem: how was he going to eat?

Meals out were one of the few luxuries a cop could afford himself. But if he was going to be working in Sweet Auburn, that meant Negro restaurants. Not only was he the only white cop around, he was the only white *person* around. Sometimes during the day, sure, a municipal worker might be fixing light poles or phone lines or repairing a sewer, or a white delivery man might pull up in a truck. But those were short, discrete tasks. They probably packed their lunches and then returned home to their wives with stories of how they'd survived a day in Darktown (most white folks referred to any Negro area as Darktown, when in fact Darktown denoted a specific, particularly run-down area).

McInnis, on the other hand, would be there, day after day, for months. Years.

Initially, the thought of entering a Negro restaurant had seemed borderline heretical. It was something white people simply didn't do. Later he would interrogate this, would realize certain contradictions: Negroes cooked in the homes of white people and in white restaurants. So their presence around food wasn't the problem. It was the idea of eating in the same place where they ate, of exercising that role of equals. The transgression of a carefully maintained boundary.

Bonnie had seemed to see this problem coming before he had: when he'd rolled out of bed on his first day of his new assignment, she'd already packed a sandwich for him. She made him the same sandwich every day, honey ham and provolone with lettuce but no tomato, which would only have made the sourdough soggy anyway. And a dill pickle, all of it wrapped in wax paper.

He had eaten that same sandwich for years.

Bonnie had teased him more than once for his predictability, asking him if he'd like to try turkey or roast beef, but he always said no. He knew what he liked. When not in uniform, he tended to wear one of two or three outfits. He'd never changed his haircut, receiving a monthly trim so it wouldn't grow shaggy. Shaved every morning. Ordered the same thing at the same restaurants, because once you knew what you liked, why take the chance on something inferior?

Voted Democrat and never considered otherwise. Been with the same woman for more than two decades now, since the time in '33 when he and a friend had left the movie theater and walked right into a quartet of high school girls on the sidewalk. Something about the way the tall blonde one smiled at a friend's joke—like she understood it but found it wanting, and smiled along anyway, confidently superior—drew him to her. A week later he and Bonnie had their first date, and a year after that she graduated and they married.

He still loved his wife. But he grew tired of that goddamn sandwich.

The first shift that he skipped the sandwich, he wasn't driven so much by a sense of adventurousness or racial equity as by random circumstance. A stolen necklace, to be specific.

Linwood Carter, the colored owner of Linwood's Restaurant on Auburn, had been walking home with his wife late at night when they'd been held up at knifepoint by two young men, who made off with their purse, wallet, and jewelry. Mrs. Carter was particularly heartbroken over a gold necklace; her husband, a former Negro Leagues outfielder, had bought it for her years ago on a baseball trip to Cuba, which had doubled as their honeymoon. McInnis had taken down their report, noting that their description of the perpetrators matched that of a pair who were wanted for similar robberies. The very next night, as luck and bad judgment would have it, the two thieves got drunk and crashed a stolen car three blocks south of Auburn. One of them was declared dead at the scene, the other taken to the hospital. In the trunk McInnis had found a bag containing jewelry, including a necklace that matched Mrs. Carter's description.

It had been early in the evening, so McInnis made the decision, against protocol, to take the necklace back to Linwood's Restaurant himself. He knew that more white cops soon would be descending on the scene, given the death and the long list of crimes the men were accused of, and he had a bad feeling that some of this recovered loot would not be filed in official reports and would mysteriously vanish.

Linwood's was only a few blocks away, so McInnis walked over. Mrs. Carter worked there too, as hostess, so he told her about the crash, mentioned they would do their best to recover what else they could, but, in the meantime, ma'am, here's your necklace.

She'd thanked him profusely and refused to let him leave until she'd found her husband in the kitchen so he could thank McInnis, too. They'd insisted on fixing him a plate, on the house. He wasn't supposed to be on break yet, but he *was* hungry, and it *did* smell delicious. So he ate it, right there at a table.

The lone white person in the restaurant. He did not receive any dirty looks from other patrons, but quite a few wary ones. As a cop, he was used to that. But this was different. Though invited, he knew he looked like an invader of their space, that perhaps he was doing more harm than good to be there.

Both Carters made a point of checking in on him a few times, making conversation.

"You work with one my best friend's sons," Mr. Carter mentioned as McInnis was finishing. "Ray Hanrahan? I've known him since he was a baby."

McInnis smiled. Hanrahan had started a few months earlier, the youngest of his officers, green as an early strawberry. "Ray's a solid officer. Pleasure working with him."

"He tells me he loves his job. 'Cept maybe for that time the fellow got him with the rolling pin."

"Yeah, that was rough," he said, remembering: a domestic dispute gone unpredictable, four stitches. "We all get our scars eventually."

"We do. Anyway, Ray speaks real well of you. Glad to see you're back on your feet."

McInnis realized he must have been referring to the fact that McInnis had broken his ankle the previous month and was only recently off crutches. He sat there marveling at the fact that this man knew so much about him. Maybe he was not the stranger here he'd thought he was.

On his way out, Mrs. Carter told him to come back any time. He imagined her other patrons didn't feel the same way.

Still, he did come back, occasionally. Not monthly, but a few times a year. Usually sitting in the back, at times when they weren't busy. Over the years, he worked a few more restaurants into his routine, places where he'd already met the owners, where he figured he wouldn't alarm them by showing up. Sometimes he ate with some of his officers, but usually he was alone.

While he ate, people might walk over and introduce themselves, offer a tip, a request that he look into something, or thank him for having done something for their uncle or grandson and neighbor. He never heard complaints about the police when he was eating, something he later told Boggs he was surprised by. Boggs had grinned ruefully at that; when Boggs ate out, all he *got* was complaints. Boggs had then explained that patrons simply didn't voice their many criticisms to the white sergeant, due to etiquette, or fear of his reaction, or lack of hope that he'd do anything about it.

McInnis filed this away. Yet another sign of all the meanings and layers he didn't even know existed. Was this a sign that he was making a mistake, that his efforts were doomed, or was the learning of it progress?

Good with faces, McInnis met more people, grew to recognize who belonged where, who kept what hours. He didn't know the neighborhood nearly as well as his officers did, as they not only worked here but lived here. But he knew this beat far better than any white cop in town.

And now, if he wanted, he could take all that knowledge and walk away.

⟡

Two hours after roll call, McInnis sat alone in his basement office, flipping through reports of the previous day, when he got a call from the front desk that he had a visitor named Clarence Hunter. It took him a moment to place the name: the father of the rape victim. Who may or may not have sent nasty letters threatening Arthur Bishop's life.

A minute later a young rookie dropped Hunter off. The visitor was short, maybe five-six, but he was broad and thick. Tan pants over brown work shoes, a denim shirt in a brown jacket: a laborer's attire. His brown driving cap appeared just a bit lower on his forehead than McInnis would have liked, as though he were trying to hide his nervous blue eyes. He did not want to be here.

"Evening, Mr. Hunter," McInnis stood, walked around his desk and extended his hand. "What can I do for you?"

"You're McInnis?" Ignoring the hand.

"Sergeant McInnis, yes, sir." He left his hand out there another second before allowing the insult to stand and bringing it back to his side.

"You came by my house the other day." Hunter stood at the entrance to the office, as if afraid to enter. "I'm here to tell you to stay away from my wife and daughter. We have nothing to say to you."

McInnis let a few seconds tick past. "Very well."

Hunter contradicted himself by talking more. "You have some nerve saying something like that about us, about our girl."

"I never said a thing about your girl, Mr. Hunter. I'm sorry if others have."

"I just came here to tell you to stay away. And to see what kind of a man you are. A white man who spends all his time with the niggers." He shook his head. "Damn disgrace."

No one would dare talk to a white cop like that in any other circumstance. People acted differently around him, took liberties.

"Mr. Hunter, the kind of man I am is someone who doesn't let wrongdoing go unpunished. If I have any reason to think you or your family did anything to Arthur Bishop, then you will be seeing me again. So perhaps you should use a different tone."

"I didn't do anything to him." Hunter's voice retreated a notch. "No one in my family would do a thing like that."

Not even to defend your name, your family's honor? Isn't that why you're here?

Heavy footsteps descended the stairs. Hunter stepped back into the hallway, alarmed. McInnis heard the voice of Officer Dewey

Edmunds before he saw him, ranting, "If I have to replace another of these motherfucking flashlights . . . "

McInnis too stepped into the wide hallway and saw Dewey jogging to his desk. Dewey was so absorbed in his search for a working flashlight that it was another moment before he saw the unexpected white man, who was glaring at him.

"It's all right, Edmunds," McInnis said. "Grab a new light and get back to your partner."

Strangely, Dewey froze in place, as if he knew Hunter from somewhere.

Hunter shook his head, disgusted by the mere sight of this very dark-skinned man in a police uniform. McInnis felt an awkward, dual sense of embarrassment: at being linked to this profane Negro in Hunter's eyes, and at being linked to this angry white man in his officer's eyes.

Dewey started, "Sergeant, do you—"

"Get back on the street with Jennings," McInnis cut him off. He wanted to see what else he could get out of Hunter, and he knew the white man would clam up around Dewey.

Hunter's eyes were darting between them. In an unhealthy way. Like cornered prey.

Dewey, still not moving, said, "Sergeant, twenty-nine."

That number sent McInnis's hand to his sidearm by instinct. "Twenty-nine" meant *gun on the scene.*

McInnis kept the rest of his body still, his eyes on Hunter, who backed up another step. Now McInnis understood why Dewey had that look on his face: Dewey had seen Hunter's back when he came down and must have noticed a bulge in Hunter's belt.

Hunter started moving his right arm toward his back. That was more than enough, and McInnis drew his weapon, shouting, "Put your hands up, *now!*"

He could see in his peripheral vision Dewey drawing his weapon too. Hunter paused, a pause that McInnis could have used as justification for firing. The nervousness in the man's eyes was replaced by full-on terror.

Palms out, Hunter raised his hands. "Just keep him away from me!"

McInnis stepped up to Hunter, grabbed him by the shoulder, twisted him around and leaned him into the nearest desk. "Do not move." He cuffed Hunter's hands behind his back, then frisked him, coming away with a Colt .45 revolver. Whichever desk rookie had led Hunter down here without noticing the piece was going to get a serious chewing out later.

"I got a right to carry that!"

Forty-five wasn't the same caliber that had killed Bishop, but that hardly ruled Hunter out.

"The right to carry a gun into a *police* station?" McInnis nearly spat as Dewey lowered his own weapon. "You have any idea how stupid that is?"

"That's for my protection! I'd be crazy to come downtown at night without one!"

Dewey was shaking his head with disgust. McInnis thought for a moment, then pulled Hunter up by the shoulder, swung him around, and pushed him roughly into a chair.

"Sit."

"I didn't do anything, all right?" Hunter's cap had fallen on the floor, his hair mussed.

"You came down here to settle things with me the old-fashioned way, isn't that right? That's what the gun was for."

"No! Jesus, no! I came down to tell you what I just told you, that's all! For God's sake, I wouldn't shoot a cop!"

"Not even one who's a 'damned disgrace'?"

"Now you're just twisting my words. Having a gun in my pocket doesn't make me a killer."

"You were reaching for your piece," McInnis said. "We both saw it."

"Damn right," from Dewey.

Hunter nearly shouted, "Only because *he* showed up behind me! *He's* got a gun, don't he?"

McInnis pointed at Dewey, whose eyes were livid. "That man

is a police officer. You draw a weapon on an officer in the street, you can expect to be killed. You are a goddamn lucky man right now, you understand that?"

"Yeah, fine."

McInnis tried to wind himself down, think this out. His heart was pounding and he felt nearly dizzy, a delayed reaction.

"Any other messages you wanted to relay to me, now that you have my full attention?"

"No. Look, I came here to tell you to leave my family alone. The gun was just for my protection. I swear."

"Oh, he swears," Dewey said, shaking his head.

McInnis asked Hunter where he was the night Bishop was killed.

"I was home with my wife and daughter."

"Anyone else can vouch for that, other than kin?"

A fierce, "No."

Dewey interjected, "'No, *Sergeant*,' goddamn it."

Hunter took an angry breath, like he desperately wanted to talk back. The fact that he was cuffed and outmanned finally won out. "No, Sergeant."

McInnis didn't know what to believe about the dumb son of a bitch. Hunter had been acting squirrely from the start, but whether that was because he'd planned to shoot McInnis or whether it was just a response to being downtown at night, and then to being surprised by Dewey, was unclear. McInnis would have loved to throw him in jail, as carrying a concealed weapon into a police station was indeed illegal, but McInnis was loath to get pulled deeper into the scandal of the rape case, which an arrest would exacerbate. A white judge might even side with his "I was afraid of Negro cops" argument.

McInnis grabbed him by the arm and pulled him to his feet.

"I'm going to take the cuffs off and walk you to your car now, and then I'm going to watch you drive away." He could hear Dewey utter a note of disgust at this news. Yet he continued, "If I ever see you carry a weapon in a police station again, or in any Negro neighborhood, I will consider that ill intent and you'll spend time in jail. Understood?"

"Understood. Sergeant."

Dewey shook his head and said, "Sergeant, can I have a word, please?"

McInnis pushed the still-cuffed Hunter back into the chair as he and Dewey walked into his office, through whose window they could watch him.

Dewey spoke low enough for them not to be overheard. "Explain this to me, please."

"We arrest him for simply having a gun in his pocket and it'll be in the papers tomorrow. We'll have the captain on our ass for getting involved in the Higgs case." Which McInnis himself had instigated by visiting Mrs. Hunter the other day, an indiscretion he would pay for if this spiraled out of control, but he didn't want to tell Dewey that. "So you and I will quietly put this down in a report tonight, so it's on record in case anything else happens."

"Anything else happens?" Dewey raised his eyebrows. "I hope I *happen* to walk down the stairs at the right time then, too, Sergeant, and not a few seconds later, after he's put a bullet in you."

"We don't know that was his intent."

Dewey's flat expression wordlessly conveyed that he did not agree with this white view of reality.

"What?" McInnis asked, annoyed.

"Tell me he'd be a free man right now if he was colored."

"That's not the point."

"Then what is the point, Sergeant? *I'm* willing to get chewed out by Captain Dodd if that's what happens. I'll take that over letting a man come into the *colored basement* armed and getting away with it."

That was a direct challenge—not to McInnis's authority as sergeant, but to his willingness to take a stand against bullshit.

He took a breath. They were both charged up, him more so. He'd taken far more than his share of shit from Dodd and other white cops when sticking up for his officers over the years, so he didn't care for the implication that he couldn't take a little more.

Worse, he felt embarrassed that he'd missed the gun, and worried he'd made a mistake in visiting the Hunters.

None of that changed the fact that Dewey was right.

"Then we'll get chewed out together," McInnis finally said. He walked back to Hunter and pulled him up.

"Clarence Hunter, you're under arrest. Let's go upstairs and take some photographs."

"What?" Hunter's face went red. McInnis turned him around, leading him toward the stairs. "You said you were letting me go! You let *him* talk you into this?"

McInnis tightened his grip on Hunter's shoulder as he led him up the stairs. "I advise you to shut the hell up and concentrate on walking. People have a habit of falling down these stairs, real hard."

Only later would McInnis realize he'd never thanked Dewey for possibly saving his life.

29

STEPPING INTO A prison visiting room made Smith distinctly uncomfortable. He clutched his notebook like a life preserver, but he knew it couldn't save him from drowning, sharks, hurricanes, or Jim Crow law.

Even as a cop, he'd never enjoyed the few occasions when he'd stepped into the jail. As a mere civilian, it felt far worse. He knew how he looked to the white cops and prison guards: just another Negro unfortunate visiting family, no doubt, his bloodline forever infected by the taint of criminality None of those assumptions was true, yet his being here was a reminder that he was perpetually at risk of winding up on the wrong side of this divide.

He'd already been patted down, roughly. One guard had rolled his eyes at Smith's notebook as if surprised he could read. They wouldn't let him bring in his pencil, claiming it could be used as a weapon. He resisted making any pen/sword aphorisms and bade silent farewell to the pencil. They let him keep the notebook.

The white male guard escorted Victoria Bishop into the long narrow room. Victoria's hair was pulled back and she appeared every bit as forlorn as she had the last time he'd seen her, at her arraignment. Striped prison clothes, bags beneath her red-tinged eyes.

She folded her ringless hands on the table that bisected the room. Two-foot pieces of plywood afforded a tiny bit of privacy between them and the nearest couples. The room full of whispers.

"I'm not interested in speaking to the press," she said. "Normally I would tell you to call my lawyer, but since he's the one who said this was a good idea ... "

"I'm here beyond a reporting capacity, Mrs. Bishop. Some things have happened that make this personal for me too." He wasn't going to get into the FBI or the strange maybe-cops right yet. "I believe you're innocent, but I can't prove that. So if there's anything you could shed light on, I would love to hear it."

She watched him for a moment, suspicious. "Why do you believe I'm innocent?"

"I don't know, ma'am. An ex-cop's hunch, I guess."

"But you're a reporter now. You go based on verified facts, not just something a nice lady like myself says."

"I've been on the other side, the police side. I've seen with my own eyes how they put things on people even when they're innocent. Locking you up makes things easy for the folks in charge."

He'd gotten a bit of info from Deaderick: ballistics had determined that the .38 found in Bishop's house was probably not the same one that had shot and killed him. That wasn't ideal for the detectives' case against Mrs. Bishop, but at the same time, it didn't rule out her killing him with a different gun, then disposing of it. The lack of a murder weapon or other hard evidence might have been enough to let a white defendant off, but she had no reason to be so confident.

Smith needed more. He wished Mrs. Bishop trusted him, but he understood why she didn't. No one wanted to be in someone else's story, with other minds calling the shots, choosing the adjectives and arranging the objects into the subject's line of fire.

She asked, "What do you want to know?"

"Why did you lie to me about your having an affair?"

"Because it's none of your business."

"I'm sure it's hard, ma'am, but it would have looked better if you'd told the whole truth from the start. If there are any other secrets you've been holding back, because you were afraid maybe it wouldn't look good, I respect that, but you keeping them back will start to look less like a woman maintaining her privacy and more like a killer hiding a motive. So, please, can you tell me if either of you were involved in something dangerous, or had money problems, or anything else?"

She considered this for a while. Then she said, "He had no outstanding debts that I know of, beyond the standard workings of his business. There's always some loan or another, but nothing overly large or concerning."

"Can you tell me why you weren't at the Board of Commerce meeting the night he was killed?"

"Because I was an emotional wreck, if you must know. I wanted to be alone, and since Arthur worked so late every night, I figured being home was the best place. I hadn't realized a mundane decision like that would make me look like a murderer to some people."

"When you asked for a divorce, did you ask for money?"

"I asked for my fair share. Not as blackmail, but as my due as his wife of many years. Someone who endured loneliness," and now her eyes watered, and her voice thickened, "while he gave his entire life to that paper. I worked there, too, in the early years, without a salary. I helped build it up into what it is today."

"And Dr. Bridges . . . did he ask your husband for anything?"

"They never spoke. No, that's not true, they had met before, but they never spoke once I broke the news to Arthur. There is neither smoke nor fire there, Mr. Smith, I assure you."

"Do you think Morris Peeples had any reason to hurt your husband, ma'am? Or Celia Winters?"

"Celia?" She seemed alarmed by his change in tack. "Why on earth are you asking about *her*?"

"She's an interesting lady."

Mrs. Bishop sat up straighter. "You're embarking on what my husband would have called a fishing expedition, Mr. Smith. He always advised his reporters against those."

She still was only giving him so much. He needed to press harder.

"Ma'am, I'm sorry to say this, but at the end of the day, it won't matter how white your lawyer is or what firm he's from. You're taking a heck of a chance if this comes to trial. You don't just have city prosecutors to worry about. You need to worry about the FBI."

"What do you mean?"

"They broke into your husband's office. A few nights after he was killed. I was there. I think they broke into your house, too."

"What . . . what happened?"

He sketched a vague picture for her, not wanting to give her too much yet. "I don't suppose you'd know what it was they were looking for?"

"I . . . I haven't the foggiest notion."

"I'm thinking they were there for one of three reasons. Maybe they were investigating his murder, which I doubt, since that's not federal. Or, maybe they were investigating him for some other crime, which wouldn't reflect well on him. Or," and he floated a new theory, "maybe he'd worked with them."

"That is *ridiculous*. My husband never *worked with the FBI*." She ended her sentence with a whisper.

He paused. "Mrs. Bishop, are you absolutely sure he never met with them?"

A longer pause. "It's true that from time to time agents did *come* to the office, mostly during the war, to discuss the tone of certain stories. It was important to put forth a patriotic air, that sort of thing. But that's all." She was deploying wounded pride as a smokescreen, he thought, hoping he'd back down. He'd seen this behavior plenty as a cop.

"Ma'am, I'm really not fishing for something that will hurt your husband's reputation. I have no desire to tear a good man down." He paused. He'd only been guessing about Bishop being an FBI source, but he figured it was one possible reason they had sent an agent to his office. "But when an FBI agent points a *gun* at me, I become awfully determined to find out why."

She couldn't meet his gaze any longer. She waited a long moment, either to muster the strength or to arrange her words into a form that might mimic truth. "You need to swear to me you won't speak of this," she said quietly. "I don't want this in the paper."

"I swear it." Hand on his heart.

She took a breath. "He spoke to them sometimes. He didn't tell me at first, but one day I happened upon one of their ... meetings. He admitted it, but he excused it. He was only telling them about old colleagues who'd gone off the deep end, spouting that communist nonsense."

"Which he himself spouted once."

She looked surprised he knew. "That was long ago, before we knew each other. He'd admitted it to me when we first met, so I knew. Anyway, when he told me a few years ago that he was talking to the Bureau ..." She sighed. "I told him it was not honorable. Even disgraceful. So he told me about a couple of the people he'd ... *informed* on, and I agreed they were bad sorts. He claimed that justified it—he helped put away some potential bomb-throwers before they might do harm and set back our cause. In the process, he felt he was winning the Bureau as allies, which would dissuade them from ever trying to push the *Daily Times* around."

"Do you think he believed that?"

"Yes. But I didn't like it, and I told him as much. I thought he was being naïve, to think he could win their favor. They would only smell weakness, lean on him even harder. His going along with them would keep the paper in the government's crosshairs, forever."

"Bet he didn't like hearing that."

She laughed bitterly. "No. After I said that, he never told me what he discussed with them again. Said the less I knew, the better. But that only made me wonder, who else is he telling them about? I hadn't wanted to believe he was capable of that, but now that I knew it ..." A deep breath. "It did a lot to change the way I felt about him. You need to understand ... I hadn't just loved him, I had *adored* him. He was a leader, a success in a world that did everything it could to brand us as failures. But now ... he seemed like just another weakling who made bargains to hold onto what he had."

Her eyes teared up. She made a funny motion, and Smith realized she had instinctively reached for her purse to retrieve a handkerchief, then remembered where she was. Stripped of her purse and her dignity.

"Do you have any reason to believe your husband gave up Peeples to the FBI? Or Winters? Did they have reason to be angry at him for anything he'd done?"

She shook her head and said, "No." She was on the verge of breaking down. He'd pushed her as far as she'd go. He waited for her to compose herself.

It took a while. He felt cruel, manipulative. He hated this job sometimes. Like the other job.

"He was in Montgomery recently," Smith noted. "Is there any chance he was there to check up on the boycott, maybe see if any of his old, red friends were involved? Could he have been spying on the boycott for the feds?"

"I have no idea," she insisted. "He didn't tell me why he was there. And as far as I know, he doesn't know anyone involved in the boycott. But maybe, I suppose."

That day's paper had brought reports of a second Montgomery bombing, this time in the front yard of E. D. Nixon, a Pullman porter and the former president of the Alabama NAACP.

She added, "You asked the other day whether he may have been killed because of something he was working on. I don't know, but, as I told you, he was working on a memoir. I told you I didn't know where his memoir is, but ... I do have an idea. I didn't feel like saying this before, as it seems none of your business, but maybe ... " She shook her head. "He did have a place where he liked to hide papers he didn't want others to see. In the basement of the *Daily Times* building. There's an old custodial closet, where he kept a couple boxes of papers on a shelf, because his own office was over-crowded. I believe he'd been down there a lot lately because he'd come home with dust on the knees of his slacks, from crouching. Addie, our maid, complained to him about how he was ruining his slacks. Anyway, I would still warn you against going on any fishing expeditions, but *if* there is something secret my husband was working on, you'd be best served by looking in those boxes."

A white guard approached her from behind and told them their time was up.

~

The stairs leading to the *Daily Times* basement creaked with annoyance as Smith descended into the abyss. No light switch at the top of the stairs, and none at the bottom either. He walked slowly, blind, a hand above his head until he finally found what was either a drawstring or a terrifyingly thick spiderweb. He pulled and a light clicked on.

The basement was so messy it made the rest of the building seem neat, which was saying something. Boxes everywhere, a few stacks of old chairs, dusty signs advertising the *Daily Times*. He found the custodial closet, and there on the floor, beneath shelves holding boxes of industrial soap and sponges, he found two large cardboard boxes stuffed with notebooks and loose papers.

Good Lord. This will take weeks to read.

One at a time, Smith carried the heavy boxes upstairs to his office.

The notebook on the very top bore a title, *BREAKING THE STORY: A memoir.* Smith sipped his cold coffee and started reading.

The first few pages described a long-ago scene, the time the paper reported on a congressman's attendance at a lynching outside Atlanta. It had won the paper national acclaim but had not, alas, forced said congressman to step down. Smith wondered if this could be what Bishop had alluded to that last night, when he'd asked Smith about people who get away with murder.

In search of meaning, Smith turned the pages.

~

Early that evening, Smith drove his cranky Ford, which the mechanic claimed to have fixed, out to the secret Atlanta office of the Civil Rights Congress.

He had managed to get the police to run a reverse lookup of Celia Winters' phone number (Dewey had dodged Smith's calls, but luckily he had more than one old friend on the force, though he seemed to be running out of those). Barely a mile into the drive, already the Ford was making unhealthy sounds when idling at red lights. *Fucking mechanic*, Smith thought, ruing the thirty bucks he'd paid.

The address led him south of downtown to a modest, mixed business and residential area near, but not technically in, the Negro neighborhood of Summerhill. He passed a white elementary school, low-slung bungalows, a pharmacy, a locksmith, a carpenter's woodshop, and several dark buildings with For Rent signs. He could hear a freight train nearby, railroad tracks never very far away in Atlanta.

Maybe he should have waited until daylight, but he had a feeling these people kept unconventional hours.

He parked across the street and saw that the lights were indeed on. The building was an old wooden structure that looked like it had been a residence once then converted, like a doctor's office. Faded paint at the front suggested a sign once hung there advertising a business. He wondered how long they'd been renting the place.

As he got out and walked over, he noticed that one of the vehicles parked on the street had someone sitting in it. A red pickup, with a white man smoking in the driver's seat, and another man beside him. It unnerved him, but not enough to turn back to his car.

He knocked on the door. Blinds were drawn, but the lights shone through. After a moment, he saw a finger part the blinds, then the door opened.

"Can I help you?" The white lady from the photograph, decades later. Tall, only a couple inches shorter than him, with dark, graying hair pulled into a bun. She wore a green sweater over a gray flannel skirt. Reading glasses dangled from a cord around her neck.

"Are you Celia Winters?"

"I am. And you are?"

"I'm Tommy Smith, a reporter with the *Atlanta Daily Times*. I was wondering if I could ask you a few questions."

He heard a car door close behind him. Then another.

"What about?" she asked.

As he answered, he turned to the side to see what was happening on the street behind him. "Well, ma'am, I understand you were once a colleague of my boss, Arthur Bishop?" Two white men had gotten out of the red pickup. Two other men were coming from another car. "And as you've probably heard . . . "

He stopped himself when he saw that two of the men held baseball bats, and a third held something else—he couldn't tell in the dark, some box-shaped thing draped in cloth.

Bandanas covered their noses and mouths.

"Stay the hell back!" he shouted at them.

"Time for you to get the hell out of town, you red bitch!" yelled a man holding a bat.

Even though Smith could only see parts of their faces, they didn't seem to be the same men who'd knocked him out at the Bishops' house. Two looked to be in their late twenties, the others a generation older. Wearing workmen's jackets and boots, they didn't have the clean-cut look of FBI agents but could have been off-duty cops, or else random white enforcers here to roust the reds. How did they know the CRC was here, in an unmarked office?

The men had been walking quickly before, and now they charged forward.

Smith turned and saw that Winters was retreating into the building. He followed her; another second slower and she would have locked him out. He stumbled inside and she slammed the door, throwing a deadbolt that, Smith knew from experience, would not survive a few hard kicks.

A window shattered. Someone was taking a bat to the front windows—two down, one to go.

"Jesus!" Winters shouted. She glared at Smith. "Did you bring them here?"

"Of course not!"

They were standing in what used to be a parlor, since converted to bare-bones office space. Wood-paneled walls and two desks in the center of the room, messy with paperwork. A couple of crates on the floor, filled with more papers. A young, thin white man stood by one of the desks. Dark, slicked hair, horn-rimmed glasses, an expression of sheer terror.

"What's going on?" he asked.

"I warned you about this, Maury," she said, sounding more exasperated than panicked. She ran over to the phone and picked it up, probably dialing the police.

The first kick shook the door. Smith guessed that the second would do the trick.

The cops still hadn't returned Smith's guns. He'd been carrying a knife in his pants pocket, but that wasn't a great defense against bats.

"There a back way out of here?" he asked. Young Maury nodded, moving toward a narrow hallway. Smith grabbed Winters by the shoulder and told her, "You don't have time, let's go!"

She dropped the receiver, then shook off Smith's hand so she could grab a file from atop her desk. More windows shattered. Smith could see gloved hands reaching in, clearing the jagged pieces that were caught by the blinds.

"Now!" Smith shouted at her.

The second kick did indeed free the front door from its hinges, at least partially. It slanted to the side, the top left hinge slightly hanging on, the door on the verge of falling backwards onto the intruder.

Smith caught the scent of gasoline. *That's* what one of them had been carrying.

Smith, Winters, and Maury raced down the hallway, away from the sounds of splintering wood and shattering glass. Years ago, Smith had sat guard overnight in his sister's house when angry whites had gathered on the sidewalk, hoping to intimidate them into selling their home. No violence had broken out, but at least Smith had been holding a rifle. This was his first direct experience with a nightmare he'd heard about, read about, reported on, and woken up in the middle of the night thinking about: deranged white people invading.

His heart pounded but he tried to remember what he'd been taught, what he'd do if he still wore a badge.

"Do you have any firearms?" he asked.

"No!" Winters replied as Maury opened a door into a small kitchen. Smith drew his knife and scanned the kitchen for anything else sharp he could grab.

"Anyone out back?" he asked Maury, whose hand was already on the back doorknob.

Smith threw open what he hoped were utensil drawers, but found no other knives.

"I-I think we're clear," Maury stammered.

"If we hurry two blocks north," Smith said, "there's a big grocery store. Plenty of people around. We can find a payphone."

Smith could see that Maury was afraid to move, so Smith nudged past him, putting a finger to his lips for silence. Winters' eyes were steely and surprisingly calm, as if this had happened to her before. Smith opened the door and stepped out, looking both ways. An untended backyard, low winter grass, no fence. He didn't see anyone. He could hear voices and more violence from the front of the building, only a matter of feet away. He beckoned the others forward, then they started running.

Through another backyard, then past a house and into a road. He stuck his knife back in his pocket, mindful that a white neighbor might see him and call the cops on *him*. Maury was fast, keeping pace with Smith, but the much older Winters was lagging behind.

Another block and they reached Fulton, a wide four-lane road. A hundred yards to the right, Smith saw the grocery store. A steady stream of traffic was heading west out of the city. Feeling safe for the moment, the other two leaned on their hands, catching their breath.

"This happen a lot?" Smith asked them.

"Maybe not a *lot*," she said. "But I've been through worse."

"Who were they?" Smith asked. "Did you recognize them?"

"If I had to guess," she said, walking toward the grocery store,

"I'd say they were members of the Hunter family, or their friends and supporters."

"Has the family threatened you?"

"I didn't even think they knew who we were," she said. "Let alone where to find us."

"You've been snooping around the Higgs case," he said as they walked. Even though he was talking to her, he walked with Maury in the middle; Smith felt self-conscious to be walking with two white people in this part of town. All it took was one driver feeling like being a hero to the poor harassed white lady. "And they found out about it."

"The only way anyone in that family could have known we were here," she said flatly, "was if the police or the FBI told them we were."

Smith checked behind them to make doubly sure the white men weren't on their trail.

"Ma'am, I know this isn't the best time, but were you in town the night Mr. Bishop was killed?"

She stopped and gave him a disgusted look.

"You're right, this isn't the best time. I need to call the fire department before those rednecks burn our office to the ground. Then I need to figure out if there's any safe place in this god-damn city."

She turned and walked on with her young colleague, leaving Smith standing there.

"Mrs. Winters, we need to talk about Mr. Bishop."

"I'll call you after the dust clears," she called after him. He wanted to follow her, but could imagine how it would look for him to bark questions at a white lady who had tired of his presence. He called out his name to her, in case she'd forgotten it. Then he shook his head and swore to himself.

She was probably right about the cops or feds tracking her down, he figured. He'd read today that members of the CRC had been attacked in the past when working on trials in the South. If Atlanta cops had found out that the group was in town, they could have simply tipped off the Hunter family or some other self-appointed defenders of Southern order. That would have saved the cops the trouble of having to surveil the reds themselves and build a legal case against them. For Southern cops, it was always easier to choose violence and intimidation above actual law enforcement.

At the very least, Smith could report on what happened. But the idea of going back to their office to see if it was on fire yet was out of the question; he'd risk becoming a part of the story, in the worst imaginable way. He'd have to leave his car on the road, come back for it tomorrow, hope the white folks hadn't burned it too.

He walked toward downtown, keeping his eye out for a bus. By the time one approached, he smelled smoke.

30

"**DAMN, WE IN** the country already," Dewey said as he drove his Pontiac down sharply curving streets beneath oak branches gone spectral in the darkness. They hadn't passed a storefront or streetlight in miles, and seemed to be driving not just southeast but backwards in time, descending into a rural, isolated part of unincorporated DeKalb County. "I've heard horror stories 'bout places like this."

Boggs hadn't realized such areas existed so close to the city until he'd become a cop and sometimes had occasion to leave the protective bubble of Sweet Auburn, where he'd lived all his life. Atlanta was like that, city here and country there, two worlds superimposed on each other, awkwardly coexisting.

"Probably got a witch's cauldron in back," Dewey went on. "Scarecrow made outta human bones."

Dewey was trying to make light of it, but Boggs was filled with disquiet. A city boy, he didn't have many fond memories of trips to the woods, but he had plenty of bad ones.

He had dug into old personnel files and learned that Warren Floyd had been disciplined several times for excessive violence, including one suspension. With the unruly state of the Department back then, a suspension would have required quite a lot of violence indeed. Floyd was hot-tempered, people said, and likely would have been fired eventually had he not left for the war.

"Shoulda done this in the daytime," Dewey said.

"He *works* in the daytime," Boggs said. And then, as much to himself as to Dewey, he added, "We'll be fine."

Perhaps because Floyd made his living as a snoop, he himself had chosen to live far from prying neighbors. Dewey nearly missed the turnoff, as the street sign was almost completely obscured by thick privet bushes ten feet tall, even in winter. Floyd lived off an unpaved road, dirt dampened to mud by rains and then frozen into jagged ruts.

"Damn, I just had this girl washed and waxed," Dewey complained as the car bounced along. "Where the hell are we?"

Another half mile in, they hadn't passed a single house. Then they found the mailbox they were looking for, number 15, as if they had somehow passed fourteen invisible homes. No name on the box. Beside it an even narrower dirt driveway, a good two hundred yards long.

"Think he's the kind of fella shoots at traveling salesmen?" Dewey asked. His lights illuminated a green Buick with the familiar tags he'd run for Smith. It was parked in front of a small wood-shingled house that looked particularly squat beneath the copse of pine trees towering overhead.

Floyd's home seemed like a great place to get away from the city's hubbub, an ideal spot to lure wayward children unknowingly trapped in a cruel fairy tale, and a tidy location for burying bodies.

Dewey parked behind the Buick. The house's curtains were drawn. Amazingly, no dog barked. Seemed the kind of place a dog-owner would live. Maybe it had died recently. Maybe the owner ate dogs.

Tonight was Boggs's scheduled off night, and Dewey had traded shifts so he could be here too, so neither was in uniform. Boggs wore a dark blazer and Dewey a corduroy coat, and inside each they carried revolvers. They weren't about to knock on the door of a white investigator unarmed.

Dewey kept rambling, "I'll bet you lunch he answers the door with a gun."

"In his hand or just on display?"

Dewey thought. "In his belt or in a holster we can see."

"I say it'll be on him, but we won't be able to see it."

"That's a bet."

They got out, carefully studying the surroundings but seeing nothing that alarmed them. A grill along one wall, the outline of a small shed faintly visible in the moonlight. A barred owl issued its guttural comment, nocturnal rodents rustling through decomposing leaves. Otherwise this was some kind of quiet.

Dewey knocked on the door twice, but surely Floyd had already heard their car. Boggs, taller by a few inches, stood slightly behind Dewey, one hand resting on his belt out of habit.

"Who is it?" a voice demanded.

"Officer Edmunds and Officer Boggs, Atlanta Police Department."

The door opened and Warren Floyd greeted them not with a gun but an opened pocketknife. He held it in his right hand, and in his left was a foot-long chunk of pine he'd been whittling. Thin lengths of wood littered the floor behind him.

Floyd stood average height, with red hair that looked slightly darker on his unshaven cheeks. The long birthmark beside his right temple was his most notable feature. His gray tie had been loosened around his neck and he stood in his socks. Over a cardigan he wore a dark tweed jacket, unbuttoned, and it was hard to tell if he wore a shoulder holster.

Behind Floyd a mantel nearly overflowed with an army of small wooden statues from other whittling projects. Boggs saw tiny bears, horses, some oddly shaped humanoid figures. The sheer amount both impressive and disconcerting, as if they had stumbled into a lair haunted by small, paralyzed woodland spirits waiting to be animated.

Their creator observed, "You sure don't look like police officers to me."

"We're not on duty, sir," Boggs said. "We're just here as curious citizens. Curious as to why you were rifling through Arthur Bishop's place the other day."

"Now, who would that be?"

"A man who was killed recently," Dewey said. "Which means

that your being at his house, well, that's not only trespassing, it sounds a whole lot like someone trying to plant evidence."

Floyd slowly, carefully peeled off another strip with his knife, watching the blade as he did. "I don't know what you're talking about." Eyes back on them. "Y'all can run along now."

"We know you were there, Mr. Floyd," Boggs said. "You and two other men, driving that car right there."

Dewey added, "And we know you're aware of the law, or at least you should be, seeing as though you were a cop once. But maybe that's why you didn't last very long."

"I lasted longer than you will."

"I don't think so." Dewey stared him down.

Floyd smiled as he whittled another strip. "Ooh, you're a tough one, ain't you, shorty? Got a little Napoleon complex going."

"Nah, I ain't complex. I'm real simple. I simply don't like you."

"Mr. Floyd," Boggs said, "why don't you just tell us what you were doing, and then we can decide if it's worth our sharing it with the detectives on the case."

The white man's smile faded only slightly. "Because you're real chummy with them, huh? You and the detectives sit down together to plan out your moves? Play pinochle together on weekends? Separate as fingers but united as the fist and all that?" Boggs was surprised: Floyd was paraphrasing Booker T. Washington of all people. "You go and tell them whatever your heart desires. I'm sure they'll be fascinated. Be sure 'n tell 'em I said hidy. That is, if I don't talk to them first."

He nodded a farewell and reached with his wood-holding hand for the door. This time Boggs spied the handle of a gun from its perch in his shoulder holster.

Boggs asked, "So you're working with the detectives, then?"

Floyd's expression was flat. More annoyed than anything else. "Both of you get the hell off my property before I tell your superior officer that a couple of cops were here out of uniform, trying to provoke a licensed investigator who has every right to do his job."

Nothing more to say, Floyd shut the door.

They walked slowly back to Dewey's car. Shoulders high, trying not to look defeated.

"That went well," Dewey said.

They got in the car and Boggs repeated, "'Has every right to do his job.' But what job, for which client?"

"He planted something for Homicide. Must have."

"I just can't see it," Boggs said as Dewey started the car and began pulling out of the long driveway. "If Homicide wanted to plant something, they'd plant it themselves. They wouldn't ask some flunky rent-a-cop to do it for them."

"So someone else hired him? Who?"

"I don't know. Tomorrow I'll hit the library and read a whole lot of *Daily Times* to see which important people Bishop had ticked off lately."

"Meantime, you owe me lunch," Dewey said.

"No, *you* owe *me*. You called 'on display,' I called 'hidden.' The gun was hidden."

"But we *saw* it."

"It was still hidden."

Dewey laughed as they drove off, debating the exact definition of "hidden" and parsing the deeper meaning of how to keep anything truly concealed in this multilayered world.

31

LOOKING BACK ON it, McInnis would blame his stressful week on the scene he accidentally caused that night at the school parents' meeting.

He hadn't even wanted to go. Bonnie managed the domestic sphere and he took care of earning their keep—that had always been their arrangement. But she wanted him there because tonight they'd be discussing the school integration concerns.

More than a hundred parents of high schoolers and middle schoolers sat in hard plastic chairs in the cold auditorium. The attire on the men served as evidence for the varied classes here in Kirkwood: ties and topcoats on the businessmen, attorneys, and journalists; casual jackets and boots on carpenters, railway workers, and millhands. Fedoras and derbies alongside drivers' caps and wool hats.

The speakers, who had formed a special group to monitor legislative activity and work with the school boards, reminded the gathered crowd that the governor remained staunchly opposed to desegregation. The state legislature was busy debating different solutions; options ranged from simply ignoring the Supreme Court, to defunding any Georgia school that tried to integrate, to allowing a very small number of schools to admit an even smaller number of Negroes. That last idea was met with boos.

"We don't support that one either," said the speaker, Cassie Rakestraw. She had short blonde hair and seemed like the kind of vigorously energetic mother who embodied all the reasons McInnis never wanted to attend these meetings. "I'm just giving y'all the rundown."

She noted that some legislators had floated the idea of closing down all public schools, then reopening them as private, but taxpayer-funded, all-white academies.

"I see that as a doomsday option," Cassie explained. "As of now, our goal is to keep our schools the way they are—to save them, not close or alter them."

Applause all around.

Time ticked slowly past as the speakers noted the different ways parents could help, such as by writing letters to their legislators, or teaching their children valuable political lessons about the need to resist tyranny and oppression. Parents of high school seniors were invited to encourage their children to participate in the upcoming essay contest on "Why We Must Protect Our Southern Way of Life"; three winners would receive $250 toward tuition at any state university.

McInnis did have mixed feelings about school desegregation, but listening to these alarmed mothers narrate their battle plans for fending it off just gave him a headache. As a cop, the idea of defying a court's ruling went against his nature. He didn't always agree with judges—hell, he disagreed with one almost every day—but it was his job to obey their rulings. Whenever courts sided with defense lawyers and dismissed hard-won evidence on some technicality, he swallowed his pride and kept doing his job. That's what grown-ups did. The thought of all these civilians in their comfortable homes deciding that they were immune from the rule of law did not sit well with him.

Still, the vision of his kids in school alongside Negro kids did make him uncomfortable. Why? Perhaps it was no different than his earlier discomfort about Negro restaurants, and this too would pass. His seven-plus years of workplace integration felt like a success, but they'd also been challenging, and he had a hard time seeing kids negotiating the process as ably as he had. The possibility for disaster altogether too high. *Maybe* it could work out, but he found himself wishing some other generation could be the one this trial befell. He didn't want it to fall on his children.

No one at the meeting expressed such mild reservations, so he didn't dare voice them either. This was not the place to ponder nuance. He kept his mouth shut and waited for this to end.

↞

He'd finally met with Chief Jenkins that afternoon. Word tended to get around when a sergeant met with the chief, and he knew he had no shortage of enemies, so he hadn't officially scheduled a meeting. Instead, he'd casually dropped by when he was confident the hallway outside the brass's offices would be less crowded than usual.

"The other day I was visited by some Montgomery police detectives," McInnis explained after sitting down, "looking into dirt on Reverend King, Jr."

Jenkins, his hair gray and thick, sat tall in his chair as McInnis explained. The chief as always wore his formal dress jacket with epaulettes on the shoulders and stripes on the sleeve, his tie the same deep indigo. His walls were decorated with commendations, fishing trophies, photographs of Jenkins alongside mayors and a couple famous athletes. Out his third-floor window dark clouds gathered in the west.

"And two of my officers saw a couple of white men in jackets and ties staking out King Sr.'s house a few nights ago. They drove away before they could be questioned. I don't know if it was the Montgomery boys, but the plates were Georgia, belonged to one Jason Matthews, thirty-seven, no record. Maybe a friend of theirs, maybe unrelated."

"These Montgomery detectives still in town?"

"I told them they weren't welcome here, so I hope not."

Jenkins thought for a moment. "I'll let King know they're looking into his son. Man must be worried sick already."

"Given that the son's place in Montgomery's been bombed, should we be watching the father's place here?"

"I don't want to have officers stationed there. But do keep your details passing by more often than usual. I'll get some day shifts to do the same. If you see any other stakeouts, I want to know about it."

"Yes, sir."

"I've a feeling things are gonna get quite a bit messier before they get calmer. Way the son's pushing, he's getting folks mighty angry. The pitchforks are gonna start coming out of the woodsheds, and you and your officers will have a job on your hands. Let me know what you need."

McInnis moved on to the Bishop case. No one had yelled at him for arresting Clarence Hunter for bringing a gun to the station, yet. He imagined Dodd would chew him out for it soon. Hunter had spent a night in jail before being let out with a fine.

"There's one other thing: I had a run-in with the FBI." He'd been wondering how much of this to divulge, but he decided to roll the dice. He explained how Agent Marlon had broken into Bishop's office, and how that led to a meeting with Doolittle. "He told me this in confidence, sir, said he'd deny it if it came out. But he says Mrs. Bishop couldn't be the killer because his men had been following her, and she was at home all night."

"Why were they following her?"

"Wouldn't say."

A pause. "Well why in the hell would he tell you anything?"

"That's what I've been wondering. He alluded to the fact that we're going to be damn near swimming in federal agents soon. They think communists have their sights on Atlanta and we're fixing to be the site of a Bolshevik race revolution or something."

"Christ."

"He seemed to be asking me to be his personal spy into the Negro community."

"And you said . . . ?"

"I talked my way around it. He implied that he'd been giving the Department intelligence about radicals that wasn't trickling down to me, but should be. So in exchange for him directly telling me things, like Mrs. Bishop being innocent, he wanted me to keep him in the loop if I ever learned anything about reds. I made like I'd consider it, but he rubbed me the wrong way."

"Yeah, I don't trust Hoover's boys one bit. I'll talk to Doolittle."

"If you ask him about Mrs. Bishop, though, he'll know it came from me."

"So what do you expect me to do, keep quiet while a possibly innocent woman sits in jail?"

McInnis hated the layers of political and legal manipulation constricting him.

"I don't know that I believe him or not. I just need a little time to figure things out, and I'd rather do that while he thinks I'm an ally."

Jenkins tapped a pencil on his desk. "I can't have prosecutors moving to convict someone if we have or know of evidence that exonerates her. I will give you forty-eight hours to figure out whatever it is you need to, but after that time I'm getting Doolittle on the phone to air this out. Understood?"

"Yes, Chief."

McInnis rose to leave. He was nearly at the door when Jenkins added, "I understand Dodd's offered you a transfer. After all these years, you can let this cup pass from your lips."

"That's true."

"Do you plan to take him up on the offer?"

"I'm ... I'm still thinking on it, Chief."

Jenkins picked up some paperwork. "Do what you feel's best, for you and your family. Like I said, things are only going to get messier for a spell, and I'll need to have the right man over there." He put on reading glasses and started signing some forms. "Seems to me you're pretty good at it, and not everyone would be."

—⭒—

Back at the high school, Mrs. Rakestraw mercifully seemed to be closing things out after ninety long minutes.

"The values we pass on to our children are our most important legacy. We all know what mixing in schools would lead to. We absolutely cannot allow ourselves to be complacent, because that leads to defeat. Let's all agree to stay active and work with each other to keep our community safe. Thank you."

"I like that Cassie Rakestraw," Bonnie said as they rose to leave after the applause died down. "She's got spunk."

That's when McInnis recognized the name. *Rakestraw.* She had written one of those angry letters sent to Arthur Bishop right before his murder.

Mental gears, rusted from the interminable meeting, began to turn in his mind.

He still couldn't shake the idea that the fallout from Bishop's story about the rape case had something to do with his murder.

Parents were lining up to grab fliers and sign their names to petitions at tables up front. Bonnie got in one line and McInnis wandered through a crowd until he was close to Cassie.

"Hi, I'm Joe McInnis," he said after she'd finished a chat with another mother. He preferred to leave his job title or rank out of social conversations. You never knew how people might react. "Listen, I was wondering. In all your research into these issues, have you ever read the colored paper to get their perspective?"

She wrinkled her brow. That was, admittedly, a strange thing to ask another white person. "No. Why?"

"Is there any chance you wrote a letter to their editor recently?"

Her expression changed, her body visibly tightened. "How would you know that?"

"Well, ma'am, I'm a policeman. When I heard your name, I happened to remember that you'd signed—"

"My husband is a policeman too," she snapped, folding her arms. *Of course,* he realized too late; that explained why her name had seemed familiar when he'd seen the hate mail she'd written. He'd never worked with Officer Rakestraw, but he must have heard that name somewhere at the station.

He said, "That was a very . . . angry letter, ma'am."

"Are you *accusing* me of something?"

Other faces turned toward them.

"I'm not accusing anyone of anything, ma'am. I was just wondering how you'd even come across that story you were writing him about. Given it's not a paper folks like us ever read."

She looked him up and down, as if committing this new enemy's appearance to memory. "I read that story because a Negro raping a white girl is exactly why we're here. To protect our daughters, and our sons. Some smart-mouthed black reporter trying to blame it on the poor girl . . . " She looked away and shook her head, finding no words for Bishop's offense.

"Did you know that the man who wrote that story has since been murdered?"

"You're *questioning* me, aren't you? How dare you! What I might have written him is none of your business."

He was tempted to reply that it *was* his business, quite literally, but before he could say that, Bonnie appeared at his side.

"Is something wrong?" Bonnie asked. A small circle had opened around them, people watching.

"Just a misunderstanding," McInnis said.

Cassie looked at Bonnie and appeared to recognize her. Her expression switched, like she'd pulled a lever. McInnis was impressed by the way her winning smile snuffed out the hatred that had been burning in her eyes a second ago. She'd make a great politician.

"It's Bonnie, right?" Cassie asked. "Erin's mom? Your husband's a real charmer. I hadn't realized both our husbands are cops. They should get together sometime."

Then she turned her back on them, finding another audience. Bonnie gave him a questioning look. As they left, he heard in the mumbling of the crowd someone say, "He's the one works with the nigger cops."

✦

He fumed on the cold walk home.

Perhaps this was not the best time for him to finally tell Bonnie, "I've been offered a transfer out of the Negro neighborhoods. The new assignment's not great, but I'd oversee white officers."

She stopped and looked at him. "My goodness! That's wonderful news."

"I guess it is." He kept walking, too cold to linger on the sidewalk. Or maybe just wanting to avoid her gaze. Oak and poplar branches crisscrossed over the street, stripped of leaves and pointing accusations at each other.

"Are you kidding me? You should be ecstatic. What's wrong?"

Over the years, when he'd told trusted friends and relatives about his job, most had responded with a mix of sympathy and pity. They might have been wary of the idea of Negro cops, but they understood that McInnis's role was to paternalistically pass on his expertise so that the Negro officers could learn how to police themselves. He was crossing a line only so that they could keep order on their side of it.

That had changed since the schools case. Now people saw him as helping colored folk at a time when they were already emboldened and trying to take what did not belong to them. In every other white person's eyes, McInnis was working for the wrong side, giving aid and comfort to an existential threat.

"It's not a promotion," he explained, "just a different assignment. And I need to consider a few things. Like whether there are any strings attached. And why now. I don't know. I just need to decide if it's the right time."

He'd felt thrown by the compliment from Chief Jenkins that afternoon, that McInnis was the best man for the job. Had Jenkins really meant that, or was he just blowing smoke up McInnis's ass, and the chief simply didn't want to deal with breaking in a new sergeant in these tense times?

"Why on earth wouldn't it be? Joe! You can finally ... wash your hands of all this."

"Yeah. Clean the stench off me."

"I didn't mean it like that."

He stopped. "Just like they said in there. Being around the colored makes white people suspect. I get it. Get it all the time at work, get it at bullshit meetings like that, and now I get it at home, too."

She looked hurt. "What's gotten into you tonight? You used to complain all the time about how much you hated that assignment."

Was that true? Even if it was, he hadn't done so lately. Had he?

"You've *settled*, and you've settled for too long." Her breath hung white in the air before them. "You were the good soldier and you took the assignment, but now you've gotten used to it, used to thinking you don't deserve better. But you *do*." She put a gloved hand on his forearm. "You're one of the best, smartest, most honest cops they have. You shouldn't be ashamed to want more. You deserve to be out of there."

He didn't know what he deserved, what anyone deserved.

Bonnie hugged him, and maybe she'd meant it to be congratulatory, but it felt like pity.

She put her arm in his for the rest of the walk home, but with the cold and so many layers of shirts and sweater and jackets, he could barely feel her.

32

MORRIS PEEPLES' LAW degree had not earned him a fine address, Smith noticed. Or perhaps the communist liked being among the salt-of-the-earth working class, the honorable proletariat, the dirt poor. He lived on the first floor of a three-story subdivided house that was in need of a paint job and new shingles, the siding warped along the edges. It sat on a dead end block in Darktown— one of the many now slated for destruction. Smith himself had been called to this street many a time when he'd been a beat cop, intervening in domestic disputes turned violent, complaints from neighbors about strange sounds or smells upstairs, gunfire.

He carefully checked the street before making his approach. No one lingered in any parked car, no figures smoked in an alley.

He knocked on the door. Nearing six o'clock, the sun had set, the lampless street dark. His Colt .45, which he'd finally gotten back from the police that morning, was nestled in a shoulder holster concealed by his jacket—after his incidents at the Bishops' house and at the Civil Rights Congress office, he wasn't going unarmed.

"Who's there?"

"It's Tommy Smith, *Atlanta Daily Times*."

"I am not interested in conversing with you, sir."

"Please don't make me talk to this door, Mr. Peeples. It doesn't look like it could handle a hard stare. I just need to ask you a few quick questions."

"I do not have any answers."

"Please, Mr. Peeples. I'm trying to help you."

The door opened, barely. Enough for Smith to see the handle of a revolver sticking out of the old lawyer's pants. Peeples rested one hand upon the gun and kept the door from opening any further with the other.

"I have asked you to leave. I have not granted you permission to cross my threshold. Even if you were still a policeman, I am aware of my rights."

Smith stepped back and held his hands up as if the gun was pointed at him, hoping to show he wasn't a threat. He'd come here because he was tired of dancing around the subject of communism and whatever the hell Bishop had done in the past, or the present.

"I was just wondering if you might have any idea why the FBI would break into Bishop's office after he was killed."

The lawyer's face had been a mask of rage, but it softened to something more vulnerable. "Jesus. I warned you, didn't I?"

"You didn't straight out warn me about anything specific, Mr. Peeples. Just implied a whole lot and lectured me about the history of policing." He slowly lowered his hands to his sides. "Though you did say we were being watched. So I thought you might like to know you were right about that."

"You thought I might *like* it? Oh, I am over*joyed*." He opened the door wider. "Come in and stop braying on my doorstep."

Smith followed him inside. Peeples closed and bolted the door. A small parlor, a threadbare sofa and a wooden chair topped by a thin cushion. A coffee table held three mugs, and something about their positioning and the floating circles of old cream made it look less like Peeples had recently had guests over and more like he just never cleaned up after himself. Smith counted at least six stacks of books along the room's periphery, and a pile of papers and folders on the coffee table. He'd cooked fish for dinner.

"Don't sit down, don't make yourself comfortable," Peeples commanded, his gun still in his pocket. "Just say whatever it is you want to say and then leave."

"Have the police visited you yet? Or the FBI?"

Headshake.

"Sir, I don't believe Mrs. Bishop is guilty. If I can figure out what the FBI was doing in his office, I'm hoping that'll help me figure out who really killed him. I'm wondering if you could help with some of that, given how well you knew him."

"Is this for your newspaper? Some sensational story you're to write?"

"No, sir. This is for Mrs. Bishop. And for Mr. Bishop. You told me before that you were supposed to meet with him but you didn't, but you didn't have an alibi. Is that true?"

"Yes. I was here, working alone, as I often am. As I am tonight." He extended his hand to display the lonely scene before them. "It's not very glamorous, and no, I have no witnesses who can vouch for my ceaseless endeavor for a better world."

"Why couldn't you meet with him that night?"

"A case I was working on was rescheduled for the following morning, so I needed to change my plans and prepare for it. *That* you can probably verify with the Fulton County docket, if you don't believe me. Now what's that you said about the FBI breaking into his office?"

"I was there, scared the agent away. And I know someone else, possibly FBI but maybe not, was in his house right after his wife was arrested."

"The police, surely."

"No, sir. The police had come and gone, and then another group showed up. No badges. Wouldn't give their names. Whatever they were looking for, I have no idea. I was hoping you would."

Peeples sighed. "I told you before: Arthur and I had our disagreements over the years, but I have no desire to drag his name through the mud."

He'd said that at the cemetery. At the time, Smith thought communism was the mud. Now he knew differently.

"You mean, you don't want people knowing Bishop worked with the FBI."

The lawyer's voice was slow, resigned: "I don't know what you're talking about."

"He talked to them. Gave them names."

"I will not confirm anything."

"Maybe he named you, or one of your friends?"

"I will not . . . " and Peeples sat down. Leaned back in the chair, stared at the ceiling. "Jesus. You have no idea what it's like. To see men crushed because of what they believe in. To see them jailed for things they *said*. To see hard-working men and women lose their jobs, become unemployable, because what they say is incorrectly considered *dangerous*." Much as he'd claimed not to want to get into this, he clearly needed to vent, needed a witness to his anguish. "I wish I could make you understand. But I don't have that kind of energy anymore."

Ever since Mrs. Bishop had told Smith about her husband talking to the feds, Smith had realized that the killer could have been someone Bishop had betrayed. Or someone he was *about to* betray. Or someone who feared Bishop might *one day* betray.

"You need to tell me," Smith said, "who all he named."

"How would I know? *I* don't work with the FBI. I haven't a clue."

"Then how do you know he ever named names?"

"When enough lives are destroyed by a storm, you look for the epicenter. Too many people who'd once been close to Arthur have found themselves afoul of the government."

"Please, tell me who those people are. Mr. Peeples, sir, his wife could get the chair unless I can prove—"

"I'm sorry. She's a lovely woman. Hopefully she can hire an attorney more skilled than myself. But I have lost enough, and my friends have lost enough, that I am not going to sacrifice anyone else on the altar of Arthur Bishop's ego."

"Do you know why he went to Montgomery a week before he died? Was he spying on the boycott for the FBI? Did he know anyone involved over there?"

Peeples threw up his hands. "I have no idea. *I* don't know any of the people involved, if that helps. Hard as this might be for some to believe, the boycott does not appear to be a communist plot. Good God, I know some white folks think that, but I hope *you* don't."

"Of course not."

"So maybe Arthur simply went there to cover it."

Bishop had told Smith he had not been covering it. Maybe he'd lied.

"So what was it you were going to talk to Mr. Bishop about that night," Smith asked, "if you hadn't canceled? Anything to do with Celia Winters and the Civil Rights Congress?"

Peeples shook his head, but it seemed less like a denial than a partial surrender. "My God, you are one persistent son of a bitch. I would admire that if you weren't so annoying."

"Sir, what would it hurt to tell me?"

Peeples sighed again, exasperated. "Look ... Arthur and Celia were old friends, but they'd become enemies. I tried to tell Arthur that they both wanted the same thing, rights for Negroes, only they had different ways of going about it. Celia's way was to find particularly egregious cases where Negroes were trampled by Jim Crow, and use those cases to raise awareness. They did that in Mississippi with the Willie McGee trial. They considered that a success, because they raised a lot of money and made McGee a household name. To Arthur, though, what mattered was that McGee still got the chair. He *hated* the Civil Rights Congress for 'using' a suffering Negro like that."

"And he was afraid they were going to do the same thing with Randy Higgs, right?"

"Exactly. Arthur couldn't abide the idea of the Civil Rights Congress swooping into his own backyard and using it as the backdrop for their communist agenda."

Smith nodded. "That's why Bishop wrote his story about the case. He usually didn't want to touch those kinds of stories. But he wrote it hoping to pressure APD to drop the case, or at least coerce the plaintiff into confessing that she'd made it all up. That would have kept the case from ever going to trial."

"Thus depriving the communists of their next rallying cry, yes."

"I know Winters is here in town—I saw her the other day." He chose not to mention the attack or the arson. "Do you know if she'd met with Bishop?"

"I don't know, but I'm the one who told him she was here." He sighed. "It's all my fault. I was afraid Arthur would use his editorial column once again to slander the Civil Rights Congress. Despite everything I've been through, I still don't enjoy seeing one old friend publicly attack another. So, yes, I met with Arthur a couple weeks ago and politely requested he bury that old hatchet, that he stop attacking the CRC. Apparently, my request had the opposite effect, because it only alerted Arthur to the potential importance of the Higgs case."

This explained Peeples' orneriness, Smith realized. In addition to his well-won suspicion of all reporters, Peeples felt guilty. He feared he had accidentally set in motion events that left one of his oldest friends dead.

"The Civil Rights Congress must have been sore Bishop was trying to steal their thunder," Smith said, "trying to end the case before they could use it."

"Perhaps. But they're not *murderers*. I would advise you not to share your fellow Americans' obsession with communists."

Smith thought about the bourbon in Bishop's office, the close range from which he'd been shot. McInnis had let slip that the detectives suspected a woman had shot him; they had zeroed in on Mrs. Bishop, but what if it had been a different woman?

"Have *you* met with Winters since she came to town?"

"I've told you enough."

"You said he and Celia were friends from way back, but . . . " Smith recalled Farley's description of the avant-garde's time in Moscow, the romance and quarrels, *everyone sleeping with the wrong people*. A revolutionary time when all the old taboos faded. Is *that* what the feds had on Bishop? "Is there any chance they were more than that?"

"Let's not go there."

Mrs. Bishop had recoiled at the mere mention of Celia Winters. Was that because she was a red, or her husband's former lover?

Smith pressed, "Were Bishop and Winters lovers over there? It ended badly, and that's part of what really turned him against the reds?"

"How is this relevant?" The hurt in Peeples' eyes turning to anger. Smith had spoken the unspeakable. "As I told you before, I don't want old, unfounded gossip to harm Arthur's reputation. Now, I've been more than generous enough." He looked defeated, almost ill, as he pointed at the door. "Our conversation is over."

He was on foot again as he left, as his car had been towed for being parked illegally outside the CRC's office and he'd been too busy to get it back. He'd been outside less than a minute when he heard a footstep, more the scrape of a sole against the sidewalk, then he was hit in the head by something very hard.

Numbness erased his legs. He caught himself on the sidewalk by his palms. A second later he could feel his knees again, the coldness of the sidewalk through his pant legs.

Someone kicked him in the stomach.

"Have I broken any bones yet?" a voice asked. No, but the next kick, in the ribs, did. "Then we'd be even."

Adrenaline, fear, rage, pain, years of push-ups and weights and boxing, plus memories of seeing the bodies of men who'd been beaten to death: all of that combined to propel Smith from the ground. The right side of his midsection felt crumpled; he couldn't stand up straight, yet he charged into his attacker and pushed him back. He reached into his jacket for his gun.

Before he could grab it, another blow found the back of Smith's head.

Two men, he'd later put together when trying to make sense of it. Another thing that didn't make sense: he hadn't fallen down despite the second blow to his head, despite his legs giving out again. Whoever had struck him there (with a billy club? a brick? a safe?) had wrapped an arm around Smith's neck.

The person in front grabbed Smith by the hair, as Smith's hat had fallen off, and pulled his head up. It was the FBI agent from before, Talbot Marlon. His right hand in a cast.

"But I don't aim to be just *even* with a nigger."

He let go of Smith and punched him in the face. Aiming for the nose, probably, but Smith's head had slumped again. Marlon reached into Smith's jacket, relieved him of his weapon.

"Well, well. This might come in handy later."

A second punch, then the man in back released Smith, who fell. This time his palms weren't able to catch him. He hit the ground hard.

"Hey, I got a twist on that joke," Marlon said to his unseen assistant. "What's black and white, and red all over?" He filled the pause between Q and A with another kick to Smith's ribs. "A colored reporter after I'm through with him!"

Another kick. Smith tried to roll himself into a protective ball. He tensed every muscle, as if that could protect him. Another kick. He felt one of his fingers snap.

"Stay the hell out of our way, Tommy. Stay the hell away, or next time it's a bullet."

"Lights," the other voice observed. Smith would hate himself later for the fact that he didn't get a single look at the second man, couldn't even remember if he'd sounded as young as Marlon or maybe a senior agent. "Let's go."

"Do you understand, Tommy?" Marlon didn't want to stop. Enjoying this too much. Another kick.

Smith said that he understood.

Another kick for goodbye.

As they walked away, Smith lost consciousness just as he heard Marlon observing to his accomplice how strange Negro hair had felt.

PART THREE

33

MCINNIS WAS HOME reading the newspaper the next afternoon when the phone rang.

"Sergeant McInnis, this is Warren Floyd," the man said. McInnis didn't recognize the voice, though the name was familiar somehow. "Sorry to bother you at home like this, but I'm calling about an incident regarding two Negroes who claimed to be officers of yours."

"What happened?"

"Well, I'm a licensed private detective. These boys came by my house a couple nights ago, Boggs and Edmunds, though they weren't in uniform and didn't bother showing me any badges or ID. Honestly, it was hard to understand what it was they were saying—you ask me, they'd had a few drinks first, kind of slurring their speech. But I was left with the impression they were threatening me," then he chuckled, "or trying to."

"What exactly do you mean?" He certainly caught the "boys," but didn't want to correct the man until he heard more. The idea of Boggs being drunk seemed hard to imagine; Atlanta cops were forbidden from drinking, and though McInnis knew plenty of white cops who partook, the Negro officers knew damn well that any indiscretion could get them fired. Preacher's son Boggs was the last person McInnis expected to catch with booze on his breath.

"Well, I won't lie to you," Floyd said, a phrase that always set off alarms in McInnis's head, "it so happens I had some business recently in a Negro neighborhood. Nothing I'm not empowered to do thanks to my license. But they were all huffy that a white detective like me would enter 'their territory,' as they said. Since you're their superior officer, I figured you'd like to know they were throwing their weight around. I don't think intimidation is a good habit for officers to be having."

"No, it's not, Mr. Floyd. Though I think I'd like to hear their side of the story first."

"Oh, you go ahead and do that. Now, I know I could file a complaint with the Department, go through official channels and all, but I imagine you already have your hands full with a group of unruly Negroes over there, so I don't see any reason to make you look bad by letting *your* superior officers, like Captain Dodd, know that your boys are running amok. I figured I could just reach out to you like this, so you could handle it quiet. Your boys need to be reminded that private detectives like myself have a right to do our job."

McInnis hated him. Hated the implied threat. He wondered how well this fellow knew Dodd. "If you really do want to file a complaint, Mr. Floyd, you know where to find the station."

"What's that?" Floyd chuckled again. "You think you can call my bluff?"

"I'm not calling anything. Now, I don't suppose you'd care to tell me what exactly it was you were doing in a Negro neighborhood that allegedly angered my officers?"

"Afraid not, Sergeant. Sure you understand, us private dicks need to play things close to the chest. But I'll thank you in advance for talking to your boys and telling them not to interfere from here on out. You have a good day."

***

The only time McInnis saw his kids was the short window between school's end and when he left for work, at 5:30. Generally speaking, these were not calm hours. Even so, he was taken aback, not long after his call with Floyd, when the front door was thrown open so hard it slammed against the wall.

"I said I'll be fine!" Jimmy shouted.

"I'm just trying to *help*!" replied Erin, his younger sister.

McInnis stepped into the parlor to see why all the commotion. Jimmy had been rushing to the kitchen but he stopped when he saw his father. Jimmy had blood on his upper lip, trickling from his nose, and a purple bruise around his left eye. The knuckles of his right fist were bloody, his shirt ruined with stains.

"Jesus. Are you all right?"

"Yes, sir."

Bonnie came downstairs and gasped. Erin backed up a step while Bonnie tended to Jimmy, asking him what happened, was he hurt, who did this.

"It's not as bad as it looks. I'll be fine."

Bonnie had Erin fetch some ice in a cloth while McInnis asked Jimmy, "What happened?"

"It was . . . the same thing as before. We were off school grounds, like you said. Just a few blocks away, but they cornered me. I had no choice."

McInnis had told Bonnie about Jimmy's previous brawl but had not mentioned the fact that Jimmy had been called a "nigger lover."

"What has gotten *into* you?" she asked him.

"I'm not gonna let them get away with calling me that," Jimmy insisted. "Dad said I should stand up for myself."

Erin brought Jimmy ice wrapped in a cloth, and Bonnie led him into the bathroom to get him cleaned up. McInnis stewed in the parlor.

Minutes later, Bonnie returned as Jimmy stayed in the bathroom.

"I know boys will be boys," she said, "but two fights in a week?"

"I can talk to the other parents," McInnis said.

"I know what they've been calling him," Bonnie said. "Why did you tell him not to tell me that? We aren't supposed to keep secrets from each other."

"I didn't want you blowing it out of proportion."

"What, blow the fight out of proportion, or what they're calling him?"

"Either."

"This, Joe, *this* is why I can't believe you're even *considering* not taking that transfer." She pointed at the bathroom door. It was shut, so hopefully Jimmy couldn't hear them. "Do you think this would happen if you weren't working with Negroes?"

"I have a job, so I do it."

"But you don't have to do that job anymore. You can leave."

He searched for words. He hadn't said he *wasn't* going to take the transfer, only that he'd wanted to think about it. Yet she was acting as if that was tantamount to insanity.

"It's not Dad's fault," Erin said. She had silently emerged from the kitchen, half-eaten apple in hand.

"Excuse me?" Bonnie snapped at her.

Erin stared at the floor. McInnis told her, "This isn't a discussion for you, young lady."

"It's just . . ." Erin kept her eyes down as she fumbled for words. "It's not on account of Dad's job, it's on account of Tessa."

"Who is Tessa?" McInnis asked.

The next voice was Jimmy's, booming out of the bathroom. "Don't you say another goddamn word!"

Bonnie's jaw fell at the cuss. Before she could scold Jimmy, McInnis asked Erin again, "Who's Tessa?"

Erin's voice shrank. "A girl he likes. A colored girl."

"*What*?" husband and wife said in unison.

Jimmy charged in from the bathroom, too late. "Don't listen to her! She's just gossiping—"

"About what?" McInnis demanded. "Who's Tessa, young man?"

Jimmy thought long and hard. Lowered his voice. "She's just a girl I talk to on the way to school some days."

"A colored girl?" McInnis asked.

"She waits for her ride out there alone and I . . . joke around with her. That's all."

"How are you even crossing paths with a colored girl?" Bonnie asked, confused. No Negroes lived near them; the closest colored neighborhood was a good mile away.

"She catches a ride to her high school outside the five-and-dime on Oakview, where her dad works," Jimmy explained. "Her uncle picks her up on his way downtown. It's easier for him to get her there than at her house."

"You seem to know an awful lot about this girl," McInnis observed.

Jimmy looked down. "We just talk, is all."

"They talk a *lot*," Erin said. "And they joke a lot."

"I said, can it!" Jimmy yelled, stepping toward her.

Erin pleaded to her parents, "They call him a nigger lover because he's all moony-eyed around her, and—"

"Shut up!" Jimmy stepped forward and pushed her to the ground, hard.

Bonnie shouted at Jimmy, and he froze there as if amazed at what he'd done. McInnis stepped forward, grabbed his bloodied son by the shoulders, and steered him into the hallway. They could hear Erin crying behind them while McInnis pushed Jimmy roughly against the wall. Family portraits bounced on their nails, misaligned.

"Is that true? Or are you calling your sister a liar?"

He hadn't manhandled his son like this in years. Jimmy was his height now, though hardly the experienced brawler the sergeant was.

"Have you been carrying on with a colored girl? And out in public, where anyone can see?"

"I haven't *done* anything," Jimmy whimpered. Eyes wide with fear.

"Maybe not yet, but you're working your way up to it?"

"You told me it was okay." Tears in his eyes now.

"*What?*"

"You said they're just folks."

He slapped Jimmy across the face, open-handed. Jimmy slunk down the wall into a crouch.

"Don't you *dare* try and twist my words around!"

Jimmy sniffled. "You said only white trash would say—"

"I told you white trash is who *says* 'nigger lover,' but that doesn't mean you have permission to *flirt* and carry on with a colored girl!

Are you out of your mind? You have any idea what could happen to you, or her?"

"Joe, stop it," Bonnie said, her voice far calmer than anyone else's.

He held out his palms to show he wouldn't touch Jimmy again. "I surely did not raise a son so stupid as to not know that. You knew what you were doing."

Jimmy shook his head, face red, tears running down his cheeks. McInnis could see that nothing else he said would sink in, so he turned and left the hallway, wondering how his family had come unhinged.

✦

He would later reflect on how well his son had played him the day he'd gotten into his first fight. Jimmy had claimed at the time that he'd been teased because of his father's job. An expert move indeed: the thought that Jimmy had swung at a bully not just to defend himself but to defend his father's honor had sent an unmistakable bolt of pride through McInnis. Blinding him to the true reason for the fight.

He stood in the front yard, seething, trying to regain control of himself.

He wondered how Jimmy and Tessa could have possibly flirted, or even spoken, for so long without some busybody neighbor reporting back to him or Bonnie. That's what neighbors did for each other, right? The only reason no one had told them, he realized, is because the neighbors already saw the family as beyond hope. The McInnises had fewer friends than they used to, socialized less. He liked to think that was because he worked nights, but in his heart he knew it was because of whom he worked with.

The McInnis family could not be trusted.

He paced in the yard, too angry to go back inside yet. A car drove down the road and he recognized the driver as an old man who lived around the corner. They made eye contact but neither of them waved as the car drove past.

After roll call that night, Boggs and Dewey stood in McInnis's office, looking distinctly uncomfortable. He'd sent their partners, Jones and Jennings, out together so he could talk to these two alone.

He sat in his chair but had made a point of dragging his guest chairs out of the room before they got here so they'd have to stand. He paused for a moment, letting them steep in their guilt, and waited until the sounds of the other officers heading out receded.

"Mind telling me what you two were up to on your night off?" No answer. Sheepish looks. "Anything that would explain why I got an angry call this afternoon from Warren Floyd?"

"Sergeant," Boggs said, "he broke into Victoria Bishop's house just a few hours after she was arrested. Him and someone who works with him. We wanted to know why, so we asked him."

"Where did you hear about the break-in?"

Boggs waited, and his eyes turned toward Dewey, who said, "Tommy Smith called me and asked me to run the tags of the car driven by the intruders, and I did."

"You ran tags for Smith? For a newspaper reporter?"

"Yes, sir. I realize it was a mistake."

"I'm glad you *realize* it, Officer. I'm glad you're not such a fool that you thought running tags for civilians was actually *allowed*. Jesus. Smith is not a cop anymore. Cops do not get privileges for life. If you'd like to learn more about exactly how few privileges ex-cops receive, I can make that happen for you."

"I'm sorry, Sergeant."

"Christ." He shook his head. First his family, now his officers. Everything that was supposed to be within his control was spiraling beyond it into chaos. "And you stormed over to Floyd's house, what, to try and intimidate him?"

"We certainly weren't intimidating to a man like that," Boggs said. "We were just there as private citizens, discussing a private matter. We didn't break any rules doing that."

McInnis pinched the bridge of his nose, where his headaches usually set up beachheads, sending their troops marching across his skull.

"I swear, Boggs, when you talk like that you remind me of my own kids trying to weasel out of trouble. In uniform or not, you were hardly discussing a *private* matter. You were talking police work. And I'm not so much interested in the letter of the law here as I am by the fact that two of my men are out freelancing like that." He paused, then planted an index finger on his desk. "You should have come to me first."

"Yes, sir," Boggs said, and Dewey echoed him.

"I know I'm not perfect, but I'd like to think I've earned your trust over the years."

It appeared to take them a moment to realize that he wasn't just angry. He was insulted, even hurt, that his subordinates had conspired behind his back.

"I'm sorry, Sergeant," Boggs said. "We do trust you. We should have come to you."

He wasn't sure he believed Boggs, if they really trusted him at all. Just another white man playing by obscure, unknowable rules. Perhaps he was wrong when he thought he had made progress here. His son kept secrets from him, his officers kept secrets from him. He'd failed at both jobs.

"If either of you ever runs a tag for a civilian again, and if you even think of throwing your weight around like that off the clock, I will have you suspended. Understood?" They said they did. "When you have a problem with someone, for God's sake, come to me. Don't go sneaking around like skunks. I've stuck my neck out for you I don't know how many goddamn times, but I will not stick up for men who abuse their positions."

He told them not to share anything else they'd learned with Smith: not Floyd's name or what he did for a living. Smith was a civilian, period, and he would be kept in the dark.

Then McInnis told them what he'd learned when he'd looked up Floyd's file a few minutes ago: Floyd was an ex-cop, four years

McInnis's senior. Their paths hadn't crossed much. Floyd had left the force, voluntarily, soon after the anti-corruption sting that McInnis had led. That kind of timing made him wonder if Floyd had been a dirty cop then, too, one who had been fortunate enough to escape the probe unscathed, and who had decided to get out before his luck expired.

McInnis wondered aloud, "Why in the hell is a private eye breaking into the home of someone who'd just been arrested for murder? Who's Floyd working for?"

Boggs floated the theory that Floyd had planted Bishop's murder weapon in the house, or some other false evidence that might implicate the widow.

"But Homicide hasn't mentioned any big discoveries in that house," McInnis said. "There's got to be something else." He was troubled by the parallels between what the FBI had done in Bishop's office and what Floyd had done in Bishop's house, but he didn't yet want to share what Doolittle had told him in confidence.

"Maybe the Hunter family hired Floyd to teach Bishop a lesson," Dewey offered.

"Or to look through Bishop's files to find something incriminating," Boggs said.

"I don't know," McInnis told them. "I'm not a big fan of the Hunters, but ... I have trouble seeing it."

"Not even after Hunter came down here with a gun?" Dewey asked. "And not even after what happened to those communists?"

No arrests had been made for the fire at the Civil Rights Congress's secret office, which had occurred in a part of town that only white officers patrolled. From what McInnis had gathered, white cops had known about the arson in advance; they'd even notified the fire department to be ready, not to protect the building but to keep the blaze from spreading to other houses. Which meant white cops had either been the arsonists themselves or had tipped off the arsonists on where to find the communists so they could literally smoke them out of town. Clarence Hunter might have been one of the arsonists; he'd been released from jail the night before, so a like-minded cop could have passed him the information, knowing what he would do with it.

Doolittle, McInnis realized, had tried to sick him on the Civil Rights Congress first, by giving him Celia Winters' name and office address. When McInnis didn't take the bait, Doolittle turned to other cops.

"Sergeant," Boggs spoke cautiously, "I don't think we should underestimate how angry and irrational the Hunter family might be in a case like this."

"I'm not."

But was he? He realized how he looked then, a white man refusing to believe the worst in other white people. It made him defensive, questioning his own reactions and motives.

He asked, "If they had the Attorney General suing the paper, why send private eyes too? *After* Bishop was killed? And for that matter, why kill him? Why sue him *and* kill him?"

"Maybe they wanted to see him dead *and* kill his business," Dewey said. "Sends a heck of a message, doesn't it?"

McInnis still didn't buy it. He hadn't told them about Doolittle's tip that Bishop's wife was innocent; he still wasn't sure whether he believed the fed's story.

"Give me a second," he told them, fishing inside his desk for Doolittle's card.

Boggs and Dewey exchanged glances while McInnis dialed the number and asked the receptionist to patch him through to Special Agent Doolittle. He hurriedly ran through the pleasantries with Doolittle, then asked, "There's something I need to know about how you boys operate. Have y'all ever hired Pinkertons down here? Or ex-Pinkertons?"

"God, no." The G-man sounded offended by the suggestion. "Mr. Hoover would never allow that."

"Not once?"

"I've been with the Bureau since '42, and in that time I have never heard of us contracting work like that. *We* are the best at our jobs. We would never hire someone else. Why do you ask?"

"I've got a private dick sticking his nose someplace I don't want him. I couldn't help wondering if it had anything to do with you boys."

"I assure you, it doesn't. But why would you think it? Care to tell me any more?"

"Not right now, no."

"All right. Are you any closer on the Bishop case?"

He still didn't understand why Doolittle cared. If the G-man wanted to see the widow exonerated so badly, he could just tell Homicide that his agents could vouch for her alibi. Why was he giving McInnis just enough information to realize that justice was not being served, but not enough information to serve it?

McInnis played dumb by asking, "You mean, the murder case for which detectives have already arrested their suspect?"

"Yes. That one."

"No. But if you'd care to offer any help, I wouldn't say no."

"I did help you. That ball's in your court, Sergeant. Have a good day."

McInnis hung up and relayed Doolittle's side of the conversation to Boggs and Dewey—at least, the parts he wanted them to know.

"Where does that leave us?" Boggs asked.

"It leaves me still plenty goddamn angry at both of you. But even angrier that we've got so many sons of bitches who think they can call the shots in our territory."

He could see Boggs and Dewey were surprised by this. Yet he couldn't hold back his anger any longer. He was enraged by the fact that first the FBI, then Montgomery cops, and now a group of private dicks were throwing their weight around and acting like they were the authorities here. The time had come to show that this was *their* neighborhood.

"Floyd expects me to warn you to leave him alone. Well, fuck him. I don't know what the hell he was up to over at the Bishops', but we are going to find out."

Then his phone rang. A voice he didn't recognize told him Tommy Smith was in the hospital.

34

"HALT," SMITH REPEATED from the top of J.J. "*Halt!*"

"Is it the ditch?" asked Dart, the too-talkative gun loader, after the tank finally stopped. "Is it the ditch?"

Their second day of battle. They'd named the tank J.J. after Jack Johnson, former heavyweight champ. Charlie Company of the 761st Tank Battalion had just entered Morville-lès-Vic. Two years of training, and perhaps Smith's entire life, leading to now. This moment right here. A line of tanks making a complete stop in a hostile area, something they should never, ever do.

They had navigated past all manner of obstacles and minefields and bridgeless rivers, but they had heard rumors yesterday that the Germans had dug an impassable ditch, the mother of all trenches, somewhere in the vicinity. Judging from the fact that the lead tank was now motionless, they'd found it.

J.J. was powered by two Cadillac V-5 engines. In better times, they'd joked that this was the closest they'd ever come to a real Cadillac. Those engines still hummed but J.J. was terrifyingly immobile.

Smith, the tank commander and therefore literally the highest-up of the five-man team, gazed out the rectangular glass of his hatch. They were the fourth tank in the line and he could just barely see the ditch, a long tear in the earth as if God had dragged a fingernail across the frozen ground. Marking them.

The ten tanks had been moving closely together, which meant they were now bottlenecked. They would have to wait for the rear tank to reverse and move in a different direction, then the ninth, et cetera.

They would be here for minutes. Which was forever.

"Shit shit shit," Dart was muttering.

They were thirty tons of motionlessness. A beautiful target.

"Periscopes," Smith told them. Meaning, *We need more than my one pair of eyes right now.* He heard the others manipulating their sights as he scanned every direction he could, wondering where the ambush would be coming from.

The tank reeked of body odor and Chesterfields and a tiny bit of mint. Telly, the gunner, less than three feet from Smith, was nervously chewing his Wrigley's open-mouthed.

Then Smith saw them, German infantry hurrying from behind a patch of trees at ten o'clock. On one of their shoulders a *panzerfaust*, like our bazookas but stronger. Tank killers.

He started reading the coordinates to Telly, although he knew the Sherman's heavy 75-millimeter main gun wouldn't get there in time. Sensing this, Baines, the A-driver, called for Smith to pop the hatch so they could get to the .50 machine gun mounted atop the turret.

A risky idea and a good thought, but the *panzerfaust* flashed red and they felt the rocket move so fast Smith never even saw it.

Felt it. Didn't so much hear it.

Deaf for a moment, and the cold November air went hot like *that*. Smith hit his head against the turret and something weird happened under his feet. Numb already. He wasn't sure if his feet were still there. He was opening the hatch, too late. He gave the order to evacuate, though he wasn't sure if anyone could hear it. He couldn't hear it himself.

Out and exposed now, the cold air bracing, he grabbed the .50 and started firing before he even saw the Germans with his naked eyes. Gunfire all around, other men from C-Company firing at Germans who'd emerged from more hiding spots like fire ants back home. He stayed at the gun and fired, fired, mowing them down while the men below him crawled out. Those men who could. Only two, Dart and Baines.

He reached back for the others but saw only fire. Felt it at the bottom of his feet, his calves. The entire left side of J.J. had crumpled like aluminum foil. The driver, Lester, must have been killed instantly. Smith saw the shiny top of Telly's helmet, his head slumped. He knew he should have run, but he climbed back into J.J., where already it felt hot enough to melt metal, and reached for one of Telly's shoulders. When he pulled, the weight was so loose and light that it took him a moment to realize he was only pulling the top half of Telly, that the bottom half of his friend had been shorn off.

More explosions as *panzerfaust* guns punched holes into the other disabled prey. Smith never actually saw Telly's face, never saw his eyes, never had confirmation he was fully dead yet. He would always, always wonder.

Morphine. They needed morphine.

Everyone screaming. Everyone in pain.

Smith needed it, too. He felt it all over his body, in his soul.

He had seen the wonders morphine could perform on men many times, but he'd never felt it himself until now. He opened his eyes, barely, in some brightly lit room.

"How are you feeling?" a voice asked.

He opened his jaw, which ached. He didn't remember being kicked in the face. Maybe he'd fallen on it.

He slowly took stock of the world around him. His feet were the usual distance from his face, or at least he thought those two bumps beneath the thin hospital blanket were his feet. He wasn't sure if he could feel them. He wasn't sure of a lot of things. He tried to twitch them, felt conscious of the effort of actually sending that mental message to his extremities. It took an alarming amount of time, but the two bumps moved, more or less the way he'd wanted them to. Thank God.

"Don't try to sit up," the voice said. "Take it slow."

He hadn't realized he'd been trying to sit up at all, but then he saw his hands braced at the sides of the bed. His body seeming to perform acts without his mind's permission. Or trying to perform them. He winced now that his brain was able to process the fact that one of those hands was half in a cast.

Dizziness converged on him from all sides, turning his stomach. He leaned back again.

The one thing he liked: this pillow. This was the most comfortable goddamn pillow in the world. He'd have to steal it when they let him out.

"You have three broken ribs, two broken fingers, some pretty bad bruising all up and down your right side." Smith thought he recognized the voice. "You had some internal bleeding, so we needed to go in and clean you up. That's why you've got the stitches in your chest." He said that as though Smith already knew he had such stitches. "Your jaw isn't broken but your nose is, and you most likely have a concussion from those lumps on your head. You're going to feel mentally not right for a week or two. Maybe longer. You'll need to rest your mind for a while. I know that sounds strange, but it's important."

Smith's eyes were able to focus now and he recognized the doctor's face, somehow, somewhere. From another world.

Finally he understood. He wasn't in France, he was at the Gradys in Atlanta.

And before him stood Dr. Luther Bridges, the lover of Victoria Bishop.

"Oh," Smith said. "Hi."

"Yes, funny meeting you here."

Dr. Bridges asked him a few insulting questions, like his name and the name of the President. Which, actually, he might have gotten wrong—it was Eisenhower, right? Or was Ike still a general, and Smith was back in the war? It was 1956, not '44?

Everything felt so difficult and strange.

"How'd I get here?"

"Maybe you asked a complete stranger some personal questions about his love life, and he didn't handle it as well as I did."

Touché, Smith thought, sparing his ribs the pain of voicing it aloud.

The doctor, his points duly scored, explained, "Someone called for an ambulance and said you'd been attacked. As I understand it, he refused to leave his name."

Peeples, maybe. Or a random neighbor.

Bridges had been standing, but he stepped closer and lowered himself onto a chair. Or maybe he was just hovering, levitating. Smith felt like *he* was levitating.

The doctor asked, "Does this have anything to do with what we talked about? What's happening with Victoria?"

"Thought you wanted me . . ." His voice was weak, long sentences challenging. "To rest my mind."

"True. You said you used to be a cop, right? Should I call the police for you?"

Smith managed to read the clock on the wall behind the doctor. One o'clock, and the light in the window suggested that this was p.m. Which meant no Negro officers were on duty for another five hours.

"Not til after six," he said, closing his eyes.

⚡

He dreamed of his father, his true father, the one he'd never met. He owned a sole photograph of Benjamin Thomas Smith. Whenever Smith dreamed of his father, he was wearing his army uniform, even though Smith had never laid eyes on it. The uniform he surely had been proud to wear and the one he had been killed in. The one that had driven whites to a rage, set to madness at the mere sight of a Negro in uniform. And so Smith himself had signed on to the army in the next war, and had worn that uniform with pride. A few years later came the police uniform.

In his dream his father, like everyone else, asked him why he didn't wear the uniform anymore. Smith tried to answer but his jaw wouldn't move. He couldn't find his voice. He couldn't move. He was in too much pain.

And he didn't know what he would say in reply.

Later. The clock too fuzzy for him to read this time. Sitting in a chair beside him, not in uniform but wearing a dark slicker over a plain gray shirt, was McInnis.

"He's alive."

"Yes, sir." Even after six years, it was hard to drop the "sirs" around his old boss.

"Need some water?"

Smith nodded, which hurt, and McInnis stood, walked over to a side table, and brought a cup to his lips. No straw, so Smith had to tolerate the pain throbbing in his skull as he lifted his head.

Smith slowly exhaled as if that might parcel out the pain into more manageable portions.

"You look like hell."

"Damn," Smith said. He hadn't yet seen a mirror and would not ask for one. "The ladies."

"I'm sure they'll find their way to you soon enough."

In a bed behind McInnis, someone who sounded very old or very sick, or both, coughed. Coughed so long that Smith began to worry the person was running out of breath. Then he stopped.

McInnis leaned forward. "Warren Floyd do this?"

"Who?" Smith didn't understand. McInnis looked away, perhaps realizing he'd spoken more than he should have. Smith hoped he would remember that name through this haze of pain and drugs, for later follow-up, but he probably wouldn't.

"It was that FBI man," Smith explained. "Marlon." He could only say so many words before pausing for breath. "One who broke into Bishop's office. One who you wouldn't tell me why he was there."

"Son of a bitch. How'd it happen?"

He didn't like the idea of betraying his sources, and he didn't like how McInnis still hadn't told him what he'd learned from Doolittle. The FBI had done this to him, and he would see them punished for it.

"I was talking to an old friend of Mr. Bishop's, Morris Peeples. Former communist." He paused. "He'd brushed me off once. And I didn't like how he'd done it. So I went to his place."

McInnis looked like he wanted to ask for a follow-up, but he waited for Smith to marshal his strength and keep going.

"We talked. He told me why Bishop had written ... about the Higgs case. Bishop was afraid the Civil Rights Congress, a communist group ... would use the case as PR for the reds. One of their old friends is involved. White lady. Celia Winters. Bishop didn't want them doing their thing here in town."

"The arson the other night," McInnis said. "Doolittle had mentioned Winters and her group to me, too, but I didn't know why."

"I was at that fire," Smith said. "Four white men. In bandanas."

"What?" McInnis sat up a bit. "Wait, one thing at a time. What happened last night?"

"Peeples said he doesn't know who killed Bishop. Then I left. And, boom. Somebody hits me over the head. Marlon. Told me it was payback." Smith closed his eyes, hating that he had to admit weakness. It was slightly easier to do so when the evidence of his weakness was so obvious.

"Do you have reason to suspect," McInnis asked, "that this Peeples fellow had anything to do with Bishop's murder? That he wanted to pay him back for ... "

"For being an FBI snitch?"

Smith had always admired McInnis's poker face. It was one of the reasons he never fully trusted the man. McInnis could maintain a blank stare when being insulted, when on the verge of violence, when lying. "Where did you get that idea?"

"Ain't that what Doolittle told you?" Smith asked. "In that conversation I'm not allowed to know about? Because Peeples always suspected it. And he ain't the only one."

McInnis looked down at the floor for a moment, then scooted his chair even yet closer to Smith's bed. He was leaning, elbows on knees, so far over he could have kissed Smith good night. Only the drugs made this not extremely uncomfortable.

"I am telling you this against my better judgment," McInnis said quietly. "You can't repeat what I'm about to tell you."

"I might not *remember* what you're about to tell me." He closed his eyes again, opened them. McInnis was still there.

"Yes, Bishop was an FBI informant. That's why they raided his office, to make sure he hadn't left behind any evidence they'd ever spoken. And they were following his *wife* the night of the murder. She couldn't have killed him, because Doolittle's men were surveiling her at her house that night, and she never left."

"Shit." Smith's synapses were hardly firing at full strength. Each neuron that tried to pass information to the next one instead dropped it like a quarterback making a poor handoff, fumbling into the ether. His mind was a series of footballs hitting the ground, bouncing in weird directions. Yet this news still registered as amazing. Despite the painkillers and depressants, despite all those fumbled footballs, he sat up a bit straighter. "The feds need to tell Homicide."

"They won't. They refuse to admit they'd been following her."

"Why have they been?"

"They wouldn't say. Maybe she's a red, too. Seems like the best guess."

"She's no red. She's a damned business owner. Capitalist as they come."

McInnis only leaned back and shrugged, unwilling or unable to engage in political hairsplitting.

"Sergeant. You can't sit on this. It could get her sprung. She'll hang otherwise."

McInnis leaned close again, conspiratorial. "And that, Mr. Reporter, is why you're going to write about it in your paper."

That was about the last thing Smith had expected to hear. He wondered if he'd fumbled another football or twelve.

"Thought you said I couldn't tell anyone."

"You can't let anyone know you got it from *me*. But we need to get that information out in the public so the FBI will either fess up, or at least go behind the scenes and admit it to Homicide—and her defense attorney. Either way, it gets her out, and it finally focuses Homicide on looking for the right person."

"Okay. Wow. I don't even know if my editors would run it. It's risky."

"You've always struck me as a fellow who enjoys risks."

"I do. My editors don't. And I'd need a second source for verification."

"Just say *you're* the first source. You were there when the FBI broke in, and that's when they told us about her being home all night, right?" McInnis winked.

So, lie. Treat his journalistic ethics the way he'd once treated his police ethics. No matter what job he took, he brought the same self along.

"You'd have to be the second source," Smith noted.

"I'll vouch for the story with your editor, but I can't be quoted."

"'An unnamed source in the Police Department.'"

"That sounds all right."

Smith grinned. "'An unnamed white sergeant in the Negro precinct.'"

"Not funny."

Smith put his smile away. "Now hold up. You're asking me to lie, in print, about having heard with my own ears something I'm only hearing from *you*. You're asking me to put a lot of trust in you."

"If there were another way, I'd do it. I don't have a document, or Doolittle on tape. Don't name any of the feds—Jesus, this will tick them off enough without you naming names. You say you saw with your own eyes that the FBI broke into the office and was rifling through his papers, then you fudge the part about hearing them say how Victoria Bishop was home all night while under FBI surveillance."

Smith thought a bit longer. "You *swear* to me Doolittle told you that?"

"Yes." The poker face did slip sometimes: McInnis looked offended that Smith would doubt him.

"Then, why? Why are you doing this?"

"You really need to ask me that?"

McInnis meant, *because it's my job and I take it goddamn seriously*, Smith knew from their years working together. Still, Smith wanted more.

"Why take the risk? You could get screwed by the Bureau, or the Department. Why bother?"

"For the same reason you're nearly getting yourself killed trying to find out the truth."

Smith wondered if that could be true. Hoped so. Wasn't sure.

"Enough is enough," McInnis said, folding his arms. "First the Bureau jerked me around, and then they beat up one of my former officers."

"I'll leave that last part out. Still have my pride."

"I don't start fights, but I finish them. I know we can't take the FBI down, but we can cause them some serious pain for messing with us. Once this story is out, hopefully Mrs. Bishop gets released, and we see how the FBI and Homicide respond. Then we get another chance to find out who really killed your boss."

Smith nodded, which, speaking of serious pain, hurt. "Okay. Soon as I remember how to spell, I'm on it."

35

THE NEXT NIGHT, Boggs learned about Call Me Becky.

A woman had called the station earlier, her call triaged to McInnis, and asked to speak to one of the Negro officers. McInnis had told her that he was their commanding officer, but that hadn't been enough for her. She'd agreed to come in later when Boggs was available.

McInnis laid low inside his office with the door shut, lest the presence of a white officer scare this mystery caller silent, while Boggs sat at his desk. The young woman who was escorted down the steps was short and plump, with a gray skirt and pink sweater set, straightened hair pulled back, dark skin and nervous eyes. She stepped carefully as she looked around, clearly unimpressed by the environs.

Boggs asked how he could help as they sat down.

Hands tightly over the purse in her lap, she said her name was Natalie Washington and that she worked as a copyeditor at the *Daily Times*.

"It's a great paper," he said, trying to make her feel comfortable. "Read it every day."

"I need to talk to you about what happened to Mr. Bishop. I mean, I don't *know* what happened, who did it or anything. But, about three weeks before it happened . . ." Her eyes were welling up. She opened her handbag and started digging around for a tissue. She found one, but without using it she looked up at him again, steeling herself. "I was approached by a white lady one night, leaving work. She knew my name. And she knew that I"—deep breath—"she knew I'd been carrying on a bit with a fellow at the *Daily Times*, a fellow who's married."

Boggs tried to look nonjudgmental as she explained how the white woman, Call Me Becky, had coerced her into spying on Mr. Bishop. How she had been vague at first, but later had pressed for information about train porters, or Montgomery, or an old murder. "Didn't tell me *what* murder, or anything about it, just wanted to know if I'd heard him say anything."

Train porters? An old murder? Boggs didn't understand. He asked what Call Me Becky looked like, and Natalie shrugged, blew air from her lips, and described an unremarkable middle-aged white woman. Professional, cold. Graying hair cut in a bob. Neither tall nor short, fat nor skinny. Two eyes, a nose.

"About a week before Mr. Bishop was killed, he went out to Montgomery to research a story. I don't know what the story was, though I assumed it was the boycott. When he got back, I tried to ask him real casual, but he didn't tell me anything." Then she mentioned, almost offhand, that she had Call Me Becky's phone number.

"Would you mind sharing that number with me?" he asked. She reached into her purse and handed him a slip of paper.

He asked, "Have you seen her or spoken to her since Mr. Bishop was killed?"

"No. That's the thing." She took another breath and her eyes teared up again. "I didn't like doing that for her, but I didn't want to lose my job. And I figured, how bad could it be? I was just telling her if Mr. Bishop was looking into this one story, and I didn't even know what it was. But then when he got *killed* . . . " She looked down and dabbed at her eyes, took a moment. "And when she wasn't there when she was supposed to be, and time went by and I never heard from her again, it just . . . seemed more and more likely she was involved."

She looked at him searchingly, and he realized she was hoping he would tell her that surely the murder had nothing to do with her spying for this white lady. But he couldn't say that, because he didn't know if it was true. So a long and difficult moment passed as she silently pleaded with him for absolution he could not grant.

"I was afraid to talk to the police," she finally continued. "Then, when I found out how Tommy Smith got beat up, I decided, that's it. I needed to tell someone."

"Do you have any reason to think what happened to Smith is related?"

"I don't *know*, but come on! Our publisher gets killed, then one of our reporters gets beat half to death. How can it not be related?"

"Have you told any of this to Smith?"

"I haven't told this to *anyone*. And please, *please* don't tell. What I did, it's not against the law, right? But I know it doesn't look good. I don't want to lose my job."

"I don't want you to lose your job either." He asked her more about what "Becky" had been looking for and why.

"There was a name." Natalie fished inside her handbag for another scrap of paper. "Here it is: Henry Paulding. I said I'd never heard of him, so she just told me to forget about it. Keep looking out for the porters and forget she even asked about Paulding. Like she regretted she'd mentioned him. But I kept the note right here."

Boggs leaned back in his chair and thanked her for coming forward. He assured her he would keep her confidence, but he took down Natalie's number and address just in case.

After he'd escorted her out of the station, he returned to the basement and briefed McInnis. Both of them wondered why some white lady was interested not only in porters but also in Henry Paulding, the white owner of one of the development firms slated to tear down Darktown and part of Sweet Auburn.

~

McInnis called Records and requested a reverse phone number lookup. Boggs, accustomed to being delayed, insulted, or outright refused by the white clerks whenever he needed information, marveled at how quickly McInnis was granted what he'd requested.

McInnis hung up. "It appears to be one of two numbers for the offices of Floyd Investigations."

So not only had Floyd and another man broken into Bishop's

house, they also had a woman running a spy in Bishop's office. They knew how to cover their bases.

"Didn't know there were lady detectives," Boggs said.

"Having one on the payroll is a wise move. They can get access to things we can't. A strange white man might have scared the bejesus out of Natalie, but a woman knew how to manage her."

So Floyd's mystery client was worried Bishop would write a piece involving porters, or Montgomery, or an old murder, or Henry Paulding. Boggs tried to align this with what little he knew so far: Floyd was a former Pinkerton, and Pinkertons often worked for big businesses that needed to quash labor disputes. Pullman porters, all of them Negro and most of them Southern, long had been prevented from joining a white union, so they'd formed their own, the Brotherhood of Sleeping Car Porters, decades ago. After years of struggle, the Brotherhood had been officially recognized by the Pullman Company back in the late thirties or so.

Boggs recapped some of this for McInnis, who shook his head, unconvinced such political history was relevant.

"Maybe it's about Randy Higgs after all," McInnis wondered. "Is his father a porter? Could this be part of a campaign to run down the family's reputation?"

"I don't know. We can check into his family."

McInnis picked up his phone again. "It's high time we paid a visit to Floyd Investigations. You free tomorrow morning?"

36

AFTER THREE NIGHTS in the hospital, Smith walked into Laurence's office and announced, "I have a story."

"Welcome b—" Laurence started talking before he looked up, but when he saw Smith's face he stopped. "Good God. Are you feeling well enough to be here?"

No, he wasn't. His fingers were still in a cast, his ribs hurt when he breathed too deeply or moved too fast, and he'd suffered a few dizzy spells already. His left eye was swollen shut, his head pounded despite some aspirin, and he feared morphine withdrawal might kick in at any moment. Still, he explained as much as he could about the story he intended to write: the FBI break-in here, their surveillance of Victoria Bishop.

"Will you run it?" Smith asked.

The look on Laurence's face was that of a lifelong pessimist who'd just had more of his beliefs about humanity confirmed.

"Why was the FBI following her?" he asked. "You're saying she's innocent of Arthur's murder, but that she was also under government suspicion for something. What?"

"I still don't know. But given everything else, that seems less important than the fact that she's innocent of murder."

Laurence picked up his phone. "Write it and bring it to me. I'll call some people together and take it from there."

As if Bertha wasn't already a pain in the ass, typing on her one-handed (left-handed at that) was torture. The only positive was, it forced Smith to think extra hard about every word, his fingers slowed down to the pace of his addled brain.

After two hours of typing out a rough draft with Toon's assistance, and crossing parts out, scribbling in the margins, rearranging things in his mind and out loud with Toon, Smith slowly made his way back into Laurence's office. Another dizzy spell caused him to lean against a wall for a moment, but he made it. He watched while Laurence read and asked a few clarifying questions. Laurence crossed out a few lines with his furious red pen. Then Laurence handed it back to him and told him to type up a new, immaculate version. "I'll call you over once I have the lawyers here."

Back in his office, Smith caught up on all the news he'd missed. While he'd been in the hospital, whites had rioted at the University of Alabama to protest Autherine Lucy's admission, and the school had responded by suspending her. The governor blamed the riots on "outsiders." In industry news, the *Chicago Defender* had just become a daily, meaning the *Daily Times* had lost its claim to being the only Negro daily in America.

Smith's phone rang. A woman with a Northern accent said, "Hello, Mr. Smith. This is Celia Winters. I'm sorry it took me so long to get back to you, but as you can imagine, I've been rather busy."

He grabbed a pencil and flipped open a notebook, any notebook, the first he could find.

"Are you still in Atlanta, ma'am?"

"I'd rather not say. I'm using a phone that I *believe* is not tapped by the FBI, but then again, one never knows." She sounded flippant, long accustomed to government surveillance.

"I'm sorry about what happened to you the other night." The CRC office had been completely destroyed.

"Thank you. Now, you said you wanted to talk about Arthur Bishop?"

"Yes, ma'am. I understand you met Mr. Bishop during your trip to Moscow in the thirties?"

"That's correct."

"When was the last time you saw him, ma'am?"

"A long time ago. We had a falling-out, so I didn't bother looking him up when I came to town."

"Well, with him being killed when you happened to be in Atlanta, Mrs. Winters, I'm afraid I have to ask where you were the night he died."

"My, you just come out and say it. I like that. On the night he was killed, I was attending a political meeting of the sort Arthur never would have attended—at least, not anymore."

"Any names I could verify that with?"

"The naming of names is a big no-no with us, Mr. Smith. I'm afraid I will decline the opportunity to tell you who saw fit to meet with an evil, communistic spawn of Satan such as myself. I don't see any reason to have their reputations run down, either by your paper or the police."

"Well, ma'am, it would be easier if you had an alibi someone could vouch for."

"Let me put it to you this way. If the FBI thought there was any chance at all that I didn't have an alibi for that night, would I be walking free right now?" A good point, he silently conceded. "You see, an alibi isn't really necessary for me. I walk the earth in full awareness of the fact that any law I break, I will immediately be arrested for it. At first that's a rather constricting feeling, but, over time, it becomes quite liberating. And speaking of arrests and alibis, I understand you were a policeman once?"

"Yes, ma'am." Wondering what else she knew about him.

"But then you rightly decided that being part of a corrupt system was perhaps not the best way to reform it."

"Maybe I just didn't like people shooting at me."

"Or maybe you realized that the best way to bring justice to a corrupt system is at the root, not at the prettily adorned tips of some branches."

"And maybe I don't like being analyzed over the phone by someone who doesn't know me."

"I'm sorry. I can be rather brusque when someone I don't know accuses *me* of crimes. But I understand, it's your job. I like your new job better than your old one, even if your boss hated us."

"But he didn't always hate you in particular. Once upon a time, he even loved you."

Silence. Then the hint of a sound, but nothing, like she'd started to talk and found her voice wouldn't work, a catch in her throat.

"I don't know what you're implying," she finally said, her voice slower than before, "but we both know the sorts of terrible things that can happen down here when those kinds of allegations are made."

"Did Mrs. Bishop know?"

Another pause. "Did she—who I never actually had the pleasure of meeting—did she know about something that might have happened many, many years ago, in fact many years before she and Arthur had even met? I have no idea. You'd have to ask her. Although, again, you might not want to, since the mere suggestion can make people act unpredictably."

"Is there any chance at all he was still carrying a torch for you? And that you coming to town this month, it made him—"

"None." Like a door slamming. "We hadn't spoken in years. I didn't even attend his funeral. I considered it, as I was in town, but I feared my presence there would only create problems for his family." She sighed. "It's not much fun, Mr. Smith, this feeling that you're carrying a stench around with you, that polite company would run screaming."

"It's better than being shot and killed in your office."

"That nearly happened to me too, as you saw. Maybe they weren't carrying guns that night, but those bats looked more than adequate. Why aren't you looking into *them*?"

"I've been trying, ma'am." His attempts to learn anything had been blocked by police headquarters. *Possible arson, possible electrical malfunction, no witnesses, investigation ongoing.* Pure bullshit.

He ran down his theory that Bishop had written about the Higgs case as a way of preempting Winters' Civil Rights Congress from capitalizing on a crooked trial to raise money for their cause, and she agreed it sounded plausible. But when Smith ventured that Bishop's staunch anti-communism might have made her or some of her fellow travelers angry enough to kill, she didn't take the bait.

"Please. We have enough on our hands. We may have disagreed with Arthur about a lot of matters, but no one here would stoop to that." She sighed. "I'd like you to not see me as your antagonist, Mr. Smith. I'm an ally. You think I'm trying to *use* the Randy Higgs case? And that I'm a bad person for trying to take a horrible situation and make it into something good? Look, maybe the city will drop the charges against Higgs now that they know about those love letters Arthur put in his story. Maybe the CRC *won't* raise any money because the trial will never happen. And you know what? I would be happy. That would still be better than having yet another legal lynching for us to bear witness to."

He didn't much like her, yet he found himself wondering if Peeples was right, that Smith was spending too much time on communists. Everyone's hesitance to talk about the subject had piqued his curiosity, but perhaps it had distracted him from more important secrets.

"Good luck with your reporting, Mr. Smith," she said. "Meanwhile, if you're ever looking for a way to cause some *real* reform, look us up."

Minutes later, Toon walked in.

"I didn't have a chance to tell you yet, but we've turned up something else that might relate to Bishop's murder. A money angle."

Toon explained that Crispin Bishop, the Bishops' eldest nephew, had been staying in Atlanta after the funeral. A lawyer from Boston who advised corporations up north, Crispin had examined the paper's accounting and made some odd discoveries. Arthur Bishop had transferred $100,000 from his personal account into the newspaper's account a month before his death. Days later, $93,000 was moved to another company, and the other seven grand went to Eric Branford, Bishop's longtime attorney and friend. The only people with access to the newspaper's account were Arthur and Victoria Bishop and Branford himself. Crispin had shown the paperwork to Laurence, who in turn showed it to Toon.

"Looked to Crispin like someone was embezzling."

"I don't get it," Smith said. "If Bishop had moved money from the paper and into his private account, then yeah. But he did the opposite."

"True, but the seven grand going to Branford was suspicious. And that amount of money being moved around, that alone was strange. Me and Laurence weren't sure what it meant at first. Crispin was the one who found it, and it seemed awfully convenient for him to find information that might incriminate one or the other of his rival board members." Crispin, Victoria, and Branford comprised the board; if Victoria was acquitted, it remained unclear whether she would be appointed publisher, or if Crispin might take over, or if they'd choose someone else. "So Laurence and I made a trip to Branford's office to ask him about it."

This was the most shocking news of all. "Laurence went outside again?"

Toon smirked. "We *drove* the three blocks. *I'm* the one who drove; he pulled his fedora down so low he might as well have been blindfolded."

"Proud of him. Come a long way."

"Branford says Mr. Bishop had moved the money to invest in a real estate venture with Clancy Darden, a former VP at Atlanta Life Insurance. Branford says he doesn't know the specifics, but it had something to do with the redevelopment plan."

"What?" Smith remembered Darden from the funeral, but he hadn't realized he'd been a business partner of Bishop's. "Bishop knew about the redevelopment but didn't break the story?"

"Looks like he stood to profit from it, so maybe he didn't *want* the story to break yet. And here's the other thing: according to

Branford, Bishop later changed his mind. Branford claims that Bishop called and told him he wanted the money moved *back* to the newspaper, that the real estate investment no longer seemed like a good idea. And a few hours later, Bishop gets killed."

Smith leaned back in his chair.

"Branford claims he'd been too busy to move the money that day," Toon went on, "so the next morning, when he hears Bishop's been killed, he felt that any big financial move like that would be untoward, possibly illegal. So he had to leave the money exactly where it was when Bishop died."

"Which is where?"

"A real estate company he co-owned with Clancy Darden."

"Jesus. We need to talk to Darden."

"I left a message at his office. Haven't heard back yet."

"Do you think Branford's clean? What about that missing seven grand?"

"He claimed it was money Bishop owed him for services rendered. I don't know, I think I believe him. He was awfully annoyed at us for accusing him of doing anything wrong."

Which meant nothing, Smith knew. Could be outrage, could be guilt. Before he could think this through, he heard Laurence calling for them.

＊

The very people Toon and Smith had just been discussing were now gathered inside Laurence's cramped office. Sitting in the guest chair was Eric Branford, the white-haired attorney who may or may not have embezzled from the paper. He wore an expensive-looking pinstriped suit, complete with watch chain dangling from a pocket. Beside him stood young Crispin Bishop, whose shirtsleeves were rolled up and tie loosened. He nodded hello to Smith, then awkwardly started to reach out for a handshake before pulling back when he realized Smith had a cast on his right hand.

Branford held the most recent draft of Smith's piece. The old attorney passed it to Crispin and, without giving him a chance to read it, said, "My advice as the *Daily Times* attorney is that you absolutely do not print this. In fact, I advise that you burn this piece of paper, and whatever other drafts he typed up."

"With all due respect," Smith started, but Crispin waved a hand for silence.

"Please, let me finish it."

Smith didn't like the kid, but he waited. Two minutes later, Crispin looked up at him as if for the first time, assessing Smith's injuries like he hadn't noticed them before. Then he turned to Branford.

"I disagree," he said in his high-mannered New England accent. "I say we run it."

Before Smith could linger over Crispin's use of *we*, and what it might mean for the paper's future, Branford said, "Laurence, I just *today* managed to get the Attorney General to drop the libel lawsuit out of respect for the dead." This was news to Smith. What other information might Branford be withholding? "If the paper turns around and prints this nonsense about the FBI, then they'd find a reason to shut us down."

"Mr. Branford, I'm sorry, but it's not nonsense," Smith responded. "It's the truth."

Branford took a long eyeful of this whippersnapper who'd contradicted him. "I'm not impugning the veracity of your piece. I'm telling you that if you put this in print, the Attorney General will reload some double-aught buckshot for this paper, and this time he'll have the FBI firing alongside him."

"Tommy," Laurence said, "there are other considerations we need to balance."

"Have you called the FBI for comment?" Crispin asked Smith.

"I told him not to yet," Laurence said. "I want to call them late enough in the process that, if they try to mobilize and stop us from running the piece, they'll be too late."

Branford looked like he was surrounded by fools. "The fact that you realize they could do that to us, and yet you're still even thinking of running this, is insane."

"Mr. Branford," Crispin said, "I respect all that you've done for this paper over the years. But if the FBI is withholding evidence that my aunt is innocent, that's news we cannot hold back."

"I'm not Mrs. Bishop's criminal attorney," Branford explained. "If I was, then maybe I would say to run the piece. But as the attorney tasked with keeping this paper out of legal trouble and making sure the lights stay on and the reporters and editors and clerks still have jobs next week, and don't wind up in jail cells, I say, unequivocally, do not run that piece."

Crispin looked at Laurence. "The board hasn't voted on new leadership yet. So, as managing editor, Mr. Laurence, it's your call."

"Shouldn't we get Mrs. Bishop's take?" Smith asked.

"No." Laurence all but scowled. "This is an editorial decision. Victoria's not on the masthead."

Silence for a few beats. Toon asked, "Have we fact-checked yet?"

"I wanted my lay of the land first," Laurence said, looking at Smith. "Who's your unnamed police source?"

Smith stepped toward the desk, picked up Laurence's phone, and dialed McInnis's home line. When McInnis answered, Smith was succinct: "It's Smith. My editor has a few questions for you."

He handed Laurence the phone. He and Toon exchanged glances while they all eavesdropped on half the conversation. They could tell McInnis was confirming everything.

Laurence thanked him and hung up. "It checks out."

"We need to run it," Crispin said again. "If some corrupt cracker government tries to shut us down because of it, then so be it. We need to draw a line in the sand."

"This isn't Boston, young man!" Branford snapped. "We don't draw lines in the sand, *they* do. If we cross them, people *die*. You still have that nice law practice up north to run to, but we *live* down here 365 days a year."

"I'm not being cavalier," Crispin insisted. "I understand the risks. But I will not let them do this to my family."

"If anyone cares what I think," Toon offered after a loaded

pause, "I say we run it too. Look, they've broken into our offices. They've beaten Smith. They've followed our publisher's *wife* around, at night. God only knows what else they've done." He looked around the room. "Are they following another one of us, or our wives? Our kids? Do they have one of us on their payroll right now? We *can* draw a line in the sand."

Crispin nodded. "Everything that my father and uncle built is meaningless if we can't expose this."

Then Branford played his trump card, judging from the look of dignified anger on his face. "Arthur never would have run a story like this."

"You're right," Laurence said somberly. "And maybe that's why he's not here with us." He picked up his phone again as Branford shook his head. "Smith, who am I asking for at the FBI?"

"Special Agent Doolittle."

Laurence made the call and was blocked by a secretary, so he left his name and number and asked for Doolittle to call him back as soon as possible.

"He's probably out boiling communists in oil," Smith said. The politics in the room already more than enough for him, he headed for the door. "Let me know when he calls back."

✤

Minutes later, Smith's phone rang, and the voice of his old partner came over the line.

"Do you know if Bishop was working on a story in Montgomery?" Boggs asked.

"I know he went out there, maybe a week or so before he was killed. Why?"

"What was he doing there?"

Smith hated how Boggs had ignored the question and proceeded with his own. Smith said, "I don't know. You gonna tell me why you're asking? And how about those tags on that car I told you about? When do I get to find out whose they were?"

"Look, Tommy, McInnis has already rapped our knuckles

enough on this. We can't be giving you privileged information. Maybe if you still had your badge—"

"Oh, you'd *love* that, wouldn't you?"

"Let's not do this. I need to go by the book right now, and I'm not apologizing for it."

"By-the-Book Boggs."

"Listen, I got a tip last night. Somebody says they were black-mailed into spying on Bishop, told to keep an eye on whether he was writing anything about porters or an old murder, possibly in Montgomery, possibly involving Henry Paulding."

"Wait, spying on Bishop?" Smith's head spinning. "You talked to the FBI?"

"What? No, it wasn't . . . Look, Tommy, I can't tell you who it was. Sorry. But it wasn't the FBI, okay? At least, I don't think so. Anyway, this person, you don't have to worry about them anymore. I just wanted to know if that other information means anything to you: porters, an old murder, Montgomery, Henry Paulding?"

It galled Smith that he'd been risking his life trying to solve this, and meanwhile Boggs was getting helpful dirt, probably from McInnis, and maybe from the feds—and maybe even the same ones who beat him up. Had McInnis been straight with him after all?

He tried to tamp that down and focus on what Boggs had told him.

"Henry Paulding—why do I know that name?"

"He's a white builder, makes a lot of money, greases a lot of wheels. His name came up in those city council memos—if the city tears those blocks down, his firm is on tap to get a big, fat contract."

Synapses fired in Smith's head. All of the fumbled footballs bounced off the turf, landed snug in the hands of hungry running backs who had the entire field in front of them. He still didn't know how some of the pieces fit—communists, FBI agents, the bus boycott, love affairs, and now train porters—but he finally had a connection: real estate.

He asked, "You know the name Clancy Darden?"

"Sure, my brother worked for him. Why?"

"Bishop and Darden had formed a real estate company, and they'd been planning to get in on that same redevelopment project."

"*What?*"

Smith told Boggs what Toon had just told him: how Bishop had decided to invest with Darden, then changed his mind and tried to pull the money back, only to be killed before his lawyer, Branford, could do the paperwork.

Silence on the line.

Boggs finally said, "Darden lied to me. I specifically asked him if he thought there was any chance Bishop would have been working on a story criticizing that plan. He said no, but he *also* said he hadn't even known about the redevelopment until he read about it in the paper that day. Why would he lie?"

"I'd say he had a hundred-thousand-dollar motive."

"Jesus Christ," Boggs said.

Smith envisioned a headline: *LUCIUS BOGGS CUSSES.*

"Are you sure about all that?" Boggs asked.

"Pretty sure. When did you talk to Darden?"

Boggs recapped their brief talk from a few days ago. "He made like he'd never heard of the redevelopment plan before. And he all but begged me not to dig into Mr. Bishop's affairs. I'd thought he was just being overly proper, but—"

"He was trying to keep you off his tracks. We're hoping to get a comment from him. You might want to talk to him, too."

"There's this thing I need to do this morning, but then I'll pay him a visit," Boggs said. "Please, don't talk to Darden just yet. Let us do it. I need to hear it from him myself."

"But what about the rest, porters and Montgomery? What did your spy find out? This spy I ain't allowed to know about."

"She wasn't my spy, I mean . . . " Boggs sounded like he'd already said more than he'd meant to. *She.* "They never found anything important, they say. But that's what they'd been told to look for."

After they hung up, Smith looked down at the two boxes of

Bishop's papers he'd exhumed from the basement. He'd spent hours reading through them and was nowhere near finished, having already combed through all manner of memoir drafts, old half-written articles, story ideas, letters sent and not sent. He'd even read through a few short fiction pieces Bishop had tried to get published, all of them surprisingly pulp-like: in one, a freedman starts a successful new life after the Civil War in a far Western town before being run off by jealous whites; in another, an elderly butler working for a wealthy white family is drowned in a back-yard swimming pool by a psychotic member of the household; in another, a gambler in Savannah flees north after a night of cards turns deadly. He'd also found transcripts of Bishop's long-ago WPA interviews, and, now that he thought of it, some of those had been with train porters. He'd only glanced at them before, but now he'd go back and reread them.

Henry Paulding. Porters. Montgomery. An old murder. At least now he knew what needles he should be looking for in these haystacks.

37

THE OFFICE OF Floyd Investigations occupied half of a small, one-story gray building on the western edge of downtown. The block was hemmed in by train tracks on one side and a freight yard on the other, a dead end. Noisy freight cars clanked in the background and few cars drove along the pothole-riddled road, though there were some cars parked along the curb. This wasn't a business that expected much walk-in traffic.

McInnis had set up this 10 a.m. meeting by calling Floyd the previous night and asking, as politely as he could muster, if they could talk in private.

Admittedly, he was not at his best that morning. He hadn't slept well, plagued with guilt from the blowup with Jimmy and his argument with Bonnie about his job. If Erin already knew that her brother was flirting with a Negro girl, then McInnis was worried about who else might know. Despite his crystal-clear warning to Jimmy to stay away from her, he feared their transgression might have already set in motion things he wouldn't be able to stop.

McInnis had never excelled at teaching children lessons, he realized. He had hoped that the example he set—to work hard and treat others fairly—was straightforward and easy to follow. But he saw now that he'd been deluding himself. His path these last years had been difficult enough for *him* to walk; he shouldn't be surprised that his son couldn't manage it.

His job sent mixed signals to his boy. Perhaps Dodd's transfer offer was a godsend. He could switch out of the basement, leave the Negro officers to some other sergeant, and show his children how to navigate a far easier path.

It was against his nature, however, to leave a mess for another man to clean up. That meant figuring out what was going on with the Bishop investigation and chasing out the feds and private dicks and Alabama cops while he was still putatively in charge of the Negro district.

The door to Floyd Investigations was locked, surprisingly. McInnis knocked, wondering if Floyd might have stood him up. The long, narrow window was blocked by blinds, the reflected morning sunlight forcing McInnis to shield his eyes. Then a bolt slid and Floyd opened the door, inviting him inside with a smile. The big redhead wore a white Oxford and black tie, tan slacks.

"I sent the girl out on some errands, figured we could talk privately," Floyd explained. The waiting room had two upholstered chairs, a coffee table, and a small desk where a secretary would be. But it looked unused and McInnis had an inkling that Floyd had been lying about employing a secretary.

Floyd led McInnis into his office, behind one of three doors in a small hallway. Large desk, file cabinets, guest chairs, but no photos of family, no framed credentials on the walls. A small, lone window with a view into an alley. Being a cop had its downsides, but McInnis saw that being an ex-cop private dick was worse.

"So what can I help you with?"

"I need quite a lot of help," McInnis said. "And you may be the perfect person to talk to. If we handle this right, we'd be helping each other."

"All right, let's hear it."

"It's the fucking niggers," McInnis said, uncomfortable with his language but getting into character. "They're driving me mad, and I think I've finally figured a way to put a stop to it. You said it yourself: they're running amok over there. I mean, Jesus, the Department has been expecting me to make *officers* out of them. I didn't ask for that job, but I follow orders, so I've been busting my ass over there, smacking my head into a brick wall, over and over. I got one hell of a hard head now."

"Hard as theirs, probably," Floyd laughed.

"That's my biggest fear, that the longer I spend with them, the more their damned madness is gonna seep into me." He was playing a role, yet he felt uncomfortable with how these sentiments mirrored some of his own fears. "I deserve the goddamn Nobel Peace Prize on account of what I've been doing all this time. Anyway, I thought you should know, my boys just won't stop looking into this Bishop murder. They're convinced it wasn't the widow. They can't get it into their heads that a 'refined Negro lady,'" pronounced like that was an absurdity, an oxymoron, "might actually have committed a crime like that. They're convinced some white person did it and the Department is just pinning it on her, and they've been spending most of their time snooping around. I'm afraid that at this point they've mussed things up so much they might actually damage the case against her."

Floyd listened patiently, revealing nothing just yet.

"And they've been watching *you*, in case you haven't figured that out yet. Coming by your house was the least of it. They know you were at Bishop's place right after she was arrested, and they know you've got eyes inside the *Daily Times*."

"What are you talking about?"

"I'm telling you, Warren, they're like a goddamn hive or something. One of them thinks something, then they all know it. It's eerie. I don't know if it's voodoo or some conjurer's trick they brought over from the Congo or what. But one of them saw you going through the Bishop place, and another knows your associate was talking to a Negro at the newspaper, keeping tabs on Bishop before he was killed. Whatever one of them knows, the rest of them do, too. Trust me, there isn't a white man in America who's had to work more closely with Negroes the last few years than me." He laughed bitterly. "I'm like the reverse Jackie Robinson. I understand them better than anyone."

"So what do they think about the murder?"

McInnis rolled the dice. "They think you were working for Henry Paulding, they figure that's why Bishop was killed, and they're hell-bent on proving it. At the same time, and here's what worries me, they don't care about being able to prove it in a court of law, the way you or me would. They have their own style of jungle justice, and they're fixing to bring it to you *and* Paulding."

"You've got to be joking."

"Wish I was. I've done everything I can to get them to back down, but they're damned uncontrollable. I just need to prove that to Captain Dodd, fast, before they do something like kill a white man."

"I ain't scared of them." But Floyd's tone of voice said otherwise.

"Well, they've already figured out you were working for Paulding," and McInnis couldn't help noticing that Floyd hadn't contradicted him the first time, "and I don't know what they'll find next. We need to stop them before they make their next move."

"Well, goddamnit, you're their sergeant. Tell them to back the hell off."

"You think it's that easy, do you? Want to trade jobs? The thing is, I need to know what's going on before they figure it out. I gotta stay a step ahead of them. Frankly, I'm tired of being a step *behind* them and three steps behind *you*. I can't keep them off you if I don't know what the hell it is they're fixing to discover next."

Floyd shook his head, exasperated. "This damn job is so much more trouble than it's worth. Paulding sure isn't paying enough for it."

"What *is* he paying for?"

Floyd held up a hand. "Look, don't go telling anyone this. You confide in me, I'll confide in you, and hopefully we can set this mess straight."

"Absolutely."

"It's all bullshit, really. Paulding needed me to help stave off a smear campaign. He heard Bishop was trying to ruin his reputation, so he needed me to keep that from happening."

"What was Bishop trying to smear him with?"

"There's some old story Paulding was afraid would get out. A long time ago, we're talking back during the Depression, he and some buddies were up drinking on a Pullman train one night, telling stories. Everyone trying to outdo each other. So Paulding spun some crazy yarn about some terrible thing he did when he was younger, making the whole thing up for laughs. Now, he wouldn't tell me exactly what it was he'd said on that train back then, but he implied that he'd bragged about doing something criminal. Which has me thinking, murder. He says the story wasn't true, just something he told for laughs, but that if the story got out and people misunderstood, it would be bad for him and his business."

Floyd continued, "Now, at the time of that train ride, Paulding was only in his twenties, a rich brat. So he tells this tale—about what, I don't know—and he says the only folks in that train car were three friends of his, who knew he was making it up, and this young Negro porter who waited on them. Anyway, he says he could tell that the Negro *believed* him. Thought it was more than just a tall tale. And before long, Paulding started hearing the rumor come back to him, and he realized the story he'd told that night was spreading among the coloreds somehow."

McInnis clarified, "This story about some awful thing Paulding talked about doing, but didn't actually do?"

"Yeah. The blacks think it's true, and that bothered Paulding at first, but then he figures, hell, it makes him seem more like a tough guy, someone not to be crossed, so he lets it go. Figured it was a good way of keeping the help in line." Floyd shrugged. "But now, skip ahead about twenty years, his old man has passed and now Paulding runs the family business. Turns out they're fixing to handle a big redevelopment plan that'd knock down a lot of the Auburn Avenue neighborhood, and they expect that a lot of coloreds will be up in arms about it—that's happening already, the story broke before the city had planned on announcing it. But even before that happened, Paulding was afraid that now of all times would be when that story, about him doing some terrible *something*, way back, will hit the front pages to cut him out of the deal."

McInnis nodded. It didn't sound like Floyd was lying, and it finally explained the connection between Paulding, porters, and the Negro press. But he wondered whether Paulding really had kept the mysterious something from Floyd, or if Floyd in fact knew what it was.

"And then," Floyd continued, "just as the announcement of the big redevelopment plan nears, Paulding hears that *Bishop*, the very man who runs the black *Daily Times*, has been interviewing a bunch of retired porters. Trying to track down the one who'd supposedly heard Paulding tell the story so many years ago."

This must be why the lady detective had been so angry when she'd realized Bishop had traveled to Montgomery without their noticing. Maybe Bishop, after years of talking to the FBI, knew how to throw off a tail, travel unnoticed.

"So you needed to track down the porter first," McInnis said, "and silence him."

Floyd folded his arms. "I didn't kill the porter. I'm a private detective, not a hitman. Far as I know, the porter's alive and well."

"But Arthur Bishop isn't. You're telling me Paulding wanted to make sure Bishop didn't write a story, and then Bishop gets killed, and you don't know anything about that?"

"I don't. Now why don't *you* tell *me* how I can keep your boys away from this. Even with Bishop dead, Paulding's still afraid someone else is going to run with that story and use it to stop his project. Like that ex-officer of yours who writes for the *Daily Times*, maybe. A story like that could cost Paulding a hell of a lot of money."

"I'd say. Sounds like Paulding had quite a motive to kill Bishop himself."

Floyd shook his head. "Paulding's a ruthless son of a bitch, but he's a businessman. I can't see a snooty ol' fart like him driving into a Negro neighborhood at night for a whore, much less to kill someone."

"All right," McInnis said, unsure whether he agreed. Then he stood. "I appreciate the conversation."

"Wait, hold up. What's the plan for taking your Negro officers out of the picture?"

"Well, Warren, I'm afraid you're just a tiny bit too gullible. No wonder you couldn't cut it as a cop."

Oh, the look on Floyd's face right then. McInnis treasured it. It was all about the eyebrows. First they were a bit tight, puzzled, then they narrowed a bit as Floyd attempted to make sense of what McInnis had just said, and finally they lifted high as the reality dawned across the rest of his face.

"You . . . " But he couldn't find the words. He jumped to his feet. "You were playing me?"

Yes, and it had felt awkward and dirty, not to lie to this man but to speak the language of a fire-breathing Kluxer. The act had won McInnis what he needed, but even now, he felt unsettled, as if the language and attitude he'd adopted had left a mark.

"Settle down there, Warren. Just doing my job. Thanks for pointing out a few things. Makes a lot more sense now."

McInnis left the office and walked through the waiting room. He thought he heard the sounds of car doors outside, but that was overpowered by Floyd shouting behind him, "You weren't here to fuck over those niggers at all! You've been lying this whole time!"

Any detective should know that lying went with the territory, so it wasn't just McInnis's subterfuge that enraged Floyd. McInnis's true offense was that he had allied himself with Negroes against a white man, that he'd bamboozled the wrong race.

"Yes, and I'm so terribly sorry for that." He stopped and turned, facing Floyd, who'd followed him into the waiting room. "But you've been real helpful, bless your heart. If you really thought you could get a sergeant to betray his officers to you, well, it really has been a long time since you wore a badge. Now here's some advice: keep your ass out of my beat, and stay the hell away from my men. Because maybe I *was* telling the truth when I said I can't control them as well as I'd like."

He turned back around and was a foot from the door when it opened up. In walked a man and a woman, both in their forties. The man was a bruiser, with three inches and maybe fifty pounds on McInnis. He wore a long dark trench coat and his fedora angled up as if he faced a great wind. The red tinge in his eyes, his unshaven cheeks, and his poorly done tie suggested that here was a drinker, maybe even this morning. The woman beside him, whom McInnis assumed was Call Me Becky, wore a red sweater and long wool skirt, her graying hair cut in a bob. The man closed the door behind him and they stayed there, blocking McInnis's path.

"Ma'am, sir," McInnis said, stepping toward the door again. "I was just leaving."

They didn't step away from the door. Becky asked, "What's going on, Warren?"

"This son of a bitch tricked me! Goddamn nigger lover made like he needed help getting those boys tossed out of the force, but he was really prying me for dirt."

McInnis was surrounded, and his mistake was to take offense at what Floyd said. He turned and pointed. "That's enough. You and your little playgroup here had better stay the hell out of my territory from now on."

But when he turned toward the door again, not only did the other two still block his path, but the man was pointing a gun at McInnis.

"Keep your hands up," the big fellow commanded.

McInnis went cold. "You're making a mistake."

"I've made plenty, so one more won't cost me. Get your goddamn hands up."

McInnis obeyed. He couldn't believe he'd let them get the drop on him. Hands up, he swiveled his head between them and saw that Floyd too was drawing a gun.

"Now, let's everyone just cool off," McInnis said. Realizing he had no leverage, he tried to make nice. "I know y'all have just been doing your jobs, and I'm ready to leave you be. But if you don't put those guns away right now, that changes."

"What did you tell him, Warren?" Becky asked in a tone between angry and panicked.

"Nothing," Floyd said, embarrassed. "I swear."

The dynamic in the room had shifted even before the gun had

come out, though McInnis couldn't tell why. Floyd may have headed his namesake detective agency, but he certainly wasn't acting in charge of the other two. He seemed scared of them.

That fear grew contagious, fast.

Becky hadn't drawn a weapon yet, but she stepped to the side, removing herself from any potential line of fire.

"Bullshit!" The big man nearly spat at Floyd. "You talked! You're selling us out!"

Floyd held out his other hand in appeasement. "No! I didn't. Sam, we're good."

McInnis wasn't clear on what they were talking about, what this Sam fellow was afraid Floyd had said, but he had some ideas.

Sam's gun was still aimed at McInnis's chest.

"Mr. Floyd," McInnis said, trying to project impatience while remaining calm despite being hemmed in by two armed men. "I'd like you to remind your associates here that I'm a police sergeant, and you need to put those pieces away. Whatever it is you're worried about, and whatever trouble you may be in, we can figure a smarter way out of it, all right?"

Silence for a beat, then Becky said, "He's right." She held her palms out. "Maybe we should just talk this through, Sam."

"No," Sam said, his eyes gone cold. Behind them McInnis sensed a series of steps had been planned out, haphazard and ill-considered, but already fated. "There's been enough talking."

38

ALONE IN HIS office, Smith was catching up on all the news he'd missed, reading a review of the new Chester Himes novel, when Laurence appeared in the doorway.

"No word from the FBI yet. If I don't hear in another hour, I'm calling their Washington office and demanding someone answer our questions."

The boxes of Bishop's old writing filled Blackmon's chair and forced Laurence to stand as he asked, "Tell me, Tommy. Whose side are you on here?"

"Excuse me?"

"You knew about that break-in, you *witnessed* it, yet you kept it from us for days."

"I'm sorry. Sergeant McInnis told me I couldn't write about it."

"He's not your sergeant anymore. Any other reporter would have come straight to me with it. Yet you took orders from your *previous* boss. I find that odd."

Smith had agonized over this. He likened himself to a maverick blazing his own trail, but now he wondered if he'd granted McInnis too much power over his thoughts, his actions.

"If you want to work with the police for scoops, that's one thing," Laurence said. "But if you plan to be keeping secrets with them, and go running around doing what looks more to me like police work than reporting, it makes me wonder if you have the wrong job."

Smith was about to respond when Toon came running down the hall. "Laurence! FBI's on the line."

Laurence hurried back to his office, Toon right behind him,

the wobbly Smith a few paces back. Crispin sat in the guest chair; Branford wasn't present, having returned to his law office. It looked to Smith like Laurence took a moment to gather himself before picking up his phone.

"Good morning, sir. We plan to run a story on the FBI's involvement in the investigation into Arthur Bishop's murder. Could you explain to me why one of your agents broke into Mr. Bishop's office that night? ... Well, I have an eyewitness, sir, one of my reporters ... Yes ... Nonetheless, we're within our rights to report this ... His name was Agent Talbot Marlon, as a matter of fact. Apparently his wrist was broken during an altercation ... Really? Well, a source at the hospital has already confirmed that a man by that name was indeed treated for a broken wrist that night ... No, we weren't going to print his name, but you asked." He rolled his eyes for the benefit of his audience. "So I'll put that down as neither confirming nor denying?"

This silence was far, far longer than the others. The skin at the edge of Laurence's lips and eyes looked as though it was being tugged down by a gradual but persistent force. Finally he snapped, "I don't need you to explain that to me. I've been doing this a long time. And while we're on the phone, sir, I'd also like to know why the Bureau was following Mrs. Bishop the same night that Arthur Bishop was murdered ... Yes, sir ... Were you planning on informing Atlanta police about this, or were you just going to stand by and withhold evidence while an innocent woman was tried for a murder you know she couldn't have committed?"

It burned at Smith not to be able to hear whatever Doolittle was saying just then. He'd never met the FBI agent, but if he was the man who'd sent Talbot on his little mission, the sound of his voice issuing impotent denials would have been priceless.

"Oh really?" Laurence snapped. "Yes, I suppose you could, and I could accuse you of trying to impede the work of a free press ... So, to be clear, you do not confirm that your agents were following her? Great, thank you, that's all I need."

He hung up and exhaled. Smith was dying to break the tension with a quip, but instead they all waited.

Laurence grabbed a pencil and said, "We run the story. We add that the FBI denies breaking into the office and denies following Mrs. Bishop." He was scribbling as he spoke, then he handed the sheet to Smith. "Reach out to Mrs. Bishop's attorney for comment, now—I want this in production as soon as possible." Then he looked at Toon. "Tell Mrs. McClatchey downstairs to lock the doors and let me know if anyone tries to get in."

Smith winked at Crispin, who looked more nervous now that the plan he'd been pushing was actually happening. "Welcome to the South."

39

"**I DON'T LIKE** this," Dewey said as they watched the white couple hurry into Floyd's office.

"Me neither," Boggs said.

Though McInnis had wanted to meet with Floyd alone, he'd realized it presented the possibility of his walking into an unsafe situation. He didn't think a licensed detective would do anything *too* stupid, but still, McInnis had always preached safety to his men, so he exercised it here as well. He'd asked Dewey and Boggs (both in their civvies and both armed) to follow him in Dewey's Pontiac, parking at the far end of the block. The isolation of Floyd's office came in handy, as two Negroes sitting in a parked car might have seemed suspicious had anyone noticed.

Glad that morning wasn't as cold as some, and sipping thermoses of warm coffee, they'd been sitting there about fifteen minutes when they'd seen a DeSoto park in front of the building, driven by a white man. He and his passenger, a white woman who matched the description of Call Me Becky, hurried out of the car as if they were late for something.

"Why are they moving so fast?" Dewey asked. "Looks like an ambush."

"Maybe they're just late."

They waited another minute. The seconds crawling past.

"We should get closer at least," Dewey said. "See if we can hear anything."

They got out and closed their doors. They had parked on the opposite side of the street, and they walked across the empty road. They were less than ten feet from the building when they heard a gunshot.

"Frisk him," Sam told Becky.

Though enraged, McInnis knew nothing good would come of his escalating things. He wondered what Boggs and Dewey were doing as Becky patted him down, removing his .38 from its shoulder holster. As she stepped away, Sam extended his free hand and said, "Give it here."

"You all are making a serious mistake."

Becky handed McInnis's gun to Sam, who slid it into his belt.

"Why's that?" Sam asked with eyes gone blank. Eyes like McInnis had seen only a few times. "You're barely even a cop. More like a zookeeper. No one'll miss you."

McInnis realized how badly he'd miscalculated. These people weren't just working for someone who'd killed Bishop—*they* had killed him. That was the only explanation for why they would take the chance of holding a cop at gunpoint.

"The way I see it is, you came here to order Warren around," Sam explained. "Things got heated and you drew your weapon, firing at Warren, but just barely missing him. Hit that wall behind him, maybe. So Warren had no choice but to shoot back. Right, Warren?"

Floyd seemed to consider this calmly and McInnis went even colder.

"Wait," Becky said. But instead of stepping forward to intervene, she was stepping back again to remove herself from the imminent crossfire. "Let's think this over a minute."

"There's nothing to think about," Floyd said. "You have any idea how much fucking trouble we're in if he walks out of here? The time to think was last week, when—"

"Can it!" Sam snapped.

Despite the trio's bickering, this had attained a momentum McInnis needed to stop. "Everyone needs to calm down," he said, shifting his gaze between the two armed men, "and put your guns away."

Floyd too stepped back so as not to be hit by a stray bullet from Sam's gun. Sam then placed his own weapon in his hip holster, but that was not the good news it had at first seemed, because then he took out McInnis's pistol and aimed it at McInnis.

He was pinned in a corner by a trio, two of them with weapons trained on him, a third with her hand reaching for yet another gun. It was a small room and no one was very far from a wall or piece of furniture.

Then something seemed to distract Becky. She stepped closer to the window, where the two blinds were mostly but not completely closed. She widened the gap between two of the slats with her fingers, and said, "There are two Negroes walking over here."

"What?" Floyd asked. He started walking over to the window to see for himself, which meant McInnis was no longer hemmed between Floyd and Sam. Sam turned around to face the door.

For that one brief moment, all of their backs were turned to McInnis.

He charged at Floyd, wrapping his left arm around his throat and reaching for his gun with his right. They struggled for the gun, which fired into the ground. McInnis knew that Sam would be pointing his piece at them, but now Floyd was the one in the middle.

It had seemed his best play, but it still wasn't a good one. He and Floyd stood there locked together, and McInnis tried to keep his feet planted while he freed the gun from Floyd's grip. He slammed Floyd's hand into the wall and the gun fell. Then Floyd used his now-gunless hand to reach for McInnis's left arm, still wrapped around his neck, and he twisted his body, the two of them rotating sideways.

Another gun fired.

"Police!" he heard Dewey and Boggs shouting outside. "Come out with your hands up!"

McInnis released Floyd and he stumbled back, dizzy. His ears rang in a way they never had before, like something inside them had come loose, vertigo overtaking him. Floyd slipped to the ground, then dove for his gun. McInnis looked up at Sam, who still stood with his back to the door, facing him, and then McInnis fell.

Not until he looked down at himself did he realize he'd been shot. He smelled cordite and singed wool, and the way his jacket had fallen open he could see the redness spreading so very quickly across his white shirt.

McInnis went cold, parts of his body rendered immobile. Sam pushed Becky out of the way so he too could look through the blinds. Sam stepped back and fired through the window, three times.

Becky ducked down and started crawling on the ground toward the back rooms. McInnis was glad at least one of them was sane, but sanity did not seem to be winning today. To his left, he could see Floyd starting to pick himself up, and no doubt looking for his gun.

Another shot, this one from outside, shattering another panel of the window. Sam ducked beneath the window, then rose up again and aimed through one of the holes in the blinds, firing twice more.

No more shots from outside. McInnis had drilled into them the importance of not firing unless their lives depended on it. They couldn't see inside yet, didn't know where people were standing. They had fired once in retaliation but they must have realized they didn't have a decent shot and didn't want to take the risk of hitting McInnis.

He would have called instructions out to them, told them where to fire, but his voice wasn't working.

He was half lying on the floor, half leaning against the nonexistent secretary's desk. His right leg was bent. He thought about pressing a hand into his wound to staunch the flow. He tried to be rational. He'd been hit well below the heart, below the lungs. He could survive, maybe. But when he moved an arm toward all that red, some animalistic imperative took over and he could not touch himself there.

Becky had done a half-assed job of frisking him and hadn't checked for an ankle holster, so that's where McInnis reached, pulling out his .38 special.

He aimed at Sam, who was still firing through the window.

Two shots and Sam went down.

McInnis moved his arm again, which still seemed to be working but might not be for much longer. He couldn't see Floyd or Becky. Furniture stood in his way. They were impassable mountains to him.

He was exposed and knew he needed to move. He wasn't sure he could.

He put his left hand against the wall and tried to push himself up, but he felt a stabbing pain in his side. *Stabbing* didn't do the pain justice. It was as though the bullet had nailed him to the wall. He gasped and dropped his gun and slumped further down.

The gun was only a few inches from his hand. It shouldn't have been that hard to pick it back up. But he knew he never would.

Floyd stepped out from somewhere—McInnis couldn't quite tell where—and was standing before him now. Aiming a gun at McInnis's head. McInnis stared at the son of a bitch and hoped at the very least that Floyd would remember this expression for the rest of his life.

The shot loud but not as loud as it should have been.

Floyd's head burst. Blood spattering the wall to McInnis's right.

Floyd dropped and landed in a heap just inches away. McInnis managed to swivel his head just enough to see Becky standing near the desk, gun outstretched.

He still wasn't quite sure which side she was on, but that was a hell of a vote in her favor. He tried to thank her but it came out small, a whisper, and he coughed.

Wood splintered as the door was kicked open, nearly hitting McInnis. Boggs's gun and outstretched arms reached into the room like some lethal proboscis, twitching this way and that, and then Boggs himself stepped inside.

"Police!" Boggs shouted. "Drop your weapons!"

Sergeant and officer made eye contact. McInnis could feel Boggs's eyes sweep across his bloody stomach—even someone looking at it hurt—and then Boggs continued scanning the room. McInnis wanted to warn him that Becky still had a gun and was in perfect position to shoot Boggs, but his voice was gone, his body shutting down.

40

NONE OF THE Negro officers had ever been shot. McInnis was white, of course, but this still was the first time Boggs had seen one of the men he worked with closely lying on the ground with a bullet wound.

He stared an extra second longer than he should have.

"Don't shoot!" a woman's voice called.

He moved his gun and saw her standing in the corner of the room, near the desk. A gun in her hand. It wasn't aimed at him, but that could change in a heartbeat.

"Drop your weapon!" he shouted.

Her fingers straightened and she let the revolver fall onto the desk.

He shouted at her to keep her hands high and she obeyed. Her eyes wide, in shock and fear. He probably looked the same way.

Keeping his gun on her, he scanned the room. Near the window, one white man lay flat on his stomach, the back of his jacket torn and bloody. Just in front of McInnis, another white man lay on the ground, half his head missing. Some of it seemed to be on the wall a few inches from Boggs.

"I don't know what happened," the lady said. "Warren and Sam just went crazy. They . . . they were going to kill him!"

Boggs told her to put her hands against the wall. He pulled her wrists behind her, stuffing his gun into his belt holster and using that now-free hand to grab his cuffs and fasten them on her wrists. Cuffing a white person for only the second time in his life.

"Oh my God." Her eyes wide as he pushed her roughly onto a chair. "This wasn't supposed to happen. They—"

"Be quiet. Not a word."

He frisked the woman, who must have been Call Me Becky, finding no other weapon than the one he'd already put in his pocket. He had three guns on his person now. He found her ID in her purse. Real name, Lisa Collins. He tried to commit that and her address to memory, though his nerves were firing so fast right then he couldn't be certain he'd remember later.

"I'm the reason he's still alive!" she snapped. "I shot Warren before he could put one in his head."

Boggs looked at McInnis, his face whiter than usual. The sergeant nodded slightly, confirming what she'd said. Or maybe he was going into spasms.

Boggs heard the sound of a back door being kicked open, and Dewey's feet stomping inside.

"We have two dead in here, and a third cuffed!" Boggs shouted. "McInnis has been shot!"

Dewey yelled "Clear," from another room, then stepped into this one. He surveyed the carnage but focused on McInnis.

Boggs grabbed a man's jacket that had been slung over one of the chairs and crouched before his sergeant. He balled it up and pressed it into McInnis's midsection. McInnis sucked in his breath. It looked like McInnis was trying to move, but the wound was an anchor, tethering him to this spot. The nearest hospital felt light years away.

Boggs had seen plenty of civilians shot, a few even shot in the chest or gut like McInnis. Some lived, many didn't. He often guessed wrong.

"Call headquarters," Boggs told Dewey, holstering his gun. As Dewey found a phone and relayed the news to dispatch, Boggs pressed the jacket again into McInnis. The sergeant screamed.

"You need to hang on for me, Sergeant."

Dewey redid Becky's cuffs, fastening her to the desk's metal leg.

"More officers are on their way here now," he told her. "If you even attempt to escape, we will hunt you down and shoot first next time."

She started to explain again that she hadn't been a part of this, the men had just gone berserk and she'd done what she could to help, until Dewey took advantage of this rare opportunity to tell a white lady to shut the hell up.

~

Dewey took the wheel and Boggs stayed in back, holding the jacket against McInnis's wound. The potholed road felt even bumpier than before. Boggs could see that every jostle made McInnis wince.

"Listen," McInnis rasped.

"No, Sergeant, don't talk. It tenses your stomach. I need you to relax, all right?" Yet he knew his own voice was anything but calm. "We'll be at the hospital soon."

"You need to know," McInnis said, and Boggs understood it as *otherwise, if I die, the information dies with me.* "Paulding was their client. He hired them . . . because there's some old rumor . . . about Paulding . . . didn't want the story out."

In any other circumstance, Boggs would have asked him for more information. But all he could think right then was, *Hurry up, Dewey.*

"Sergeant, I need you to relax and stop talking."

Within blocks they were in a busier part of downtown, Dewey leaning on his horn. Boggs glanced out the window and flinched as another car, headed straight at them, slammed on its brakes just inches away. Dewey was blowing through intersections, his foot heavy on the pedal, liberally deploying his horn in lieu of a siren, though it certainly didn't cause the same response from the other drivers. How ironic if a white cop would become the first to die as a direct result of the Negro officers not having a squad car.

McInnis kept rambling. "Don't know if it's true . . . Bishop was trying to . . . track the porter down."

"Hold tight!" Dewey yelled, and the car lurched to the left, Boggs's head hitting against the window.

When Boggs looked down, McInnis's entire body had gone

tense, his back arching, his chin high, head pulled back. *Oh Jesus, oh Lord, this is it.*

Then he realized McInnis was actually laughing. Or trying to, his ribcage and mouth and mind at war with each other, some strange thought gripping him but his body fighting it.

"Sergeant, just hang on for me, all right? Look at me. Look me in the eye."

"Funny," McInnis managed to say. "Dodd offered me a way out . . . Said I could . . . work with white cops again . . . " His cough became a laugh. Or the other way around. Boggs wondered if it was a good sign that no blood had come out of his mouth. His training lessons in first aid had barely touched on gunshot wounds, and that deficit seemed so glaring now, unforgivable; he would write to the Chief to complain.

"Just hang on there, Sergeant."

Dewey slammed on the brakes. Boggs lurched forward and nearly tumbled over the seat and into the front.

Dewey leaned on his horn and screamed, "Move, goddamnit!" Two seconds that felt like forever. *We cannot afford to be motionless. We must hurtle ever forward, otherwise death.* The engine revved again. Dewey shouted back to them, "Less than a minute, Sergeant! Don't make me come back there and slap you in the face!"

McInnis continued his delirious ramble. "Looks like . . . I'll be leaving the Y . . . just not . . . the way I thought."

But they hadn't been stationed at the Y in years. The skin around his eyes seemed to be relaxing, his eyes glassy.

Two minutes later, Dewey pulled up in front of the hospital. McInnis hadn't spoken another word.

PART FOUR

41

THE FOLLOWING MORNING, as the *Daily Times* story about the FBI tailing Mrs. Bishop was being read across Negro Atlanta, and hopefully some other places as well, Smith and Toon made the long drive to Montgomery.

They arrived in time for lunch, having left at sunrise. Tired, legs cramped and bladders full, they'd gone a long stretch between areas where they would have been allowed to use the facilities, so they hadn't stopped. Smith had never set foot in Montgomery before, but his handy Green Book guided them to Holt Street, the main thoroughfare of the city's colored district.

They passed an unusual number of men and women on foot on the sidewalks, and on streets that lacked sidewalks. The boycott of the city's transportation services appeared to be in full swing even on that bitterly cold morning. Frost had glazed the ground and tree branches in Atlanta when they'd left, and now in Montgomery hours later the gray skies were low and a harsh wind whipped people's scarves and fluttered their jackets.

A crumpled copy of that morning's *Daily Times* lay on the floorboards, Smith having read various stories aloud to Toon, since he couldn't do any of the driving himself with his right hand in the cast and one eye still swollen mostly shut. Still no arrests had been made in the bombing of Reverend King Jr.'s home.

Though they were in a rush to reach their destination, they stopped at a deli to eat and use the restroom. The man at the counter said, no, he hadn't ridden a bus since early December, and neither had anyone who worked for him.

Back in the car, they checked their map for the right street. On the way there, cold rain began to fall. They were about to pass an older woman, shoulders hunched, clutching a paper bag but not an umbrella, when Toon pulled over.

"Can we give you a ride, ma'am?" Smith asked.

She took a moment, then decided these gentlemen looked trustworthy enough and climbed in.

"Thank you. I normally do carry my umbrella, but today I forgot. Skies just can't make up their mind."

They talked about the weather, unpredictable in February. And every other month.

She explained that she had just picked up a few items for her niece, who'd given birth two days ago, and who lived on the other side of town. Used to be your whole family was on the same block, but times were changing.

Toon asked if she had ridden the buses since the boycott started.

"Oh, no. And I know it's cold, but I'm still walking." After a pause, she said, "This a nice car you have. Guess you don't need to use the bus, huh?"

"We're from Atlanta, ma'am," Smith said.

She thought for a moment. "You riding the bus over in Atlanta?"

"I have a car, too," Smith said, then considered lying but admitted, "it's in the shop a lot, and when that happens, yeah, I do ride the bus."

She didn't say anything, didn't judge him. But he judged himself.

"Turn right up there," she told Toon. "What brings y'all to Montgomery?"

"We're reporters, ma'am, for the *Atlanta Daily Times,*" Smith said.

"You writing about the boycott?"

"Not today. We're reporting on something else."

﹀

Ten minutes later, after dropping her off, they arrived at a block of tightly packed bungalows that would have been shaded by massive oak trees had this been two months later. No driveways here. A few scattered cars were parked on the street, none of them occupied. The rain had already stopped, but the cold hadn't, so their jackets were buttoned and collars high as they knocked on the door of Maurice Vincent, retired Pullman porter.

The man who opened the door was tall enough that Smith imagined him ducking to fit through the passages between train cars. Age bent his shoulders in a mild stoop. Gray flannel shirt, blue sweater vest, a full head of white hair and a matching mustache.

"Good afternoon, Mr. Vincent?" Smith asked.

"Who's asking?" He stared at Smith's bandages and swollen eye.

"Sir, my name's Tommy Smith, and this is Jeremy Toon. We're reporters for the *Atlanta Daily Times*. We were hoping we—"

"Oh, Lord, no." It was as though Smith had said they were representatives of the Grim Reaper and he was late for his appointment. Vincent looked over their shoulders, checking for a scythe perhaps. "No more reporters."

Toon asked, "Sir, have you already spoken with our publisher, Mr. Bishop?"

"I'm not talking to anyone," and he started closing the door.

But not before Smith put his foot in it. "Mr. Vincent, please. We know about Henry Paulding. We know you haven't done anything wrong, but we'd really like to talk to you. We drove all the way from Atlanta."

"Sir," Toon said, "we were hoping you could repeat whatever you told him, because he never had a chance to tell us. Mr. Bishop's dead."

The old man slowly lifted a hand to his heart. Looked shocked. And scared.

"I told him no good would come from this."

～

Minutes later, after he'd invited them in, they sat drinking coffee the old man had insisted on making. The home was tidy and well-kept, wood banister and molding recently shined, windows spotless, tables uncluttered. Photos on the walls bore evidence of a large family.

They sat at an old dining room table, the dark wood scratched here and there, Smith noticing some indented numbers as from a child's pencil pressing hard while doing homework.

"What happened to you?" he asked Smith.

"Car accident, sir," Smith lied. Concealed by his jacket, his revolver hung heavy in his shoulder holster. "I'm all right."

After countless hours of reading through Bishop's various papers, Smith had finally found the old interview notes that had caused Mr. Bishop so much trouble. Notes featuring a porter. Bishop's killers may have stolen some of Bishop's files on this story, but they hadn't found these years-old papers, which finally put Smith on the right trail. And thanks to the Pullman Company's strong record-keeping and its healthy network of retirees, he and Toon had found the right porter.

Smith still didn't know much about yesterday's shoot-out between police and Warren Floyd's crew. He'd reported on it as best he could for today's edition—two men were dead and a woman was being held, but thus far she hadn't been charged with murder. Boggs and Dewey had vanished, though, either suspended or in some kind of bureaucratic lockdown. None of the other Negro cops would answer Smith's calls, and when he'd cornered some of them outside their apartments or when walking their beats, they all shook him off. *This is serious as hell and I ain't losing my badge. Go away, Reporter Man.*

The Department itself was giving out almost zero information. The only thing they were saying was that two white men had been killed in a shoot-out with police and that Sergeant McInnis was in critical condition. Investigation ongoing.

"How long were you a Pullman man, Mr. Vincent?" Smith asked.

"Thirty-one years. It was a good job. Now, I don't kid myself, it was being a waiter, a janitor, a go-fetch-me-this-now. Back before I started, they used to call all porters *George*, like you didn't have your own name. Just George. And there were a few times I got called worse than that. But I put up with it, because it paid. There were some bad shifts, some *long* shifts, let me tell you, but then I'd get home and cross paths with this old friend who still couldn't find no job, this fella just got out of jail because he robbed somebody to feed his pregnant girlfriend, this fella I used to look up to but now the only job he can find is emptying trash somewhere, and I'd think to myself, okay now, riding the rails ain't so bad after all." He nodded. "I made some good friends. Saw the whole country. We looked out for each other. Had to learn a lot. A *lot*."

Smith nodded along, not wanting to be impolite, but fearing this would go on forever.

"Now, I grew up in a small town in central Tennessee, understand, and I knew how to navigate that world. The rules, the law. The unwritten rules. Unwritten ones the most important, understand?"

"That's right," Smith agreed.

"And you may know the unwritten rules in your own hometown, but what rules they got in Chattanooga? How 'bout Lexington, Cincinnati, St. Louis? We went everywhere, boy, and had to learn the rules right off. Had to know which direction to walk once you left the station, whether you were in Pittsburg or Lynchburg. I knew some fellas ran into some serious trouble just 'cause they got bad directions and walked into white parts of town at night, got hassled, got beat, got arrested." He shook his head. "You had to learn *quick*."

"Mr. Vincent," Smith gently prodded, "what can you tell me about Henry Paulding?"

"You want to hear my story but on your own time, huh? All right. Here's how it was. Sometimes the passengers treated us okay, sometimes they treated us downright nasty. But most of the time they just treated us like wallpaper. Refill their glasses, have their newspaper ready, prepare their bed, all that, but without them even noticing you. But the wallpaper sees things. Saw married men taking other women into their sleepers. Sometimes married men taking *men* into their sleepers. Gambling, drugs—Lord, men traveling alone like to get in trouble. And when the only people watching 'em are colored men in porter uniforms, well, to them it must have felt like nobody was watching at all."

Smith shot a look at Toon, who widened his eyes slightly. They were just going to have to hear this fellow out.

"When folks got to drinking at night, well, that's when the *real* trouble occurred. So this Paulding fellow, he was . . . he was memorable. I wouldn't have remembered the exact day or year, but that other writer who came by, Bishop, he'd done his homework and said it was probably April of '25. All I remember is, I was young. I'd started in '18. Anyway, we were heading south from Chicago. Loved Chicago. Had a lot of great times there. Thought about moving there, honestly . . . " and he rambled on for a spell, about the wonderful Midwestern capital and its promise of freedom, but finally he picked up the thread.

"One night, real late, the dining car is full of men drinking. Now, that's where the porters are supposed to sleep, and there *is* an official closing time, per the Pullman Manual, which was our sacred text. But the Manual *also* said we were never supposed to kick paying passengers out of that car if they were still up and enjoying themselves. Now that there is a challenging contradiction. But when there's a contradiction, you figure it in the white man's favor. So me and another porter, fella by the name of Antoine, we were both waiting these white boys out. Four of 'em. Young, like I was, but acted older 'n they were. Acted like they got the whole world at their feet, when really they only been outta their mama's house a few years."

He sipped his coffee. "It's two, three in the morning, and me and Antoine just dying to get some sleep, but they ain't showing no sign of slowing down. Now this one, Henry Paulding, he's got shaggy blond hair, he seemed the least drunk. He had this way about him. Steely. More he drank, more in control he seemed. Got to the point they were telling stories, you know, about the worst things they'd ever done. One of 'em admits he got three girlfriends pregnant already, arranged back-alley doctors for all of 'em. One almost bled to death." He shook his head, still offended after all these years. "Anyway, apparently Paulding felt he had to one-up that story. So he did. He started telling his story about a Negro butler his father had, back in Atlanta, and how Paulding never could stand that butler. Said he was haughty, didn't know his place," and he raised his eyebrows at those well-worn phrases. "Now, as he's telling this story, me and Antoine look at each other, wondering if really he's talking to *us*. Talking to us without actually talking to us, you know how they do."

Toon scribbled notes, Smith feeling nakedly pen-less due to his cast.

"Then Antoine gets rung by a passenger, so he heads out of the car. Now it's just me and the white boys. And Paulding goes on and tells these three friends of his, with me standing not more 'n ten feet away from him, about how he decided to *teach that nigger a lesson*. His words. One day just a few years earlier, he says, Paulding visited his daddy's house when Daddy wasn't there. And while the butler was out in the backyard, cleaning up, Paulding says he lured him over to their pool and knocked the man down, and pushed him in the pool. Then . . . "

He paused for a moment, distraught. His mind lingering on the memory.

Smith finished for him: "Then Paulding got in the pool with him, and held the butler's head underwater and drowned him. And he told people later he'd found the butler there in the water, that he must have had a heart attack and fallen in."

"Yes," Vincent said, surprised. "How'd you know? Did Bishop tell you?"

"No, but I've been reading through his old papers. He wrote a short story about this, years ago. I'd thought it was fiction but, turns out, it was based on the truth."

Bishop's unfinished memoir had included a passage about his early days interviewing porters for the WPA and hearing their tales of mistreatment, including a few times when inebriated white passengers had confessed, in front of the horrified porters, that they'd committed crimes. One white man had even admitted drowning his parents' butler, the memoir had noted, without giving any other details. When Smith read that, he remembered how one of Bishop's old, unpublished fiction pieces had featured a similar murder by drowning: a young white man of privilege decides to kill an old Negro butler for fun, drowning him in his parents' pool—and getting away with it.

Bishop had disguised the truth in fiction. After Smith had seen the reference to a drowning in Bishop's memoir, he'd gone back and reread the "fiction" and realized that Bishop had barely even changed the killer's name: the fictionalized Henry Paulding was "Paul Henry."

"What happened next, in the train car?" Smith asked.

"I have never felt tension like that in my life. Now, *he* laughed a few times. But the other three were silent. Uncomfortable. It was like Paulding just thought he was topping their stories, that's all, and he felt like he'd won the contest, but the other three . . . " He shook his head again. "One of them decided to call it a night, and they all went off to bed. So finally I could, too. But I couldn't sleep. I just felt . . . disgusted. Sick to my stomach. Then a couple hours later it was time for the workday to start. And a few hours after that, Paulding wakes up, comes out to the dining car, and he seeks me out. Smiles. Even puts his hand on my shoulder. Says he hoped I didn't mind, it was just a tall tale. Nothing to worry about. See how he did that, letting me know that I wasn't the wallpaper at all? He'd known I was there listening the whole time." Another pause. "I just nodded and said, oh, I understand, sir. And I walked away from him fast as I could without *looking* like I was running away."

Smith asked, "But you believe Paulding's story was true, Mr. Vincent?"

Vincent's eyes pressed into his. "Without a doubt."

"You told Mr. Bishop about this, years later, in the thirties?" Toon asked.

"That's right. He was interviewing porters for that WPA project. Government was paying him and a bunch of other writers just to interview folks and write their stories down. I talked to Bishop for hours. I got to thinking about that night, probably a decade earlier, when Henry Paulding had told his tale about killing a Negro with his bare hands like it was no worse 'n driving over a squirrel. And I told him."

Smith thinking, first Henry Paulding tells a story to his friends and an eavesdropping porter. Then, years later, the porter retells the story to a young WPA reporter who, many more years later, becomes the editor of a newspaper. Vincent was convinced Paulding's story was true, but how could they prove it?

It was only after hearing from Boggs about how someone had been blackmailed into spying on Bishop, and then reading the part of Bishop's memoir about porters, that things came together for Smith: Henry Paulding had hired private detectives because he was afraid an unflattering story would get out and sabotage his urban redevelopment project. The story had something to do with a horrible crime he'd once confessed to a porter, whom Bishop had been trying to track down.

The story *must* be true, or Paulding wouldn't have tried so hard to suppress it. But, again, how could they prove it?

"Mr. Bishop found you again, recently?" Smith asked.

"That's right. Years had gone by since that WPA interview. Two decades or so. I'm retired. Worked long, worked hard, raised a family. Five children, twelve grandchildren. A great-grandchild on the way." He smiled, gazing into space. Smith felt conscious of all the framed photographs surrounding them, the many generations pretending not to eavesdrop. "One day I get a knock on my door, and there's this fellow I don't recognize one bit. He reminds me of our talk for the WPA, and I certainly remembered that. I'd only told a few people about Paulding, and each time was memorable, believe me. Bishop tells me he's now the editor of the *Atlanta Daily Times*. And that fills me with some pride, because I read that paper many times, passed it around the trains, helped move it across the country in my small way. And he tells me he wants to talk about that Henry Paulding story again." He sighed with dread.

"Had you forgotten the details?" Smith asked.

"I won't forget a detail of what Paulding said as long as I live. I have nightmares about it still. Bishop said he wanted to look into it, find the butler's death record, find people who knew him, or knew Paulding back then. Find whatever there was to find. Said he'd always meant to go back to that story, but life kept him busy and he never got around to it until now. Said Paulding had become a big shot in Atlanta, and now Bishop needed to know for sure if he really was a stone killer."

Toon asked, "And you believe he's a stone killer?"

"With every fiber of my being."

Vincent let that sink in a spell, then continued, "Bishop told me that, if he determined it really was a murder, he was going to write about it in his paper. He was asking my permission to finally go public with what I'd told him. He pointed out I was an old man now, retired, couldn't nobody hurt me for talking." He laughed. "I finally told him, yes, he could use my story, but," and he pressed his finger into the table to punctuate each syllable here, "I did not want to be named." He gestured to the framed photographs. "Don't tell me I can't be hurt."

"An unnamed source," Toon said.

"That's right. I would be his unnamed source, but that's it."

Smith asked, "What happened next, sir?"

"Nothing. We talk a good while, then he leaves. That was, what, three weeks ago? Four? Then you show up here today and tell me the man is *dead*. How am I supposed to feel about that? How safe am I supposed to feel? And my family?"

"Sir, I don't have all the answers here," Smith explained, not wanting to offer false hope. "I still don't know who killed Mr. Bishop or why. I don't know for sure that it had anything to do with this. I do know that Henry Paulding was concerned this story might come to light, and he suspected Bishop was looking into it. But I don't know that Paulding knew about your recent talk. And I can tell you, sincerely, no one but the three of us knows we're here, no one followed us, and no one is watching us right now."

"How would you even know?"

"I used to be a policeman, Mr. Vincent. We were not followed. There's no one outside watching us."

Vincent's eyes stayed on Smith's. "An ex-cop, huh?"

"Yes, sir."

"Why aren't you a cop anymore?" He glanced again at Smith's cast. "Too many 'car accidents'?"

Smith leaned back. Being asked so often didn't make answering any easier. "It's hard to explain, sir. Partly because I got tired of hearing about things like this and not being able to do anything about it."

"What can you do now?"

"At the very least, Mr. Vincent, I can shine a spotlight on it. And I can still try to get this into the hands of someone who *can* arrest him."

"So you're going to write about it." Vincent sounded disappointed but resigned.

Toon said, "We can leave your name out of it if you'd prefer."

"Make me an unnamed source again?"

"Unnamed source works for us, Mr. Vincent," Smith said.

The old man looked Smith in the eye as he nodded his assent.

⤙

They had researched Henry Paulding before making the drive. Born in '05, fifty years old. His father, Horace, had built a number of grand homes in Inman Park, a tony neighborhood just east of downtown (so Smith had been told; though it was less than two miles from his office, he had never laid eyes on it). Henry was the eldest of four children. Vanderbilt graduate, got right to work with his old man, who passed away in '42, at which time thirty-seven-year-old Henry took the reins. Over the last few years, some of Paulding Builders' biggest jobs had been commercial: two downtown towers, an office development south of Buckhead.

Neither Henry Paulding nor his father had ever been arrested, nor had any relatives the reporters could identify. Henry belonged to all the important fraternal orders and donated liberally to charities, sat on a few boards for arts associations and a hospital, was a regular at Crackers games. He appeared to be well-liked, a pillar of the community.

He maybe killed a man with his bare hands once.

"For the sake of discussion," Toon said as he drove Smith back to Atlanta, "do you think there's any chance Paulding didn't do it, and he just made it up to talk big and impress his bratty friends?"

"Mr. Vincent was convinced. That's good enough for me."

"Me too. I was trying to be a skeptical reporter, but … it just makes too much sense."

They were quiet for a spell, both filled with silent rage. A rich white man kills a Negro for no reason. For kicks. Because he can. Then goddamn *brags* about it. Like Emmett Till's murderers, selling their story to *Look* magazine.

The key difference: Till's killers had already been exonerated by a sham trial before they started yakking, but Paulding could still be tried.

In theory.

He was a powerful man, and this was a decades-old crime.

Smith stared at Toon's notes. As the doctor had warned, his head still felt fuzzy. Too many sentence fragments dancing there without punctuation. Objects deprived of subjects. Effect missing cause. The more he tried to concentrate, the more his mind turned back into that fumbling quarterback, footballs bouncing everywhere, their meaning elusive.

This much was easy to focus on: another white person had killed a Negro. Which made Smith think again of the father he'd never known, murdered by a mob that simply couldn't stand the sight of him. An event he had no memory of, yet it was the defining moment of his life, and its echoes kept haunting him no matter how long he lived or what he tried to do about it.

He tried to focus.

"So Paulding hired the detectives because he caught wind that

Bishop was looking into the old story. Bishop must have pulled legal records, called the butler's surviving relatives, done *something* that tipped Paulding off."

"The killer stole Bishop's notes from his desk. That's why his desk was messy that night."

Something else clicked in Smith's mind. "And remember those financial records that Crispin dug up? Think about it: Bishop's going to invest with Clancy Darden in the big urban redevelopment, but then he hears an old rumor that Paulding, one of the key builders in the plan, killed his own butler once. He asks around and realizes it's the same story he himself heard way back for the WPA project. He wonders if it's just some myth, a bogeyman tale, but if there's any chance it's real, there's no way he'll do business with a white man like that. So he tries to verify it, he digs up his old notes, tracks down Mr. Vincent. He hears what we just heard and he decides, hell yes, Paulding *was* a killer. So he tells his attorney, Branford, that he doesn't want to invest after all and that Branford should pull Bishop's money out of his deal with Darden. Which makes Darden a suspect, since he wouldn't have wanted to lose that money. But meanwhile, from Bishop's perspective, pulling out still isn't enough; he's also going to write an exposé to take the white man down."

Silence for a quarter-mile as they considered the angles, mentally double-checked Smith's theory.

"That works," Toon said. "But we still don't have *proof* Paulding killed anyone, either the butler or Bishop."

"Night he died, Bishop asked me how I felt when murderers got away with it. He knew Paulding had gotten away with it, after all this time." Smith stewed as he stared out at leafless trees, fallow farms, an ancient land inscribed with forced toil and blood. "And it's only gotten worse since then."

42

THE FIRST TWENTY-FOUR hours after the shoot-out passed in a haze for Boggs, a long nightmare leaving his senses raw. First the rush to the Gradys, not knowing if McInnis was even alive anymore, then getting his own wounds tended at the other side of the hospital, the one that treated Negroes (he had belatedly noticed that his neck was bleeding, as gunshots into the wall behind him had driven woodchips into his flesh). With his neck stitched up, barely able to nod or shake his head without causing himself more pain, he endured the endless interviews from Captain Dodd and white homicide detectives who refused on principle to believe anything he told them.

Why were you even there? Why were you investigating this case? Why did you discharge your weapon? And from the opposite tack, *Why weren't you beside your sergeant, why were you cowering outside?* The questions more pointed over time, the higher-ups outraged that Boggs and Dewey had been doing police work off the clock and outside any Negro neighborhoods, outraged that a sergeant had taken the bullet, outraged that Boggs had fired his weapon near white people, near *a white lady* of all things.

Interviews at the hospital, at the station, in offices, in interrogation rooms. Even Chief Jenkins dropped by; he was the first person to make Boggs feel that perhaps he had at least one white ally left, but he wondered if that was enough.

They'd allowed him only one call to his wife, Julie, as if he were under arrest, a felon and not a cop. When he finally walked home after midnight, she was still awake, bleary-eyed on the couch. She held him a while, and even that hurt his neck, then he told her he needed rest. He hadn't eaten since breakfast, yet he collapsed into bed and fell asleep immediately.

He slept fitfully, his stitched neck and his frayed nerves waking him again and again.

He finally dragged himself out of bed in the late morning. He called his colleagues for an update on McInnis. Then he ate, carefully showered from the neck down, changed, and called Dewey. The white lady, Lisa Collins, was claiming she'd tried to help McInnis fight the other two off, and had shot Floyd to save McInnis. The other two were loose cannons, she'd said, and she the lone voice of reason at that agency. Ballistics was still trying to see who had shot whom; she was being held in custody, but if the tests confirmed that she shot Floyd then she'd probably be released. The police didn't seem much closer to finding out who had killed Bishop, but surely the file cabinets in Floyd's office would point them in the right direction.

After Boggs had taken all this in, he told Dewey his plan.

Clancy Darden looked ashen as he greeted Boggs at the door.

"Lucius, are you all right?"

"Cut myself shaving, Mr. Darden. May I come in, please?"

Again he was offered coffee, again he declined, and again he found himself sitting in Darden's impressively appointed den. This time, though, he would not be lied to.

"Surely you're joking about the neck?" Darden's face twisted a bit, like a man in pain trying but failing to smile.

"I am, Mr. Darden. I was shot at. Me and some other officers were shot at. Our sergeant's in critical condition."

"Oh dear. I'm so sorry to hear that."

Given Boggs's exhaustion, and the pain behind his eyes, it was all he could do not to stare at Darden so hatefully the man would recoil, run away. And Boggs could hear it, from the quiver in Darden's usually forceful voice, and see it in the way Darden kept readjusting himself, as if his chair was not soft leather but a concrete block in a prison cell.

Darden felt cornered.

"It's a hard job, Mr. Darden." Boggs's voice quieter than usual. "I've been doing it nearly eight years now, and parts of it have gotten easier. Parts haven't. But my father, he's always pushed us to believe we could do more if we really tried, if we stuck with it."

"Yes. You should be proud."

Boggs knew he played a role, even if it was one that often made him uncomfortable. Like standing on those stages for Mayor Hartsfield's rallies. Men like Bishop and Darden played roles, too, and Boggs finally saw how that had contributed to this convoluted affair.

When Reverend Boggs had tipped off the *Daily Times* about the redevelopment plan, the paper's story had caught the city councilmen off guard. The white papers had paid no notice, as they looked down on the Negro press and didn't like to acknowledge the fact that their perceived inferiors could scoop them. So the *Constitution* and *Journal* had simply ignored the story, deciding they would cover it once the city made its proper announcement, which still hadn't occurred yet.

Boggs realized that the city councilmen hadn't wanted to announce the plan until they had some Negro partners involved. With prominent businessmen like Bishop and Darden lined up, the project would have been protected from charges that it was bad for the community. Bishop was doubly important, since his participation would have kept the influential *Daily Times* on board.

"Reginald always spoke well of you, Mr. Darden. He said you were a fair boss. And I've always respected you, sir, all that you've accomplished. People like you and me, and my father, and Mr. Bishop . . . we're different than most folks. Aren't we? We accomplish more, we're capable of more."

Boggs was saying what Darden needed to hear. He himself wasn't so curdled with pride, at least he hoped he wasn't. But he believed to his core that a man like Darden *did* feel this way, assured of his status and the rightness of all that he had.

Boggs continued, "I know that other people, they look at how low they are and how high we are, and they resent us for it. I mean, the things I have to do in this job, the sacrifices I have to make, every day, every night? It's easy for them to mock me, call me the white man's house slave. I know they say that about me. Probably say plenty about you, too. People like them could never understand what happened that night at Mr. Bishop's office. But I do."

Darden's brow knit, concern on his face. "I don't ... I don't follow."

"Other people don't know what it's like to deal with all that we have to deal with every day. They don't understand the pressures we're under. How success has *costs*. And it takes risk to get there. When Bishop told you he was going to pull out of that real estate deal, that would have financially ruined you, right?"

"Lucius ... "

"Your years of hard work would have blown up, just because he got cold feet. If Bishop had pulled out his money and the plan collapsed after you'd already invested in all that shoddy real estate, I mean, you would have lost a *lot*, right?"

Darden's voice was choked, small. "Not a lot. *Everything*."

Boggs waited.

"I never should have ... " Darden looked down and took off his glasses, his hand shaking. "I made bad decisions, overleveraged myself. But I still would have been all right if the city hadn't used eminent domain to take half my properties last year. I got pennies on the dollar, nearly ruined. People see how I dress and where I live and they just assume, *assume* everything is always fine and dandy, everything roses. They don't see the work and the sweat and the ... the fear. I *needed* this deal."

"You didn't mean for that night to go like it did, did you, Mr. Darden? You were just trying to talk him out of it, and things got heated. You never meant for the trigger to go off."

"Wait, no." The twitching in Darden's body ceased and he went rigid. "I didn't shoot him! My God, you need to believe me."

Boggs had only been guessing, and maybe he was wrong. The more likely explanation was that the private detectives had killed

Bishop, but he still had no proof. All he knew at this point was that Darden was far more involved than he'd let on before, that he was hiding something, and Boggs wasn't going to leave until he found out what.

Darden explained, "I did try to talk Arthur out of reneging on our deal that night, yes, I admit that. I went to his office and we had a drink. I asked him to reconsider, and then he told me what he'd learned about Henry Paulding, even showed me the research he'd done. I agreed it looked . . . very bad. Paulding, years ago, may have . . . killed someone. Arthur was going to run a story on it."

Silence for a long while, as if Darden hoped the story could end there.

Boggs said, "You asked Mr. Bishop not to pull out of the deal and not to write the story about Paulding."

"I did, and he refused. We argued, yes. But I didn't *shoot* him, I swear it. I left. And then . . . "

"Then what?"

"I hadn't . . . gone to see him of my own accord. I had been *advised* to go. By a white man, Warren Floyd. Some sort of security consultant for Mr. Paulding. He explained that they'd done due diligence into the project and had learned . . . that Arthur was digging around for some unflattering story about Paulding, that Arthur was going to use that as an excuse to kill our side of the deal. Floyd thought I would have better luck talking Arthur out of it than they would."

He paused again.

"I failed to talk Arthur out of it. He was . . . unyielding. So I left the office and walked toward my car, trying to make sense of how I could survive financially if everything fell through . . . and there was a white couple leaning against the hood of my car. Not Floyd, but they told me they worked with him. They asked me how it had gone, and they didn't like what I told them. They'd been drinking, too, I could smell it on them. The man was belligerent. Threatened to 'teach me a thing or two about how to persuade someone,' but then she told him to back off. And she told me . . .

she told me to go home, and said that they would 'finish the job.' I didn't ... I just ... "

"What happened next?"

"I got in my car, and I saw the two of them arguing with each other. I drove off and at the first light I checked the rearview mirror and ... I saw her going into the *Daily Times* building. The man seemed to be waiting outside."

"It was the woman who went in, are you absolutely sure?"

"Yes. Lucius, I ... I suppose I should have known what they meant to do, I see that now, but at the time, I never thought ... "

"You thought she was just going to *talk* to Mr. Bishop? You didn't think she'd go up there and shoot him?"

"No, never!"

Boggs waited a moment, considering this. He asked Darden for the names of the white people, but Darden didn't know. He asked Darden what they looked like, and his descriptions matched those of Floyd's accomplices Sam Wilton, who'd been killed alongside Floyd yesterday, and Lisa Collins, aka Call Me Becky. She'd been claiming that yesterday's shoot-out had been instigated by her overly aggressive colleagues, that she was as much a victim as McInnis.

Boggs felt fooled yet again. The lady detective had put on a good show—had possibly even shot Floyd so he couldn't live to contradict her tale, had expected them to fall for her act—but she was the one who had killed Bishop.

"So you yourself didn't shoot Mr. Bishop," Boggs said, tasting the words to see if they felt truer on his tongue. "Yet when you learned that he had been killed that night, right after this white lady had gone in to see him, you didn't tell this story to anyone. You kept silent. And you lied to my face, said you'd never even heard of the redevelopment plan."

"Because she called me the next morning." Elbows on the desk, Darden clasped his hands in front of his face, nearly blocking Boggs's view of his mouth. "She said she'd taken a glass from Arthur's office. A glass with my fingerprints on it, that could put me at the scene of the crime. She said if I opened my mouth, she'd feed me to the police. *Feed me*, those were her words. Between that and . . . what could be construed as my financial motive, I'd look like the killer."

His story made sense. It explained why Collins and Wilton had panicked, racing over to Floyd's office once they'd learned McInnis was talking to Floyd. It explained why the PIs had drawn weapons on a police sergeant; McInnis had unknowingly cornered the murderer. Perhaps Floyd himself had never wanted them to shoot Bishop, and *Collins* was the loose cannon, driven by drink or rage to "finish the job." Maybe she'd only meant to threaten Bishop with her gun, or maybe she'd planned the murder the moment Darden told them Bishop was writing the story. Regardless of whether she or Paulding had planned the murder, it seems Floyd had decided his best bet was to cover their tracks and hope they would evade suspicion. Figuring that the murder of a Negro wouldn't rate too highly with APD, that they'd manage to skirt away unscathed.

"You could have come to me, Mr. Darden. I could have helped you."

Darden nodded, tears in his eyes.

Boggs wanted to say so much more. *You let them arrest his grieving widow. Mrs. Bishop is in jail because you didn't come forward. Would you have let her hang, too? My sergeant is on death's door because you hadn't told us the truth. I was shot at. All because you couldn't lose a deal, couldn't lose this house, your fancy car, your Jacob Lawrence painting, your status.*

"Let's go to the police station, Mr. Darden. Everything you just told me, I need you to tell it again."

"Lucius, please . . ."

"We can go there together, Mr. Darden, or I can call white officers to come here with a wagon." Boggs didn't know whether he bought the blackmail story about the bourbon glass, but right then he didn't even care. He felt he was doing more than Darden deserved, offering to help him save face for an hour or two, until he was charged with murder or accessory or obstruction, or *something*, goddamn it.

Darden finally nodded and lowered his hands to his sides, to the arms of his chair perhaps. Or to a drawer containing a gun.

Boggs leapt to his feet. "Keep your hands where I can see them!"

Darden froze and stared at him, stunned it had come to this. He lifted his empty palms.

"Would you mind if I called one of my children?"

"Yes, I'm afraid I would." He stared at Darden for a second. "Keep your hands where I can see them. *I* have a call to make."

He picked up Darden's phone and called the station, asking for Captain Dodd. After getting Dodd on the line, he asked if Collins was still in custody.

"Yeah, but her lawyer's causing a fuss. Looks like she really was the one who shot Floyd, like she said. Saving your superior's ass."

"Well, I have a witness who can put her at the scene of Bishop's murder. We can't release her just yet."

"I am the one who'll decide what we can and can't do, Officer," Dodd snapped.

"I understand, Captain. But if you could just give me ten minutes, I'll have a witness in the station."

Dodd grumbled that he should hurry up then, as her hearing was in less than an hour.

Boggs hung up, told Darden it was time to go.

Once they were outside, the door to a parked white Dodge opened and out stepped big Champ Jennings, Dewey's light-hearted but massive partner. At the wheel sat Dewey. Boggs had called them beforehand, told them to wait just outside but knock if he was longer than ten minutes.

"We'll give you a ride, Mr. Darden," Boggs said, guiding Darden into the back.

No one spoke during the ride, which took five minutes yet must have felt like the longest of Clancy Darden's life. Boggs sat beside him in the back, wondering how he would tell his father and brother, and trying to appear calm as he studied Darden out of the corner of his eye, watched the way the businessman stared tear-streaked at his city, so much here built and sustained by his company and work and connections. Unspooling before him slowly and then replaced by the edifice of the police station and its tall, unforgiving stone steps.

43

MCINNIS LOST DAYS to unconsciousness, to surgeries and transfusions. The bullet had passed through him, too low to hit his heart or lungs, but it did plenty of damage. The first day, doctors had warned his wife he might never wake up. They said the same thing on day two.

Bonnie had been the first person he'd seen when he'd opened his eyes, on day four. He'd tried to speak to her, failed. Her hands on his. Then he'd drifted off again.

In and out the images had come, flickering through his dreams. Bonnie and the kids. Friends, some of them the very people he thought had abandoned him, afraid of getting too close to the racial taint of his job. Father Larry from church.

"Don't be giving me last rites just yet," he'd managed to say to the white-haired old priest, his voice dry.

"I'm afraid I already did, three days ago."

McInnis had closed his eyes again. "Give 'em to me again in about thirty years."

One day, the face he saw was Captain Dodd's.

"Have I died," he asked, voice weak, "and gone to bureaucratic purgatory?"

"That part comes after you've recovered more." Dodd's stern expression seemed comically misplaced, as he was surrounded by well-wishers' gifts of lilies, lilacs, and gerbera daisies. A dumpy police captain overtaken by horticulture. "Gave us quite a scare, Mac. And left quite a mess at my feet."

"How's that?"

"Two dead bodies jog your memory? You at the office of a private investigator named Warren Floyd? With two of your officers?"

"I was there to find out why Floyd had broken into Arthur Bishop's home. Set up the meeting the night before. I wanted Floyd alone so he'd talk. Hadn't expected to be ambushed."

"Yet you brought two of your officers?"

"Maybe I half expected to be ambushed, then. Quarter expected. They were hanging back, just in case."

"And the two dead men?"

McInnis shut his eyes. "Talk to Boggs and Edmunds. They'll tell you."

"They have. I'd like to hear the story from a white man, too."

"I trust my officers, Captain. If trusting them is too much for you, then . . . then that's your fucking problem."

"I'm gonna attribute that to the pain medicine."

"If it makes you feel better. What's the lady detective saying? She in jail, I hope?"

"She is. Had you figured out she was the one who killed Bishop?"

"No." He opened his eyes. "How did you?"

"Your boy Boggs gets credit for this one." Dodd told him about Boggs's arrest of Darden and what Darden had said about the night Bishop was killed. "When we went through her apartment, we found way back in her cabinet a certain leaded glass, matched the one from Bishop's desk. It looks like how Darden says: she shot Bishop, kept the glass to keep Darden from talking."

McInnis felt dizzy but he tried to follow. "What's this mean for Mrs. Bishop?"

"As a matter of fact, she's gone free. Just about the time you were doing your John Wayne impression, a story broke that the FBI had been tailing her and knew she couldn't be the killer."

"What? Jesus."

Dodd asked, "Any idea where a colored reporter who used to be one of your officers could have possibly gotten that information?"

"The FBI, I would assume." Lying was quite easy when in this state. His voice only had one setting right then, extreme exhaustion, so honest statements and flat-out falsehoods sounded exactly the same. Unless Dodd had questioned him earlier, when he was half-conscious and too drugged to censor himself.

In which case, he was fucked.

"I did speak with Special Agent Doolittle, and I have to say, he did not sound the slightest bit disappointed to hear you'd been shot."

McInnis would have shrugged were that physically possible. "Who's running my officers?"

"Sergeant West. Hates my guts now, I can tell you, but somebody's gotta do that job. He'd best get used to it."

The shock penetrated the painkillers. "Wait, you mean it's his job, permanently?"

"That's right. Once we get you patched up, you're on a new beat."

"I never got back to you," he noted. "Never officially said I wanted that."

Dodd rolled his eyes. "Like you said, we can talk when you aren't on the hard drugs. But I'm sure you understand what's good for you. The new assignment, it's a slow area, but slow is probably what you'll need once you make it out of here."

McInnis felt cheated, robbed of a decision he'd been afraid to make.

Later, with Bonnie at his side, he asked her why none of his officers had come to see him.

"They aren't allowed," she said slowly, as if afraid his mind wasn't right yet.

A white hospital. Of course. "Tell the nurses I said it's okay."

She looked uncomfortable. "I'm not so sure what you say is what they go by, dear."

"Well, tell them anyway. I need to talk to Boggs. Tell 'em it's police business and that I need one of *my* officers present, and that means a Negro. If they don't like it, then I can have a talk with the fire inspector about their latest violations. Just get Boggs over here, please."

McInnis was awake one afternoon when Jimmy walked in, knapsack slung over his shoulder. He'd been catching a city bus to the hospital after school every day to check on his old man, but this was the first time father and son had been alone together, without Bonnie.

"Feel like a walk?" Jimmy asked.

"Just did an hour ago. Maybe in a little bit." He'd recently made it as far as pacing up and down the hallway, leaning on a cane.

"All right."

"How was school?" McInnis had been in the hospital so long that the bruises from Jimmy's fight had completely faded.

"Fine." The usual unhelpful response. Been that way since he started elementary school, when a child's life first becomes mysterious for his parents. A mystery, McInnis understood, that was not his to solve.

"I wanted to talk to you about Tessa."

Jimmy looked down. "I haven't talked to her since we spoke, sir."

"I just wanted you to understand . . . It's not that *I* care about you talking to her. It's everyone else. It's the way folks see things. How they see things becomes how you are, how you're judged, what you can do." He paused, hoped he was getting through. "I'm sure she's a fine young lady. I'm sure she's a good person. But you go acting that way around a colored girl, you're putting yourself in a bad situation. You're putting *her* in a dangerous situation. You don't want to do that to her, do you?"

"No, sir."

"You've got a big heart, Jimmy. I've always been proud of you for that. But it can get you into a tricky spot if you're not careful."

Jimmy thought for a moment. "Is that what landed you here, sir? Having a big heart?"

He didn't know how to answer. Part of why he'd been livid

at Jimmy that awful afternoon, he realized, was because of fear. And the sense that he had failed. With Jimmy almost sixteen, and schools becoming the new Southern battlegrounds, McInnis saw that the younger generation would be paying the toll that McInnis's generation had tried to avoid. Not only could he not protect his kids, he felt a sense of shame that this failure had put his kids in greater danger.

He was pondering this when Boggs appeared in the doorway. Civilian attire, a blazer and tie. The right side of his neck covered in a large white bandage.

"Sergeant. Good to see you."

"Your father been offering any prayers for me?"

"The whole congregation, in fact. He mentioned your name from the pulpit. Usually that costs a pretty donation."

"Well, I'm cheap. Figured getting shot would be easier."

Jimmy had stood up, and McInnis introduced them. Father approved of how his son did not flinch or pause when Boggs extended his hand, saw that they looked each other in the eyes as they shook.

"Is this a future cop?" Boggs asked with a grin.

"Let's hope not," McInnis said, looking at Jimmy still. "This look fun, son?"

"No, sir."

McInnis asked Jimmy to run to the cafeteria and buy three Cokes. Once Jimmy had left, McInnis motioned for Boggs to sit.

"What happened to your neck?"

Boggs explained his injury, and how he'd at first assumed the blood was McInnis's.

McInnis said, "At least you were already at a hospital."

"Well, I had to go to the other wing."

"Oh. Yeah."

A nurse stepped in, stopped, and walked back out.

"I believe I'm making the staff nervous," Boggs said.

McInnis coughed, his throat on fire. Boggs offered him a glass of water, angling the straw just so.

"Thank you." Boggs nodded, and then McInnis clarified, "Thank you for saving my life. They were fixing to shoot me and bury me in the woods someplace. You did real good."

"I'd do it again."

"Let's pray you don't have to. So where do things stand on our murder case?"

"Lisa Collins still denies she shot Bishop, says the glass must've been put in her cabinet by Wilton, who's conveniently dead. And as for our shoot-out, she still claims she was trying to calm everybody down and did what she could to help us. But I think prosecutors feel good about the case."

Boggs also explained how Smith and his *Daily Times* colleagues had tracked down the retired porter who'd once heard Paulding brag about the years-old murder of a butler, how Bishop had been digging for the facts behind that story, and how Bishop's research had convinced him to back out of the redevelopment plan and commit to exposing Paulding.

As the facts came together, McInnis realized that, despite all the concerns about Bishop's communist past, it was good old capitalist greed that led to his death.

"The catch is, this still lets Paulding off," Boggs pointed out. "He instigated everything. By killing a man a long time ago and bragging about it, and then by hiring detectives to make sure Bishop wouldn't report that story. Even if Paulding never told them to kill Bishop, even if the murder was because one of the detectives was a hothead who didn't like hearing no from a Negro, the fact remains that Paulding has his finger-prints all over everything, but we don't have anything on him that'll hold up."

McInnis considered this, his head swimming but not from the pain medicine.

"How are things working out with Sergeant West?"

"Fine." The preacher's son was not one to speak ill of a superior, so that terse reply was his way of biting his tongue.

"He doing such a fine job that y'all don't even notice I'm gone?"

"Let's just say, we're being reminded how fortunate we were to work with you."

The past tense stung. "Let's not rush to conclusions. I never said I was walking away."

"Dodd said you were taking a transfer. The injury just accelerated the timing."

"Not exactly." He felt angry, at Dodd, and at himself for not having made the decision before now, at the whole untenable situation. "He'd *offered* me a transfer, and I'd said I'd think on it. I just . . . wasn't sure if I wanted out or not."

He realized that may have sounded insulting to Boggs, so he continued, "You know I've liked working with you. I just mean, we both know the whole situation is . . . complicated, and all. Seemed if I could take another post, I don't know, maybe that'd make sense. I just wasn't sure."

It wasn't like McInnis to hedge so much, to sound so unsure of himself in front of one of his officers. He felt stupid and spineless.

"That must be interesting," Boggs said as he rose to leave. "To have a choice."

44

DETECTIVES FROM SHOOT-OUT *HAD BEEN WORKING FOR HENRY PAULDING*, the page one headline read, with the subhead: *Builder For Redevelopment Plan Spied On* Atlanta Daily Times.

And a story below it: *SUSPICIOUS '25 DEATH OF BUTLER COMES TO LIGHT.*

The two stories on Paulding were not nearly as damning as Smith had wanted, but days of research and reporting had only unearthed so many details. They had found the thirty-year-old death record of one Leander Gower, a sixty-two-year-old butler for Henry Paulding's father, whose official cause of death had been listed as a heart attack, although the police report had noted that his body had been found floating in the Pauldings' swimming pool. They had testimony from Mr. Gower's son, Terrence, now a carpenter in his forties, who told them that his father, a few days before his death, had noted an altercation with Henry Paulding and had even confided that he feared the young man. Terrence also recalled that the Paulding family had attended his father's funeral, the white family paying tribute to a Negro who had served them dutifully for decades, but that Henry Paulding had been a no-show for reasons unexplained.

Smith and Toon also had found three different people (other than the retired porter Mr. Vincent, who went unnamed in the piece) willing to go on record that they had heard Henry Paulding brag about drowning a Negro in a pool. Most damningly, Smith had tracked down a former attendant at the Capital City Club who retold an eerily similar scene to the porter's tale only five years ago: a handful of white men deep in their cups after a day on the links in '51, telling wild stories. Henry Paulding's story had been identical to the one he'd regaled his buddies with on that train many years earlier.

Smith had been unable to get a single comment from Paulding, whose underlings and secretaries took messages but clearly weren't interested in conversing with a member of the Negro press.

Boggs and Dewey had refused interviews, though Smith himself had written a short piece praising their heroism under fire. He'd also heard through the grapevine that McInnis had recommended them for a commendation, but that it hadn't been approved by the brass.

"I do wish that we'd found more evidence," Laurence said, visiting Smith and Toon in Smith's office the morning the stories ran. Now that Laurence had been named publisher (the board, which included Victoria Bishop ever since the charges against her had been dropped, had voted unanimously), he had revealed himself to be even more willing than his predecessor to anger the halls of power. He initially hadn't wanted to implicate Paulding without any evidence beyond hearsay, but the case unnerved him. As did the fact that this white man had actually hired people to spy on the *Daily Times*. The FBI hadn't burned the paper to the ground for its story on feds tailing Mrs. Bishop, so it seemed relatively less risky to take on a politically connected builder.

"I wish we had, too," Smith agreed.

"It was the perfect crime," Toon said, shaking his head.

"That's an oxymoron," Smith countered. He realized after he'd said it that he'd learned that response from McInnis, years ago.

Smith thought of another memorable phrase, something Mr. Vincent had said: *The unwritten rules are the most important ones.* True. Just like the untold stories are sometimes the most important. At the very least, they had made sure that Leander Gower's murder would no longer be an untold story. Henry Paulding's late-night, alcoholic, sadistic brags would no longer be the loudest voice invoking Mr. Gower's memory.

Deeper in the paper was a story about tonight's big meeting, led by Reverend Boggs, to discuss the redevelopment plan and formulate a community response. Laurence had insisted the Paulding stories run no later than today so that the public could digest them in time for Reverend Boggs's meeting. The full city council was scheduled to vote the following week on whether or not to move forward with the plan.

Smith felt no satisfaction at seeing the Paulding stories finally in print. An empty sense of sadness and loss pervaded the office.

He walked around the corner to Victoria Bishop's new office. After taking some time to recover from her adventure with the Southern legal system, she had asked Laurence if it would be possible for her to write for the paper again.

"How's the space working out for you?"

She looked up, pen in hand. This tiny room had been a storage closet for years, then it had belonged to Tim Pinckney, the writer Bishop had fired a few weeks ago for writing a piece he'd been bribed to write by a developer. That developer was Henry Paulding, Pinckney had told Smith; it had meant nothing to him at the time, but now Smith saw that it had been part of Paulding's plan to get positive stories in the Negro press in the weeks leading up to the redevelopment announcement.

"It's a good deal quieter than I'd expected," she said. "I remember the other writers being a lot louder."

"Oh, we can do loud. You haven't been here that long."

He didn't know if she was still seeing Dr. Bridges, didn't know if they still intended to wed or if they'd postponed out of respect for her departed husband, or even called it off. He wasn't going to ask, more than happy not to wear his reporter hat around her anymore.

"Good job on today's stories," she said.

"I hope it's enough to get that son of a bitch in jail," Smith said.

"I highly doubt that, but I appreciate your hard work all the same."

He closed the door behind him. "There's something else I've been meaning to ask you."

She put down her pen. "You want to know why the FBI was watching me that night."

"It has bothered me, yes, ma'am."

She said simply, "I don't know the answer."

He felt she owed him more than that. "Mrs. Bishop, I kept my word and haven't said anything about him being an FBI informant. I could have put that in one of our stories, but I didn't want to do that to him." Indeed, despite Darden's arrest and the shootout at the detective agency, Arthur Bishop's reputation remained unsullied: a successful businessman and important writer who'd worked long and hard to educate, inform, and inspire. Who chased difficult stories even at the cost of his life. Smith still didn't know whom Bishop had betrayed to the feds over the years.

Her lack of forthrightness annoyed him. If not for Smith, she'd be on death row. He pressed, "You really don't know anything else?"

"Maybe they knew about my affair and wanted to find some . . . incriminating evidence they could use against me or Arthur. Or maybe one of the many people I know have red skeletons in their closet, so the FBI wanted to see if I did, too." She shrugged.

He wondered whether her politics could be more complicated than she'd let on, and whether the FBI would continue to be a troubling presence in her life, and his.

"There's something else, something I thought you might want to read. Mr. Bishop wrote it a long time ago." He handed her a twelve-page story, which he'd retyped, as the old copy had been stained and torn. He wondered if she'd ever seen the original. "There's this thing I was thinking about doing."

DAYS LATER, A rare ice storm paralyzed Atlanta, scattering fallen trees on every major road and plenty of minor ones. Even thieves were too uncomfortable to venture out, as crime seemed to be on holiday, overwhelmed by the novelty and romance of a Southern blizzard. Chainsaws buzzed in the air as men cut through fallen oaks to clear the roads. Tree branches glazed with ice like melted sugar, kids turning cookie sheets and garbage lids into makeshift sleds on every street with a halfway decent incline. On day one, Smith was sent to report on human interest stories of how people were coping with the near shutdown of an entire city. By the second day, though, with power out everywhere, the cold tested everyone's patience. Icy fender-benders led to fistfights, trashcan fires spun out of control, and cabin fever turned homicidal, leaving Smith with plenty of material.

When the city finally returned to life as usual, the news about Henry Paulding had spread to the white papers, albeit in watered-down form. Paulding's link to Darden and to the detective who had shot Bishop made it in, but no hint of an old murder was made, no deceased butler was named. Smith marveled at the way those reporters could dance around a subject without naming it. Across the country, other Negro papers ran stories about this unexpected coda to Arthur Bishop's life story, demanding that all those responsible for his death be brought to justice.

Though homicide detectives tried to keep Boggs far from what could only loosely be described as the investigation into Arthur

Bishop's death, he did his best to stay involved. Collins, through her lawyer, still claimed to know nothing about Bishop's death, saying that perhaps Wilton had been the shooter and had put the glass in their cabinet. Fortunately prosecutors believed Darden's story (offering him a lighter sentence in exchange for his testimony), as well as young editor Natalie Washington's reports about Collins using her to spy on Bishop. They seemed confident that they had enough to convict her, though Boggs was afraid they'd settle for manslaughter rather than murder one.

Even so, going after the rogue lady detective was one thing; getting involved in the business of Henry Paulding or wading into the murky waters of city revitalization projects was quite another. Homicide expressed no interest in looking into Paulding beyond a cursory interview.

Boggs wondered, as he often did, if his being a detective would have helped. Wondered if that would ever happen, or if the city would continue to stymie the Negro officers' bids for advancement. From his hospital bed, McInnis had written a recommendation that Boggs be considered for promotion, but Boggs had already received an official letter informing him that a promotion would not be coming this year.

The letter ended with "You are welcome to reapply next year." Boggs wasn't sure if that was intended as a taunt or a challenge, but he treated it as both.

A couple weeks later, Smith received the fourth rejection letter for "The 'Accidental' Drowning." With Mrs. Bishop's blessing, he had submitted a copy of Arthur Bishop's old unpublished work of "fiction," listing Bishop's name as author, to Scribner's, which tersely declined to publish the story. *Esquire* and the *New Yorker* also regretted that it was not right for their pages. Now it was *Ebony's* turn to say no, thanks. Smith had sent them a more thorough cover letter, figuring that their editors would recognize Bishop's name and would wonder how it was he could be submitting fiction posthumously. *Ebony*'s reply paid due compliments to Bishop's body of work at the *Daily Times*, but explained with apology that the story was too "inflammatory."

That damn word again, the same one Laurence often used about Smith's writing. Maybe what the world needed was some inflaming.

Finally, tired of how long this was taking (getting fiction published seemed as tedious and time-consuming as police work and newspaper reporting), Smith dropped a copy in the mail to *Dime Detective Magazine*. He'd flipped through a few issues before and he doubted it was the sort of journal Mr. Bishop would ever peruse, but hell, it was worth a shot.

McInnis walked into Linwood's Restaurant for the first time in many weeks.

Since finally returning to active duty, he had been consigned to a desk, his recovery slow. Doctors weren't sure when he'd be up to the physical tasks of policing a street again, so he pushed paper now. More administrator than cop, and hating it. He no longer commanded the Negro officers, sometimes going many days without seeing any of them. This little field trip had been both a physical test and an attempt at a salve.

His body could take it, the seven-block walk not as bad as he'd feared. Until recently he'd still used a cane on some days, but hopefully that was behind him. Short jogs were in his immediate future, he hoped.

It was late for lunch, so only a few tables were occupied, one by an older man he recognized, and they nodded at each other. He took a table in the back but not all the way in the corner, as that would have seemed too obviously like hiding. And as a cop he was constitutionally unable to sit facing the back, so he faced the entrance, even though that meant all would see his white face when they walked in.

He sat there in his uniform, the shirt feeling looser in the chest but snugger in the belly now that he hadn't been lifting weights as much, and he endured the awkward greeting from a new waitress who didn't know him. He wondered whether this was a mistake. As if he were seeking some forgiveness or communion that wasn't his to receive or theirs to grant.

He had brought a folded *Constitution* with him, and he tried to escape into it, reading the latest back-and-forth between Ike and the Soviets, the governor's insistence that Georgia schools would never integrate, and the modified plan to redevelop part of Darktown, which had been approved and was set to begin shortly.

He had called Boggs a few times to check in, catch up on old cases. That was a decent tonic, but only that. He sorely missed the energy of the streets, missed Dewey's cussing and Boggs's strict lectures to the young men lollygagging on street corners; even missed teaching the kinds of rookies who he knew in his bones would not last a year.

And loath as he was to admit it, he missed being special.

He was just another cop now.

"Hey there, Sergeant." In the door walked Linwood, dressed in jacket and tie. He walked to McInnis's table and they shook hands. "How you feeling?"

"Like I got shot a few weeks ago. Otherwise, all right."

"Cousin of mine got shot in the Pacific. Shoulder. Never could use his left arm the same way again. Otherwise he's strong as a bull, but it took a while. You'll get there."

"Thank you. Tests the patience, though. How's business?"

"Fine now. I'm worried about what'll happen once they start knocking down buildings, but we'll see."

Linwood excused himself to check on a few things. McInnis looked to his side and saw, on an empty table, a copy of the *Daily Times*. He reached over and picked it up, looking for Smith's byline.

⟡

Randy Higgs was found guilty of rape.

Despite the love letters from Martha Hunter, the jury had not been swayed. The defense attorney had been afraid to call Martha Hunter to the stand and ask her to verify her love letters, figuring the jury would sympathize with her and would punish Higgs for daring to put her on the spot. The letters were admitted into evidence but did little to sway the jury. Whether she and Higgs ever had been a true couple (difficult as that was for some to imagine), that still didn't preclude the possibility he'd raped her on that particular night.

Higgs was sentenced to twenty years' hard labor. The fact that he didn't get the chair, and wasn't dragged from his jail cell to be lynched, was, to some white people, a sign of progress.

A local chapter of the NAACP announced that very afternoon that it would appeal. A lawyer in town told Smith they'd made that decision lightning-fast as a way of keeping the Civil Rights Congress at bay, essentially declaring this an NAACP matter, no reds allowed. Still, Lord knew how long the appeal might take, and how many months or years Higgs would spend behind bars.

Smith wondered if Higgs would spend any of his time reading those old love letters.

Later still, news from Montgomery: police had launched a mass arrest campaign, locking up at least fifty participants in the boycott, including King and thirteen other ministers. All were quickly out on bond, but they'd been accused of inciting an illegal boycott and causing "racial tension and violence."

They were unbowed. The sidewalks of Montgomery would remain well traveled.

Dogwoods had shed their confetti of white petals and the hardwoods were putting forth their lightest-green leaves in March when the city began smashing the buildings into the past.

Windows shook all down Auburn Avenue and beyond, utensils jumped on tabletops and dogs got to barking. Then it happened again, and again, like the city was under attack.

Which it was.

In minutes, three blocks of old tenements in Darktown were rubble. Streets had been closed on all sides, the army of bulldozers and wrecking cranes came chugging along, a phalanx of dump trucks close behind.

"Out with the old," Reverend Boggs said somberly.

"And in with Lord knows what," Boggs replied.

They had been having coffee in a diner but had stepped outside so they could watch from about half a mile away. They bore witness as the tops of buildings shimmied and danced, then fell, disappearing behind the tops of nearer structures, and then all the smoke and dust rose even higher than those buildings had ever dared. *Like their ghosts*, Boggs thought, *set loose to haunt the city*.

The outrage from the community—not to mention the scandal of Bishop's murder, Darden's arrest for accessory to murder, and the sordid implications about Henry Paulding—had helped blunt the city's initial plan, but not stop it entirely. Paulding's company had been pushed out by pragmatic city councilmen, so at least he personally wasn't profiting from this. And Reverend Boggs had managed to get the city to back away from its larger plans to take part of Sweet Auburn through eminent domain.

But blocks of Darktown were being demolished. Hundreds of people had just lost their housing, and the officers had already noted the changes in their beat, the sudden diaspora of the poorest in their community taking root in this block or that, wandering rootless and in desperate need of shelter and food, with few ways of finding them.

The only good news, as far as Boggs, his father, and their peers were concerned, was that the city was not trying to tear down Sweet Auburn.

Yet.

Because as they both stood there, watching as the breeze blew the dust further than anyone would have imagined, they feared what the city had unleashed. They wondered how long the diner they'd just eaten in would survive the white man's wrecking ball.

They noted how their community was becoming surrounded, that those armies of bulldozers and dump trucks were inching ever closer.

Boggs's kids still had to go to a poorly heated, insufficiently funded elementary school, yet white people had no trouble finding the money for a civic center. At this rate the schools would never integrate, and while rule-followers like Boggs waited and waited for the Supreme Court's ruling to be obeyed, he feared he would look up one day to see that his people had been driven from the city that he still, despite himself, loved.

His father, shoulders slumped, walked back inside as one of the clouds of dust approached, but Boggs lingered on the sidewalk. Across the street he saw a mother with two young children, boy and girl, covering their ears and staring. His own children, the younger ones at least, loved to watch construction trucks, could spend hours standing on a sidewalk marveling at all that activity.

He was glad they weren't seeing this.

Early April, pollen season, the sidewalks so yellowed that Smith left footprints as he walked to work. He passed a bus stop crowded with maids on their way downtown and he thought of Montgomery. Two weeks ago, Reverend King Jr. had been found guilty of conspiracy for his role in the boycott; he was sentenced to a year in jail, but was out on appeal. The boycott continued, though it hadn't spread to Atlanta or any other city, as far as Smith knew.

He was whistling to himself, walking an unfamiliar route to the office because he'd spent the night at Patrice's house. He'd slept there only a few times, taking things slow for the little girl's sake; usually he'd skulk off before sunrise. This morning was the first time the three of them had breakfast together—Smith had snuck out early again, then bought doughnuts down the street before coming back and ringing the doorbell, as if he'd just happened to be in the neighborhood again. He wasn't sure if the daughter fell for it or not, but as they'd sat at breakfast he'd found he enjoyed what might become a domestic routine.

Patrice was worried about her business still: the white boycott was going strong, and she'd let another employee go recently. She worked nearly every waking hour, so they didn't have much time for each other. But what they had was *good*. He still wasn't quite sure where they were going, but this felt right so far, and maybe that was enough.

At a newsstand a block from the office, he saw a new edition of *Dime Detective*. He stopped and opened it, glancing at the table of contents. There it was, Arthur Bishop's name alongside the story's title. The editors hadn't even sent Smith a letter thanking him for the submission, or any payment, not that money was his reason for doing this.

Smith bought four copies.

The story was mostly as Bishop had written it, though Smith had pared back at some passages that struck him as overripe. He had not changed the basics: a young, rich white man drowns his father's butler in their pool. Police arrive and question the young man, but they conclude the old butler suffered a heart attack. The young man reads the newspapers obsessively for a few days but concludes he got away with it. In the final scene, the murderer proposes to a young lady and wonders whether he should hire the dead butler's son to be their driver. Twelve pages, four thousand words, zero remorse.

Smith had chosen to keep the autobiographical blurb brief and matter-of-fact: *Arthur Bishop served as the editor-in-chief of the* Atlanta Daily Times *for sixteen years.*

Back in his office, he scribbled a short note and paper-clipped it to page 37 of one of his copies, which he slid into a large envelope, with his name on the return address, and mailed it to Henry Paulding.

His note would have made his ex-partner proud. He'd heard it at Bishop's funeral and had committed it to memory.

*When justice is done, it brings joy to the righteous but
terror to evildoers.*

PROVERBS 21:15.

We're still watching you.

Over those first few weeks, Sergeant West, the new superior for
the Negro officers, occasionally stopped by McInnis's desk to
seek his counsel. How might he go about unruffling the feathers
of this minister, or what would be the wisest way of settling this
dispute between families caught in the throes of a blood feud, or
how exactly could he go about getting his officers to despise him
a bit less? For the most part, though, West kept away, so McInnis
did the same, not wanting to seem like he was hovering over and
judging his successor.

Until the day McInnis walked into the basement, his calves
still sore from his longest run since the shooting. Roll call was
thirty minutes away. The place smelled as musty as ever, and the
mousetraps in the corners of the hallway appeared newly reloaded.

He found West alone in McInnis's old office.

He asked, "How are you getting on?"

"I still don't like them and they still don't like me." West was tall
and thin, bug-eyed, looking like some half-starved Confederate
deserter lost in the wilderness, minus the facial hair.

"You know, I just heard there's an opening for a sergeant in
the Second."

"Doesn't help me. I was strictly instructed, I do at least two years
down here. Unless of course I can get someone to trade with me,
but that ain't gonna happen."

"What if I told you I'd trade?"

West stared. Thought maybe he'd misheard.

"I'd think either you were teasing me, or that you were crazy,
but I'd keep that second part to myself and just say, sounds good,
let's trade right now."

"All right then. Let's set up a meeting with Chief Jenkins, see what we can't work out."

Given some of the bad stories McInnis had heard about West's leadership, he figured he could exact a few more concessions from Chief Jenkins before making this official. Like a step raise, and a facilities upgrade in the basement. And some goddamn squad cars for his officers.

He'd rehearsed how he would explain this to Bonnie, how he might justify himself. Had even written some of it down, half arguing with himself and half hoping that, even though he doubted he could win her over, at least he could explain why he needed to do this.

"Wait, wait." West held up a hand. He seemed certain McInnis was playing some prank. "You're serious? You really want back down here?"

"I know this job isn't for everyone." He looked around at the chipped walls of this shitty office. "But yes. Hell, yes."

In early May, the air already summer-hot and Smith so pleased to see the ladies in their sundresses again, he arrived at his desk to see a copy of the *Atlanta Constitution* on his typewriter. It was folded to page A-5, a headline circled in red ink, with an exclamation point drawn at the end of the headline.

DEVELOPER DIES OF HEART ATTACK ABOARD FLIGHT.

It took Smith a moment to understand.

On a Washington-bound flight the previous afternoon, Henry Paulding had died. Pilots had diverted the plane to Charlotte, but Paulding was declared dead on the scene.

Smith read the article twice. Leaned back in his chair.

His first emotion was celebratory. A mere month after Smith had mailed Paulding the pulp magazine, his empty heart had failed. The power of the pen mighty indeed.

But the elation faded fast, as did Smith's grandiosity, the sense that this was somehow his doing. After all, Paulding was fifty-one, and plenty of fifty-one-year-old hearts gave out.

No, Smith hadn't killed the man. Nor had guilt. Or even justice.

He lit his first cigarette of the workday, and he reflected on Henry Paulding's full life. He had lived for years as a free man beyond the reach of the law, had reshaped the city whose riches he had inherited, and had ultimately died wealthy, with his wife beside him as they coursed through the heavens in their first-class berth.

The proverb had it wrong: Paulding had never seen justice, and Smith felt no joy.

He dropped the newspaper and looked at his new typewriter, the one Laurence had finally agreed to buy a week ago. His fingers still weren't quite used to its stolid keys, its unwavering focus. He put his hands on either side of it, felt its weight.

He was angry enough to throw it against the wall. He started to lift it.

Then Laurence, standing in his doorway. "You saw the story?"

"I did." Smith guiltily moved his hands away from the new Victrola. Then he repeated what he now realized Bishop had been saying to him the last time they spoke, months ago. "He got away with it."

"He did."

They stared into the familiar void for a moment.

Smith said, "I never . . . never found it."

"Found what?"

"The piece of evidence. The one thing that would've put him away. I just . . . It was so long ago."

Laurence folded his arms. "Did you really think you could have found something that would have locked that man up?"

"Of course. Otherwise, why bother?"

They held each other's gaze a moment. Then Laurence nodded and said, "Good. Hold onto that attitude, Mr. Smith. Bring it with you to the office every day."

Then Laurence checked his watch and reminded Smith that his next story was due in four hours, and the editor's red pen awaited.

ACKNOWLEDGEMENTS

Big thanks once again to my family, friends, agents Susan Golomb and Rich Green, editor Ed Wood, and the many publishers, publicists, marketers, and booksellers who have helped put my work into the hands of readers.

This is a work of fiction. As in my past books, I have made efforts to ground the narrative in as realistic a historical setting as possible, but all characters as well as the plot are works of the imagination.

On January 3, 1938, W.A. Scott, the publisher of the *Atlanta Daily World*, Atlanta's black newspaper, was shot on his property at 181 Ashby Street. He later died from his injuries, and his murder was never solved. I first learned this fact years ago when I was conducting preliminary research for *Darktown*. I filed the information away. Since I was hoping to extend that book into a series, I was intrigued by the idea of including a book that further explored both the role of the black press in the early Civil Rights movement and the inevitable tensions in the relationship between police and the press.

This book is not an attempt to tell the story of Scott's murder, not least because it's set in a different decade. The company and employees of my invented *Atlanta Daily Times* are not modeled on any actual figures, and none of my characters' secrets, shadowy pasts, criminal acts, or political backgrounds should be construed in any way as a criticism of the dedicated individuals who worked so hard to create and deliver the real *Daily World* to readers over many decades.

In 2018, when I was deep into a late draft of this manuscript, historian Thomas Aeillo published *The Grapevine of the Black South: The Scott Newspaper Syndicate in the Generation Before the Civil Rights Movement* (University of Georgia Press, 2018). Since my manuscript was nearly finished, I chose not to read Aeillo's book until my novel was complete, as I didn't want any discoveries at that point to sway me from where *Midnight Atlanta* was going. That said, I've since read it, and I highly recommend it to anyone wanting to know more about the *Daily World*, the other papers the Scott family published, and the vital role these journals played in American history. Aeillo includes an entire chapter dedicated to Scott's murder and a subsequent trial.

Emory University's archives of the *Atlanta Daily World* was invaluably helpful as I've researched all three books in this series.

In 2006 I published my first novel, *The Last Town on Earth*. I was extremely fortunate in the book's critical reception and publicity—and indeed I feel fortunate to still be publishing books fourteen years later. But three months after the book's publication, *The New York Times* ran a story about how novelists increasingly were including bibliographies and long acknowledgements at the end of their books; several critics were quoted dismissing the practice as pretentious and off-putting. The critics' argument, apparently, was that bibliographies were for nonfiction books only, that novelists should simply be assumed to conduct research for their art, and that to openly acknowledge such research was akin to bragging or seeking undue praise. Bibliographies dispelled the magic of fiction, and they were unseemly.

One of the offending writers that the paper of record mentioned was myself. While it was flattering for this then-rookie novelist to see his name grouped with esteemed authors like Norman Mailer, Thomas Pynchon, Charles Frazier, and Martin Amis, I also felt called out, all for doing something that just seemed the decent thing to do: thanking the writers who'd gone before me and pointing curious readers in their direction.

I did include a bibliography for my second novel, *The Many Deaths of the Firefly Brothers*; for my third, though, I only included a brief note pointing people to a blog post on my web site, which listed books I'd found helpful in my research, and when *Darktown* was published in 2016, I decided not to run a bibliography at all, digital or otherwise. I'd done a great deal of research for that book, but I'd perhaps overinternalized those critics' remarks over the years. I'm sure my decision was also made because I wasn't sure if it was odd for a crime novel to reveal all its evidence, so to speak, and show where my imaginative fingerprints lay. Also I feared it might look defensive to include a long list of books I'd read, as if it were justification for wading into the thicket of mid-century race relations, like a conscientious student showing his work. I decided it was better to let the book stand on its own.

But I've always felt torn about the decision.

After all, authors of historical fiction stand on the shoulders of the historians and journalists who conduct often painstaking primary research: combing through old diaries, chasing down legal files and arrest records, sorting out census tracts and property deeds. While I do spend a fair amount of time in archives and talking to people, the majority of my research has always been in the form of reading nonfiction books that are the direct result of other writers' efforts.

When giving speeches and talking to book clubs, I've always made a point of mentioning many of the books I found helpful in writing *Darktown* and *Lightning Men,* but I've come to regret the lack of bibliography, and I regret the fact that I allowed myself to be cowed years ago by some grumpy critics. So, overdue though it is, I'm including here a bibliography of the many books I've found helpful during the years in which I've worked on *Darktown, Lightning Men,* and *Midnight Atlanta.*

I'm a fiction writer. I don't claim to be a historian. I make things up, I bend dates and facts to my will, all in service of what I hope is a good story that moves people, which isn't to say I'm being falsely modest here: I think fictional storytelling is as important as anything, and is perhaps more sorely needed now than ever. At the same time, I've always had the deepest respect and appreciation for the many historians and journalists whose work make mine possible.

In 2007, when I was at the award ceremony for the Society of American Historians in New York, one of the winners, historian Jennifer L. Anderson, waxed poetic about the joys of archival research. She described the thrill of finding some once-neglected records that were so old and undiscovered that, when she flipped through them, a dead moth slipped from the pages. The audience (most of them fellow historians) nodded and murmured to themselves knowingly. I thought, *These people are crazy. But thank God for them!*

Indeed, thank God for all of these books and the writers who produced them. If you're interested in learning about 1940s–50s American history, the Civil Rights movement, Atlanta, policing, and other sundry subjects covered in these novels, I recommend you check out any of the following. Not all are intended for lay readers, but all were instrumental in helping me build the fictional world of Boggs, Smith, Rake, and McInnis:

ATLANTA-SPECIFIC

Courage to Dissent: Atlanta and the Long History of the Civil Rights Movement, by Tamiko Brown-Nagin, Oxford University Press, 2011

The Temple Bombing, by Melissa Faye Greene, Da Capo Press, 1996

Atlanta Life Insurance Company: Guardian of Black Economic Dignity, by Alexa Benson Henderson, University of Alabama Press, 2003

Daddy King: An Autobiography, by Reverend Martin Luther King, Sr., William Morrow & Co., 1980

Living Atlanta: An Oral History of the City, 1914–1948, edited by
    Clifford M. Kuhn, Harlon E. Joyce, and E. Bernard West,
    University of Georgia Press, 1990
Where Peachtree Meets Sweet Auburn: A Saga of Race and Family,
    by Gary Pomerantz, Scribner, 1996

CIVIL-RIGHTS-ERA AMERICA

Parting the Waters: America in the King Years, 1954–63, by
    Taylor Branch, Simon & Schuster, 1988
*This Nonviolent Stuff'll Get You Killed: How Guns Made the
    Civil Rights Movement Possible*, by Charles E. Cobb Jr.,
    Basic Books, 2014
Atticus Finch: The Biography, by Joseph Crespino, Basic Books,
    2018
*The Eyes of Willie McGee: A Tragedy of Race, Sex, and Secrets in
    the Jim Crow South*, by Alex Heard, Harper, 2010
*Devil in the Grove: Thurgood Marshall, the Groveland Boys, and
    the Dawn of a New America*, HarperCollins, 2012, and
    *Beneath A Ruthless Sun: A True Story of Violence, Race, and
    Justice Lost and Found*, by Gilbert King Riverhead Books,
    2018
*Simple Justice: The History of Brown v. Board of Education and
    Black America's Struggle for Equality*, by Richard Kluger,
    Knopf, 1975
The *March* graphic novel series, by John Lewis, Andrew Aydin,
    and Nate Powell, Top Shelf Productions, 2013, 2015, and
    2016
*Mothers of Massive Resistance: White Women and the Politics of
    White Supremacy*, by Elizabeth Gillespie McRae, Oxford
    University Press, 2018
*A Spy in Canaan: How the FBI Used A Famous Photographer to
    Infiltrate the Civil Rights Movement*, by Marc Perrusquia,
    Melville House, 2018

Sweet Land of Liberty: The Forgotten Struggle for Civil Rights in the North, by Thomas J. Sugrue, Random House, 2008

The Blood of Emmett Till, by Timothy B. Tyson, Simon & Schuster, 2017

A Man Called White: The Autobiography of Walter White, by Walter White, The Viking Press, 1948

THE PRE-CIVIL RIGHTS SOUTH

Slavery by Another Name: The Re-Enslavement of Black Americans from the Civil War to World War II, by Douglas Blackmon, Doubleday, 2008

I Am A Fugitive From A Georgia Chain Gang! By Robert E. Burns, The Vanguard Press, 1932

Speak Now Against the Day: The Generation Before the Civil Rights Movement in the South, by John Egerton, Knopf, 1994

Defying Dixie: The Radical Roots of Civil Rights 1919–1950 by Glenda Elizabeth Gilmore, W. W. Norton & Company, 2008

Blood at the Root: A Radical Cleansing of America, by Patrick Phillips, W.W. Norton & Company, 2006

THE PRESS

Ida, A Sword Among Lions: Ida B. Wells and The Campaign Against Lynching, by Paula J. Giddings, Amistad, 2008

The Defender: How the Legendary Black Newspaper Changed America, by Ethan Michaeli, Houghton Mifflin Harcourt, 2016

The Race Beat: The Press, the Civil Rights Movement, and the Awakening of a Nation, by Gene Roberts and Hank Klibanoff, Knopf, 2006

South of Freedom, by Carl Rowan, Alfred A. Knopf, 1952

A Question of Sedition: The Federal Government's Investigation of the Black Press During World War II, by Patrick Washburn, Oxford University Press, 1986

HOUSING AND RACE

Arc of Justice: A Saga of Race, Civil Rights, and Murder in the Jazz Age, by Kevin Boyle, Henry Holt & Company, 2004

White Flight: Atlanta and the Making of Modern Conservatism, by Kevin Kruse, Princeton University Press, 2005

The Color of Law: A Forgotten History of How Our Government Segregated America, by Richard Rothstein, Liveright, 2017

CRIME AND POLICING

One Righteous Man: Samuel Battle and the Shattering of the Color Line in New York, by Arthur Browne, Beacon Press, 2015

Black Police in America, by W. Marvin Dulaney, Indiana University Press, 1996

Locking Up Our Own: Crime and Punishment in Black America, by James Forman Jr., Farrar, Straus and Giroux, 2017

Keeping the Peace: A Police Chief Looks at His Job, by Herbert Jenkins, Harper & Row, 1970

The Klan Unmasked, by Stetson Kennedy, University of Alabama Press (reprint), 2011

OTHER TOPICS

White Rage: The Unspoken Truth of Our Racial Divide, by Carol Anderson, Bloomsbury, 2016

The Cold War and the Color Line: American Race Relations in the Global Arena, by Thomas Borstelmann, Harvard University Press, 2001

Strom Thurmond's America, by Joseph Crespino, Hill & Wang, 2012

The Black Panthers: A Story of Race, War, and Coverage; The 761st Tank Battalion in World War II, by Gina M. DiNicolo, Westholme Publishing, 2014

Son of the Rough South: An Uncivil Memoir, by Karl Fleming, Public Affairs, 2005

J. Edgar Hoover: The Man and His Secrets, by Curt Gentry, W.W. Norton & Co, 1991

The Fifties, by David Halberstam, Villard, 1993

White Trash: The 400-Year Untold Story of Class in America, by Nancy Isenburg, Viking, 2016

The Bureau: The Secret History of the FBI, by Ronald Kessler, St. Martin's Press, 2002

Red Summer: The Summer of 1919 and the Awakening of Black America, by Cameron McWhirter, Henry Holt & Co., 2011

Grand Expectations: The United States, 1945–1974, by James T. Patterson, Oxford University Press, 1996

The Separate City: Black Communities in the Urban South 1940–1968, by Christopher Silver and John V. Moeser, The University Press of Kentucky, 1995

Race: How Blacks and Whites Think and Feel About the American Obsession, by Studs Terkel, The New Press, 1992

Rising from the Rails: Pullman Porters and the Making of the Black Middle Class, by Larry Tye, Henry Holt and Co., 2004

Baseball's Great Experiment: Jackie Robinson and His Legacy, by Jules Tygiel, Oxford University Press, 1983

The Warmth of Other Suns: The Epic Story of America's Great Migrations, by Isabel Wilkerson, Random House, 2010

Atlanta, 1948. In this city, all crime is black and white.

On one side of the tracks are the rich, white neighbourhoods; on the other, Darktown, the African-American area guarded by the city's first black police force of only eight men. These cops are kept near-powerless by the authorities: they can't arrest white suspects; they can't drive a squad car; they must operate out of a dingy basement.

When a poor black woman is killed in Darktown having been last seen in a car with a rich white man, no one seems to care except for Boggs and Smith, two black cops from vastly different backgrounds. Pressured from all sides, they will risk their jobs, the trust of their community and even their own lives to investigate her death.

Their efforts bring them up against a brutal old-school cop, Dunlow, who has long run Darktown as his own turf – but Dunlow's idealistic young partner, Rakestraw, is a young progressive who may be willing to make allies across colour lines . . .

*Soon to be a major TV series from Jamie Foxx
and Sony Pictures Television.*

**A brilliant blending of crime, mystery, and American history.
Terrific entertainment'
Stephen King**

**'Magnificent and shocking'
*Sunday Times***

Atlanta, 1950. Crime divides, the fight unites.

Officer Denny Rakestraw and 'Negro Officers' Lucius
Boggs and Tommy Smith face the Klan, gangs and
family warfare in a rapidly changing Atlanta.

Black families – including Smith's sister and brother-in-law – are
moving into Rake's formerly all-white neighbourhood, leading
his brother-in-law, a proud Klansman, to launch a scheme to
'save' their streets. When those efforts leave a man dead, Rake
is forced to choose between loyalty to family or the law.

Meanwhile, Boggs has outraged his preacher father by
a domestic, whose dangerous ex-boyfriend is then
om prison. As Boggs, Smith, and their all-black
ntend with violent drug dealers fighting for turf
itory, their personal dramas draw them closer to
that threaten to consume Atlanta once again.

**Written with a ferocious passion
that'll knock the wind out of you'**
New York Times